"T[...]

His lordship bit off a[...] his angry gaze raked over the sobbing figure before him.

"Here, take mine." The marquis thrust a large clean handkerchief into her flustered hands. "My name is Richmond. At your service, ma'am."

"I do beg your pardon," she said in a watery little voice. "I should not have hit you, only I didn't hear you approaching and you gave me such a fright!"

"I am sorry, Miss...?"

"Clifford. My name is Corisande Clifford," supplied the enchanting damsel.

"Well, Miss Clifford. We cannot stand in the middle of the road all day and there's a very good posting house at Beckhampton if you will accompany me."

A tide of colour flooded Miss Clifford's cheeks.

"Are you certain it is quite safe to accompany you?" she said doubtfully.

"Certainly not if you intend to box my ear again!" he teased, and was rewarded with the sound of laughter no angel could dare match.

A MOST
UNSUITABLE DUCHESS

GAIL MALLIN

Harlequin Books

TORONTO • NEW YORK • LONDON
AMSTERDAM • PARIS • SYDNEY • HAMBURG
STOCKHOLM • ATHENS • TOKYO • MILAN

Original hardcover edition published in 1990
by Mills & Boon Limited

Harlequin Regency Romance edition
published October 1991
ISBN 0-373-31160-5

A MOST UNSUITABLE DUCHESS

Printed in U.S.A.

CHAPTER ONE

"WALK 'EM, DICKON. I shan't be long." The tall young man flung this command at his groom as he sprang lithely from the elegant yellow-bodied sporting curricle and ran lightly up the steps of a handsome town house.

The door had already been thrown open by the porter, and Swale, his father's butler, stood waiting in anticipation, a welcoming smile on his lips. "Good afternoon, my lord. May I say what a pleasure it is to see you again?"

The Marquis returned this greeting with one of his charming smiles for the elderly man who had saved him from the dire consequences of many a youthful scrape.

"His grace is expecting you." Swale coughed discreetly. "Perhaps it would be better to stable your cattle, my lord."

This piece of sound advice caused the young man to shake his dark head abruptly. "I think not," was his cool reply.

Trained to hide his feelings, Swale swallowed an instinctive protest and proceeded to lead the way to the wood-panelled library where the master of this splendid establishment was at present ensconced. "The Marquis of Dene, your grace," Swale announced loudly.

The silver-haired man seated at the satinwood writing table did not look up. Only a brief wave of his white hand acknowledged that he had heard, but the gesture served to dismiss the butler, who melted away from the scene wishing it had been possible to offer some words of cheer to fortify one whom he still thought of as naught but a reckless lad.

"You may sit, Dene."

"Thank you, I prefer to stand." The Marquis replied in an equally curt tone.

The apartment was large, but was heated to the kind of high temperature favoured by the Prince Regent at Carlton House although the April day was a mild one. In spite of its enormous fire, however, to the Marquis the room felt as chill as a tomb, a strange sensation which he knew of old to emanate entirely from the austere figure of his parent. Strolling nonchalantly to the window, he gazed down into the quiet street below. To all appearances he seemed merely bored, but as his father continued to read the document spread out before him on the polished surface of the desk it grew harder to maintain this indifferent pose. Feeling his temperature beginning to rise at this cavalier treatment, the Marquis thrust his hands into the deep pockets of his many-caped driving-coat, which he had refused to relinquish to Swale, and set his teeth.

At last the Duke of Weston looked up. His eyes travelled with disdain over the tall person of his son. From the crown of his dark head to his highly polished boots Marcus John Charles Richmond, Marquis of Dene presented the very picture of a man of fashion. The Brutus crop, tidily brushed for once, the bottle-green coat by Stultz, the pale yellow pantaloons and the gleaming Hessians all bore mute testimony to the fact that the Marquis had taken especial pains for this unwelcome meeting with his father.

However, neither his son's handsome looks nor his elegant mode of dress appeared to afford the Duke any satisfaction. "I suppose I should count myself honoured that you saw fit to obey my summons," he said sourly.

"You call, sir, and I obey."

This flippant answer brought a tinge of angry colour to the Duke's thin cheeks. He drew in a deep breath and then continued as if the Marquis had not spoken. "I posted into town to ask you whether it was true that you had been out with young Royston." At his son's nod, his lips tightened. "You fool, how dare you risk engaging in a duel? I warned you last time that I would not condone such behaviour now that you are my heir."

"It was an affair of honour, properly conducted, and, moreover, Royston did not expire."

"I am glad to hear it. It is no part of my plans for you that you should be obliged to flee the country." The Duke's irritation seemed profound.

Marc quelled the impulse to tug at his immaculately tied cravat. His father was the one person in the world who had the power to make him feel like a scrubby schoolboy once again. "Was there anything more you wished to say to me, sir?" he demanded, his dark eyes defiant.

The Duke inclined his head. "You may choose to disregard it, but thanks to my influence this business with Royston has been smoothed over."

"Thank you, but I'm capable of attending to my own affairs." The Marquis sounded anything but grateful.

"Damn you, Dene, I don't want your thanks." The Duke glowered at his son for an instant before regaining control of his emotions. "Pray excuse me, I forget my manners."

Marc shrugged lightly, concealing his surprise. He could not remember his father ever having displayed such feeling before. The Duke of Weston had a reputation for cold austerity and his son had better cause than anyone to know it was well-deserved.

"My purpose in asking you here today was not to discuss your latest vulgar brawl. I am willing to consider that incident closed. But there is another matter."

Richmond shot him an intent look, his black brows rising.

"Sit down, I do not care to have you towering over me." When this command had been obeyed the Duke nodded. "Good. Let us try to act like civilised beings for once." He gave a short laugh. "God knows we have little love for one another, Dene, but you are my heir. It is time we both faced that fact."

The Marquis was suddenly pale and a muscle twitched at the corner of his mouth. "As you please, sir."

The Duke snorted. "I am very well aware that you would like to remind me that the position was not of your choosing, but Edward's death left me without the luxury of choice no less than you." As usual his grace's precise voice had unconsciously softened on his elder son's name. "I will not pretend that I find you a satisfactory substitute, but you are a Richmond and, frankly, there is no one else. I trust I make myself plain?"

"Perfectly." The answer was indifferent, but a fierce light shone in the Marquis's eyes.

"Excellent." His father seemed uncaring that Marc's temper had been aroused. "Since we are in agreement I am sure you will follow my reasoning," murmured the Duke sardonically. "You are almost five and twenty and it is high time you were married."

"Married!" Lord Dene repeated in blank surprise.

"Of course. I hesitate to appear feudal, but the notion of grandchildren has begun to hold an attraction for me." The Duke laughed gently.

His son recovered from his astonishment. "And you have someone in mind, do I understand?"

"Naturally. After due consideration I have decided that you should pay your addresses to Lord Marlow's daughter."

"Augusta Marlow." The Marquis rolled the name around his tongue. Then he shook his head. "No," he said simply. "I'm sorry, sir, but no."

"I am not interested in your sorrow, Dene," his grace retorted with cutting sarcasm. "You do not appear to have a proper understanding of the matter. I am not asking you to marry the lady in question, I am ordering you to do so.''

The Marquis's long-fingered hands clenched upon the arms of his elegant Hepplewhite chair. Yet when he spoke his voice was even. ''And if I still say no?''

The Duke picked up the document he had been perusing when his son had been announced. ''This,'' he said, ''is an account of your current debts. Do I need to inform you of the disgraceful total?''

''No doubt your spies are accurate, sir.''

''I shall ignore your impertinence, Dene, it does not alter the facts.'' He smiled coldly. ''You are in no position to argue with me. Refuse to do as I say and I will disinherit you. Edward's death broke the entail and I may dispose of my property as I please. How long do you think it would be before every dun in town was at your door when it became known that you were no longer heir to Amberfield?'' His smile took on a wolfish aspect.

''Jupiter, I believe you would do it!'' An unwilling laugh broke from the Marquis. He had no particular love for his boyhood home, but Amberfield had been the magnificent symbol of the powerful, wealthy Dukes of Weston since the seventeenth century. ''The scandal would not weigh with you, would it, Father?''

''My credit would survive the misfortune of your disgrace.'' The Duke laid the sheet of paper back upon the writing-table. ''But it need not come to such drastic measures. Be reasonable. Is it such a disagreeable prospect?'' He observed his son in silence for a moment. ''The girl is young and handsome enough and I will settle these in return for an announcement of your engagement in the *Gazette.*'' He tapped the list of debts with one forefinger.

''A bargain, no doubt, sir, but I have no desire to enter the parson's mousetrap,'' replied the Marquis drily.

''We must all marry in time.'' His grace disposed of this objection with an impatient wave of his hand. ''You are not supposing yourself in love with another, I hope?'' he added with an expression of distaste. An amused chuckle answered this query. ''Very well, then! What is there to prevent you from obliging me in this matter?''

''A fancy, absurd as it may seem, to find my own bride.''

''Edward knew his duty.''

''It is precisely the idea of taking up my late lamented brother's leavings that sticks in my gullet, sir.'' Lord Dene's answer rapped out. ''For God's sake, Father, I am not Edward, and saddling me with Augusta will not turn me into him.''

For a second the Duke's natural pallor faded to a bleached bone-whiteness and he looked every year of his advanced age. An apology sprang to his son's lips, but before it could be uttered Weston had recovered. "You need not remind me of it," he said bitterly. "I am past expecting miracles. In exchange for a son I could be proud of, what have I in his place? I'll tell you: a gamester and a wastrel."

"If you think that, it would have been better had you let me remain in the Army!"

The Duke greeted this impassioned cry with a shrug of his thin shoulders. "I knew my duty, even if you do not know yours. When Edward died you had to return to England, though you have shown precious little interest in fulfilling your new obligations."

This unfair accusation led the Marquis to quit his chair and take a hasty turn about the room. It was useless to protest that the opportunity to learn his new role had been denied him. His father might speak of permitting him to take up the reins, but in truth he had no intention of delegating one jot of his own control over the vast Richmond holdings. These included Amberfield and no less than six other country seats, ranging from Cornwall to the Lowlands of Scotland, the handsome town residence in which they now sat and many other varied interests, which added to the Weston coffers.

"Sir, I gave up my commission in the Tenth Hussars at your request, but I cannot marry the lady you have chosen," Marc said hotly. "If Edward had not broken his neck on the hunting field he would have offered for Miss Marlow. You must see that it will not do!"

"The reasons which made Augusta Marlow a suitable choice have not altered. I gave the match my blessing precisely because she would make an excellent duchess." The Duke raised his quizzing-glass and surveyed his son through it. "Do you dispute Miss Marlow's qualifications?"

"Of course not!" The Marquis flushed.

"Well, then!" A faint smile curved the Duke's thin lips as he opened his snuff-box, a gold case painted in the grisaille style. He held a pinch of the King's Martinique specially blended for him by Messrs. Fribourg and Treyer to one nostril before he spoke again. "I fail to understand this reluctance on your part." His tone was languid, but his pale blue eyes danced with malice. "You cannot prefer destitution to the lady."

"I'd as lief marry an opera-dancer!"

"It would not surprise me in the least if you so far forgot what is owed to our name. You have committed every other indiscretion." The Duke flicked the lid of his snuff-box shut.

Controlling his rage, the Marquis responded with an exquisite bow. "No doubt you speak from experience, sir." And had the savage satisfaction of knowing this hit had reached its target as the Duke's mouth tightened.

"My past is none of your affair, you insolent puppy," his grace snapped. "However, you can take it that I do understand all the temptations open to a young man in your position." A sour grimace touched his narrow face. "Temptations which you can no longer afford." He rose abruptly to his feet. "I will give you until the end of the season to make your mind up."

The Marquis bowed and turned sharply on his heel, but as he jerked open the door the cold voice halted him.

"One thing more. Do not attempt to leave the country without my permission. I should regret the necessity of detaining your departure. Remember, it is Miss Marlow or disinheritance." And his Grace of Weston laughed.

HIS FATHER'S mocking laughter continued to ring in Lord Dene's ears as he drove his matched pair of Welsh-bred chestnuts away from Grosvenor Square, at the spanking pace only such bang-up paragons of blood and bone could achieve.

"I knows they be sixteen-mile-an-hour tits, guv'nor, but springing 'em down Brook Street!" complained his skinny young Tiger, a London lad named Dickon, who was hanging on to the straps behind the Marquis.

"Quiet!" His devoted servant received this curt reprimand with a plaintive sigh, but lapsed into obedient silence.

In a rage his lordship was apt to drive with very little regard for whatever other vehicles might chance to cross his path. Luckily, Dickon possessed the requisite iron nerve needed for one in the service of the Wild Marquis, besides being devoted to his lordship's interests, a trait shared by Dickon's fellows. Cheerfully willing to endure danger to life or limb, the Tiger did no more than wince as they brushed wheels with a smart phaeton driven by a stout young man and feather-edged a corner at almost full speed without overturning, although for a moment it seemed as if they must.

Having thus worked off the worst of his rage, the Marquis steadied his pair and the rest of the journey to Manton's Shooting Gallery was conducted at a more suitably decorous pace. Here, his lordship proceeded to further relieve his feelings by gulping wafer after wafer, causing several gentlemen to nervously remove themselves from his vicinity.

"Remind me never to let you call me out." A cheerful voice hailed him, and the Marquis swung round to greet his favourite cousin, the stormy look vanishing from his lean features.

"Tom! I thought you had gone into Somerset."

"Tomorrow." Mr. Lavenham smiled. He was a pleasant-faced young man of almost the same age as the Marquis, but his fair looks were in sharp contrast to his cousin's black-browed swarthiness. Not as tall as Marc, who topped six feet, he none the less had a trim figure which was clad with great neatness in a well-cut coat of blue superfine cloth, fawn breeches and top boots.

"I was hoping to find you here. I thought you might care to dine with me."

"Still playing guardian angel, Tom? Did Fanny send you?"

This shrewd remark forced a reluctant laugh out of his cousin. "I warned Fanny that you would guess." He laughed, but then his round face grew more serious. "Did Uncle Montague take the affair with Royston badly?"

"He rang a fine peal over my head, to be sure," replied the Marquis casually as he turned to surrender his pistol to a waiting attendant. He flung a companionable arm about Tom's shoulders. "Are you driving your greys? No? Then let me take you up," Marc offered. When they were beyond the range of listening ears he added in a different manner altogether, "Tom, I must talk to you!"

Startled by the sudden intensity in his voice, Tom blinked at him. The brilliant light smouldering in those dark eyes portended mischief. Marc was well known for his crazy starts. His madcap behaviour since he had sold out after the Battle of Toulouse, which had ended the war in the Peninsula, had earned him the sobriquet of the Wild Marquis, and Tom eyed him uneasily.

By the time they had arrived back at the Marquis's lodgings in Ryder Street, Tom was sure his suspicion was correct. His cousin was ripe to embark upon one of his distempered freaks. And, if Fanny was to be believed with regard to the state of the Duke's present temper, then truly the fat would be in the fire.

The Marquis's apartments bore the unmistakable signs of being a bachelor's residence. There were riding-whips and spurs scattered about, newspapers and journals littering most of the available surfaces, sporting prints and advertisements abounded on the walls and altogether an air of comfortable disorder reigned supreme.

"You know, I can't understand how the Four Horse Club accepted you as a member, blessed if I can!" moaned Tom weakly, staggering to an old-fashioned but comfortable armchair and collapsing into it.

His cousin ignored this gibe and strode to the mahogany sideboard, which supported a wide array of bottles, assorted tankards and a large silver punch-bowl. Dashing off a handsome bumper of brandy, he drained its contents in one gulp and as he refilled it asked, "What will you have?"

"Ale," Tom replied with a look of mock horror. "My stomach ain't up to balls of fire at this hour," he continued severely, accepting the tankard thrust towards him.

A gleam of appreciation lit his lordship's gaze. "Ah but I have a need of it," he murmured. "A man must be pot-valiant at least when about to throw away rank and fortune and take the King's shilling."

This piece of intelligence made Tom sit up straight so abruptly that his ale spilled over his immaculate fawn pantaloons. Disregarding this sartorial disaster he spluttered, "Good God, man, what did his grace say?"

"I've thought it over, Tom, and it's the only answer." Marc sat down heavily. "I'll enlist under a false name and if they won't take me as a trooper then I'll join a line regiment." He gave an abrupt laugh. "I fancy they might find me a handy fellow, though."

Since Captain Lord Richmond had been one of the most brilliant officers in the Hussars, Tom did not care to dispute this statement. "It's a pity my uncle insisted on you selling out," he agreed. "Not that it wasn't understandable, a fine state the succession would have been in if the French had blown a hole in you at Waterloo."

"I wish to God that they had." Marc grimaced savagely. "I sometimes think that that fate would have been preferable to trying to fill Edward's saintly shoes."

"But what did my uncle say to you?" Tom pressed, an anxious frown creasing his smooth face. He had known Marc all his life but he couldn't ever remember seeing him in such a black mood. He could only be glad that he had persuaded Fanny to stay at home; hearing her brother talk so wildly would have sent her into hysterics.

"Behold, Tom, you see before you the latest aspirant to the hand of the Iceberg."

"The . . . the Iceberg! Uncle Montague wants you to marry Augusta Marlow?" Tom said in a daze. "Great Jupiter!"

"Quite so, dear coz. Now do you see why I'm for showing him a clean pair of heels?" The Marquis sighed, thrusting a hand into the thick tangle of his black locks. "His grace has already warned me not to try and leave the country." He laughed harshly. "I shouldn't be surprised if he has set armed guards to watch the Mermaid."

His beautiful yacht lay at Newhaven but, as he informed Tom, much good that would do him. "I've had a devilish run of luck of late, the dibs are out of tune and he knows it, damn him! If I refuse to take Augusta my gentle Papa tells me that he will set it about that he will disinherit me, which will bring the vultures flocking."

"Surely he wouldn't...I mean, dash it all, you are his son!" Tom expostulated, his eyes widening.

"Since when has that ever weighed with his grace?" Marc spoke matter-of-factly. The days when, as a small child, he had wept bitter tears over his father's cruel indifference were long gone. "If that happens, it's the cent-per-cent bloodsuckers, and we all know how they can ruin a man once they get their hooks into him."

"Aye, that's true enough," agreed Tom fervently. He coughed. "If there's anything I can do—"

"Thanks, Tom, but I'm not so far gone as to borrow from my friends yet," interrupted his cousin swiftly.

"Augusta is an heiress," Tom pointed out a moment later, breaking the gloomy silence which had fallen. "And she ain't ill-favoured neither." He considered the matter.

"She is also, or rather was, Edward's chosen bride," Marc retorted. He had been striding restlessly about the room, but now he halted by the tall marble mantelpiece. "It must be exile of some sort," he declared, drumming his fingers impatiently against the cluttered shelf. "There's no other help for it. I will not...cannot marry her."

Tom gazed at him helplessly. This was worse than Fanny had thought. Thinking Tom might succeed better than herself in so delicate a mission, she had begged him to keep a watchful eye on the Marquis, knowing that he was prone to drinking sprees and rash folly after contact with the Duke. But Tom didn't know what to say. Long acquaintance with his uncle had proved how that gentleman always seemed to achieve his aims. It was disagreeable to have to own it of a member of one's family, but the whole world knew that the Duke of Weston would stop at nothing. Tom suspected that his sinister reputation was entirely well-deserved.

In plain words his uncle was a selfish, cold-hearted despot. The only person he had ever been known to show any affection for was his elder son. Lord Edward had inherited his father's callous, arrogant disposition and had been highly unpopular among the younger members of the *ton,* unlike Marc, who for all his faults was universally well-liked. Edward's death had disturbed no one save the Duke but, seeing the angry misery in his cousin's eyes, Tom could almost wish Edward back again.

"Thing is, Marc," said Tom, coughing discreetly, "what's to prevent m'uncle from discovering your whereabouts? Don't want to cast a rub in your way, old chap, but he is very acute and it's all Lombard Street to a China orange he'd have you brought home again. Dashed awkward!"

"I'll be hanged if I'd submit tamely to any attempt to drag me back," was the alarmingly ferocious reply.

"Look, why don't you sleep on the idea of enlisting?" persuaded Tom. "His grace can't expect you to ask the wench out of hand. He don't, do he?" he added anxiously.

Marc shook his head. "No, he doesn't want to set tongues wagging if he can help it. Apparently I'm to pay court to the lady." He snorted in disgust. "I've till the end of the season to finish the job."

"No need to rush into any hasty decisions, then," Tom said brightly. "Why don't you come down and visit the Place instead? We could put our heads together to think of some plan without distraction there?"

The smile of hopeful encouragement which accompanied this eager remark made the Marquis laugh slightly. "Jupiter, if ever I knew such a fellow!" he said, gripping Tom's shoulder in silent affection, his haggard frown chased away.

By an unspoken but mutual consent the topic of his lordship's nuptials was abandoned and they fell into a discussion about the forthcoming sparring contest to be held under the auspices of Mr. John Jackson at the Fives-Court, Westminster. An habitué of Gentleman Jackson's Bond Street Boxing Salon, the Marquis was a notable amateur, who kept his tall lean figure in training and was reckoned a knowledgeable connoisseur of the Fancy.

By the time they had thrashed out the various merits of the contenders the Marquis's black mood had lifted and his temper so much restored that he accepted Tom's repeated invitation to dine with him. They repaired to the set of chambers Tom occupied in the Albany and after he had changed his clothes he suggested that they essay the dining-room at the Clarendon. The best and most expensive dinner in town was said to be had at this exclusive hotel and Tom declared that he was in funds, thanks to a lucky bet placed at Watier's the previous evening.

On their arrival, the *maître d'hôtel* recognised them and himself bowed them to a table reserved for distinguished patrons and presented a large bill of fare. Unfortunately, no sooner had the soup been removed and the fillets of turbot with Italian sauce, the chickens *à l'estragon*, the lobster patties and the other assorted dishes been set upon the table than another party entered the room. While Tom exclaimed, "Great Jupiter!" in disbelieving tones, the Marquis merely set his teeth and schooled his expression to a polite civility he was far from feeling.

"Ah, Dene. Lavenham." The portly gentleman in satin knee-breeches who accompanied the two ladies hailed them with a wave of one fat, beringed hand.

"Sir Lucius." Marc returned the greeting coolly. He had never cared for any of the Marlow family and thought Lady Marlow's brother little better than a Captain Sharp. There was something untrustworthy, something repellent about those pale eyes set in that perpetually smiling plump face.

It was a pity that Miss Marlow had inherited the same almost colourless eyes, for otherwise she was a strikingly personable young woman of three and twenty. Bowing to her, Marc repressed a shiver. Like her mother, Augusta was a tall, full-figured blonde and in her first season had been hailed as a Beauty. However, her manner was so remote and haughty that it had earned her the unflattering title of the Iceberg among the young bloods. In spite of her handsome dowry, it was believed that none of her suitors had come up to scratch or at any rate she remained unwed.

"I hope I see you well, Miss Marlow."

"Perfectly, I thank you, my lord." Augusta's cool voice was flat-toned, just as her smile seemed prompted only by disinterested civility rather than any genuine pleasure. Even her movements were measured and formal and the Marquis secretly likened her to a marble statue as she stood there in her white gown.

The two parties exchanged banal pleasantries for a moment longer and then Sir Lucius led his sister and niece away and the two cousins sat down again.

Surveying his dinner, the Marquis found his appetite had deserted him. The only consolation seemed to be that the Marlows did not appear to be aware of His Grace of Weston's plans. Marc was sure that Sir Lucius at least would have been unable to refrain from twitting him with it if he had known.

"How could even Edward have contemplated leg-shackling himself to that . . . that iceberg!" Tom spoke in accents of awe, wiping his brow with a large silk handkerchief. "Uncle Montague must be insane!"

"No, you're out there, Tom." His lordship shook his head. "My father always knows exactly what he is doing." His long fingers clenched convulsively upon the stem of his wine glass. "Only this time he has gone too far. I wouldn't wed Augusta Marlow if she were the last woman left single." His mouth twisted. "Anyone, a Bath miss, opera-dancer, beggar-maid, I don't care which, but any other woman in the world would be preferable!" the Marquis of Dene declared as the glass in his hand snapped in two with an audible crack.

"HERE, GUV'NOR, cast your daylights to the right," recommended Dickon in some anxiety.

The Marquis's moody gaze was fixed at a point somewhere above the ears of his horses. In the distance there was a huge gold and green accommodation coach rocking and swaying on its ponderous journey west. The surface of Marc's mind was idly considering the fact that he would have to pass this hinderance eventually, but his inner thoughts were turning over the recent interview with his parent, searching for a solution.

Thanks to his preoccupation he did not immediately heed his henchman's advice, but when he did turn his head the Marquis saw to his astonishment that there was a young woman tramping along directly in their path, a shabby valise clutched in one hand. To his lordship it was as if she had been conjured up by some magician, but fortunately his hands remained rock-steady on the reins as the curricle went flashing past, so close that the body of the vehicle almost brushed the flapping ends of her brown cloak.

The girl's startled shriek as she leapt aside mingled with Marc's curses as he skilfully brought his team to a halt. Ordering Dickon to their heads, he sprang down and hurried back to aid the fallen pedestrian. The girl, who had tumbled to her knees in her haste, had narrowly avoided ending up in the ditch, an escape which had left her clutching her hat and gasping for breath.

"I beg your pardon, ma'am, I did not see you."

"Ooh!" His victim emitted a loud shriek, which if he did but know it was of sheer rage, and ignored his outstretched hand offering aid.

"Good God, must you make that abominable noise?" the Marquis demanded brutally, hauling her to her feet without any more ado.

"Oh, how dare you?" she gasped indignantly, her bosom swelling, and, reaching up, promptly boxed his left ear.

CHAPTER TWO

THERE WAS NO telling how the furious Marquis might have reacted to this unexpected treatment, for no sooner had the blow landed than its perpetrator burst into tears.

"The Devil!" His lordship bit off another more violent expletive as his angry gaze raked over the sobbing figure before him.

She was a very young lady dressed in a faded round gown beneath her cloak. An unbecoming chip bonnet was perched lopsidedly upon her tangle of red-gold curls, its strings tied in a bravely saucy bow beneath her rounded chin.

"Here, take mine." The Marquis thrust a large clean handkerchief into her flustered hand as she sought in vain for her own in her reticule.

Miss Corisande Clifford gave one final sniff and began to mop her cheeks. "Thank you."

He stared down into the pair of slightly blurred but celestially blue eyes she lifted to his face and made the discovery that she was beautiful. Dazed, he wondered how he could have been such a clodpole as not to see it until now. Her features had a charming delicacy and even the bout of tears had failed to spoil her lovely rose-petal complexion.

The Marquis blinked and then recovering his usual aplomb made her a graceful bow. "My name is Richmond. At your service, ma'am."

She acknowledged this with a regal inclination of her head and then rather spoilt the effect by saying in a penitent voice, "I do beg your pardon. I should not have hit you, only I didn't hear you approaching and you gave me such a fright!" A watery little smile hovered on her lips. "You must think me a regular ninnyhammer to behave so, but for one awful moment I thought you were Horace."

"Horace?" queried the Marquis still bemused, his attention almost wholly occupied in wondering how it would be to kiss that delectable rosebud mouth.

"Mr. Hepburn." A shudder racked her slim form. "He is the most odious creature."

"Then I'm sorry to remind you of him, Miss . . . ?"

"Clifford. My name is Corisande Clifford," supplied the enchanting damsel. "Oh, no, you don't look at all like him, it's just that I thought he had followed me and I couldn't bear it." Her soft voice was filled with revulsion.

Sensing a mystery, Marc's black brows rose. "Why should he wish to follow you?" he asked. "And come to think of it, Miss Clifford, why are you out here all alone on foot? Where's your abigail?"

A gurgle of laughter escaped her. "I don't have one. Paid companions don't, you know."

"You're a servant?" ejaculated the Marquis incredulously. Everything about the girl, from her manners to her pleasant voice, spoke of gentle breeding. Forcing himself to concentrate, he realised that her clothes were of cheap material and then his glance fell on the shabby valise which she had dropped earlier at her feet. "Good God, are you a runaway?"

A shadow darkened the lovely face. "Yes, I am," she admitted. "But I won't go back, so you needn't try to make me."

"My dear girl, I have no intention of doing so."

At this, the mutinous look faded from the blue eyes. "Good, for if I did, I would only have to hit Mr. Hepburn over the head again with another vase and Lady Maltby would be sure to find out and then I should be dismissed anyway."

An involuntary chuckle greeted this doleful pronouncement, but as the Marquis hastily apologised for it Miss Clifford let it go without comment. "Er—forgive my curiosity, Miss Clifford, but why did you hit this Hepburn fellow in the first place?" Marc asked gravely, controlling his amusement.

"He kissed me," she explained sharply. "Yesterday, when Lady Maltby was resting in her room. It was horrid and the only way I could think of to make him stop was to seize that vase. Luckily, it did not break for, although it is quite hideous, Lady Maltby seems to value it and I wouldn't have been able to think of an explanation of how it came to be broken, I'm sure." A little giggle escaped her. "Well, leastways, not directly, though I dare say I should have done in the end."

A pair of enchanting dimples peeped at him and the Marquis found himself weakly agreeing with the propriety of her decisive action.

"The trouble is, you see, Mr. Hepburn is Lady Maltby's nephew. He is a great favourite with her and can do no wrong in her eyes."

Corisande sighed. "You can have no idea how awkward it has been trying to avoid his attentions these past few weeks."

"He sounds a curst rum touch. No business running after a baby like you."

"I'm not a baby!" cried Miss Clifford indignantly. "I'm turned eighteen—well almost," she corrected herself, incurably honest.

"Well, you don't look it in that rig," his lordship informed her frankly. "Damme, you don't even look old enough to be turned out on the world. What can your parents be thinking of?"

"I'm an orphan," Corisande explained. Receiving his embarrassed apology, she reassured him that she was used to it. "My Mama died when I was a baby. I was brought up by my Grandmama, Mrs. Dalton, my Mama's mother, who was a widow. We lived near Oxford, but when she died last spring there was no money and so I had to find employment."

"Haven't you any other close relatives?"

"Oh, yes, an uncle, in fact, but he lives in Northumberland and Papa quarrelled with him years ago before he disappeared while in Africa."

"Africa!" The Marquis had the disconcerting sensation of sinking deeper into what promised to be a morass of tangled explanation. "Look, I think we had better continue this discussion elsewhere. We cannot stand in the middle of the road all day and there's a very good posting-house at Beckhampton."

"No." A tide of colour flooded Miss Clifford's cheeks.

The free and easy tone of their conversation had not led him to suppose that she might regard him with suspicion. "Don't be missish! I haven't any nefarious schemes in mind, I promise you. You are quite safe with me."

"Are you certain?" A doubtful look accompanied this question. "It is quite wearying, you know, having to defend one's honour all the time."

The Marquis gave a crow of laughter. "Quite certain, but I'll make sure there are several vases to hand, Miss Clifford, if it relieves your mind."

HAVING APPARENTLY decided that the Marquis was no "Hardened Deceiver", Miss Clifford docilely allowed herself to be handed into the curricle. She bestowed a friendly smile upon the startled Dickon and exclaimed in admiring tones, "Oh, how very comfortable this is!" with all the air of one happily prepared to be pleased.

Gathering the reins in his hands, Marc ignored his henchman's enquiring gaze. "Stand away from their heads." Dickon obeyed and as the curricle moved forward jumped up nimbly behind, muttering loudly to himself as he did so. "Danged if I knows what your lay is this time, guv'nor! Running off with a gentry-mort! A rare dust-up there'll be when a certain old cull gets wind of it!"

Since the Marquis, in common with most of his friends, was conversant with cant terms, he had no difficulty interpreting these dark remarks. Glancing at his passenger's face, he saw from her puzzled expression that the Tiger's meaning had been lost on Corisande and was thankful for it. However, Dickon's warning prompted him to say, a little mendaciously, "Seeing you are a runaway, I think we'd better give the Beckhampton Inn the go-by." Corisande looked at him in surprise. "They know me there and it would be all round the countryside that you were with me." He met her wide-eyed stare. "I'm the Marquis of Dene." He coughed apologetically.

"Oh!" Miss Clifford received this information with an interested look. "Then you are the Duke of Weston's heir?" she ascertained.

"Just so." He inclined his head in acknowledgement. "You appear to have the advantage of me, Miss Clifford."

"I have heard a great deal about you," she agreed unabashed. "Lady Maltby is very fond of gossip and she was forever talking about you. She said that your extravagance was a scandal and disgrace and that you would be the death of your relatives."

"Hah!" retorted the Marquis. "She can't have met my father."

"Isn't it true, then?" asked Miss Clifford innocently. "It did sound rather dashing, but now I come to think of it you don't seem much like a libertine."

"What!" exclaimed his lordship furiously. "I'll thank your Lady Maltby to keep her tongue off me. Libertine indeed! I might keep a fancy piece or two, like everyone else, but I've never ruined anyone's reputation yet."

"Then you aren't a gamester either?" His passenger sounded disappointed.

"No! Well, maybe I am, but what has it got to do with some old cat?" he demanded wrathfully. "And what business had she discussing such things with a chit like you? I'd like to know. A fine thing to be filling the ears of a schoolroom miss with such tales!"

This testy declaration induced Corisande to apologise shyly. "And you see, in any case she is so very old that I think she often forgot precisely who I was. At least she frequently called me by the name of her particular bosom-bow, a lady who died several years ago according to the servants. It was worst when she drank, for then she could never remember anything!"

"Good God!" exclaimed the Marquis in accents of disgust. "Never heard of such a shocking thing in my life!"

He was a good-natured young man and the picture she had unwittingly painted readily engaged his sympathy. The idea of such a lovely girl being shut away with some addled old woman, who probably bullied her, besides being obliged to fend off the attentions of the rum customer of a nephew, horrified him.

"It strikes me," he said severely, "that it was a curst good thing you loped off when you did. No place for a young girl like you."

"I'm so glad that you think so! It did worry me a trifle having to slip away early this morning without a word, but if I hadn't left while Lady Maltby was still abed I should never have got away."

"Didn't you leave a note?" Marc asked, wondering if he was going to be required to rectify matters, since no matter how unsuitable a guardian Lady Maltby had proved to be, it was not *bon ton* to leave her in ignorance of Miss Clifford's fate. "Don't want the silly old gudgeon to think you've fallen into a river, or some such."

Miss Clifford gurgled with laughter and assured him that she had indeed left a missive explaining her intention of seeking fresh employment.

"Well, that's all right, then," he said relieved.

By this time they had reached the outskirts of the little town of Calne and Miss Clifford began to make an attempt to tidy her dishevelled appearance.

"Here, you'd best straighten your bonnet while you are about it," advised her companion.

Friendly to a fault, she did not take exception to this remark but merely thanked him and rectified her omission. Such rational behaviour delighted the Marquis. Females in his experience were apt to fly off into a pet at the least hint of criticism.

"That's the ticket, you'll pass muster now." He gave her an approving smile.

Corisande felt her pulses go bump in an alarming manner. Although she did not know it, hearts more experienced than hers had fallen for that engaging smile, but she was wise enough to silently chide herself for her foolishness. Grandmama had often warned her that her besetting sin was a reckless impulsiveness and here she was plunging into intimacy with one who, by repute at least, was a dangerous, hellraising, womanising blade. It would be outside of enough to compound this original folly by placing any personal emphasis upon his carelessly caressing smiles.

It was therefore an accordingly subdued Miss Clifford who followed his lordship into the Red Lion. This modest hostelry rarely entertained the gentry, but there was a clean homely air about the place that Corisande found reassuring. The landlord came bustling up at their entrance and his repeated bowing made her want to laugh. Not that it surprised her that he was so eager to please. The superb cut of his lordship's drab Benjamin and his unconscious air of command as he bespoke a private parlour for their use proclaimed his quality as surely as if he had handed out his card.

Once ensconced in the snug little parlour Marc said, "Shall I order some food for us both? I don't know about you, but I'm devilish sharp-set. I left London early and have been travelling ever since."

A delighted smile lit up Corisande's small face. "Oh, please do. I am excessively hungry. There wasn't any time for breakfast this morning."

"You poor child," the Marquis said.

"Now you are bamming me."

"Yes," he admitted. "Do you dislike it?"

"No, I've always wished I had brothers to laugh with, to share a joke with and tease a little." There was an unconsciously forlorn catch in her voice that prevented the Marquis from replying as he wished. He had no desire to be seen in a brotherly light by so pretty a girl, and it was a novel but dampening experience, he decided glumly as he moved to pull the bell and summon the waiter.

"May I ask where you are heading?" Corisande, thinking she ought to break the silence, put this question to him rather timidly a few moments later. There was suddenly something withdrawn about his darkly handsome face, reminding her of the great gulf between them. A peer of the realm and a pauper!

The remote expression vanished as Marc replied cheerfully, "I'm on my way to visit my cousin, Tom Lavenham. He lives near the village of Marshfield at a house named Lavenham Place."

With these words he was once again the friendly young man she had encountered so unexpectedly and Corisande's queer feeling of isolation and depression vanished. She smiled at him in relief and Marc decided that any crumb of her interest was better than nothing at all. He couldn't remember when he had last been so attracted!

"And you, Miss Clifford, what are your plans?"

"I'm not precisely certain," she confessed, wrinkling her little nose thoughtfully. "I was hoping to have caught the stage to Bath at Marlborough, but I missed it. It took me much longer to walk into town than I had reckoned on but, having arrived there too late, I thought I might as well continue on foot."

"You cannot have intended to walk all the way to Bath," objected the Marquis.

"No." She grinned at him, her dimples dancing. "But I am rather short of funds, you see." Her expression darkened. "Not long before we met I did catch up with the stage, quite by accident. You might even have seen it yourself, it was bound for Bristol, but it had stopped because one of the leaders had got a leg over the trace. Anyway, I seized the opportunity to ask the driver if he would convey me to Chippenham, where the Bath road goes off, but he said no, he had his full complement of passengers. He seemed in a very bad temper, but I dare say if I'd been able to grease his palm he might have found room for me after all."

"Very probably," concurred the Marquis sympathetically.

"Now you are teasing me again," Corisande laughed. "But truly I was never so glad as when you offered to take me up. My boots were pinching and I was very cross and hungry."

"It's a wonder you did not murder me," said her companion, his eyes twinkling. "I salute your restraint."

Corisande blushed. "I am not normally so ill-tempered," she said in a small voice. Her behaviour seemed very shabby now, particularly in light of his subsequent kindness. "You must excuse my bad manners, sir," she added, her head drooping in embarrassment as she recalled how hard she had slapped him.

"Gammon!" This admonition brought the red-gold head up abruptly. "I deserved it. Driving like the veriest whipster! To tell you the truth, I wasn't concentrating," he admitted with a rueful grin.

This revelation appeared to ease Miss Clifford's conscience. Her fingers ceased their nervous pleating of her already sadly creased skirts, which were not enhanced by such rough treatment.

Beneath the ugly lines of the gown her slim body curved in all the right places, prompting Marc to think that she was a young lady who would certainly repay the dressing. She was not tall, which was the *mode,* nor was her hair a fashionable brunette shade, but her figure was excellent and her small oval face classically lovely. Were she dressed in elegant clothes, he'd back her to cast all the current London Beauties in the shade.

As Corisande chatted brightly, pouring out her life's history, Marc wondered if she was truly as unaware of her stunning looks as she seemed to be. Her disposition appeared to be so open and unaffected that he rather thought she might be. He could not think of any other female of his acquaintance who would be so unselfconscious in the same circumstances. Miss Clifford seemed oblivious of embarrassment at finding herself alone in a private parlour with a virtual stranger. Quickly dismissing the thought that she was altogether too innocent to appreciate the potential danger of such a situation, he came to the conclusion that she trusted him.

If he had been a vain young man, Marc might have felt affronted but, as he was not, he was rather touched by her confidence in him. It was a novel feeling, if nothing else, to have his morals so uncritically approved—a sensation that was not dulled by the gradual realisation that Miss Clifford's nature was a blithely confiding one. A silent laugh shook him as he half listened to her chatter. As a means, though he doubted it was deliberate, of depressing any hopeful young blade's amorous pretensions, it was a masterly stroke, since a man needs must be a hardened rake to attempt seduction under that trusting wide-eyed gaze.

"So I shall see if Miss Tidcombe will employ me," Corisande was saying. "I am tolerably certain that she will." Something in her suddenly doleful tone caught the Marquis's attention.

"Who the devil is Miss Tidcombe?"

"Oh, I wish I could see her face if you said Miss Tidcombe to her in that tone and put up your brows at her just so!" Miss Clifford chuckled. "She is the most disagreeable woman."

"Forgive me, but in that case why do you wish to seek refuge with her?"

Realising he had not been properly attending, Corisande patiently began again. "Miss Tidcombe owns a small seminary in Bath. She was my governess for a time before she inherited the school from a relative. I wrote to her offering my services when Grandmama died, but then Mr. Thruxton, Grandmama's solicitor, obtained for me the post with Lady Maltby. He said that it was a more appropriate means of earning one's living for a young lady in my position," she explained. "I cannot think he could have known Lady Maltby very well," she added thoughtfully.

"Apparently not," the Marquis said, amused.

An answering gleam lit the blue eyes. "Yes, but at the time I thought being a paid companion would be preferable to working for Miss Tidcombe. She is a nip-cheese, you see, and I know how it will be!" She sighed. "I dare say I shall soon grow accustomed to it and at least it is respectable employment and beggars cannot be choosers."

"Are you really so low on funds, Miss Clifford?" The amused note had fled the deep voice and Corisande nodded, not in the least offended by the question, sensing his genuine concern as he added abruptly, "Haven't you any money at all?"

"Only a small annual allowance. My grandfather, the Admiral, made a settlement on me in his will. He knew of course that Papa was not a practical person and I suspect he felt that he had better do something for me in case Papa forgot. Papa was not interested in money, or in his family, for that matter. He was forever disappearing off to distant places. Rare plants were his passion, you see." Her pretty mouth drooped. "He would never let me accompany him, he said it was too dangerous and, of course, he was right, for he disappeared in Africa and we never learnt what became of him."

The advent of their waiter to lay the covers brought this interesting conversation to a halt. Seeing that talking about her father had upset her a little, Marc curbed his curiosity on that head when the waiter went to bring up their meal. However, as soon as the man had set the savoury omelette, together with a dish of potatoes and a cold beef pie, before them and departed, he put another question which had been vexing him.

"You, Miss Clifford, are unquestionably a lady, but just who are your family?" He knitted his black brows together. "I fancy a female of your breeding should not be hiring herself out as a governess."

Corisande looked up from the cup of tea she had been pouring for herself, having declined to join his lordship in testing the inn's best home-brewed. "You sound just like Mr. Thruxton," she announced, much diverted. "Only, as he could not tell me what I should do otherwise, I could not very well heed his advice." Noticing a look of impatience gathering on his lordship's face, she went on quickly, "My papa was Admiral Sir George Clifford's younger son and on my mother's side I am related to the Morleys. They are a very good Yorkshire family, I understand. Do you know them, by any chance?"

"Good God," said Lord Dene faintly. "My dear girl, if you are a connection of the Morleys of Ravensthorpe, then we must be cousins of some sort. Lady Charlotte is my great-aunt and the most fearsome old dragon you could ever have the misfortune to meet."

"No, is she really!" Miss Clifford giggled. "And we are related, how very droll, sir! But it cannot signify. I only mentioned their name because they sound the sort of people you would know, but really Mama was only a distant connection of theirs."

"None the less, you had best write to them at once."

"I could not consider doing so," she declared indignantly, her busy knife and fork suddenly stilling. "I will not be an object of charity, beholden to a set of people I have never laid eyes on in my life."

"It would be more suitable to make your home with them than become a drudge in some seminary."

"I do not think so." Corisande's chin lifted defiantly. "I prefer to pay my own way, sir. Moreover, there is no reason to suppose that they would wish to take me in. My uncle, Sir Robert, wouldn't do anything for us when Papa disappeared, although Grandmama wrote to him. I know he and Papa were not on speaking terms, but still! I place no reliance, sir, on family feeling," she concluded firmly.

It was a remark which struck a sympathetic chord with the Marquis and he decided to abandon the argument. Who was he to preach? Anyway, watching Miss Clifford consume a large helping of jelly with apparent calm, he shrewdly guessed that there was a good deal of determination behind that lovely face.

"Well, I do not blame you for being wary," he conceded. "People who feel obliged to help one only because they perceive it as their duty are usually dead bores."

Miss Clifford considered this. "But you have helped me yourself," she pointed out. Then she gasped and an apologetic smile appeared. "Oh, dear, perhaps I shouldn't have said that. Grandmama used to say that my tongue ran away with me."

The Marquis regarded her with amusement. "I dare say I shall survive your criticism, Miss Clifford. Have some more pudding."

"Thank you, no. I couldn't eat another bite."

"Then, in that case, perhaps we can be on our way."

Corisande's large blue eyes opened wide and she stared at him, obviously taken aback by his suggestion.

"Do you have some objection to leaving straight away?" he enquired. "You did say you wanted to go to Bath, did you not?" She nodded, speechless. "Then time is pressing if we are to reach our destination before nightfall."

"Yes, but . . . no," Corisande's confusion was rife. "I cannot travel with you, sir."

"Why not?" he asked. "You have already done so, you know."

"But that was different," she protested. "But I cannot allow you to convey me to Bath. You are going to visit your cousin."

"Tom can wait." He smiled at her mockingly. "Or have you changed your mind and decided that I am not trustworthy after all, Miss Clifford?"

"Oh, fudge!" Corisande dismissed this flippant remark with an impatient toss of her head. "I may be a schoolroom miss to you, sir, but I am not completely stupid."

"Did that unfortunate remark rankle? I apologise for my crass mistake, ma'am," he said, keeping his countenance grave.

"Now you are teasing me again," she declared and her rather worried frown eased itself away. "Of course I trust you." She smiled at him. "You are being too absurd!"

Corisande thought of the laughter which had frequently warmed his eyes and her instincts told her she was right, no one who could laugh with his eyes like that could be a villain. "But you must see that it is nonsense for you to say that you will escort me to Bath."

"Why?"

His simple question threw her. "Well, it is," she declared at last. "I cannot let you involve yourself in my tedious affairs just because we met on the road."

"We didn't just meet. I almost ran you down," he reminded her. "Like it or not, Miss Clifford, I am already involved. I don't care to leave a lady in distress and, in any event, you are a cousin of mine, several degrees removed no doubt, but I feel justified in claiming a responsibility for seeing you safely bestowed."

This somewhat arrogant speech brought a frown to Corisande's face. "You said only a moment ago that people should not help other people out of a sense of duty," she muttered rebelliously.

He grinned at her. "Don't be missish, it doesn't suit you," he ordered. "Anyway, who said I was doing anything out of a sense of duty? I want to make sure you arrive there in one piece. Only pity my state of mind, dear girl, if I let you go off alone." His expression grew pained. "I shouldn't sleep sound for imagining you fallen in a ditch somewhere."

"Oh, well, in that case!" she laughed and abandoned her conscientious attempt to dissuade him. "I must own that your help would be nice." She stood up, smoothing her skirts. "It is rather awkward travelling on one's own. I didn't realise it until today, for I never had to do so before."

Corisande picked up her unmodish bonnet and turned to the mirror, saying as she did so, "Mr. Thruxton made all the arrangements for me to travel to Lady Maltby's and escorted me himself." She bundled her luxuriant tumble of curls beneath the bonnet's brim. "And I hardly ever went anywhere while I was living there."

His lordship found this artless speech revealing, the complete lack of bitterness in her tone surprised him. For someone whose short life could not always have been a happy one, Corisande Clifford was singularly devoid of self-pity. She seemed blessed with a sunny nature and a practical determination to make the best of things.

"You know, I think it must be so much easier to be a man," said Corisande, drawing on her gloves. "I have frequently wished I had been born a boy. Then I could have sought out some more exciting way of earning my living—perhaps even have made myself a fortune. Females are so restricted!"

"Ah, but you would have been wasted as a boy, Miss Clifford," the Marquis murmured wickedly and then regretted it as her startled eyes flew to his.

"Is that a compliment?" she asked doubtfully.

"Yes," he admitted, rather amused. "It was meant to be, I'm afraid."

"Oh!" The soft colour stole into her cheeks, making her look prettier than ever. "I wasn't perfectly certain. I haven't met many men, you see. Grandmama was often too poorly to go out into society so we lived very quietly. And, in any event, I was too young to make my come-out in those days."

Her eyes began to twinkle. "Mr. Hepburn did say several pretty things to me, but he always dressed in the most peculiar way I could not feel his taste was to be trusted." The Marquis chuckled.

"But truly, sir, he did. The shoulders of his coats were so wadded he looked like a duck and the points of his shirt-collars were so starched he could scarcely turn his head." She surveyed Lord Dene's expertly tied cravat and wondered if the muddle Mr. Hepburn displayed to the world had been intended as a copy of this elegant artistry.

Corisande decided to forgo this question as it was obvious that the Marquis was wanting to be off, so she informed him that she was ready instead. He opened the door and ushered her downstairs, where he proceeded to settle their account, an action which brought a look of consternation to her face.

No sooner had they crossed the threshold of the inn than she said urgently. "I must pay for my own meal, sir."

"You are short of funds, Miss Clifford. Pray permit me to be your banker."

A swift shake of the head answered him. "Indeed, I could not. It would be a shocking piece of impropriety; one should never be beholden to strangers."

He wanted to smile at her, but knew she would be offended if he told her to keep her shillings. "Let us call it a loan, then," he suggested soothingly. A doubtful look passed over her face so he added gently, but with a firmness that brooked no argument, "We can discuss it later if you like, but I'd rather not keep the horses standing."

Thus appealed to, Miss Clifford sensibly consented to take her place in the curricle without further ado and a moment later it drew out of the innyard to resume its journey westwards.

CHAPTER THREE

DUSK WAS FALLING as Lord Dene's curricle swept into Bath. Miss Clifford had explained that the seminary she sought was in Gay Street and she looked about her with interest as they negotiated the impressive streets. This desire to inspect her surroundings was hampered when the Marquis made an urgent request for her to lower the veil on her bonnet.

"I'm sorry, I should have thought of it myself," Corisande said apologetically. "You cannot want to be seen with someone like me." The sight of so many fashionably clad pedestrians had brought home to her the dowdiness of her apparel.

The Marquis, who was delicately manoeuvring his vehicle between a hackney drawn up on the right of the road and a rider having difficulties controlling his lively mount, could not spare the time to deny this suggestion beyond a shake of his head. He did not care a button for what anyone might think of him but, unlike Miss Clifford, was wordly-wise enough to realise that being seen in his company in such circumstances could seriously damage her reputation if it ever became known.

"Do you know which house it is?" he asked, as they turned into Gay Street.

"I'm not proioely sure," confessed Corisande. "I have never been in Bath before and I was going to enquire the direction when I got here."

"Dickon, get down and ask that crossing-sweeper over there," ordered his lordship, slowing to a halt.

Nothing loath, the Tiger hurried to accost the grimy urchin standing on the nearby corner leaning on his broom. The child nodded and gestured with one arm down the street towards Queen's Square. The Marquis flipped a coin to Dickon who handed it over to their delighted informant and they set off once more.

The house was tall and narrow and seemed singularly unwelcoming to Corisande who stared at it in distaste.

"The Devil!" exclaimed the Marquis, viewing the house in equal dismay. "I beg pardon," he added as Corisande turned a startled gaze upon him. "But don't you see, Miss Clifford, there can be no one at home. The shutters are up and the knocker is off the door."

Corisande bit her lip, the colour draining from her face. "Perhaps if I enquire at the next house I might learn when Miss Tidcombe will return." Her shaky voice betrayed her attempt to appear calm.

"Stay here." Bidding Dickon to mind the horses, he went to perform this task himself. A maidservant answered his imperious knock and his engaging smile soon conquered her look of suspicion during the short conversation that ensued. Corisande watched them anxiously but his charming smile swiftly faded as the Marquis returned to the carriage.

"I'm sorry, it isn't good news." He took one of her cold little hands in his own, in an unthinking gesture of comfort. "Miss Tidcombe has moved away and the house has been sold. Apparently the school was losing money and she decided to give it up and go and live with her married sister. The woman did not know of her exact whereabouts."

Corisande became even paler. Unconsciously she had been pinning all her hopes on securing employment in Gay Street. Swallowing hard she said, "Thank you, sir. You have been most kind, but perhaps I could trouble you further to convey me to the nearest respectable hostelry? I would not ask it, but it is growing dark and I do not know my way around Bath."

His lordship, whose knowledge of Bath hotels was confined to such fashionable establishments as the Christopher, York House or the White Hart in Stall Street where the mailcoaches stopped, restrained a groan. He could well imagine the reception an ill-clad young girl with only one shabby valise and unaccompanied by so much as an abigail would receive at these select hostelries. In any event, he doubted if Miss Clifford could afford to pay the shot at even a very modest inn for more than a night or two. "No, it won't serve," he announced. "You cannot stay here in Bath."

"What else can I do?" she blurted in a rather desperate tone. "I haven't the money to travel further and what purpose would it serve to do so? No, I shall look for some cheaper lodgings in the morning and then seek other employment." She tried to smile. "I shall do very well, sir. You must not worry about me."

The Marquis stared at her, a queer expression in his eyes. "I thought I knew your sex, but I was wrong," he murmured. Every other female of his acquaintance, in such circumstances, would have been in tears by now or casting themselves upon his neck demanding that he save them. Not so Miss Clifford!

Corisande did not understand his enigmatic remark, but it scarcely mattered. Her thoughts were in such confusion it was hard to make sense of anything. It was as much as she could do to maintain her appearance of calm.

Fortunately, the Marquis was too busy to notice the involuntary nervous convulsions of Corisande's slender hands. He had seen that they were beginning to attract attention.

"I think we had best remove ourselves from this vicinity."

Corisande sat back, trying to compose herself and make fresh plans to meet this disaster. It was no use crying or even cursing Fate as she longed to do. She had precisely five guineas in her purse, which was all that she had been able to save out of the pittance Lady Maltby had paid her. It was imperative that she find a post at once without wasting time on tears!

"Sir, we are heading out of the city!" Corisande was suddenly jerked from her contemplations. "I beg you to turn back at once."

"Don't be flying into a pucker," advised the Marquis kindly. "There's no need to fret, I've decided to take you to my cousin's."

"You've decided . . ." Corisande's bosom swelled with indignation. "Please, turn this carriage round immediately. I cannot possibly accompany you to your cousin's house."

"Why not? It seems to me, Miss Clifford, that you haven't much other choice," he retorted with some asperity. "It's the best solution, you know," he added in a softer tone, watching her catch her lower lip between her little white teeth. "It might prove difficult to find immediate employment. Have you references?"

Corisande shook her head. "I could hardly ask Lady Maltby to furnish me with one when I was intending to run away," she pointed out with a ghost of a smile, "But I'm sure I could find some other kind of work. I could be a . . . a milliner's assistant."

"They only take apprentices and you could not pay their fees. Besides, it might not suit you to be bound to some stranger; she might turn out worse than that Maltby woman."

Corisande shuddered.

"And it is difficult to break indentures, I believe," added the Marquis for good measure.

"Oh," said Miss Clifford, quite cast down.

There was a moment's silence.

"I wonder, sir, if you would care to furnish me with a reference?" Corisande asked impulsively.

His lordship quirked one eyebrow at her.

"No, of course, how stupid of me. You are a single gentleman and any recommendation must come from a respectable matron," Corisande murmured.

It seemed that she failed to realise that the Marquis's reputation was such as to positively discourage any prospective employer and he decided not to enlighten her.

"I could become a chambermaid perhaps?" Corisande suggested hopefully.

"No," said the Marquis brutally and refused point blank to enlarge upon his reasons, much to Corisande's chagrin.

Privately, he would have wagered what remained of his fortune that so lovely a girl would be in danger of being molested within an hour of obtaining such a post. She was altogether too innocent, and her beauty too tempting, for such rough and ready work. The idea that some drunken buck might try to force himself upon her made Lord Dene grind his teeth and vow he would do all in his power to prevent such a fate befalling her.

Running out of ideas, Corisande fell silent. No doubt something would occur to her presently. She sighed softly. What a coil she had created for herself by her impulsive decision to leave Lady Maltby's! But no girl of spirit could have done otherwise. The lonely tedium of her life in the bleak old manor had been bad enough, but the arrival of Horace Hepburn had made it intolerable. In spite of her attempt to make light of her difficulties to the Marquis, she had been badly frightened by his odious attentions.

Corisande ventured a swift glance at his lordship's averted profile. Now here was a very different kind of man! Unlike Mr. Hepburn, the Marquis affected no airs and graces. Corisande knew little of the world of the *ton*, but she was willing to wager that his lordship's courtesy owed less to good breeding than to his own character. She had no claim upon his help, no matter what he might argue, but he had been friendliness itself.

"We haven't very far to go. I hope driving in the dark don't alarm you, Miss Clifford," remarked the Marquis.

"Not in the least, sir," Corisande responded, earning herself a grin of approval.

Heartened by the warmth of his smile, she ventured to ask a question that was troubling her. "It will not incommode your relatives to receive me, will it, sir? I do not wish to be an inconvenience."

"Nonsense, Miss Clifford, you couldn't inconvenience anyone," Marc replied bracingly. "As a matter of fact, Lavenham Place is a deuced barracks with room for dozens of guests. Tom's always delighted to receive unexpected visitors and his staff are used to them.''

Her anxiety somewhat relieved, Corisande smiled and turned her attention once more to the vexing question of her future employment, leaving the Marquis free to concentrate on his driving and the devout hope that his cousin would keep any startled exclamations to himself.

Half an hour later they reached a handsome pair of wrought-iron gates and Corisande strove to marshal her disordered thoughts as the gatekeeper came hurrying out of the lodge to admit their carriage. It was too dark for her to discern much of her surroundings, but she had the impression of a large well-kept building as they swept up the long drive and came to a halt before a lighted portico.

Bright lights, warmth and a welcoming bustle of servants broke in on her senses as they stepped inside and Corisande suddenly realised how weary she was. The day had been too full of surprises, but she made the effort to smile as a fair-haired young man came striding towards them.

''Marc! Good God, man, where have you been? Peabody arrived an hour ago with your baggage. We've been keeping back dinner until I thought Pierre would offer his resignation, you know how temperamental he is—''

Tom's cheerful greeting came to an abrupt halt as he espied the slight figure standing at the Marquis's side. He cast an open-mouthed look of astonishment at his cousin.

The Marquis, who had turned to draw Corisande forward, now gave the small hand in his a comforting little squeeze. ''I know you won't mind, Tom, but I've brought a guest with me. This is Miss Clifford.''

While Corisande dipped a curtsy Marc flashed his cousin a warning look and taking the hint Tom curbed his curiosity.

''Delighted to make your acquaintance, ma'am.'' He shook hands politely with Corisande. ''Do come and sit down,'' he invited, leading the way into his library. He pulled a chair close to the fire and urged Corisande to take it. ''You must be chilled travelling at this hour.''

Corisande thanked him with a shy smile. ''It is a cold evening for a drive in a curricle,'' she agreed.

Tom swallowed hard. No stickler for propriety himself, he was aware none the less that many eyebrows would be raised at this artless confession. His mother held to the old-fashioned notion that no lady ought to travel in an open carriage on the public highway where any buck might ogle her if he chose. The fact that their unexpected visitor had done so without even a maid to chaperon her would only make matters worse in Mrs. Lavenham's opinion.

While a room was being prepared, Tom rang for refreshments and when the wine arrived he dismissed his butler and poured for them himself. "Let me give you a glass of this ratafia, Miss Clifford. Then when you have finished it you might like to go upstairs and take off your bonnet."

Tom's orders had been relayed to his housekeeper, who arrived some ten minutes later to conduct Miss Clifford to the room which had been made ready for her. No sooner had the door closed behind them than Tom abandoned his social chatter and rounded on his cousin. "Marc! An enchanting little piece, I'll grant you, but really!"

His cousin's dark brows snapped together. "Good God, Tom. Do you take me for such a ramshackle looby that I would bring my *bien-aimée* to this house and attempt to force her acquaintance upon your mother?"

Tom, colouring, begged pardon for his mistake. "But I don't perfectly understand. If Miss Clifford is a respectable young woman, how comes she to be alone in your company?"

Marc let out a crack of laughter at this inept remark, then rapidly sketched in the details of his acquaintance with Miss Clifford.

"I understand now. Poor little thing!" Tom exclaimed. "But it's a devil of a coil, though, Marc. What's to be done with her?"

"I was rather hoping your mama might have the answer to that," his lordship admitted with a faint crooked grin.

Tom chuckled. "In that case, we'd best go and acquaint her with the facts before Miss Clifford comes down."

Marc agreed with alacrity to this sensible suggestion and they made their way up the handsomely carpeted staircase to the drawing-room on the first floor, where his aunt was impatiently awaiting them.

"SALLY, HERE, will attend to your wants, miss. If there is anything further you require please ring and I'll do my best," announced the black bombasine-clad housekeeper with majestic hauteur.

"Thank you," Corisande murmured, feeling almost inclined to apologise for putting the woman to the trouble of escorting her to this elegant bedchamber.

Fortunately, Sally, the housemaid, whose services she was being lent, was young and not at all alarming. She had brought up hot water for Corisande to wash her hands and face and she unpacked a gown from Corisande's shabby valise while Corisande performed these ablutions.

"Shall I tidy your hair, miss?"

"Heavens, it is windblown, isn't it!" Corisande chuckled ruefully when she caught sight of herself in the dressing-table mirror.

It was an unaccustomed treat to have someone dress her hair, but Corisande had already come to the conclusion that Lavenham Place was a house where gracious living was the order of the day. Country bred, she had never encountered such style and out and out luxury and the effect was rather overpowering on her already strained nerves. She couldn't help wishing that the Marquis's cousin lived more quietly, though she knew she was being absurd.

As if his relatives could be anything other than grand, she thought to herself, amused at her folly. I must not let his kindness blind me to the fact that he is a peer of the realm! What does it matter if I feel uncomfortable amid all this grandeur? I have no business here and will be gone tomorrow, she reminded herself.

An unaccountable feeling of flatness invaded her at this realisation.

"There, that's better, I reckon, miss."

"Indeed it is. Thank you, Sally."

Corisande smiled at the maid, determined to shake off her ridiculous depression. What was the matter with her tonight? It must be that she was tired for it was foolish to give way to the vapours now. She had escaped from the clutches of Mr. Hepburn and the merest glimpse of Lavenham Place was enough to reveal that the lady who could command this household must be someone acquainted with all manner of respectable persons.

Surely at least one of Mrs. Lavenham's friends would be in want of a companion or governess or know of someone who was? Her troubles would soon be at an end, she thought with a return of her usual optimism, and this new dawn of hope enabled Corisande to follow Sally downstairs with more equanimity than she would have dreamt possible half an hour before.

Meanwhile, from the stony expression on his aunt's face the Marquis was realising that his explanation for his tardy arrival had not found a sympathetic audience.

His heart sank, but before he could say another word the very young lady seated on the velvet sofa next to her mama exclaimed, "Oh, Marc, how very gallant of you to rescue her! It is like something out of a fairy-story."

Miss Lavenham was a romantically minded sixteen-year-old. Not yet out, she was inured to her elder brother's criticisms and did not take offence at his curt, "Letty, be silent, if you please!" She merely tossed her dark curls and continued to keep her big brown eyes fastened soulfully upon her cousin's face.

"Indeed, Letty, you go too far," admonished her mama, but without her usual severity.

Mrs. Lavenham thought her giddy daughter had hit the nail upon the head. It sounded as if Marc had been taken in by some pretty-faced hussy who had spun him a tissue of lies. Modern manners were not what they had been in her youth, but even in these degenerate days it was inconceivable a real lady would have so little care for her reputation!

"Ah, Miss Clifford, come and meet my aunt."

Corisande smiled gratefully at her benefactor. She had the uneasy suspicion that her entrance had brought the conversation to an abrupt halt. This feeling deepened as the Marquis performed the necessary introductions and Corisande became aware that Mrs. Lavenham was regarding her with a cool disdain.

Corisande sat down, perching nervously upon the edge of her spindle-legged chair. She was miserably aware of the inadequacy of her simple evening gown. It looked positively shabby set against the expensive toilettes worn by the other two ladies. But she need not look down her long nose at me because I cannot afford such lovely clothes, Corisande thought rebelliously, deciding that Mrs. Lavenham must be disagreeably proud.

Just as she reached this conclusion Corisande chanced to meet Letty's frankly curious gaze. For an instant she stiffened, wondering if Miss Lavenham was cast in the same mould as her mother, but then following her natural impulses she smiled. Letty answered with a friendly warmth that made up for the chill of her mother's icy demeanour.

"Well, now that you are here at last, we will go in to dinner. Marc, you may take my arm." Mrs. Lavenham led the way into the dining-room.

Corisande's normally hearty appetite deserted her during the uncomfortable meal that followed. It was almost a banquet, so wide was the choice of beautifully cooked food, but her hostess spoilt it for her by pointedly ignoring her existence. In spite of the Marquis's efforts to draw her into the conversation Corisande felt excluded. She felt sure it was a deliberate snub and she dreaded the moment when they would have to leave the gentlemen to their port.

When Mrs. Lavenham rose and gave the signal that it was time for the ladies to withdraw Corisande could not prevent herself from flashing a look of entreaty at his lordship. With her eyes she begged him not to linger over his wine as she followed her hostess from the room. It was cowardly, she knew, but Mrs. Lavenham terrified her!

Tom, who had also understood her silent message, coughed and fingered his neckcloth. "Mama is a stickler for propriety, I'm afraid," he murmured apologetically. "I believe she had taken Miss Clifford in dislike."

"Obviously, though the fault is not Miss Clifford's but mine, since I brought her here uninvited." Marc directed a rueful glance towards his cousin. "I had not thought my aunt would take it so amiss. No doubt she is wishing me at the Devil." He raked his fingers through his dark hair. "But hang it, Tom, what was I to do?"

"Don't refine upon it, I dare say Mama will come round." Tom's tone lacked conviction.

"Only the veriest monster would have abandoned such an innocent to her own devices in those circumstances," the Marquis continued, pursuing his own thoughts.

"Anyone would have done the same," Tom agreed vigorously. "And she's such a taking little thing, too."

The look of obvious admiration on his face forced a rather harsh laugh from the Marquis. "Bedazzled, Tom? I never thought to see you ready to dangle after a petticoat."

"Well, I'm not much in that line," Tom concurred amiably. "But Miss Clifford is a nonpareil, quite out of the ordinary way!"

Tom noted that his enthusiasm did not altogether please his cousin and said shrewdly, "You may tell me to mind my own business if you choose, but is it wise to involve yourself in any female's affairs so soon after your interview with his grace?"

The Marquis raised his black brows in haughty silence.

"Oh, don't play your grand airs off on me, my lord Marquis," Tom begged, goaded into reluctant laughter. "You may fool the rest of 'em, but I know you better!"

Lord Dene's eyes gleamed with appreciation. "To tell you the truth, I was hoping your mama would offer to keep Miss Clifford by her until I could get word to that uncle of hers, but I can see it won't serve." He stared into the ruby heart of his wine glass. "The fellow lives in Northumberland, of all places. It will take weeks before anything firm can be arranged."

"But didn't you say that Miss Clifford didn't want to make her home with him?"

"Aye, but she's no other relatives." The Marquis shook his head. "Not that I blame her reluctance. God knows I've cursed mine often enough, but it must be a strange and uncomfortable thing to find oneself entirely alone in the world. She is too young and inexperienced to be cast adrift. When a girl is so beautiful there must always be a risk of a loose screw like that Hepburn fellow trying to take advantage."

Realising that Tom was regarding him with a stunned expression, Marc laughed. "Oh, I know my reputation is not so sweet I dare preach morality," he said, shedding his serious tone. "However, Miss Clifford is neither a Cyprian nor a fashionable young matron whose amorous intrigues are winked at by a complaisant husband. Jupiter, she has no more worldly sense than Letty! Could you see Letty in a like case without making some push to help her?"

"By God, you are right!" exclaimed Tom, much struck by this presentation of the matter. "We must make Mama understand our view. I'm sure she'll see reason and invite Miss Clifford to stay once she gets over her fit of pique."

ALAS FOR MR. LAVENHAM'S sanguine hopes, the scene in his mother's drawing-room was not going at all as he and the Marquis would have wished. Corisande, while mindful of her manners, was in a fair way to losing her temper!

Her earlier timidity had been destroyed by a growing annoyance. Corisande could understand that Mrs. Lavenham might resent her presence, but there was no need surely for her to be so uncivil?

"No, ma'am, you mistake the matter. It was my *paternal* grandfather who was the Admiral." Her response to Mrs. Lavenham's continuing inquisition was made through gritted teeth as Corisande strove to control her temper.

"Indeed?" drawled Mrs. Lavenham. "And you have a connection with the Morleys, did you say? Pray explain the relationship in more precise detail, Miss Clifford."

Civility forbade Corisande from refusing to answer, but her clenched fingers and set expression indicated that she thought it a great impertinence to cross-question her.

It's as though she thinks I am making up a Banbury story, Corisande thought indignantly. Does she think I'm some brazen lightskirt trying to inveigle my way into her house? If she hadn't been so angry she might have been amused at the idea.

"Thank you, Miss Clifford. I believe I have it all now." Mrs. Lavenham's tone dripped acid. She didn't believe a word of this farrago. A father lost in Africa! What nonsense, and so she would tell her nephew. She would not have thought Marc so green as to be taken in by a pair of admittedly fine eyes.

If Tom chose to disregard her advice and house the girl, then that was his prerogative, of course, but she had no intention of allowing the wool to be drawn over her eyes by some cheap little adventuress. The fact that the wench aped a certain modest gentility in her manner was nothing to signify good breeding. It showed merely that she had more cunning than most of her kind, but not enough to fool any person of sensibility into thinking she was a genuine lady of quality.

The gentlemen walked in as Mrs. Lavenham finished speaking. The Marquis's dark eyes travelled to Corisande and he had to restrain a whistle of surprise. He had not imagined she could look so stormy, all trace of her sunny smile having vanished.

It was equally clear from her rigid back and compressed lips that Mrs. Lavenham's feelings were ruffled and Tom, deciding that this was not the moment to solicit his mama's sympathy for Marc's protégée, hastily asked Letty to favour them with some music.

Letty gaped at him. Her performance at the pianoforte had been known to make her brother groan aloud, but then she realised his motive. "Oh, yes, of course."

She hurried to take up her new position. "Will you turn my music for me, Cousin Marc?"

He joined her and the uncomfortable tension in the room was soon dispelled.

Corisande's anger fled to be replaced by sympathetic amusement. Letty's rendering of Mozart's sonata was unusual to say the least! Mrs. Lavenham listened in exasperation, but her daughter's lack of skill served to distract her.

The arrival of the tea-tray relieved Letty from her task. Seeing Mrs. Lavenham's attention had been claimed the Marquis bent to whisper his thanks into his young cousin's ear. "A most heroic sacrifice," he murmured, making Letty giggle and feel rather pleased with herself.

"I think Miss Clifford was about to reply in kind to Mama's prodigiously ill-natured remarks when you and Tom came in," she informed him in a whisper. "When I consider how Mama lectures me on the necessity of behaving with courtesy at all times..." Letty's voice trailed off darkly. It was not good manners to criticise one's mama, but frankly she did not wonder at Cousin Marc's sudden frown.

The Marquis reined in his annoyance. Letty was too young to understand her mother's anxieties. Unless he had missed his guess, Mrs. Lavenham had noted the admiring glances Tom had been bestowing upon his visitor all evening and strongly disapproved.

Aunt Lavenham was a devoted mother and he had long suspected her to be possessive of her influence over Tom. Now, whether or not he could convince her of Corisande's claim to respectability, she would continue to hold the girl in dislike if she thought Tom might develop an unsuitable *tendre* in that direction. She would certainly wish to be rid of Corisande at the earliest opportunity.

It was all damned unfortunate, but he could hardly say so to Letty, or even to Tom. He would have to think of some other immediate solution while he attempted to contact Corisande's uncle.

Marc's suspicion that his aunt would not relent in her hostility was confirmed as they drank their tea. She made several barbed comments culminating in an acid assent when Corisande begged leave to retire. "Escort Miss Clifford, Letty, in case the size of a gentleman's residence confuses her and she loses her bearings."

Tom winced and flashed his mother a pleading look, but to Lord Dene's relief Corisande stood up well to this broadside of studied insult. In fact he thought he detected a glimpse of merriment in her blue eyes as she swept a curtsy to her hostess.

"Thank you, ma'am. It has been a most interesting and enlightening evening."

"Enlightening?" Mrs. Lavenham was bewildered.

"Concerning the conduct of a true lady," Corisande replied sweetly. "Had I the need of instruction I should now know what to avoid."

Mrs. Lavenham went puce in the face and began to fidget with her fan as she strove in vain for an answer.

"Touché," murmured the Marquis under his breath, his desire to wring his aunt's neck slightly softened by her obvious embarrassment as she smarted under this fully justified retaliation.

Corisande's first fury had faded, but the opportunity to retort in kind had been too irresistibly tempting. Now, she felt a little sorry for it as she observed the older woman's acute discomfort. But it was too late to withdraw her remark if she had wished to do so.

"I'm sorry," she murmured softly to the Marquis as he escorted her to the door and bent over her hand bidding her goodnight. "I fear I've embarrassed you by upsetting your aunt. Truly it was not my intention!"

"The embarrassment is all on my side. I did not realise my aunt had it in her to be such a sour-tongued virago," he replied quietly. "I must apologise to you for subjecting you to such incivility."

He pressed a kiss upon Corisande's hand, a warmer kiss than custom dictated. "Sleep well and don't worry. We'll discuss an alternative arrangement for your future in the morning. I have another idea that might work," he said, releasing his grip on her slender fingers at last.

Colour bloomed in Corisande's cheeks, but she tried to hide her discomposure as she concluded her farewells.

"Marc, I demand that you remove that creature from this house. If you do not do so I shall retire to the Dower House on the morrow and so I warn you!"

Mrs. Lavenham's angry voice rose shrilly the instant the two girls had left the room.

The Marquis turned from his unwitting staring after Corisande's departing form with a look on his handsome face that quelled the further accusations bubbling from her lips. She gazed at him uncertainly, suddenly afraid for no reason she could name to continue her tirade.

"La, nephew, you need not stare at me like that," she exclaimed nervously. "I never saw you look so like your sire!"

This checked the Marquis's fury as nothing else could have done. "I beg pardon, ma'am," he said with a freezing civility, holding his temper on a tight rein. "I brought Miss Clifford here in the hope that you might extend compassion to one in less easy circumstances than your own. However, I see I was mistaken in thinking you would show sympathy for her plight."

"I have no sympathy to spare for such a designing hussy! She has clearly bewitched you." Mrs. Lavenham sniffed. Far from showing remorse at his behaviour, her undutiful nephew was throwing all the blame on to her!

"Mama, won't you pray reconsider? I'm sure Marc will find a new home for Miss Clifford as soon as he can contrive it, won't you, Marc?" Tom intervened, anxious to promote peace. If his mother retired in high dudgeon to the Dower House it would place him in a fine pickle, since no bachelor could entertain a lady without someone to act as his hostess! His sister was far too young and in the event would be forced to accompany their Mama.

Tom was feeling horribly embarrassed. He had invited Marc down here to sort out his troubles and now his mother was adding to them by her unreasonable behaviour. What the devil had got into her?

Mrs. Lavenham fluttered her lace-trimmed handkerchief with a deadly skill. "I'm sure I had no intention of setting your back up, Tom, my love," she sighed plaintively. "Very well, if that is how you both feel I'm sure I can raise no further objection to entertaining Miss Clifford for a few days longer." Her face crumpled into peevish lines. "Pray be so good as to give me your arm as far as my dressing-room, Tom. I am feeling most unwell."

"Of course, Mama," Tom replied, shooting a rueful glance at his cousin.

"Goodnight, Marc. I hope I shall see you in a better humour tomorrow."

His lordship bowed gracefully but vouchsafed no answer and she swept from the room in an angry rustling of silken skirts.

"Oh, the Devil take it!" swore the Marquis of Dene softly.

CHAPTER FOUR

"You have done what, sir?"

Corisande's outraged demand brought a frown to Lord Dene's face, a frown which deepened as she added hotly, "You have no right to do such a thing. I will never consent to live with my uncle, even if he should invite me to do so. It was folly to write to him!"

She glared at the Marquis. After breakfast he had asked her to join him in the morning-room and Corisande's hopes had risen expectantly, but it seemed that all his plans for her involved the charity of her uncle.

Anger stirred in Marc, but only for a moment. She reminded him too much of a furious kitten spitting defiance and testing its claws. Trying to keep the amusement out of his voice, he said, "I'm sorry you dislike my interference, but there's no help for it. You cannot stay here, my aunt would make your life a misery."

Corisande acknowledged the truth of this with a little inclination of her head. "I know that, sir, but it is my hope that Mrs. Lavenham might know of someone in need of a governess or companion."

"You think she would recommend you?"

His lordship's sardonic laugh caused Corisande to flinch.

"Don't be a fool," he snapped, irritated with himself for his thoughtlessness. Deciding he might as well continue now he had already offended her, he added with brutal logic, "She thinks you an adventuress. Once I depart she will think of some way to send you packing."

Corisande's chin came up. "Then the sooner I leave this house, the better," she declared. "I did not ask to be brought here and I'll not stay to be insulted."

"Why, you silly chit, you have no place to go!" Frustration roughened Marc's tone. He was handling this very badly. He hadn't even told her yet that he had also written to his sister Fanny to beg her aid. The moment he had admitted that he had dispatched a letter to her uncle Corisande had flown into a fury. "You would be in the suds in no time."

Correctly deducing that his lordship thought she was incapable of handling her own affairs, Corisande felt a fresh wave of anger sweep over her. Coldness settled around her heart. What a fool she had been to think it could be otherwise! Why, no doubt, he was already bored by her and anxious to be rid of a burden he had undertaken on chivalrous impulse!

"Perhaps I shall make a mull of it, but you must give me leave to go my own way," she announced, ignoring his protest. "I admit I had thought to approach your aunt with a request for introductions, but I shall do well enough on my own if you'll but arrange for me to be conveyed back to Bath."

"No." The Marquis shook his head.

"You cannot keep me here like some . . . some pirate!" A gasp of indignation escaped Corisande's lips. "It's . . . it's positively feudal of you!"

A muscle twitched beside the Marquis's well-cut mouth.

"And don't you dare laugh at me." A longing to throw something at him began to possess Miss Clifford.

"Then, for God's sake stop behaving like a heroine in some cheap melodrama!" retorted the Marquis instantly. "I confess I wish my aunt's attitude were different, but in spite of her incivility you'll do better here than anywhere else until my sister arrives."

"Oh, so I'm to await the pleasure of another member of your family, am I? If your sister is as much a harpy as Mrs. Lavenham then I don't think I care to waste my time."

The black-barred frown that descended upon his face told Corisande that she had gone too far.

"You little baggage, I ought to turn you over my knee and spank you for that remark."

Hastily Corisande retreated behind a sofa as he advanced towards her. "Stay where you are," she shrieked at him, suddenly remembering Lady Maltby's tales of his notorious temper.

Abruptly Marc halted and nervously Corisande watched him battling to regain control of his rage.

"My apologies, ma'am," he said, in such a cold tone that Corisande felt herself shiver. "I had no business to make such a threat."

Corisande touched her dry lips with her tongue. She wanted to apologise, too, for her rudeness, but his expression overawed her. Gone was the friendly young man of last night and in his place stood a magnificently haughty aristocrat. Feeling completely cast down and foolish, Corisande could only stare at him in embarrassed confusion.

"You are free, of course, to leave at any time, but I would advise against it until I have had time to consult with Mr. Osborne, the local parson. He may know of a suitable position available hereabouts and my cousin Tom's word would weigh in your favour. Would such an action meet with your approval, ma'am?"

Corisande contemplated the toes of her slippers, gathering the courage to meet his scornful gaze. "Thank you," she whispered. Then, recovering a little of her spirit, she added, "It is kind of you to go to such trouble on my behalf, but you have done your duty by me already without the need of further assistance, sir."

Breathlessly she waited for him to deny it, to tell her that he was helping her because he wanted to and not because she was a tiresome charge. The longing to hear that teasing note in his deep voice brought the hot blood to her cheeks.

"Perhaps." The Marquis shrugged.

Corisande's blush deepened and she bit her lip in mortification at his indifference.

Marc's anger began to cool. She looked like a guilty schoolgirl standing there gazing at him with wide-eyed apprehension as if she truly feared he might beat her.

"Corisande . . . perhaps I should not have . . ."

"Please. Let us not discuss the matter any further."

Too humiliated to pay his words proper attention, Corisande only heard his still tone.

"As you wish." His attempt to apologise rebuffed, the Marquis took refuge in pride and made her a cool bow before walking from the room.

"But, Corisande, Cousin Marc is only trying to establish you creditably," said Miss Lavenham.

The sapphire-blue eyes kindled. "He had no business writing to my uncle without my permission," Corisande repeated mulishly.

Letty winced. It had been two days since her brother's guests had quarrelled and in that time Letty had grown to like Corisande a great deal, but she could not pretend to understand her. "What good does such stubborn independence do you, Corisande?" she asked in bewilderment. From her cradle Letty had been taught that gentlemen preferred submissiveness. "You have only succeeded in antagonising my cousin."

"Hah, much I care for his good opinion," Corisande retorted with a complete lack of truth. "He should not have insisted I accompany him. I told him I should do well enough as a chambermaid!'' She heaved a dramatic sigh. "Our quarrelling has made everything so awkward."

Letty nodded sympathetically. "You must not worry, Tom thinks well of you, you know," she ventured shyly. "We shall remain your friends no matter what happens."

"Thank you, Letty." Corisande tried to smile brightly, but she could not dismiss the quarrel with Lord Dene so easily from her mind.

The Marquis's high-handed assumption that he was the person best suited to organise her life still rankled, but it was his sharp words that remained etched on her memory. They had hurt far more than Mrs. Lavenham's continuing snubs—far more than Corisande dared allow herself to question.

"I think I shall take a walk, Letty. I should like to be on my own for a while." Abruptly Corisande rose to her feet and went to fetch her hat.

The day was cloudy, but the air was mild and sweet with the scents of approaching summer. Corisande wandered through the immaculately kept formal gardens, drinking in the beauty of the scene but, contrary to her hopes, the exercise did not improve her spirits.

A splendid oak avenue graced the eastern approach to the park-land beyond the gardens and Corisande espied a rustic bench placed beneath the trees. She sat down to think of some speedier means of shaking the dust of Lavenham Place from her feet, since the worthy Mr. Osborne was taking such a devil of a time about the task.

"So far he has not found one lady in want of my assistance," she sighed aloud, remembering with indignation how Mrs. Lavenham had laughed with malicious triumph when the elderly cleric had sent that apologetic message earlier that morning.

Large tears brimmed to her eyes and spilled over so that she was obliged to wipe them away in some haste.

"It is stupid to cry," she murmured, but it was hard to stem the flow. "And do not pretend your melancholy lies at the door of that disagreeable woman, you hypocrite, Corisande Clifford! It is the prospect of freedom that makes you weep," she continued to admonish herself sternly.

Mrs. Lavenham was plainly delighted by the turn events had taken and had dropped several broad hints that her nephew should accede to Miss Clifford's request to be allowed to return to Bath.

It was extremely disagreeable to be thought an adventuress, Corisande decided. Another sigh escaped her, but valiantly she attempted to scrub her face clean with her pocket-handkerchief.

A flash of colour caught her eye as she lifted her head and she smiled as she saw an inquisitive robin watching her from his perch upon a branch above.

"What a fool I am!" she told him softly. "I dare say all he wants is to be rid of me and I cannot blame him for thinking me a badly behaved chit when I insulted his sister without the least cause."

How she wished it was possible to retract her words, indeed to wipe out their entire heated exchange! Since they had quarrelled the Marquis had spoken to her only when necessary, his manner cool.

"I did not realise how much I would miss his laughter until it was gone," she informed her curious audience with a despairing shake of her head.

Sunk in her dismal reflections, Corisande did not hear the footsteps on the gravel until with a trill of alarm the robin flew off and she looked up to see the Marquis approaching. Quelling the absurd desire to run and hide, Corisande sat up straighter and hoped no tear-stains remained to betray her recent occupation.

"Miss Clifford." The Marquis, who was looking particularly handsome in a blue coat, striped toilinette waistcoat and pale primrose pantaloons, greeted her with an icy formality that made Corisande's spirits plummet.

"Why are you out here? It is almost time for luncheon."

"Thank you, but I am not hungry."

"My aunt is a stickler for punctuality at mealtimes," he reminded her with a wry expression.

"I shall present my apologies to her later, not that it signifies." There was a slight edge to Corisande's voice.

The Marquis remained silent. It had not escaped his notice how their quarrel had pleased his aunt. Now for the first time he wondered if she had been so cruel as to use it as a weapon against Corisande. The idea angered him, but it was his fault if Corisande had been hurt. Nothing had been further from his intention but he had been too wrapped up in his own selfish pride until now to see how the withdrawal of his support might affect Corisande's position.

"Then if you will not come in, may I stay?"

Corisande lifted her gaze from her clenched hands in startled surprise at the sudden warmth in his tone. To her relief, he was smiling at her with that faint crooked grin.

"Is that bench clean? Peabody will throw a fit if I stain these pantaloons," he explained with a lazy smile.

Corisande laughed, but she nodded happily and he sat down next to her.

"I'm devilishly sorry I shouted at you, Corisande. It was too bad of me to try and ride rough-shod over you," his lordship admitted unexpectedly.

Corisande felt like singing; the clouds had suddenly been banished from her horizon.

"It's my curst temper," the Marquis continued. "You made me as mad as fire by talking such fustian rubbish about supporting yourself."

It was on the tip of Corisande's tongue to retort that her plans made good sense, but she curbed the impulse. She could not bear the idea of arguing with him, not now when so little time in his company was left, for she must leave here soon, no matter what he said.

"You have used me shockingly, sir," she told him primly, taking the wind out of his sails with her swift agreement, but then he saw the smile that quivered on her lips.

Marc stared at her, his gaze absorbing her delicate beauty. The desire to pull her into his arms and kiss her smiling mouth was fierce but he overmastered it firmly.

"Little wretch!" he replied appreciatively. "Shall I be forgiven if I take you out riding? I heard you say to Letty that you wished to explore."

"Oh, Marc!" Stars shone in Corisande's eyes. "Oh, I beg your pardon," she added quickly.

"You needn't apologise for forgetting the proprieties. I've been calling you Corisande for days."

"Yes, when you weren't calling me ma'am in that horrid way," Corisande chuckled, suddenly discovering that she could laugh at their absurd quarrel after all. "I would have far rather you had boxed my ears."

"I'll bear that in mind for future reference," he retorted drily, but the note of amusement in his voice did not escape her.

"Shall we go in?" The Marquis rose to his feet.

Corisande discovered that she had miraculously regained her appetite. "I am a little hungry," she admitted.

The Marquis emitted a crack of laughter. "I did wonder if you were feeling quite well," he teased.

"Of all the unhandsome things to say!" Corisande exclaimed, but couldn't help laughing.

He smiled down at her and ran a long forefinger lightly down her cheek. "Come, infant, we had best not keep my aunt waiting. I fear her temper is not equal to it and it is too pleasant a day to spoil with any more scenes."

Corisande's heart had skipped a beat at his touch, but she managed to smile as if nothing had happened to affect her. "Of course, sir," she agreed, placing her hand upon his waiting arm.

"YOU KNOW IT must be rather insipid being a proper young lady," remarked Miss Clifford as she walked across the cobbled stable-yard with the Marquis later that afternoon.

"Why should you imagine that?" enquired his lordship.

"I mean having to be everlastingly concerned with appearances," Corisande explained. "It must be irritating having to watch every word you say and know that every little misdemeanour will be pounced upon by the gossips. From what Mrs. Lavenham was saying just now, there must be hundreds of shibboleths that I never even knew existed."

"I see," said the Marquis trying not to smile. His aunt had held forth over luncheon on the behaviour she deemed suitable for a young unmarried girl and it had obviously struck dismay into Miss Clifford. "In a small place like Bath, where everyone is known to one another, it is difficult, the Bath quizzes are renowned for their gossiping, but things aren't quite so bad in London."

Corisande tilted her head on one side as she considered this. "Really? I must admit it sounded more interesting, although your aunt seemed to disapprove." Her eyes twinkled naughtily.

"Do you long for what my aunt calls frivolity?" he asked with a sympathetic grin.

She nodded vigorously. "I have always thought I should have liked to cut a dash in society. Lady Maltby used to talk of the balls, the Assemblies . . . oh, and a hundred other gaieties. It sounded so exciting!" Her gaze lifted to his confidingly. "Do you think me very silly for envying Letty?"

Miss Lavenham was to be presented next season and this shy confession made the Marquis long to catch Corisande in his arms and kiss away the slightly wistful expression on her lovely face. The presence of a groom leading out a sweet-stepping bay mare made this impossible so he contented himself with a light reply. "Little goose, how should you not? At your age, infant, it would be unnatural if you did not desire parties."

He paused and for a moment Corisande thought he meant to tell her something, but the opportunity, if he had indeed intended any confidence, was lost as Tom hailed them from the stables.

"Where's Letty? Isn't she ready yet? Drat the girl!" Tom tapped his whip impatiently against one thigh.

Corisande who had borrowed Letty's second-best riding-habit and looked extremely fetching in its severely cut style, offered to go and see what Letty was doing.

"No, I'll go myself, she'll pay more heed to me. You try out the paces of Sheba here. She's a gentle creature so there's no need to be nervous."

"Did you tell Mr. Lavenham I needed an easy ride?" Corisande laughed as Tom went hurrying off.

"You did mention that you hadn't ridden for several years."

"No, not since Papa left for Africa. Lady Maltby promised to mount me when I first joined her, but it never came to anything."

"Up with you then," said the Marquis, tossing her into the saddle. "And we'll see what you have remembered." His eyes twinkled. "No gallops mind, until I'm convinced you're not cowhanded, or Tom will murder the pair of us."

"I wouldn't blame him," Corisande declared. "Not when his Sheba is such a darling." And she patted the mare's glossy neck fondly.

They trotted out of the stableyard and the Marquis noted her good seat and steady hands with approval. "Shouldn't we wait for the others?" Corisande asked as they reached the gates.

"No, they'll catch us up easily enough." Lord Dene, who was astride Goliath, one of Tom's liveliest mounts, was handling the big raking grey with a masterly skill that excited Corisande's admiration. It was taking most of her concentration to handle her mare, but it was exhilarating to be in the saddle again. She had missed the feeling of freedom riding gave.

"Oh, this reminds me of being out with Papa!" she exclaimed impulsively.

"You were very fond of him, I collect?"

"Yes." She nodded simply. "He could not always spare much time for me, but when he was home life was more interesting."

"It is a pity he did not leave you better provided for." The Marquis frowned.

"As to that, I dare say he would have done had he thought there would have been such a stupid brangle with the lawyers," said Corisande hotly, firing up in defence of her papa.

"He did leave a will, then?"

"Of course. Mr. Thruxton said that Papa's estate would not amount to a great deal, though there is the house and some money in the Funds, but until Papa is declared officially dead I cannot touch it."

The Marquis reined in abruptly. "Let me understand this properly. Are you saying that your papa might still be alive?"

Corisande shook her head sadly. "There is little chance of that, sir. Papa was not a good correspondent, but even he would not let five years go by without writing one line of reassurance. It is impossible to believe he could be alive so long after he was last seen by anyone. Grandmama had a letter from Cape Town in which Papa told her he intended to trek northwards into the interior and he was never heard of again."

"Mrs. Dalton had enquiries made, I suppose?"

"Indeed, yes. That is one of the reasons why there was so little money left when she died. It was amazingly expensive business and yielded no results whatsoever apart from one report of someone's having sighted Papa on his travels only two months after his arrival." Corisande's explanation faltered.

"But, you see, no one was able to trace his body. Without this proof or reasonable evidence of accident the lawyers said he could not be declared dead." Her lip trembled. "It was all very upsetting at the time, but as no word of him has ever reached England I have learnt to accept his death as a matter of fact." Corisande produced her handkerchief and blew her nose in a determined fashion.

"My poor girl, how horrible it must have been for you."

"I have forgotten it, sir," said Corisande, putting away her handkerchief and forcing a smile. "Grandmama always used to say it did no good to dwell on sorrow and I try to look upon my eventual inheritance as a nest-egg for the future."

The Marquis urged the grey into motion. "Did the will not appoint a guardian for you?"

"Yes, my Grandmama," said Corisande, following suit. "When she died, Mr. Thruxton kindly promised to look after my interests since my uncle did not answer his letters and there was no one else to act as my trustee. It is not official, but he is a very good sort of man," she added warmly.

The Marquis nodded absently. Matters were in a worse case than he had supposed! If Sir Robert Clifford had declined to undertake the guardianship of his niece a year ago, then the prospect of him taking an interest in her now seemed bleak. It was as well he had taken other steps to ensure Miss Clifford's future. Half tempted to tell her of his scheme, he hesitated. There was time enough, and it would be cruel to raise her hopes only to disappoint her if Fanny failed him.

Tom and Letty came cantering up, ending their private conversation, and Tom, who was an excellent horsemen and a noted breeder of thoroughbreds, complimented Corisande on her prowess after watching her for some moments. His praise made Corisande colour happily.

"Tell you what, you shall try Solomon tomorrow," Tom vowed.

"You are honoured, Corisande," Letty chuckled. "Tom won't let me touch him."

"No wonder, miss, you cannot be trusted to stay on his back," riposted her brother, but his indulgent tone robbed the criticism of any sting.

They rode for a while in companionable silence and then Corisande said curiously, "Why is the village named Marshfield? We are in such a high exposed position, not marshy at all."

Tom grinned. "Ah, it's easy enough to understand when you know that the name derives from march, a boundary."

Corisande's puzzled expression cleared. "Oh, like the Welsh Marches, you mean? I remember reading about them once. They were the scene of much fighting, particularly during the Wars of the Roses."

"Heavens, Corisande, how bookish you must be," exclaimed Letty. "Fancy remembering such dull stuff! People will think you are a bluestocking if you are not careful."

A delightful ripple of laughter from Miss Clifford answered this accusation. "How can you say so, Letty? Even if it were true, which I can assure you it is not, then it would be a suitable talent for someone in my position, after all."

The rows of the seventeenth- and eighteenth-century cottages of Marshfield were in the grey Cotswold stone that looked so charming in sunshine. Corisande exclaimed in delight at the neat tidy gardens blooming with a dazzling profusion of spring flowers and vegetables.

As they moved down the High Street, Tom pointed out the handsome almshouse, with its spire and gables, that had been founded in 1619 by one Elias Crispe.

It was now a hot afternoon for the time of year, with the advent of the sun, and Marc's suggestion that they quench their thirst at the Catherine Wheel Inn met with favour. The landlord came bustling out of the shell-hooded doorway, a feature of the village which Tom had already pointed out to Corisande, with lemonade for the ladies and tankards of his best ale for the two men.

"Mama does not approve of my entering the inn even with Tom," Letty announced with an impish grin. "Still, she can't complain if we don't go inside! It is quite antiquated of her, of course, but someone would be bound to notice and pass comment when we next paid a social call or attended church."

The Marquis, who had dismounted, took a glass of the lemonade over to Corisande and, watching them, Tom noticed his smile as he handed it to her. A low whistle of astonishment hissed through Mr. Lavenham's pursed lips.

A little flushed with the heat of the day and the unaccustomed exercise, Corisande's lovely face looked enchanting as she thanked his cousin with an unaffected pleasure. She exchanged some remark with him that Tom did not quite catch, but it made the Marquis laugh.

Tom felt a ripple of unease slither down his spine. He was not one given to fanciful notions, but he had the disturbing impression that his cousin and Miss Clifford were locked in a world of their own, their seemingly innocuous conversation full of hidden meanings known to them alone.

He's making love to her right under our noses! Tom thought in dismay. His gulped hard, wondering if he dared remind Marc of the Duke's decree. Not that he blamed his cousin for being bewitched. If he had been a ladies' man, which thankfully he was not, he too would have been tempted by Miss Clifford.

"Tom." Letty nudged her horse closer in order to gain her brother's attention. Once she had it she said in a slightly puzzled tone, "Do you think Cousin Marc and Corisande are plotting secrets? They seem to have forgotten us."

Even as Tom shook his head Letty's expression underwent a rapid change and she went on in an excited whisper. "That must be the answer! Tom, only look at Cousin Marc, I've never seen him so happy. Wouldn't it be famous if he has fallen in love with Corisande? If she married him she would not have to seek employment and we could all stay friends."

"Don't be such a silly gudgeon, Letty." Tom's tone was sharp. "Miss Clifford is an excellent young woman, but she has no qualifications to fit her for the role of the next Duchess of Weston! What on earth would Uncle Montague say!" Privately, he was certain Marc would never be such a fool as to offer marriage, but such speculations were not for the ears of his young sister!

Letty gazed at him in chastened silence for a moment. "I suppose you are right," she conceded with a wistful sigh. "But I wish it could be so. You haven't an ounce of romance in your soul, Tom."

"No, I haven't, thank God!" her brother told her and firmly changed the subject.

"COME AND PLAY a game of billiards with me, coz," invited the Marquis that evening after everyone else had retired to bed. Unlike Corisande, who was tired after her day in the fresh air, Marc felt restless and disinclined for sleep.

Tom was happy to oblige and they were soon engrossed in their game, the Marquis puffing at his thin black cigar as an aid to concentration.

"Faugh, you'll set the table alight," Tom announced, waving his hand in mock disgust.

The Marquis flashed him a crooked grin. It was an old argument between them. "I notice you only ever seem to object to my habit when you are losing," he retorted sweetly.

Tom laughed. "You are too good for me, I need an excuse to distract you."

The Marquis had picked up the habit of smoking cigars while on campaign in the Peninsula, but of late he had abandoned it. Tonight it suited his restless mood.

"You should stick to snuff," Tom teased as his cousin prepared to light up a fresh cigar.

"Thank you, but I'll leave that to my father."

This dry retort made Tom think uneasily of his uncle and his infamous decree.

"What's wrong, Tom?" The Marquis had noted the shadow that had passed over his cousin's open countenance.

"Oh, nothing," Tom replied airily, but he could not get his mind off the scene he had witnessed that afternoon outside the inn.

"Miss Clifford handled Sheba well, I thought." Tom fiddled with his cue, hoping he sounded as if he was making mere idle conversation. "And she looked stunning in that old riding-habit of Letty's. She really is a remarkably beautiful girl."

"So you've said before."

This cool reply did not deter Tom. "Aye, but what's even more unusual is that her beauty goes hand in hand with a warm heart. And her manners are refreshing after the insipidity of most of the females one meets, don't you think?"

"I suppose so," the Marquis replied, but his attempt at indifference didn't fool Tom, who saw the eager agreement in the dark eyes and was shocked.

"Good God, I thought you were merely amusing yourself! Never say you are getting serious about the girl?" Tom ejaculated.

"No, of course not."

Mr. Lavenham's round cherubic features remained wreathed in disbelief.

"How very perceptive of you, coz. I had no idea you could be so acute." The Marquis shrugged.

"There's no need to rip up at me." Tom grinned at him cheerfully. "I shan't betray your secrets, old friend."

"I know." There had been many love affairs in his past, and Marc had never minded anyone knowing, but somehow he didn't want to discuss his feelings about Corisande, even with Tom.

"Shall you offer her a *carte blanche?*"

A black frown descended on his cousin's face. "I shall do no such thing, you mutton-head!" he growled savagely. "For God's sake, Tom, she's no Covent Garden nun!" Marc flung down his cue with an impatient oath. "Even if I should sink so low as to suggest to Corisande that she become my mistress, this is neither the time nor the place to ask her. She is in my care. Do you expect me to abuse her confidence by making love to her?"

Tom shook his fair head, wishing he had kept his curiosity to himself. It was rare for him to see this side of his cousin, but Marc was capable of the same withering sarcasm as the Duke of Weston on occasion.

There was a short silence while they resumed their game. When it was concluded neither of them wished to begin another.

"Perhaps it's just as well I must keep silent." The Marquis stubbed out the butt of his cigar with a thoughtful grimace. "Considering my dear papa's edict that I must marry Miss Marlow it would be highly inconvenient to fall victim to a grand passion now." He laughed softly. "My wishes would not sway his determination one iota."

Tom knew that note of self-mockery in his cousin's voice. "You may not choose to acknowledge it, but you are talking good sense, Marc," he said with unwonted seriousness. "In birth, rank and fortune Miss Marlow must be counted the superior. You may not like the girl, but your father is right about one thing, she would make a very suitable duchess . . ."

"And Corisande would not." Marc finished the sentence for him. "I wonder."

CHAPTER FIVE

"MAMA HAS GIVEN permission for me to go shopping in Bath since Tom has agreed to escort me. Would you like to accompany us, Corisande?" Letty came whirling into Corisande's bedchamber the next morning. "We shall leave directly after breakfast. Do say you'll come."

"I should like to," Corisande responded promptly, a new plan forming swiftly in her head. This could be her opportunity to look for employment if she could manage to give her companions the slip.

"You could look for some new clothes while we are there. I know a very good dressmaker...oh how stupid of me!" Letty's face turned crimson with embarrassment. "I should not criticise your clothes."

"Please don't worry, Letty. I'm not in the least offended," Corisande chuckled. "Only I don't have the money to spend on new dresses."

"No, of course not." Letty hung her head. Tom was always telling her to think before she spoke!

Watching Corisande finish her *toilette,* Letty wished it was possible for her friend to dress in a more befitting manner. *She* had far more clothes than she knew what to do with; Mama was most generous in that respect.

"What is it?" Corisande turned abruptly as Letty emitted a sudden whoop of delight.

Sobering, Letty considered carefully before saying in a hesitant voice. "Pray do not take it amiss, Corisande, but should you like to have some of my old dresses? I have grown a great deal, you see, this past year and many of my things no longer fit me. They are in good order and still fashionable. I'm sure they could be made to fit you without too much difficulty, since you are smaller than me," she added anxiously.

"How kind of you!" Corisande's eyes began to sparkle. Letty was blessed with the kind of wardrobe she had always longed for.

Luckily, she was handy with her needle and it would be a pleasure to work with such fine materials.

Then another consideration occurred to her. "Would your mama approve of such a gift?"

Letty tossed her dark curls. "Since they are no longer of any use to me Mama can hardly refuse without seeming very mean-spirited indeed." A naughty twinkle lit her gaze. "I know just how to put it to her. She likes to appear charitable."

Corisande managed not to wince. She could not afford false pride; and Letty did not mean to be tactless.

"Are you ready? Good, then let's go down. The sooner we finish breakfast the sooner we can leave," Letty announced gaily, unaware that she had reminded Corisande of the urgency of finding a suitable position where she would not be the object of charity, no matter how well meaning.

They were on the point of departure when the Marquis strolled into the hall. He had not appeared at breakfast, but on being informed of their plan he announced that he should like to join the expedition.

Corisande hoped her expression did not reveal her dismay. Normally she would have enjoyed the prospect of his company, but she knew that the Marquis's sharp eyes would put her plans in jeopardy.

"Must you, nephew? I had hoped for your company this morning." Unexpectedly, Mrs. Lavenham interrupted the discussion. "There are some designs for the new alterations to the Dower House on which I should like your views. You have such excellent good taste, Dene, and you are so knowledgeable about architecture. And you, too, Miss Clifford, perhaps you would care to join us? A fresh opinion would be most welcome."

While the rest of the party blinked and tried to hide their astonishment at this show of unlooked for cordiality, the Marquis alone guessed the reason for this effusiveness. Mrs. Lavenham had realised that he and Corisande had made up their quarrel. He wondered if she was secretly a little ashamed she had allowed her prejudice against Corisande to go too far and had issued this invitation by way of amends.

"Thank you, aunt, for your confidence, but perhaps another time if it is convenient?"

The Marquis's cool reply dashed Corisande's flicker of hope. So he meant to accompany them after all!

Mrs. Lavenham inclined her head politely. She had read the message in his lordship's dark gaze and knew that she was not to be so easily forgiven. A slight shiver ran through her. Marc had not

forgotten his manners, but since yesterday he had made it plain that
he found her treatment of that wretched girl intolerable. In some
ways he was more like his father than he knew!

They reached Bath before mid-morning and, leaving the carriage at the Christopher, the four of them embarked upon a tour
of the fashionable shops on Milsom Street. To Corisande's dismay Letty and Tom went on ahead, leaving her to follow with the
Marquis.

He drew her arm through his and a delicious tremor danced
along her nerves. She could no more escape to look for work than
if he had tied her to him as his prisoner, but it was hard to think of
her plight when she was so conscious of the man at her side, his
arm warm and strong beneath her fingers. Happiness spread itself
throughout her treacherous body and Corisande would not allow
herself to question it as they strolled along in the pale sunshine.

"I think Letty persuaded Tom into that shop over there." Corisande pointed out a fashionable milliner's some considerable time
later and the Marquis groaned.

"Not another one! That girl will exhaust us all."

They had become separated in the crush and were about to cross
the flagway to follow their companions when an urgent feminine
voice attracted the Marquis's attention.

He swung round to behold a lady dressed in a smart pelisse and
a bronze-green velvet hat waving at him from a travelling-chaise.

"Fanny! Bless you for coming so quickly!" Grabbing Miss
Clifford's elbow, he hurried her across to the chaise.

"Do get in," the newcomer urged and when they were seated she
leant forward to kiss Lord Dene's cheek, saying rather breathlessly, "They told me at the house that you had come into town so
I decided to follow you as your letter said the matter was urgent.
Is this Miss Clifford?" Without waiting for a reply, she hurried on,
"How happy I am to make your acquaintance, my dear. My
brother has told me all about you and I shall be delighted to have
you stay with me. Aunt Lavenham has behaved monstrously and
so I told her, but you needn't fear any such incivility in my house."

"Fanny, Fanny," interpolated the Marquis, laughing. "Let me
at least introduce you."

At this the lady broke off with a smiling apology, giving him the
chance to explain that she was his sister, Lady Linton.

Corisande turned a surprised gaze upon him and Fanny smiled
at her. "How infamous of my little brother not to tell you I was
expected. But before Marc explains let us repair to the Christopher. I fully intend to rack up there for the night, since nothing
would induce me to stay with Aunt Lavenham."

"Quarrelled with her, did you, Fanny?"

"She is a very silly woman," his sister declared roundly.

The comfortable carriage speedily conveyed them to the fashionable hotel where there was no difficulty in procuring a set of rooms for so distinguished a visitor as the Duke of Weston's daughter. While Fanny's dresser, a motherly-looking woman named Ellen Clay, disappeared to unpack for her mistress they retired to the private parlour to drink tea and discuss what had brought Fanny to Bath.

"Oh, but you should not have written, sir!" Corisande went pink. "I cannot impose upon you, ma'am," she continued, turning back to Fanny.

"Nonsense, my dear, and do pray call me Fanny. There is not the least difficulty. I have a large house and I would enjoy having you stay with me."

"You are in need of a companion?"

The suddenly hopeful note of Miss Clifford's voice did not escape either of her listeners.

"Yes, in a way I am," said Fanny picking her words carefully. "I did have a paid companion until recently, but she left my services—not wishing to winter with me in Italy. It would give me a great deal of pleasure if you would be my guest. I should enjoy the chance to take you about and introduce you into society."

Corisande's eyes widened. She cast a bewildered look at the Marquis, but he merely smiled imperturbably.

"You are too generous, ma'am, I . . . I don't know what to say."

"Why, then, say yes," Fanny laughed. "I came here to oblige my brother, but if I did not think we would suit, Corisande, it would be the easiest thing in the world to fob you off on one of my acquaintances. In helping Marc, I shall be helping myself, for I am sure I should enjoy having your company."

Corisande bit her lip. "Are you quite certain? Mrs. Lavenham did not seem to think I was respectable enough and it is rather lowering, you see, to be passed from hand to hand as if one were an unwanted parcel. Forgive my bluntness, but I'd as lief find other employment if you are only offering me a home out of pity," she said anxiously.

Fanny, who had a very kind heart, did not take offence at this forthright speech, but said quickly and with obvious sincerity, "I give you my word that is the last thing on my mind."

Corisande's consent was taken as settled and the conversation turned to practical matters concerning the arrangements for the journey back to London, giving Corisande the opportunity to sit back and observe her benefactress. Lady Linton, Corisande judged, was in her late twenties, perhaps thirty at the most. In colouring she did not resemble the Marquis; her hair was light brown and her eyes a pale blue, Richmond family traits, although Corisande did not know it. Pale-complexioned, Fanny had a look of fragility. She was much of a height with Corisande, but was even more slight, frankly thin, in fact.

However, Lady Linton's frail appearance was contradicted by her lively manner and air of elegant assurance. "Should you like to stay here tonight with me instead of returning to the Place?" she asked, startling Corisande from her reflections.

"Indeed I would," was the outspoken answer, which Corisande tried hastily to soften to a more seemly politeness when she realised what she had said.

The Marquis grinned at her. He was relieved that his sister had taken a liking to Corisande and found himself offering to escort them back to town.

"You mean to cut short your visit, then?" Fanny asked with a sudden sharpened interest. Miss Clifford's beauty had surprised her, since Marc had made no mention of it in his letter, and she felt a slight flicker of alarm. Her brother was perfectly capable of acting generously to an unfortunate orphan, but she hoped he wasn't going to take too great an interest in the girl.

Marc rose to take his leave. "I had better go and find Tom and Letty before they raise a hue and cry," he announced. "I shall have to dine at the Place, but I will drive over tomorrow morning and we can make an early start."

"Could you bring my valise with you, sir?" Corisande asked with a little worried frown and he nodded.

"You may borrow a nightgown of mine and anything else you need for tonight," Fanny offered when her brother had gone. "In fact," she added, eyeing Corisande's shabby sprigged muslin with a pained expression, "I think we had better do a little shopping ourselves this afternoon."

After luncheon Fanny changed her gown for a walking-dress of amber-coloured cambric with a vandyked hem, which quite wrung Corisande's heart with envy. Lady Linton was not conventionally pretty, her features were too thin for beauty, but she had an elegance which certainly caught the eye.

During the stroll to the mantu-maker's Fanny remembered from her previous visits to Bath, Corisande decided that her new acquaintance was exceptionally kind and good-natured. Her own slight shyness quickly melted and they were soon chatting away in a natural manner.

"Now, I think we turn here . . . yes. I was rather sickly as a girl and was despatched here to bathe and take the waters, so I know Bath quite well," Fanny remarked. "Drinking those vile waters probably did me some good, for I outgrew my weakness except for taking a chill all too easily." She smiled. "That is why I detest our English winters and travel abroad to a warmer clime whenever possible."

Corisande began to ask her about Italy and the rest of their journey was pleasantly occupied in this manner.

The dressmaker's was a refined little shop with small gilt chairs for customers to sit upon while debating the merits of the various rolls of silks, satins and other fabrics brought out for their inspection. In addition, the shop carried made-up gowns in the latest styles and it was these that Lady Linton desired to see. A figured French muslin, demurely sophisticated and outrageously expensive, took her eye.

"Do try this one on, my love."

Corisande, who had naturally assumed Fanny to be buying for herself, gasped. "Oh, I'm sure I should not," she breathed, but her expression contradicted this polite refusal.

"I simply cannot bear to see you in that dreadful dress. Do let me buy this one for you if you like it," Fanny coaxed and Corisande's scruples were swept away.

Her elegant reflection in the glass rendered Miss Clifford blissfully inarticulate while Fanny paid for the gown and bore her off to a milliner's down the street. Fanny was rather amused at Corisande's wondering pleasure and felt that her money had been well spent when she saw how the Angouleme bonnet trimmed with lace framed the delicate little face so becomingly.

Corisande came out of her intoxicated state to draw the line when Fanny wished to purchase a very handsome silk pelisse to bestow upon her and remained determined in spite of Fanny's reassurances that it was in the latest fashion.

"Thank you, but really I should be most upset if you did buy it," Corisande told her frankly. "It is priced sixty guineas, which is very nearly the sum of my annual allowance from the Admiral!"

Fanny's eyes opened wide. Having been blessed all her life with sufficient means to purchase whatever took her fancy, she had rarely considered how uncomfortable it must be to have to count the pennies.

"Heavens, my dear, that would not last me a month as pin-money!" she exclaimed, but agreed to leave the shop without making any further purchases as she could see that Corisande was becoming embarrassed.

Throughout dinner that evening Fanny turned over several schemes in her mind on how best to persuade Corisande to accept her help. So many new things were necessary for her launch into society, but it was easy to see that the child was too independent to take charity, even the most well-meaning sort!

She would have to devise some way of overcoming this reluctance, for plainly the solution to Miss Clifford's difficulties was to find her a rich husband.

IN THE MORNING Corisande was the first to wake. A maidservant answered her ring and brought her hot water for washing, with the intelligence that Lady Linton's dresser was asking to be admitted.

Ellen Clay entered, Corisande's shabby valise in one hand. "This was delivered for you just now, miss, but milady said how you were to breakfast in bed if you wished."

Ellen thought Miss Clifford looked rather like an enchanting child sitting in the middle of the wide bed, two heavy plaits framing her face, and it was with almost a child's exuberance that Corisande cried, "Oh I should much prefer to get up," as she flung aside her bedcovers.

Ellen did not share Corisande's relief at the return of the disgraceful valise and her shocked disapproval deepened when Corisande drew out a travelling-gown in muddy brown merino.

"Miss, you are never planning to wear that?"

"I'm afraid I must," Corisande replied meekly, but her dimples danced. "I know it is shabby, but it is the only suitable dress I own."

Miss Clay endeavoured to hide her appalled feelings and offered to do Corisande's hair. "Milady ordered breakfast for nine o'clock. I hope you have a good appetite, miss, for, as sure as check, the Viscountess will hardly eat a thing and it will all be wasted else."

"Her ladyship is a viscountess?" Corisande seized on the most interesting fact.

"Did you not know, miss?" Ellen preened a little. "Milady is the Viscountess Linton. The Dowager Viscountess, I should say, seeing as how his late lordship's cousin, him as inherited, got married last winter," she added gloomily.

"I'm sorry, I hadn't realised she was a widow. Has she been one for long?"

"Almost three years and not a thought in her head of remarrying, though there have been dozens of gentlemen anxious for her to say yes to them," lamented Ellen. "And her only twenty-nine, 'tis not natural.'' A sigh escaped Miss Clay's plump bosom and then she seemed to recollect her youthful audience. "Well, I mustn't stand here gossiping all day. Will you step into the parlour, miss?''

Half an hour later Fanny found her there, sitting curled up in the deep window-seat, watching the street below with interest.

"I'm sorry to keep you waiting. I'm not a great believer in early rising,'' she greeted Corisande with a smile.

Breakfast was served and Fanny poured out coffee for them both, dismissing the hovering waiter. Consuming her buttered eggs with a healthy appetite, Corisande noted how Fanny merely nibbled upon a thin piece of bread and butter. "Do try some of this ham, it is very good,'' she urged.

"I can see that Ellen has been busy already,'' Fanny laughed. "She fusses over me like a hen with one chick and I cannot bring her to believe that I am not a sickly eight-year-old any longer.''

Corisande thought privately that it must be rather pleasant to be so lovingly cosseted but she discovered that she did not need to search for a tactful answer, for Fanny was already chattering about something else with the lively animation that made her appear so attractive.

"I place no reliance upon my brother's arriving before noon and it would be a pity to waste this fine weather sitting indoors, don't you think? We could take a walk in the Sydney Gardens; they contain some pretty grottos.''

Corisande nodded enthusiastically; this plan was entirely to her taste. In the country she had gone for long walks every day. Mrs. Lavenham had said that it was fast to go out alone, but if she went with Fanny it must be acceptable.

Unfortunately for these plans, the Marquis arrived just as they were finishing the meal.

"Heavens, Marc, how early you are!'' Fanny declared in surprise as he bent to kiss her cheek.

She watched him bow over Corisande's hand and heard the underlying concern in his attractive voice as he asked her if she had slept well. Oh, dear, thought Fanny to herself, I do hope Marc hasn't forgotten Papa's edict.

"Thank you for sending on my valise,'' Corisande was saying. "Did you manage to find the time to convey my excuses to Mrs. Lavenham and to thank her and Tom for their hospitality?'' she asked, striving to control the happiness flooding over her at the mere sight of his tall handsome figure.

"Never fret, I did that pretty on your behalf," Marc grinned. "As a matter of fact, Aunt Lavenham has even sent you a farewell present."

"A present!" Corisande's eyes widened.

"She agreed to Letty's request that you should have some gowns or other. I have the trunk downstairs. Letty said you would understand."

"Oh, I do." Corisande smiled at him with such brilliance that he caught his breath. "I shall write and thank them both before we leave, if I may?" Corisande turned a look of enquiry upon her hostess.

"Of course." Fanny was watching her brother.

"Letty charged me to make her farewells. They are to come to London at the end of May and she hopes to see you then," the Marquis continued, his heartbeat steadying.

"And Tom, is he fixed at the Place until then?" Fanny enquired, hoping she was doing the right thing.

"No, he returns to London as soon as he has concluded this business with his agent."

Fanny nodded and then announced she must go and supervise her packing.

When they were alone the Marquis said abruptly, "Are you sure you wish to go to London with my sister? Fanny is the dearest soul, but if you do not care for it I shall try to arrange something else."

"Not wish to live in London? Oh, Marc!" Corisande exclaimed laughing. "London! All my life I have longed to visit it! The shops, the theatres, the Opera, the Military Reviews in Hyde Park...oh, and a host of other things to see!"

Her shining-eyed enthusiasm made him smile a little. "And the parties, the balls, the routes and Assemblies, won't you enjoy those too?"

Her responsive smile was so dazzling that he was rendered speechless, but then it faded and in a more subdued voice she said, "Such entertainments are flying too high for a girl who has no fortune. I couldn't possibly be such a charge upon your sister. I am only to be her companion, you know."

"Fanny has a handsome jointure and she would enjoy organising your début," he pointed out gently.

"But it would be so expensive and I have no hope of repaying her." Corisande's fingers twisted together in agitation. "Already she has been kind enough to buy me a new gown, but I could not go on accepting such gifts." She lifted her chin. "Would you do so in my place?"

The Marquis, who had frequently refused loans from his sister, had no answer for this blunt question. "Would you allow me to frank you instead?" he asked unexpectedly.

Corisande shook her head, her lips parting a little in astonishment. "It is very kind of you, but you must know I cannot accept," she whispered.

A lady could receive only trifling presents from a gentleman unless she wished to jeopardise her reputation, a fact Corisande was well aware of, in spite of her lack of worldly polish.

"But I want to help you," said the Marquis urgently.

"Please, do not let us discuss it," Corisande implored.

"Very well, we won't," he replied, seeing how it distressed her, and possessing himself of both her hands, he raised them to his lips to brush a kiss across her fingertips.

CHAPTER SIX

"AND DOES LONDON live up to your expectations, Miss Clifford?"

"Oh, yes," Corisande replied enthusiastically, smiling up at the broad-shouldered gentleman who had posed this question. "I have been busy since we arrived last week."

Sir Harry Vernon admired her dimples. "I am happy to hear it. May I hope you will give me the pleasure of your company driving in the Park tomorrow?"

Corisande blinked. "Don't you mean to ask Lady Fanny?" she murmured a little doubtfully.

"Ah, I think not."

Sir Harry gazed across the elegant drawing-room towards his stubborn inamorata, who sat gossiping unconcernedly with Lady Byrant, another of her morning-callers.

Corisande guessed from his momentarily unguarded expression that Sir Harry would have liked to box Fanny's ears and she could quite sympathise with him. She caught her lower lip between her teeth. She had not known her benefactress had it in her to be so provoking!

In fact it was impossible to acquit Fanny of deliberate coquetry. Sir Harry was her most devoted admirer but she treated him quite shamefully. Sometimes she would be all smiles and then for no reason at all she would blow cold. The poor man never knew where he was with her, Corisande decided.

This morning Fanny had been distinctly pettish. Sir Harry could do nothing to please her. Corisande suspected he had come across to talk to her before he lost his temper but she was also sure that the baronet would not have left without exchanging a word with her even if Fanny had been at her most charming. He had been very kind to her since she had arrived at Fanny's fashionable house in Hill Street and Corisande had taken a swift liking to him.

Unversed though she was in the ways of the world, Corisande had recognised that Sir Harry was a man to trust, a true gentleman in every sense of the word. Equally, it was plain to her that he was genuinely in love with Lady Linton.

Really, it would serve Fanny right if he decided to relinquish his pretensions to her hand, Corisande thought with a touch of indignation. Fanny's acid remarks had clearly hurt him, though he was trying hard not to let it show as he chatted to Corisande about the sights she must see while she was in town.

Corisande recalled that Ellen Clay had told her that Sir Harry had already asked Fanny to marry him and been refused, though the matter was not generally known. In Corisande's opinion his devoted persistence was touching, but perhaps even his good temper was wearing thin after months of such fickle treatment.

"It's a pity milady will not see what a perfect husband she has under her nose," Ellen had lamented. "No one can doubt the sincerity of his affection. Why, he is never in attendance upon any other lady and I've heard tell he will not dance at all unless she is his partner."

Corisande quickly discovered the truth of this for herself. Sir Harry was the despair of every hostess in town, for if Fanny did not honour him he would stand watching her progress with a jealousy more suited to a stripling than a mature man of five and thirty.

Corisande regarded him now, with an appraising eye. To her he seemed quite old, but it could not be denied that he was a very attractive man, for all of that. Dark-haired, he had a rather stocky sportsman's figure and his features were homely rather than handsome, but he had a particularly good-humoured smile and his fine grey eyes were kind. A bachelor, he possessed a large estate in Kent and was extremely wealthy, but he affected no pretensions and his manners were easy and pleasing.

"You know, you ought to hold aloof a little and see what effect that has."

Corisande was mortified to realise that she had spoken her thoughts aloud when Sir Harry turned a look of startled enquiry upon her.

He waved her hasty apology aside. "Please, Miss Clifford...Corisande, I hope we are friends. Pray do continue, I found your remark most interesting. You were speaking of my relationship with Lady Linton, I think?"

She nodded. "But it was most improper of me."

"You must let me be the judge of that." He gave her a rueful smile. "I admit I stand in need of good advice."

"I'm not precisely certain that it is good advice." Corisande was candid. "But it could not be worse than the line you are pursuing.

You see, I think Fanny does not value you as she should because you are forever at her feet."

Her brow wrinkled as she stove to clarify her argument. "What I mean, sir, is that I am convinced a little jealousy would work wonders. She is altogether too sure of you!"

The baronet, to whom the capriciousness of the female sex was a mystery, looked a little confused. "You mean I should not make my feelings plain? That I should appear interested in another lady?" he asked doubtfully.

When Corisande nodded he considered this novel idea.

"Miss Clifford, I thank you. I believe you may well have hit upon the answer," he said after a moment. "But there is a difficulty. How am I to give your notion a chance? Where can I find a lady willing to engage in the sort of flirtation you describe? My feelings for Lady Linton are so well known I fear I should never be able to convince anyone I was in earnest."

A chuckle shook his broad shoulders. "And if I did succeed, then I should be in the basket indeed, for I have no intentions of proposing marriage to anyone other than Fanny."

"I had not thought of that! It would be dreadful to raise false hopes. On second thoughts perhaps a light fashionable flirtation would do nearly as well." A gleam of mischief lit her gaze. "Or, better still, several flirtations!"

This made the baronet laugh heartily, not least at the idea of himself as a ladies' man.

Their lively amusement attracted Fanny's attention and she looked across the room in some surprise at her faithful cavalier. Sally Byrant continued to chatter, but suddenly Fanny found herself unable to concentrate upon the latest gossip.

I wonder what Corisande is saying to put him in such good spirits, Fanny fretted. She was not accustomed to see Harry so cheerful after she had administered one of her sharp set-downs. It was even more of a shock to realise that he was happily paying court to another woman.

Fanny could think of a dozen reasons why he should distinguish Miss Clifford in this manner, but none of them satisfied her. There was no doubt Harry was kind enough to want to make the girl feel at ease. Equally, there was no doubt he was taken with her protégée's lovely face and innocent charm.

A peculiar sinking sensation in the pit of her stomach assailed Lady Linton. Only yesterday Corisande had confided to her that she liked Sir Harry the best of all her new acquaintances.

Sally's words rolled over the Viscountess's head unheard as Fanny struggled to make sense of her feelings. It was a difficult task.

A chance meeting last summer at a private party held by friends who lived near Harry's home had brought him into her orbit. Until then he had been content to spend his life quietly in the country, having no desire to shine in Society, but he made no secret of his instant attraction towards her. Fanny had felt something in herself respond, but the habit of holding aloof remained strong.

We made such an odd couple, she thought reflectively. The social butterfly and the country gentleman! For a few days Harry had haunted his neighbour's house, but Fanny had believed he would forget her once she had returned to London. Instead he had immediately followed to try and fix his interest with her.

He had rented a house in the best part of town and entered into the social whirl. Everywhere she went Fanny found him waiting for her, and she was torn between a growing regard for him and a fear that he was making her look ridiculous in the eyes of the *ton* with his dogged devotion.

His persistent courtship had strengthened her desire to winter in Italy. Good breeding had dictated that Harry could not follow her when she had made it plain that she desired solitude, but no sooner had she arrived back home a few weeks ago than he had turned up on her doorstep once more.

Her pleasure at seeing him again had warred with her ingrained distaste for romantic entanglement. The intensity of his regard made her feel afraid. Passion was a trap, a snare and a delusion. She did not want Harry's love.

Why then do I dislike seeing him pay attention to Corisande? she asked herself in bewilderment. I must not be so selfishly foolish!

All the same, Fanny was relieved when Harry rose to his feet. But her relief was short-lived.

Harry made his farewells in an unprecedentedly casual manner, without any of his usual enquiries as to her future engagements. Fanny forgot she considered his habit of attending only the same functions as she did annoying and compressed her lips in vexation.

"Have you the headache, Fanny?" Corisande enquired after all their callers had departed. It was rare for Fanny to be so quiet.

"No. I'm just a little tired," Fanny prevaricated. She had no intentions of discussing her feelings for Harry Vernon with anyone.

"Then shall we stay home instead of going to watch the balloon ascent?"

Corisande's generous offer was firmly refused and accordingly at two o'clock they sallied forth escorted by Mr. Russell and Lord Thorne, members of Fanny's court.

Mr. Russell, an over-dressed exquisite whom Corisande could not like, described the outing in scornful tones. "If it were not for your celestial presence, dear lady, I vow I should loathe to concern myself with such an out-moded occasion."

Corisande sniffed. She thought him very rude to say such a thing and the ardent glances and affected sighs he sent in her direction made her feel uncomfortable. Lord Thorne was another matter. For all that he must have seen several such ascents, the middle-aged dipmatist's good-humoured attitude did nothing to detract from Corisande's enjoyment.

It was exciting to watch the huge brightly coloured silk bag being filled with gas. When this operation was completed the balloon would be released from its tethering ropes to bear its gilded gondola and crew up into the sky.

They were part of a large noisy crowd of spectators and several vendors had appeared to ply their wares. They were doing a roaring trade in selling refreshments and Corisande would have loved to have got down from the carriage to join the throng and partake of a cooling drink.

"Heavens, my dear, you must not think of doing such a vulgar thing!" Fanny whispered urgently when Corisande quietly put the request to her. The Viscountess flashed a look at their escorts, but they did not appear to have heard, thanks to the cheering which had broken out to mark the ascent of the balloon and her warning frown relaxed.

Corisande restrained a sigh. In spite of what Lord Dene had told her, there still seemed to be a great many rules governing the polite world. Fanny had been at pains to explain the most important to her, but Corisande wondered if she would ever remember them all. It seemed something so trivial as being seen in St. James's Street where the gentlemen had their clubs could seriously damage her reputation.

Such petty restrictions irked her and made her wonder if she was cut out to be a lady of fashion, which was Fanny's ambition for her. It was of no use for Corisande to protest that she was content to be just her ladyship's paid companion, for Fanny simply refused to listen.

"Of course you shall be my companion and I shall make you a suitable allowance, my dear, but why should you not have a little fun at the same time?" Fanny insisted when Corisande brought up the subject of her duties on their first day in Hill Street. "Launching you into Society and seeing you safely settled would give me a great deal of satisfaction. My life is an idle round of pleasure, Corisande; do not deprive me of this opportunity to do something useful. It is a task fitted to my poor talents and one I should enjoy."

Corisande had shrugged helplessly. Such generosity overwhelmed her, making it difficult to cling to her dreams of independence. "If you wish it, then I must be grateful for your kindness, ma'am," she said, acknowledging defeat.

Once she had gained Corisande's consent, Fanny swung into action. A host of plans were made and Corisande allowed herself to be carried along on the tide.

"I shall tell anyone who asks that you are the daughter of an old friend," Fanny announced. "That will explain your presence here in Hill Street and it is no lie to say that you are an orphan."

Satisfaction coloured the Viscountess's tone. She also intended to drop careful hints about a rich uncle in Northumberland and Corisande's connection with the Morleys, but it was not necessary to mention these facts to Corisande. Fanny was sure her protégée would protest such tactics, but the business of finding her a suitable husband was going to be difficult enough, as the child's lack of fortune could not be entirely glossed over.

Thinking of the problems ahead, Fanny coughed delicately. "You will not mention my brother's part in your affairs, will you, my love? People are apt to get the wrong idea about such things."

Corisande nodded obediently. The Marquis had a wild reputation and she could see the sense in Fanny's warning.

"Good. Then I foresee a most pleasurable season ahead for both of us." Fanny beamed at her.

Remembering this conversation as she gazed up at the gaudy balloon floating towards the sunlit clouds, Corisande wished she could recapture that mood of optimism. The reality of her debut had been far different from her imaginings. She kept on making mistakes like the one she had made just now and she had been hard put to it to curb her unruly tongue upon several occasions.

Avid curiosity and speculation were no easier to bear coming from some high-nosed dowager, she'd discovered. It made her blood boil to hear her person and prospects discussed as if she had not been present. Corisande knew she ought to ignore such irritations, but she felt strangely vulnerable. It was a whole new world, exciting and wonderful, but a little frightening, too.

Perhaps it might have been easier to laugh at her misgivings if Lord Dene had not stayed away. This thought popped unbidden into Corisande's head.

In order to lend conviction to Fanny's story, the Marquis had yielded to his sister's request that he should not call upon them too often.

"You know how everyone loves to gossip, Marc. We do not want them to think you have any special interest in Corisande. Wait until the child is more settled, at least," Fanny had begged him privately, and because he wanted to help the Marquis had agreed.

He had only visited them once. A brief formal call on one of Fanny's at-home days, during which he scarcely exchanged a dozen words with Corisande.

Corisande had missed him, though the whirl of social activity left her little time for reflection. Each day was a giddy non-stop round of engagements. Such frivolity was delightful, of course, but she longed for someone to share her thoughts with. I did not need to try and guard my tongue with him, she thought wistfully.

A high-pitched shriek of pain jerked Corisande instantly from her thoughts and to her indignation she saw a small boy being set upon by two other bigger lads. They were some distance away, but she could see that all three were dirty and badly dressed. They struggled noisily for a moment before the youngest fell to the ground.

"Will no one help him?" Corisande demanded in horror as the crowd edged away, their faces expressing indifference or distaste.

Only the flailing arms and legs of their victim could now be seen under the weight of the two older youths and Corisande shook off Fanny's restraining hand.

"If neither of you gentlemen will do anything, then I must," she announced crisply.

"Miss Clifford! Wait!" Looking rather shame-faced, Lord Thorne attempted to detain her, but he was a heavy man and slow in his movements.

Corisande jumped down nimbly from the carriage, deaf to the protests that followed her as she ran swiftly towards the combatants.

"Let him go at once, you bullies." Corisande swung the handle of her parasol to land with precision in the middle of the uppermost youth's back.

A satisfactory thud and a yelp of pain answered her.

"What's your game, lady?" The bully lumbered to his feet. He stared at her sullenly, his resentful gaze taking in her elegant carriage-dress. "We ain't doing nothing wrong."

"Then let that poor child alone. You ought to be ashamed of yourself, he's not half your size," Corisande said roundly.

The other youth had got to his feet by now and Corisande experienced a slight flicker of alarm as they exchanged sniggering glances. They began to move towards her, their expressions turning ugly.

"I am with friends." Corisande refused to show any fear, but she wished the carriage were not so far away.

Out of the corner of her eye she saw the child who had been winded recover and dart a look of thanks at her before creeping to his feet.

"Hoy, the little runt's getting away!" A yell of rage greeted his escape and one of the youths made to chase after him, but Corisande foiled the attempt by thrusting out her parasol and tripping him up.

He lay sprawled on the grass, cursing horribly and his friend swung back to Corisande, his face purple with anger.

"Keep your distance." She did not think they would dare attack her in such a public place, but the crowd had thinned out now the ascent was over and she wondered a little desperately if anyone would rush to her assistance if she cried out. Had Fanny abandoned her?

The youth she had hit suddenly made a grab for her and Corisande let out a squeak of alarm that turned into a gasp of relief as she heard a familiar deep voice behind her say, "Your pardon, Corisande," before strong arms plucked her effortlessly out of harm's way.

"And now, my buck, have you a taste for some home-brewed from someone more up to your weight?" the Marquis of Dene enquired.

Her former assailant took one look at his lordship's broad shoulders. They were only marginally less frightening than the murderous look in those dark eyes!

With a squawk of terror he turned tail and fled, closely followed by his henchman. There was no sense in tangling with the quality, particularly the kind that looked as if he could handle himself in a bout of fisticuffs!

"Thank you." Corisande's voice trembled a little. The whole incident had lasted less than a moment or two but she found she was shaking.

"What the devil were you about, you little fool?" demanded the Marquis. Now that the danger was past he could have wrung her slender neck for frightening him so!

"Nothing except trying to help, as any decent Christian might do," she snapped back at him, furious with herself for the tears that came welling into her eyes. "Those brutes were beating that

child senseless. Would you have had me stand by and do nothing?''

Precisely how the Marquis would have answered remained a
mystery for at that moment Fanny arrived with a breathless Lord
Thorne and Mr. Russell in tow. Lady Linton looked close to tears
herself and guilt rippled along Corisande's nerves. She had let
Fanny down again and she was sorry for it, though she knew she
could not have ignored that child's plight.

''Thank you, Marc,'' Fanny's voice strove for calm. ''I'm sure
Miss Clifford is obliged to you.'' She turned a stiff smile upon
Corisande. ''You really must try to remember you are not living in
a quiet country village now, my love. There is not the least need for
you to concern yourself with such matters.''

Corisande bit back the sharp reply which came to her tongue,
realising that Fanny was doing her best to smooth things over and
pretend nothing untoward had occurred.

''Perhaps you would prefer your brother to escort you home, my
dear,'' suggested Lord Thorne with exquisite tact.

The two gentlemen made their farewells, Lord Thorne with a
sympathetic smile for Corisande which contrasted with Mr. Russell's gloating curiosity.

''No doubt George Russell will have spread the story all over
town before nightfall,'' Fanny raged as they made their way back
to her carriage. ''You could not have chosen a worse witness for
your folly, Corisande.''

''Don't fret, Fanny. If I know Thorne he'll put a damper on
Russell's vicious tongue, and if he does not I'll make sure of it,''
said the Marquis grimly.

Fanny's expression brightened. ''Would you, Marc? I should
feel happier if you were to follow them now without waiting to escort us home.''

He nodded. ''Of course.''

He handed her up into the barouche and as she fussed with her
skirts and instructions to her coachman he turned to Corisande.

''Can you try to forget my boorish remark?'' he said softly,
raising her hand to his lips. ''It was a brave thing you did—if a
foolish one to put yourself at risk.''

Corisande coloured beautifully. His kiss seemed to burn her skin
through her thin gloves. ''I acted on impulse, as usual, without
thinking of the consequences,'' she confessed. ''Your interven-
tion was most welcome and I was truly grateful, in spite of how it
must have sounded when I snapped at you.''

The Marquis smiled at her. ''Then let us consider the incident
closed. Only no more scrapes mind, infant. Fanny's nerves won't

stand it." He gave her his hand to assist her into the waiting carriage and then stood back as it prepared to move off.

Corisande dragged her eyes from his retreating figure and turned to face Fanny's scolding.

"We shall forget it this time," Lady Linton sighed in conclusion, sinking back against the barouche's luxurious velvet squabs. "But really you must be more circumspect, my love."

Guiltily Corisande noticed that beneath her rouge the Viscountess looked drained. There was a tiny frown between her brows, which had first appeared that morning and now looked deeper. Fanny had denied she had the headache, but there was no doubt she looked fagged today.

"I'm sorry, I shall try not to be so much trouble," Corisande announced impulsively, hating the idea that she was responsible for causing her kind hostess any distress. "I did not want to embarrass you. Perhaps I am not suited to be a lady of fashion. Might it not be better if I sought employment elsewhere?"

"Are you unhappy living with me, Corisande?"

"No, indeed!" Corisande shook her head vigorously.

"Then let us hear no more nonsense about leaving. You just need time to adjust to your new circumstances, that is all, my love." Fanny patted her hand. "Now, shall we join the promenade in the Park or should you like to rest before this evening?"

Corisande didn't feel in the least bit tired, but she suspected that Fanny might like a nap before the party she was giving in Corisande's honour so she said she should like to return home.

They were forced to halt in the middle of Park Lane. A noisy altercation was taking place between the driver of a hackney and a stout man in buckskins standing beside an overturned cart which was blocking the road.

"Who is that lady, Fanny?"

Fanny forced herself to concentrate. "Which lady, my love?"

"That blonde girl over there in the landaulet. She is wearing a white threadnet hat trimmed with pink roses."

The Viscountess obediently looked in the required direction. "Oh, that is Miss Marlow and her mother," she answered, feeling suddenly flustered.

Corisande wondered why Fanny had begun to fidget with the carved ivory handle of her sunshade. "She seems to be staring at us."

"What? No, I'm sure you are mistaken, my love." Fanny was aware that her tone was too bright, but on top of all else that had happened today she simply could not face the idea of explaining that Augusta had almost become her sister-in-law and would indeed be so if the Duke had his way. That knowledge was still confidential, so far as Fanny knew, but there was no way Marc could escape his destiny and Fanny was beginning to think that Corisande might care too much what happened to her scapegrace brother.

"John, cannot you find a way through?" Fanny fired this question impatiently at her coachman.

He began to reply phlegmatically that it was impossible to proceed when the obstruction was cleared and the traffic began to move again.

"Oh, thank goodness! Drive on home, do, John. I am quite parched with thirst. Are you not also longing for some cool lemonade, Corisande?"

Her drooping spirits miraculously revived, Fanny began to prattle energetically, giving her young companion no chance to ask any further questions.

CHAPTER SEVEN

THE MARQUIS OF DENE caught his breath. Bidden to dine in Hill Street before the party, he was just in time to see the vision of loveliness that was Miss Corisande Clifford in her first fashionable evening-gown, descending the staircase.

Turnbull, Fanny's butler, coughed and then discreetly removed the Marquis's glossy beaver from his suddenly nerveless fingers, but Marc's eyes never wavered from the fairy-tale figure floating down the stairs.

The delicate white Italian crêpe gown with its high waist and narrow straight skirt suited Corisande's slender figure to perfection. The square neckline was modest, but low enough to display her white shoulders to advantage, while the tiny puff sleeves showed off her pretty arms. Silver embroidery edged the hem of the dress, matching the silver ribbon which was threaded through the piled-up mass of red-gold curls, dressed à la Madonna, and the silver spangled scarf draped across her arms.

Aware of the dark eyes upon her, Corisande descended the last few steps with bated breath. "Will I pass inspection, sir?" she asked with an attempt at a cheerful smile.

"My compliments, infant, you are as fine as five-pence. You will doubtless outshine every other damsel tonight." His words were teasing, but Corisande could not question his sincerity when his eyes smiled at her with such admiration. Her heart swelled with emotion, and not a little pride, as she placed her fingers upon the arm he held out to her.

"I'm glad you like the dress," she confided. "Fanny will probably ask you for your opinion of it because she bought it for me as a birthday gift."

"I did not know it was your birthday," he exclaimed with a tiny frown, and Corisande was forced to confess she had reached eighteen two days previously, a fact she had not liked to mention before in case he thought she was hinting for a gift.

She knew she owed him too much already. Remembering how he had come to her aid earlier, her heart began to race. Day by day it was growing harder to maintain her pose of easy friendship, when the least glimpse of him turned her bones to water, no matter how she tried to deny it to herself.

Tonight she thought he looked particularly handsome in his superbly cut black evening clothes. The plain white waistcoat and the single pearl in the intricate folds of his neckcloth, tied in a *Trône d'Amour,* were very much to Corisande's taste. The Marquis disliked the extremes of fashion and wore the minimum of jewellery, just one fob and his heavy gold signet ring, but he made every other man she had ever met seem insignificant.

Seated next to her at dinner, Marc was in an excellent position to observe the excitement on Miss Clifford's cameo profile. She was having difficulty sitting still in her chair and he whispered teasingly, "It's not fashionable to appear so pleased. You should try and look bored, you know."

"Bored?" Corisande gave him a sparkling smile. "How could I, or are you bamming me again, sir?" she responded.

He laughed and denied it. "Fanny must be expecting a squeeze," he commented. "Her parties are always popular."

By ten o'clock the Marquis was proved right. Lady Linton's drawing-rooms were crowded and Corisande was still at her side receiving latecomers. Finally Fanny released her from her post with an admonition to go and enjoy herself. Fanny had not held out the lure of dancing, but a great many unattached gentlemen had honoured her with their presence, none the less, and several of them gathered hovering around Miss Clifford, instead of succumbing to the temptation of the salon set aside for cards.

"Do let me take you a little out of this crush, Miss Clifford," offered the Marquis, rescuing her from the over-fulsome attentions of Mr. Russell.

"Oh, thank you! He is the most detestable man," Corisande whispered as he led her towards a sofa which was momentarily unoccupied.

The Marquis possessed himself of her fan and, unfurling it, proceeded to wave it gently in the direction of her flushed countenance. "Perhaps it is as well there is no dancing or you'd be mobbed."

Recovering her composure, Corisande smiled at him in genuine amusement. "Not if they learn I am penniless."

He gave her back her fan.

"Oh, I forgot to tell you," she exclaimed. "Lady Sefton has given me vouchers for Almack's."

"Has she indeed and are you all set to waltz?"

Corisande's eyes twinkled. "Monsieur Etienne says I have two left feet."

This was something of an exaggeration. The dancing-master Fanny had hired to tutor Miss Clifford was strict, but in private he had confided to Lady Linton that his pupil was naturally graceful and needed only to practice more diligently.

Corisande enjoyed dancing, but she was rather glad of the dictate that she must not waltz in public until one of the patronesses of Almack's gave her permission to do so. Without this approval, any girl who did so was considered fast. Older persons still considered this dance rather shocking, but Corisande could think of nothing she would enjoy more than whirling around the floor wrapped in the Marquis's arms.

"I must ask Fanny if she would like me to escort you both to King Street one evening," Marc offered nobly. He was not a habitué of Almack's, finding this inner sanctum of society distinctly insipid. The main aim of the club was dancing, so low stakes were enforced in the card-room. The rules were inflexible, the refreshments meagre. Moreover, any unattached gentleman who ventured within those hallowed portals was liable to be nobbled by the match-making mamas, but it would be worth this risk to dance with Corisande.

Corisande glanced about the crowded room. She had met several important people during her first week in society and was able to say, "Look, there is Lady Jersey talking to Mrs. Drummond-Burrell."

The Marquis nodded. "Fanny is acquainted with all the patronesses but Maria Sefton is the nicest of the bunch."

Corisande hid a grin. She had thought Mrs. Drummond-Burrell odiously haughty and Lady Jersey quite malicious when these ladies had condescended to speak to her. She had been out shopping with Fanny at the Pantheon Bazaar at the time and heeding the warning that these ladies were the true arbiters of society, able to blight any young lady's aspirations with one word, she had been on her best behaviour; a very model of decorum, much to Fanny's delight.

"Are you enjoying your new circumstances as much as you thought you would?" Marc asked quietly, watching her expressive little face.

Alarmed by his shrewdness, Corisande made haste to reassure him.

"It's quite the thing to complain, you know," he laughed. "At a crowded party like this one must always declare it to be a shocking squeeze and contrive to let the world know how little you think of your entertainment.''

"What shabby behaviour!" stated Corisande. "It would be most unkind to treat any hostess so incivilly.''

This made his lordship smile, and Corisande asked with swift anxiety, ''Will people think me a rustic if I own to any enjoyment?''

"I should imagine they will be too busy paying you compliments." His glance flicked lazily to a knot of young gentlemen hovering nearby. Corisande, who had not been aware that they were under observation, followed the direction of his gaze and experienced a heady sense of exhilaration. "Do you think they all wish to make my acquaintance?" she breathed.

"I am persuaded of it," he replied drily.

A gurgle of laughter escaped her and his cynical gaze softened. There was a look of impish mischief in her face. "Be careful how you test your claws, my little kitten," he warned her in a lazy drawl. "Some of the men you'll meet don't play fair."

Corisande inclined her bright head demurely. The temptation to try her hand at flirting was irresistible, when everyone was so busy declaring her the latest Toast, but she was wise enough to know that there was sense in what the Marquis said.

"I'll be careful, sir," she promised.

Lady Fanny came drifting up to them, ravishingly elegant in gold-shot silk and a tiara of diamonds. At her side was a red-haired young man of some nineteen summers.

"Corisande, my love, may I introduce you to Mr. Swindon? Only fancy, Mr. Swindon is here visiting his uncle the Bishop but he lives in Bath and is a friend of Tom and Letty's.''

Corisande smiled warmly at the stranger, regarding him openly without any of the self-conscious shrinking in vogue with many young ladies. She was disposed to like anyone who was a friend of the Lavenhams, even if Mr. Swindon's raiment smacked of the dandy. The wadded shoulders of his coat, his startling waistcoat and the multiplicity of his fobs, seals, pins and rings reminded her uncomfortably of Horace Hepburn, but his youthful blushes as he stammered out polite inanities were rather endearing.

"Marc, do come along with me," Fanny invited with an inexorable smile. "And let us leave these two young people to become acquainted."

It was impossible to ignore the hand she held out to him, so the Marquis bowed and they took their leave.

"A little too obvious, Fanny."

Lady Linton's hand tightened on his arm although her smile did not lose any of its blithe nonchalance. "Wretch!" she said vehemently out of the side of her mouth. "Don't you dare begin one of your practised flirtations with that child, Marc! She is a sensible little soul, but you are practically the first eligible man she has ever met. None of her country beaux could aspire to your polished address."

"Fanny, you move me deeply. Such praise!"

"Fiddlesticks! Don't try to cozen me, you rogue," his sister replied sternly, but her lips twitched. "Pray be serious, sir! I am hoping to find Corisande a suitable husband, but how shall I manage if you are going to turn the child's head?"

His lordship's eyebrows had tugged together in a frown. "Don't play match-maker, Fanny."

"And why not, pray?" she demanded indignantly. "To be sure, I am very fond of the dear girl, but she cannot live with me for ever."

"I have plans of my own for Miss Clifford's future."

Fanny paled. There was a barely suppressed anger in his tone. "Marc, what are you about?" she asked uncertainly. "When you wrote to me you implied nothing but the most disinterested motives for helping Corisande."

The Marquis's mouth tightened, but he was honest enough to admit that she had the right to be concerned. "I am not proposing to offer her a *carte blanche,* if that is what is worrying you," he said harshly.

Fanny let out a sigh of relief, which changed to a squeak of dismay when he added thoughtfully, "It would be cruel to engage her affections if I were only amusing myself."

"But, Marc, you cannot be serious . . . what about Miss Marlow? His grace?" Fanny fumbled helplessly.

"The Devil fly away with the pair of 'em," retorted her brother, exasperated.

"Marc, you simply cannot be in love with the girl," said Fanny firmly. "It is just one of your infatuations."

A faint rueful smile hovered about the Marquis of Dene's well-shaped mouth. "Oh, can't I?" he murmured softly.

CORISANDE ROSE EARLY after a disturbed night. Strange yearning dreams had set her tossing from side to side, and made her bed so uncomfortable that she was glad to leave it when she awoke to find her chamber filled with sunlight. She dressed herself without ringing for assistance. She was soon ready in the simply dimity which she had brought with her from Lady Maltby's, and a flicker of amusement passed over her face. Ellen would scold her for this independence, but she had no intention of becoming a namby-pamby miss, unable to do the least thing for herself.

Stopping only to breakfast swiftly upon a cup of coffee and a slice of bread and butter, she left the house, accompanied by Alice, the most junior of the housemaids, a quiet girl already devoted to Miss Clifford.

Too recently at the beck and call of others, Corisande was considerate to all the servants. In return, her natural kindness and lively spirits had quickly won her their regard. The general opinion was that Miss Clifford was quality, that was as plain as day in spite of her lack of fortune.

The Green Park was Corisande's destination. It was devoid of fashionable strollers at this hour and had a peaceful, almost rural seclusion. The languid promenade, designed to show off one's *toilette* to the world, favoured by the *ton* did not suit Corisande's notion of exercise. Alice had to hurry to keep up.

It was good to get out into the fresh air, but this morning the brisk walk did not banish Corisande's troubled thoughts. Last night's wonderful party had shown her how enjoyable fashionable life could be now that she was over her first nervousness. It would be easy to become addicted, especially if she could share such enchanted hours with the Marquis of Dene.

A tiny sigh escaped Corisande. It was no use trying to hide from the truth any longer. She had tumbled headlong into love with a man she could never possibly marry!

How could such a man of rank and fashion look twice at a provincial miss scarcely out of the schoolroom? She had no fortune or family to recommend her, nothing but a pretty face—and there were plenty of those to choose from in London.

Corisande shook her head in silent despair. These sensible objections made no difference to her feelings. From the day they had met she had been drawn to him, though she tried to close her eyes to what was happening.

How could I have fallen in love with him so quickly? she asked herself half-angrily. Was it just gratitude because he was kind to me? But even as the thought occurred to her she knew it was not the answer.

Almost from the first moment a liking had sprung up between them, a sense of ease as if they had known each other all their lives. But beneath their friendship lay other deeper stronger currents of emotion.

When he touches me, even just to offer me his hand to step into a carriage, I feel as if I might burst into flame! This realisation made Corisande shiver with shock. She longed for his kisses!

"Are you feeling all right, miss?"

Corisande realised that Alice was staring at her in concern. She nodded hastily, murmuring words of reassurance as she strove to marshal her wild thoughts into better order. She must not let her emotions gain control in this dangerous way. It was imperative she did not make the mistake of believing in her dreams. No matter how much she might wish it, she was not a real débutante, the sort of young lady a man in the Marquis's position could pay court to without fear of a misalliance. He might desire her, but he would never marry her.

I should never have let myself be persuaded into accepting Fanny's offer, Corisande decided sadly. Now she must pay the price for her folly. Immediate flight from the danger that was the Marquis of Dene was impossible. All Fanny's friends knew that Corisande was to spend the season with her and Fanny would look foolish if Corisande were to suddenly disappear, when she had gone to such efforts to gain acceptance for her.

I shall leave as soon as I can without disappointing Fanny. It is the only solution. Once she had made this decision Corisande began to feel a little more calm. She would scan the newspapers for advertisements wanting governesses or companions; surely there would be something!

"Oh, see, miss, don't that little dog look funny!"

Alice's comment made Corisande put aside her own concerns. The red leather collar and trailing leash worn by the small white dog running across the grass betrayed him as an escapee.

"He will do himself a mischief if that leash gets stuck!" Corisande exclaimed. Swiftly, she bent and clicked her fingers together in an enticing manner. "Here, boy. Come to me, you little rascal."

The dog, who on closer inspection proved to be only a puppy, came gambolling towards them. He halted his advance still some yards off, his head cocked to one side as he regarded them warily.

"Come on, little fellow," Corisande coaxed in a soothing voice, and he began to edge forward.

Intending to be helpful, Alice made a grab for him. She missed as he jumped aside and she went tumbling to her knees as he danced away, barking with shrill delight.

"Never mind. Let's see if we can catch him." Corisande brushed aside the maid's apology with a rueful smile.

The next five minutes were excessively lively. Their quarry obviously regarded the pursuit as a good game. He let them get within a foot or two and then pranced away, his tail wagging furiously.

"Got you at last, you little rogue!" Corisande panted.

Her captive struggled for a token moment before trying to wash her face. Corisande laughed and fondled one curly ear.

"Take care, miss. He might snap at you," Alice warned timidly.

"Nonsense, you would never be so bad-mannered, would you, sir?"

A wag of his tail and a look of bright-eyed intelligence answered her.

"What an adorable little fellow, he is. I wonder who he belongs to."

Corisande's question was soon answered. A moment later a young woman came running across the stretch of greensward. Her flat-crowned Villager hat had slipped from her head to hang by its silken strings, revealing admirably cut and dressed locks of the palest gold. The rest of her appearance was equally fashionable, but the girl's expression was distracted with worry.

Corisande waved an arm to attract the newcomer's attention and the look of relief on the blonde's face told its own story even before she reached them.

"Snowy! Oh, thank you, I am so grateful to you for stopping him," she cried in unceremonious greeting.

Corisande held out the wriggling puppy, who was barking in loud recognition.

"You bad boy." Snowy's owner took him into her arms and dropped a kiss upon his unrepentant head. "How dared you run away and frighten me, sir?" Very light grey eyes smiled at Corisande. "I cannot thank you enough. I was terrified he might have got out into the streets and he is quite unused to traffic."

"I was happy to help," Corisande replied, returning the smile.

"Oh, but you have dirtied your dress chasing after him. You must allow me to make recompense."

Corisande assured her that this would not be necessary. "Heavens, I shall get a scolding from Ellen," she added, glancing down at her grass-stained skirts.

"Is she your nurse? My own is the same. They never will admit that one has grown up."

Corisande chuckled. "I cannot deny Ellen the right to complain today, but in fact she is not my nurse but my friend's."

The girl nodded, her expression revealing that this remark had intrigued her, but she was plainly too well-bred to ask questions.

Instead she introduced herself. "My name is Augusta Marlow, but I should be pleased if you would call me Gussy."

Corisande introduced herself in turn. She had heard that name before but she could not place where. There was something vaguely familiar about Miss Marlow, but she had met so many new people lately!

Corisande studied her new acquaintance. She was older than herself, she guessed, perhaps twenty-three or twenty-four. Taller, too, with a rather buxom figure, but a surprisingly shy smile and quiet voice.

"I do not think we have met before, Miss Clifford," said Gussy. "Are you new to London, perhaps?"

"Please, call me Corisande. Yes, this is my first Season," Corisande replied, locking away the bittersweet thought that it must also be her last.

"Then we shall no doubt see a good deal of each other." Gussy sounded pleased. She put Snowy down, holding his leash very firmly in her hand. "I left my maid near the Ranger's Lodge. She will be wondering what has become of me. Would you care to take a stroll in that direction? We could have a glass of milk together there if you can spare the time."

Corisande accepted this invitation and they began to walk, chatting easily. Her rescue of Snowy had broken the ice and they quickly discovered that they had several things in common.

The herd of cows and their attendant milkmaid lent a rural air to the scene by the Ranger's Lodge, where they were reunited with Miss Marlow's maid. The milk they bought tasted warm and creamy and Corisande drank deeply, savouring this reminder of the days when her grandmama had been alive and life had been uncomplicated.

"Should you care to come home with me, Corisande?" invited Gussy shyly.

"Thank you, perhaps I could call on you another day? It is getting rather late and I don't want Fanny to start worrying."

"Fanny? Are you by any chance staying with Lady Linton?" Gussy looked taken aback. "I recollect now that I saw you with her the other day."

"You were the girl in the landaulet," Corisande exclaimed. "I thought I knew your face."

Miss Marlow nodded, trying to conceal her dismay. She felt as if a shadow had fallen between them.

"Is there something wrong?"

"No, I am just being silly." Gussy assumed a smile. "Take no notice."

It was tempting to confide the reason for her hesitation, but for a very long time now she had kept her own counsel and preserved her true feelings behind a wall of ice. The courtship she had endured at the hands of the late Marquis of Dene had revolted her and given her a distaste for the whole Richmond family, but she would not let this prejudice get in the way of her friendship with Corisande. There were few people she felt drawn to and she had the instinctive belief that in Corisande she had found a friend.

"If you can persuade Lady Linton, I should be happy to see you any morning in Arlington Street," Gussy urged as they made their farewell. "Mama is not fond of making morning-calls so we are usually at home."

Not having yet heard of Lady Marlow's renowned laziness, Corisande did not understand the reason for Gussy's faint smile, but she thanked her warmly for the invitation. Then with a final pat for Snowy she took her leave.

HAVING BREAKFASTED in her bedchamber, Lady Linton was still in her room when Corisande arrived back in Hill Street. She had time to change her dress and peruse the morning papers before Fanny joined her in the morning-room.

"Ah, there you are, my love. Did you enjoy your walk?" Fanny did not wait for an answer before rushing on. "These were delivered to me by mistake. I sent Ellen to look for you, but you had already gone out."

She held out two missives to Corisande. "I hope you won't think I was spying on you! I have given instructions that your letters must be handed to you directly in future."

Corisande sensed her hostess's embarrassment and made some soothing reply as she broke open the first seal and quickly scanned the contents.

"This one is from Letty. She asks how I am enjoying London." Corisande's smile faded as she read the other letter. "It is from Mr. Thruxton. He writes to tell me that there will be no difficulty in sending on my allowance here."

Fanny had picked up her embroidery, but her busy needle stilled abruptly. "I did not know you had written to him."

Corisande coloured a little guiltily. She had wanted to inform the solicitor that she had left Lady Maltby's service, but she was too honest to pretend this was the entire truth. "I asked him if it would be possible for me to live in my Papa's house while his will remains still unsettled," she confessed.

"But why make this enquiry now?"

"I never did so before because I could not afford a chaperon when Grandmama died," Corisande explained evasively. "It would not have been proper for me to live there alone and I was too young in any case." She glanced at the newspaper she had discarded. "However, I have discovered that it would be quite acceptable to advertise for a respectable lady, say an army widow, who would be willing to lodge with me on the basis of sharing day to day expenses in exchange for a roof over her head."

"You cannot be serious!" Lady Fanny cast aside her embroidery.

"Indeed I am!" Corisande nodded vigorously. "I should like to live in my old home. I know it would not be the same as before, but at least it is a more pleasant alternative than hiring myself out as a governess."

"But to live in such genteel poverty!" Fanny expostulated. "Who would you meet? Where would you mix with people of your own age and station? It would be no real life for you, Corisande. You are a beautiful young girl, not a middle-aged widow. You deserve far better than to be buried alive in some country village." She paused and then said in a calmer tone, "Did something happen to upset you last night? I thought you were happy living here with me."

"Of course I am enjoying my stay, but it is only a visit, Fanny." Corisande tried to smile. "I am thinking ahead to when I must leave you and trying to plan sensibly for my future."

"Your future? You must marry, my dear, that is your proper destiny," Fanny declared.

"Perhaps I shall one day." Corisande felt herself grow pale.

"Forgive me if I sound brutal, but you are not imagining a silly *tendre* for my scapegrace brother, are you?" Fanny strove to keep the worry from her voice and patted the sofa beside her invitingly. "Come and sit beside me, my love, and let me tell you something."

Reluctantly Corisande obeyed and Fanny continued in the same light tone. "Marc is a very handsome man and he can be exceptionally charming, if I may say so of my own brother, but his reputation is a disgrace. I will not sully your ears with details, but he did not gain his soubriquet entirely on account of his wild gaming, you know."

"Bits of muslin." Corisande nodded sagely.

Fanny choked. "Do not use such a vulgar expression in anyone else's hearing, I beg of you! Ladies must not admit to knowing of such creatures."

"How very foolish, when all gentlemen seem to keep them," Corisande retorted naughtily.

Fanny hid a smile. "It doesn't mean that the fact is admitted even so. You will set the *ton* against you if you do not pretend ladylike ignorance, and so I warn you, my dear."

When this point had been made Fanny returned to the subject under discussion. "Promise me that you will not refine upon it too much if Marc flirts with you. I dare say it is such a habit with him that he cannot resist dallying with a pretty girl but, believe me, he means nothing by it."

Fanny was aware of a niggling sense of disloyalty. Perhaps it was unfair to Marc to implant such suspicions in Corisande's lovely head and yet no matter how he felt the affair could go no further. The thoughts of her father's wrath helped Fanny crush her uneasy doubts.

"Please don't worry. I know very well that the Marquis means nothing by his compliments," Corisande replied. Her knuckles became white, so tightly did she clasp her hands together, but she didn't even notice. "I am in no danger of being taken in by them."

"I am relieved to hear it, my dear. I should not like you to get hurt. Falling in love is a little like playing with fire, exciting but dangerous."

The bitterness in Fanny's tone surprised Corisande. On any other occasion her lively curiosity would have been aroused, but all she could manage now was a heartfelt nod of agreement.

Unfortunately, this warning not to fall in love with the Wild Marquis was too late!

CHAPTER EIGHT

"Isn't that red-head Dene's latest charmer?" demanded Lord Marlow of his spouse as he came striding into her sitting-room one morning. "I've just seen her walking into Augusta's boudoir as though she owned the place."

Lady Marlow whose blonde beauty had run to fat shrugged with her customary indolence. "How should I know what friends Augusta makes? You know how stubborn she is. I vow I've washed my hands of her."

"Don't I just know what a stubborn ninny your daughter is," he growled. It was his habit to refer to any of the children as though they belonged exclusively to Lady Marlow when he was displeased with them and he was usually out of charity with his only daughter. A tall, big man with fair hair and a florid complexion, he was generally accounted handsome, but he had a weak chin and a petulant mouth, deficiencies inherited by his three expensive sons.

"Damn the girl, why can't she marry? She could have had Edward Richmond or a score of others, but no, she'd not lift a finger to oblige me."

Lady Marlow nodded, restraining a sigh. She had heard this same tirade a hundred times before and she let it flow over her until there was a pause and she could insert the information that Miss Clifford was accounted respectable. "She is Lady Linton's protégée, not the Marquis's."

"Hah, she's acting as her brother's pander, I've no doubt," retorted her husband unpleasantly and stomped off to bury himself in his bookroom to mull over his latest losses with a bottle of claret and a copy of the *Weekly Dispatch*. This publication contained information useful to a man of his sporting proclivities, although it could not be said that any of his certain bets had turned into winners recently.

Undisturbed by any knowledge of his lordship's disapproval, Corisande's acquaintance with Miss Marlow had moved on apace until they were now fast friends. It was their habit to walk together early in the Green Park and then retire to Arlington Street for a cup of chocolate before Corisande made her way home. This particular morning as Corisande was leaving the Marlows' elegant residence another caller was just arriving.

"Uncle Lucius, you are early. Have you come to see Mama?" Augusta enquired. "She is still in her boudoir, I believe."

"Thank you, my dear." Sir Lucius Orsett was a portly, middle-aged gentleman, but there was a distinct gleam in his pale eyes as he surveyed his niece's companion. "Won't you introduce me to your pretty friend, my dear?"

Corisande dropped a neat curtsy. She wasn't sure if she approved of the baronet's wide smile, or the way in which his fat white fingers held on to hers for longer than was customary, but she was prepared to like any relative of Gussy's so she gave him a sunny smile.

"Shall we see you at the Rutledges' ball, Uncle?"

"I haven't decided yet, my dear. Tell me, Miss Clifford, have you formed the intention of attending the event?"

Corisande nodded, explaining that she was to go with Lady Fanny and Lord Thorne, who was to be their escort.

"In that case, I'm sure I shall drop in there," said the baronet with a courtly bow.

Corisande restrained an impulse to giggle at his ponderous gallantry and thanked him prettily for the compliment, before bidding them both farewell and setting off for Hill Street.

Sir Harry Vernon was in the drawing-room when she arrived. "You are an early bird today, Harry," she greeted him with a warm smile. He had made it a habit to call on her daily and Corisande valued his friendship.

He shook hands with her. "I came to see if you would care to go and see the Tower of London. You expressed a desire to do so recently and this seems a fine morning for such an expedition."

Fanny walked in just as Corisande was consenting to this plan. Her surprise at seeing Harry so early was written on her face, but she quickly recovered her composure and graciously gave her permission for Corisande to go driving with the baronet rather than paying morning-calls with her.

An awkward silence grew after Corisande left them to go and change her gown. To Fanny's chagrin it was plain that Harry was in no haste to fill it. In the past he had been very eager to snatch a moment alone with her, now he appeared indifferent. Or bored, thought Fanny in some dismay. She struggled to cover her feelings with a flow of small talk, but it was a relief when Turnbull entered to inform her that Mr. Lavenham was below.

"Do ask him to step up," Fanny instructed.

"I'll wait for Corisande downstairs," said Harry, rising to his feet. "You will want to be private with your cousin, I've no doubt."

Fanny had no heart to contradict him.

She heard Corisande's light step on the stairs and then an exchange of lively greetings before Tom entered. Pleased though she was to see him back in town, Fanny's mind strayed during his recital of the news at Lavenham Place.

She had just made the unwelcome discovery that she was in love with Sir Harry Vernon after all, but it appeared that he had fallen out of love with her!

ON THEIR RETURN from watching a Military Review in Hyde Park the next day Fanny announced, "I fear I shall have to go and lie down for a while. Are you sure you won't take a nap, Corisande? We will be home late tonight, you know."

Corisande laughed. "I dare say you will think me provoking, but I'm not in the least bit tired."

"Disagreeable girl, wait until you have achieved my years!" Fanny riposted with a twinkling smile. "No, don't get up, stay here and finish your tea and I shall see you at dinner."

Corisande was engrossed in the latest copy of La Belle Assemblée when she heard a familiar voice on the stairs.

"No, there is no need to announce me, I'll see myself up."

The next moment the door was thrown open and the Marquis stood upon the threshold, looking extremely smart in a superfine coat of Scott's making.

"I did not look for any callers at this hour," said Miss Clifford joyfully, springing up to greet him with outstretched hands.

He closed the door behind him and crossed the Aubusson carpet in a few hasty strides to kiss her hand and smile down at her. There was such warmth in his dark eyes that Corisande had to step away, trying hard to control the blush she could feel beginning to glow in her cheeks.

"Please sit down. Shall I ring for more tea?"

"Not for me, thank you. I cannot stay long, I have another engagement," he explained, drawing up a chair next to hers. "Where's Fanny?"

"She's resting. We attend the Countess of Rutledge's ball tonight." Corisande had herself in hand now and was able to ask him calmly if he meant to go to this party.

He nodded. "That's why I came. Your dance-card will be filled the instant you arrive so I wanted to ask you to save a dance for me." Marc coughed and then continued gruffly, "I would also deem it an honour if you wear this tonight," and he produced a small flat velvet case from his pocket.

Corisande opened it with trembling fingers. "Oh, Marc!"

"A present for your birthday. The merest trumpery, I'm afraid, but I thought you would like it."

"I do, it's lovely." The gleaming pendant pearl was suspended from a fine gold chain. It trembled visibly in her unsteady hold. "But I'm afraid I cannot accept it."

"Why ever not?" demanded the Marquis. "You are too young for diamonds, but pearls are worn by all the girls. No one will think it unsuitable."

"They would if they knew you had given it to me! It is very generous of you, but I cannot take it. It would be most improper."

"Damn it, Corisande, will you stop being so missish? Who the devil is to know who gave it to you if you don't tell 'em?" said the Marquis, growing rather exasperated. "You ain't got a jewel to your name. Don't you want to wear them like all the other girls?"

Corisande bit her lip, curbing back a hasty retort. *Of course* she had felt this lack—but she replaced the pendant carefully in its box and held it out to him with great firmness. "Pray do not be offended, I know you meant well, but I cannot accept such an expensive gift."

Lord Dene threw the box angrily to one side. "You are being deliberately perverse, my girl," he said, irritated by her obstinacy. "Why won't you let me do anything for you? You accept things from Fanny, but you wouldn't even take money as a loan from me. You let Fanny dress you—"

"She does not!" Corisande's chin came up. "Most of my clothes are cast-offs from Letty or gowns Fanny has finished with, as you very well know."

The Marquis had in fact forgotten, since Corisande was always so elegantly turned out, thanks to Ellen's clever fingers helping her to refurbish everything to the latest kick of fashion. "That dress you had on the other night was no cast-off," he muttered. "Aye, and it must have cost at least as much as my pendant and yet you accepted it from Fanny."

Corisande's fingers locked together in her lap. "That was different," she stated with unanswerable logic, flinging up a hand in protest when he would have debated the point further. "Please, I do not think there is any sense in arguing on this head."

Lord Dene's jaw tightened. "I'm not accustomed to being told what to do by a chit of a girl," he snapped.

"Perhaps it would do you good! It may amuse you to play King Cophetua to my beggar-maid but it is not so entertaining for me!"

He stared at her blankly for a moment and then with gathering incredulity as her meaning sunk in. "Is that what you think? That I helped you merely to satisfy my own vanity?"

"Yes...no...oh, I don't know, but you cannot deny you have enjoyed it all the same!" She shrugged angrily, longing to accept his gift. "You have been goodness itself and I am grateful for your help, but I am not your property to be decked out at your pleasure," she added unfairly. Knowing her misery was the true cause of this quarrel, not any fault of his, did not help her temper.

"You little shrew! You don't deserve that I waste my time on you," he retorted, furious at this rejection.

"Then pray leave, sir," Corisande flashed back, as angry now as he and feeling thoroughly misunderstood. How dared he offer her expensive gifts as if she were a loose woman and then act as if he had been the one insulted? "Do not feel obliged to stay a moment longer, my lord. It was kind of you to think of my birthday, but there was not the least need to put yourself out," she said coldly, in a very good imitation of one of Fanny's crushing snubs.

Marc glared at her. "You impudent little hussy," he growled. Was this all the thanks he got for a morning wasted combing a dozen jewellers shops for something she might like? He got to his feet abruptly. "Since you wish it, Miss Clifford, I will leave you, but remember this quarrel was none of my making. When you have recovered your temper you may send me word."

On this valedictory note he stalked out with immense dignity, resisting the severe temptation to slam the door behind him.

Left in possession of the field, Corisande celebrated her victory by indulging in a hearty bout of tears.

"VERY PRETTY, my love!" said Fanny approvingly when Corisande presented herself in Fanny's boudoir just prior to dinner that evening. "I may not always see eye to eye with my Aunt Lavenham, but she has exquisite taste; nothing could become you more than orange-blossom sarsenet. It could never have looked half so well on Letty, not with those ribbons. They match your eyes exactly."

"Ellen helped me re-trim the dress with them." Miss Clifford's tone was subdued and so lacking in her usual sunny vitality that Fanny was startled. The child was so pale! Not that it mattered, she was still enchantingly lovely. She will break all hearts at the ball tonight, Fanny thought.

Corisande had sent the pearl pendant back to the Marquis's lodgings and her only ornament was a wreath of tiny artificial roses which had been twisted round the high knot of curls atop her head. It was a simple style which gave her added height, which was very useful as her small feet were shod in flat-heeled satin slippers. Long kid evening gloves completed her outfit and, all in white, she looked like a snow princess.

"Where had you those flowers?" Fanny asked leading the way downstairs. A number of boxes of flowers had been sent to the house and no less than five of these posies had been for Miss Clifford. Fanny had been amused by the enthusiastic reception Corisande had accorded these tributes. Her own bouquet was of dark red and white striped clove carnations which matched her wine-coloured satin. It had been sent by Lord Thorne, who had taken the precaution of discovering the colour of her gown. It was elegant, but not as pretty as the charming posy Corisande carried of white moss roses tied up with long blue ribbons.

"Sir Harry sent them," Corisande informed her hostess, her expression brightening a little.

Fanny curbed an impulse to scream. "How kind," she murmured, struggling for composure. "Then I dare say we may be sure of seeing him in Cavendish Square tonight."

They drove to the ball in Lord Thorne's carriage. Corisande rather liked the widowed diplomat, but thought him far too old a suitor for Fanny. His aquiline countenance was distinguished, but years of good living had increased his girth. The first time they had met and Corisande had heard the faint but unmistakable creaking of his Cumberland corset she had almost disgraced herself by giggling aloud. However, his perfect manners and worldly *savoir-faire* made him an agreeable escort, and his care for their comfort was much appreciated by both ladies as they descended into the noisy hurly-burly surrounding Lord and Lady Rutledge's elegant mansion.

The comings and goings of various carriages and the heated exchanges going on between coachmen, link-boys and chairmen, all exchanging insults at the tops of their voices, resounded deafeningly around the Square. Lord Thorne shepherded them smoothly through this crush, but Corisande found it almost as noisy inside the house as they joined the slow-moving procession which was mounting the stairway.

"Lord, how hot it is already!" Fanny exclaimed fanning herself furiously. There was very little room to manoeuvre on the stairway for the sheer press of numbers and Corisande thought it very foolish of Lady Rutledge to have decorated it with a double bank of flowers and said so forthrightly. "And look how they are wilting already!"

Fanny flashed her a warning look, but Lord Thorne merely laughed and, pinching her cheek, told her she was a sensible puss.

Corisande dimpled at him, accepting the compliment in the spirit it had been intended. Her depression was lifting.

Something must occur to restore harmony between the Marquis and herself, Corisande thought hopefully. Fortune had dealt her some cruel blows in recent years, yet here she was enjoying a season in London, a miracle beyond her wildest dreams. Her pleasure in the experience might be completely destroyed if she did not take care, and she would have no happy memories to carry home to Oxfordshire.

Grandmama used to say that it was wearisome to be in the company of someone indulging in self-pity, Corisande remembered. Mrs. Dalton had been one of the most sensible people her granddaughter had ever known and Corisande knew she would have scolded her for moping over a man she could never marry.

Fanny wondered why Corisande looked so solemn. Perhaps she was nervous now they had finally reached the head of the receiving-line.

"And this is Miss Clifford, my young friend who is staying with me at present." Corisande dipped a graceful curtsy as Fanny introduced her to their hosts.

"Charming, quite charming," Lady Rutledge, a good-natured, but feather-brained grandmother cooed. "Isn't she just what one likes to see in a young gal, Rutledge?" She poked her elderly spouse in the ribs with a jewelled fan. "I do detest to see a girl scarcely out of the schoolroom decked out like a jeweller's window. There is no need for such ostentation in anyone!"

Since Lady Rutledge had covered every inch of her ample person in gems of every description Corisande reflected that she was not a woman to take her own advice, but she thanked her hostess prettily and passed on into the first drawing-room.

"Let me procure you both a glass of champagne."

"Thank you, Aubrey," Fanny responded to this offer with gratitude. "What a lamb he is," she added as the diplomat moved off to thread his way through the crush. "Heavens, what a shocking squeeze! Still, you will find it diverting to meet new people, my love."

Corisande was delighted to discover that Fanny was right. A party was the best thing in the world to take one's mind off one's troubles, she soon decided. Her natural nervousness at attending her very first ball quickly faded as she began to enjoy the sensation she was creating as her hand was sought by a score of young men all eager for her smiles.

Emboldened by Monsieur Etienne's coaching, she accepted the invitation to join a set forming for the quadrille and was so delighted by her ability to get through the complicated steps without mishap that she bestowed her most brilliant smile upon her partner. Young Mr. Bentley was heir to an affluent baronetcy, besides being blessed with good looks and a friendly agreeable nature. Dazzled, he lost no time in asking her to partner him in one of the country-dances before he led her back to where Fanny sat on one of the gilt chairs placed around the ballroom.

Fanny could hardly contain her satisfaction. Corisande was the hit of the evening, deluged on every side by invitations to pic-nics, routs, masquerades, concerts and parties of every description, and Fanny basked in the praise, feeling almost like a proud mother. Her marriage had been a disaster, but she would have liked to have had children. Corisande was too old to think of in that way, but this was how it must feel to have a daughter who was a success!

Her high-flown elation vanished abruptly when she spotted Sir Harry Vernon strolling among the well-dressed crowd, stopping to chat now and then with his acquaintances. A bloom of indignant colour lent her cheeks an unusual rosiness. It was so unlike him not to seek her out immediately that she could only stare. For one horrid moment she thought he meant to pass her by with nothing more than a small bow, but then he halted.

"Good evening, Fanny." Harry forced a carelessness he did not feel into his voice. It had been deuced difficult to keep away, especially tonight when Fanny was looking particularly lovely, but her smile, warmer than it had been in weeks, gave him sudden hope. Dash it, little Corisande is right, he thought jubilantly. "You are to be congratulated, Fanny." Harry's gaze followed the movement of Corisande's graceful figure across the floor. "Miss Clifford is the prettiest girl in the room."

Swallowing her dismay, Fanny agreed, "Isn't she, and so good-natured, too," she added with the warm generosity which made Harry love her so.

There was a pause and Harry sensed she expected him to ask her to go down to supper with him. Once he would have begged her for that privilege and it was very hard to ignore her encouraging smile and turn away to greet Corisande.

"Will you stand up with me for the next country-dance, Miss Clifford?" he asked rather gruffly, and pretended not to hear Fanny's involuntary gasp.

Eyes gleaming, Corisande accepted. If Harry wanted her help in making Fanny jealous she was more than willing to do her part, although Fanny would never be so foolish as to think her a serious rival!

Corisande could not have been more wrong! Too well-bred to refuse one of the many solicitations for her hand, Fanny none the less spent the whole of the dance trying to keep an eye on Harry and Corisande. The intimacy of the way in which Harry's dark head bent to the red-gold one stabbed her to the heart. To counter it, she immediately embarked upon a playful flirtation with her own partner and even accepted a further invitation for the next dance.

"Dash it, Corisande, do you see how Fanny allows Devlin to make her laugh and blush," muttered Harry with suppressed fury as he led Miss Clifford back to her seat.

"Do not watch them," advised Corisande. "You must try not to show that you care so much, Harry. You were doing splendidly before."

Corisande's kind heart ached for his pain. Her own knowledge of such suffering made her feel sympathetic.

"That one so fair should be so cruel!" lamented the baronet bitterly. "She has no heart."

"Oh, no, you are wrong! Think of how kind she has been to me," said Corisande in some distress. "I am persuaded she is fonder of you than she knows, Harry."

"Once I thought so... but it don't signify!" His voice became suspended and then recovering he went on gamely. "I beg your pardon. I am boring on about my affairs instead of asking you how you are enjoying your first ball."

"Oh, it is very well," Corisande dismissed this topic ruthlessly. "You are not boring me at all, Harry. Indeed, I should be very glad to do anything I can to help you."

He gave her hand a brotherly little squeeze. "Would you? You are a Trojan!" he exclaimed, a delighted smile lighting up his homely face.

From her place in the set Fanny saw this exchange and almost missed her step. Furious with herself, she resolved not to look in their direction again, but she was very conscious of the way in which they were animatedly discussing something and wondered what it could be that had brought that sparkling impish smile to Corisande's face.

Miss Clifford's evident pleasure in Sir Harry Vernon's company didn't go unnoticed in another quarter. Gloom was struck into Lord Dene's heart when he entered the white and gold ball-

room to discover his aggravating protégée beaming with unshad-
owed affection at the baronet. His long stride checked involuntarily
and jealousy seized him at their confidential manner. A jealousy
he was determined not to acknowledge.

"Marc! Where are you going in such a hurry?" Fanny reached
him just as he was about to disappear into the small chamber adjoining the ballroom which Lady Rutledge had thoughtfully set
aside for those persons desirous of avoiding the fatigue of dancing. "You cannot go and play hazard the minute you arrive!"

"Faro, Fanny, faro."

"Don't quibble," she said severely. "You have only just got
here. Come and say hello to Corisande, at least. I understood you
were engaged for the next cotillion with her and you have very
nearly missed it."

Fanny threaded her arm through his and, bowing to the inevi-
table, Marc found a way for them through the throng.

Glancing up, Corisande saw them approaching and immediately redoubled her attempt to convince the world that she was
épris with Sir Harry Vernon.

Her delicious laugh floated tantalisingly to the Marquis's ears.
His eyebrows met in a straight bar and he looked so altogether
thunderous that Fanny exclaimed in alarm, "Marc, what is the
matter?"

He ignored her. "The abominable little wretch," he grated. She
was doing it deliberately!

Fanny glanced back quickly at Corisande, who had turned one
shoulder on them. "Marc, have you quarrelled with the child?"

"Mind your own business, Fanny," snapped her brother, his
frayed temper getting the better of him for a moment before he
apologised for this rudeness. By the time they reached the other
couple he had himself well in hand. His greeting to Miss Clifford
was a model of grace and thereafter he exchanged not one word
with her, but chatted easily to the baronet.

Having spared no pains to demonstrate her indifference to the
Marquis, Corisande gained no pleasure from seeing her hints so
well understood. Regret for her impulsive action was the emotion
swelling uppermost in her breast, but it vied with strong irritation. He was paying her back in her own coin! How very like the
wretched man to take her at her word when she least desired it!

There was a grim look to his lordship's mouth when he led Miss
Clifford out for the promised cotillion. Corisande was grateful for
the figures of the dance which constantly separated them, but instead of returning her to her seat when the cotillion was over the
Marquis unexpectedly turned aside. Almost before she knew it

Corisande found herself hustled out of the ballroom and into a small deserted salon.

"Please, I must get back." Corisande strove to keep the tremor out of her voice. "It is nearly time for supper and I promised Sir Harry he could be my escort."

The Marquis received this information with a dark frown. "Why are you flirting with Vernon?" he demanded. "Everyone knows he is mad for Fanny."

The need for secrecy curbed Corisande's tongue. Quickly she decided that she must think of another reason to convince him before he began to probe her motives.

"A gentleman may change his mind, particularly if he receives no encouragement from the lady in question," she replied with a creditably saucy shrug.

The Marquis looked stunned. "You...you would knowingly try to take him away from Fanny?" he gasped, hardly able to believe he had heard her aright. "Corisande, don't you realise that she cares for him? She don't like to admit it, but she will one day. Harry might have taken a fancy to you, but he wants to marry her."

Corisande could feel her knees trembling. She dared not back down meekly now, for if she did she would begin to cry. No matter how she had tried to cheer herself up scarcely two hours ago she could not make herself follow such sensible advice now. Not when he was standing so close, his dark eyes filled with concern.

But his concern was not for her, it was for his sister! The realisation hit her like a painful blow. *She* had no rightful claims upon him at all!

Suddenly Corisande wanted to hurt him in return. Wild emotions churned within her seemingly composed frame. She could barely understand it herself, but she knew she wanted to make him pay for the anguish he had inflicted, even if he was not to blame.

"Corisande, he won't change his allegiance so easily. You will only make a fool of yourself if you persist." The Marquis's voice was gentle.

"Really? I doubt it, sir." A ripple of silvery laughter accompanied her taunting reply. "I dare say I could have him proposing marriage to me within the week, if I wished."

The Marquis stared at her in silence for a long moment.

Corisande saw the warmth die out of his eyes and then his lip curled scornfully.

"Perhaps you could, at that," he answered slowly. "My congratulations, it seems you have picked up the ways of the world in less time than I would have credited possible."

A flush rose to Corisande's cheeks. "There is no need surely to criticise me for seeking to attain a little town polish," she said in a halting voice, wishing she had not attempted to cross swords with him. She should never have tried to salve her bruised pride with such a wicked lie and she knew it!

"No, indeed," he agreed smoothly. "It was I who was at fault, but now I am amply repaid for thinking you a different creature from the rest of your sex."

"I don't know what you mean," Corisande faltered, afraid that she did.

"I imagine you do." A swift stride brought him to her side before she could think of executing a strategic retreat. "The simplest answer to your present difficulty is a rich husband and Harry Vernon is a very wealthy man."

"How dare you imply such a horrid thing?" Indignation made Corisande's eyes glow like sapphires. "As if I would marry a man for just his money!" She was so angry she would have turned on her heel and stalked out of the room if his hands had not moved to hold her by the shoulders to prevent her.

"Why not?" he jeered. "That's what most women do. Or if not for wealth, then for a fine estate or title which will bring them consequence."

Corisande's hand rose unthinkingly, but he caught her wrist before the blow could descend.

"Oh, no, my girl, you'll not strike me a second time," he said harshly.

He was now holding her prisoner so closely that their faces were only inches apart and as he stared down at her their angry eyes met and locked.

Corisande could not tear her gaze away and she heard his breathing suddenly quicken also. She felt his hands loosen their grip, but even as she swayed involuntarily towards him, so that their contact would not be broken, he slid them down to her waist.

"Corisande!" Marc spoke her name in a low whisper that was almost a groan as he bent his head towards hers.

When their lips met the emotion that they had both been hiding behind anger exploded into life. Marc's arms tightened, drawing her even more closely into his embrace. Corisande could feel the heat of his body burning her through her flimsy dress. Rational thought was banished in that instant and she surrendered to the passion that was swirling through her veins in a dizzying flood.

With knees like melting snow, she clung to him, wrapping her arms around his neck, one small hand burying itself in the thick dark hair that curled upon his neck. His lips moved to caress her closed eyelids, her cheeks, the tender line of her white throat, before finding her mouth again in another passionate kiss.

Corisande was in heaven and she sighed reluctantly when finally Marc lifted his head.

He stared down into her lovely face and laughed a little shakily. "What torment you have put me through these past few weeks, you adorable minx."

Lazily Corisande smiled at him and murmured, "Did I?" She felt as richly contented as a cream-fed cat. Every nerve was tingling with pleasure. I shall start purring aloud in a minute, she thought with a silent giggle of sheer joy.

"Little witch, you know you did! I've been under your spell from the moment we met on the Bath road and you opened your mouth to upbraid me for my carelessness." Marc touched a finger to her lips. "Your lovely kissable mouth," he added softly.

Suiting actions to words, he kissed her again, this time with a delicious butterfly lightness that left Corisande even more shaken than before. A strange breathlessness possessed her. This tenderness was something beyond passion. Was she dreaming or did he, could he, care for her?

"How beautiful you are, my enchantress." Marc gently smoothed back a lock of bright hair that had strayed from the mass of curls atop her regal little head. She looked so lovely as a blush rose to her cheeks that he was tempted to kiss her again, but he mastered the impulse with considerable effort.

It had been his intention to wait until Corisande had seen a little more of the world before he made his feelings plain to her. He had wanted her to gain some experience of life before she made her choice, but she was no child, by God! She was a woman, ripe for love and he could not regret his impetuosity.

"Corisande, I want you for my own."

The words rang in her ears, shattering Corisande's dreamy contentment. She forced herself to take a deep breath as she struggled desperately to understand them.

Loving him as she did, she had assumed his kisses meant he shared the same feelings, but with a shock she realised he had not spoken one word of love. Desire, yes, but love? Even his tenderness did not necessarily mean his intentions were honourable, but only that he was experienced in knowing how to please.

Corisande shivered. Fanny had warned her of his dangerous charm and now she knew his reputation was well deserved. He would make a perfect lover, but she had seen enough now of the Marquis's world to know that a man in his position did not offer marriage to a nobody, no matter how that nobody might long for him to do so! She did not need to ask him to make his meaning clear when the answer was staring her in the face.

"Sweetheart, have I done something wrong?" Marc's urgent voice broke into her chaotic thoughts.

Corisande strove for composure. Pride came to her aid.

"Not at all, my lord." She forced a smile. "Would you take me back now, please? Before Fanny comes looking for us," she added in a quiet voice.

"Did I frighten you just now?"

The swift question made her shake her head and deny it, but her strained manner made the Marquis think his guess was correct and he mentally cursed his own clumsiness.

He had been too precipitate! That she was ready for love he did not doubt—how could he after her sweet response to his kisses?—but she was an innocent and not one of his practised flirts. In spite of her denials, she needed more time and he must not press her to give him an answer now. He had alarmed her with his ardour and it would be foolish to rush his fences and risk upsetting her further.

"Very well, we will go back to the ballroom if you wish," he said with a reassuring smile, tucking her hand into the crook of his elbow.

Corisande inclined her head in thanks, grateful that he had not disputed the issue as she had feared he might. His unexpected tact brought a shine of tears to her eyes. He had always been kind to her.

Oh, if only she didn't love him so! What would she do if he offered her a *carte blanche?* Heaven awaited her in his arms. Would she have the strength to resist the temptation?

Corisande's imagination ran riot as they threaded their way back through the throng and though she answered the Marquis's remarks she was scarcely aware of a word she said.

"My dear, I was beginning to think I had lost you."

Fanny greeted their return with a composed smile and no sign of the apprehension which had been troubling her for the last quarter of an hour. It was not unknown for a young lady to escape her chaperone and disappear to steal a moment or two alone with a gentleman while at a ball, but Fanny had been worried when she realised that Marc was also missing. She longed to remind him of their father's command, but it was impossible in these circumstances.

"Aubrey is waiting to take us down to supper. Will you join us, Marc?" Fanny enquired with reluctant politeness, signalling with her fan to summon Lord Thorne to her side.

Before the Marquis could reply Corisande said swiftly, "Sir Harry asked if he might escort me. Look, here he comes now."

Harry's smile embraced the whole party, but his gaze came to rest on Corisande with appropriately lover-like tenacity. "Shall we go down, my dear?"

Everyone else stared at him in astonishment. Only Lord Thorne was pleased when the news sunk in. Fanny tried to conceal a gasp of dismay, while her brother experienced a sudden longing to plant the baronet a facer for daring to make such a suggestion.

When he had arrived at the ball Marc had still been angry with Corisande, though once his temper had cooled he had realised she had been right to refuse his gift. It had led him to accuse her of flirting with Vernon, a stupid mistake. It was not her fault if other men read too much into her sunny smiles.

Confidently the Marquis waited for his little love to send Harry to the right-about. Jupiter, but he could almost feel sorry for the fellow!

Corisande gulped, miserably aware of the two different pairs of eyes, dark and grey, expectantly awaiting her answer.

Silently she placed her hand on the arm Harry held out to her and he led her away with a triumphant smile.

CHAPTER NINE

THE NEXT MORNING brought Fanny an unexpected visitor.

"His Grace of Weston," announced Turnbull hastily, his eyes like saucers. Having totally lacked the courage to try and detain this particular caller until he could ascertain whether his mistress would receive him, Turnbull could think of no way to prevent the Duke from mounting the stairs and strolling into the morning-room where Lady Linton reposed *en déshabille* in a wrapper on the striped satin sofa.

"Bring up the Madeira, the best Madeira," Fanny cried, flying up to her feet in a flurry of foaming lace. "At once, Turnbull, if you please."

Recovering something of his usual aplomb, which had been shattered by this unprecedented visit, the butler nodded and bowed himself quickly out of the room.

"A very pretty house you have here, my dear. Allow me to congratulate you," said the Duke languidly. "A pity your servants are so badly trained."

Fanny flushed. Her hands, busy trying to straighten the frivolous little lace cap pinned to her loose curls, stilled at his sarcasm.

"Aren't you going to ask me to be seated?"

A quiver ran through Fanny at this gently spoken reminder. "Please," she said in a strangled tone, pointed to the most comfortable armchair.

"Thank you." The Duke moved towards it. He carried a fashionable malacca cane and it could be seen that he leant on it, if only a trifle. Still very upright, his spare figure did not show his age in the same way as did the lines of dissipation which marked his thin face. Like his daughter's, his eyes were a pale blue, but their expression habitually mocked and as usual Fanny was forced to repress a shiver at the coldness of his silky voice.

"I trust I find you well?"

"Oh, yes, yes, indeed, Papa. And you? But I need not ask, I can see for myself you are in excellent health. I did not know you were in town. Have you been so long? I had thought you fixed at Amberfield, but perhaps you have business to attend to?"

"I shall endeavour to explain my presence if you will grant me a moment's opportunity to do so." His remark cut across her nervous prattling. "I am sure you will excuse my plain speaking, but where is Dene?"

"I beg pardon, Papa?" Fanny was bewildered. "He attended the ball at the Rutledges' last night so I can only assume he is still abed. It is rather early."

A slight smile flitted over his grace's narrow face at her imperfectly concealed indignation. "Indeed, too early for callers I'll allow, but, since he is not at his lodgings, I must conclude that Dene is also abroad. An unfashionable pair, are we not? And alas before you suggest it, I have already taken the precaution of trying his clubs and drawn a blank."

A tap at the door heralding Turnbull's arrival with the refreshments gave Fanny a moment in which to think. Silence was maintained while Turnbull poured out the Madeira, but when he had gone Fanny could not come up with any answer.

"A tolerable wine, my dear." The Duke congratulated her politely and set down his glass. "So you have no idea as to where I can find your brother this morning?"

"I'm sorry, Papa." Fanny shook her head. "Is the matter urgent?"

He shrugged. "I trust not. Tell me, was Miss Marlow at the ball last night?"

Ah, now we are coming to it, Fanny thought in alarm, but managing to keep her composure returned a negative reply, "Lady Marlow said she had the headache."

"A pity. I hardly need ask if Dene made you privy to the conversation I had with him when last I was in town." His glance flicked over her averted face. "Has he said anything to you about his plans?" Fanny kept silent and he sighed. "Pray do not be provoking, my dear. I shall find out Dene's intentions whether you tell me or not."

"Papa, must you promote this match? Augusta Marlow was Edward's choice. She is not the least suited to be Marc's bride."

"I think I shall strive to forget your impertinence, my dear. It was not the custom in my day to question the decisions of one's parents," said his grace with a haughty lift of his brows.

Abashed, Fanny stared down at her hands, tightly clenched in her lap. Her face felt hot and she was as tongue-tied as a schoolgirl. It had never been easy to feel filial affection for her father. He rebuffed any effort made to get close to him and his sharp tongue left her feeling foolish and gauche.

"Amberfield at this season grows dull and it is my intention to travel to Brussels. It is quite the thing, I believe, to view the recent battlefield—so patriotic. I would not want to be thought behind the times." The Duke's manner was whimsically pensive. "I had hoped to have speech with my son before I departed. No doubt you think me sentimental, but I am persuaded it is merely a sign of age and nothing more serious."

He regarded her over the brim of his wine glass. "On my return I would be gratified to hear of Dene's engagement to Miss Marlow. Do you think me too optimistic?"

"You are a fount of wisdom, Papa," Fanny answered, recovering her spirit at this veiled threat to her beloved brother. On Marc's behalf, if not her own, Fanny was prepared to take up cudgels.

"Thank you, but I think your faith in me is too sanguine on this occasion." Fanny flinched at his sarcastic tone but her steady gaze did not waver.

A thin smile touched the Duke's mouth. He had never been in the least interested in the existence of his daughter, only Edward had been the material he needed as his heir for the future, but it gave him a sense of satisfaction to realise that Fanny had her share of the Richmond courage. "You were wasted on Linton," he remarked, slowly, voicing his thoughts.

Fanny's eyes flew to his.

"Pray do not look so worried. I have no intention of seeking a husband for you, my dear. The business of arranging one match is fatiguing enough. Now please see to it that Dene is informed of my visit. You may tell him that I intend to write to Marlow outlining certain proposals. It may serve to remind Dene of his obligations."

The Duke had finished his wine and rose to take his leave. "By the way, they tell me you have a guest staying with you. A young girl, I understand."

"Yes, Papa. Miss Corisande Clifford, the daughter of an old schoolfriend."

"Corisande...an unusual name." The Duke expressed surprise and then said unexpectedly, "I knew another lady by that name once, a most rare and lovely creature with a voice like a nightingale's." For an instant his expression softened and Fanny had the oddest impression that his mind travelled far away down some distant path of memory.

Recovering, he fired an abrupt question at his daughter. "Her people? Who were they?"

"You do not know them, sir. Her mother was a connection of the Morleys, but Corisande is an orphan." Fanny spoke casually, trying to hide her dismay at his sudden interest. Could he have possibly heard something of Marc's interest in Corisande's affairs?

"And her father?"

"I never knew him," said Fanny truthfully. "He was a botanist I believe. He died in Africa some years ago. His brother, Sir Robert Clifford lives in Northumberland. So you see, sir, Corisande is quite respectable."

"May I see this *protégée*?" The unexpected request startled Fanny. "I should like an introduction."

"I think she is still asleep," she faltered, but saw that he would not be turned from his purpose and rang for a message to be taken up to Corisande's bedchamber.

A few moments later Ellen came into the morning-room.

Dropping a respectful curtsy to the Duke, she turned back to Fanny and said, "Miss Clifford went out early, milady. Before you were up."

"She did not go out alone, I hope!"

"No, milady, one of the housemaids went with her," Ellen soothed.

Fanny sighed in relief. She wished Corisande were not so independent. "I am sorry, Papa."

"Did Miss Clifford say when she would be returning?" This question was thrown at Ellen.

"No, your grace. She is in the habit of walking in the Green Park sometimes. I think she misses the country most likely, she—"

"Thank you, I did not, I think, evince any desire for your conversation," said his grace with poisonous sweetness.

Ellen bobbed an apologetic curtsy. Eeh, but she had forgotten what a nasty-tongued devil the old man was!

The Duke seemed to lose interest in Miss Clifford. "I shall be away for some weeks. I may visit friends in Paris; I have not yet decided," he announced with a negligent wave of one white hand. "However, you may look to see me in London on my return." He moved towards the door. "You need not see me out, Fanny. I shall find my own way."

He paused.

"Oh, and Fanny, do not make the mistake of thinking you can loan Dene the money to escape his creditors. It is beyond the power of your purse and I should be most displeased to hear that you had been selling out of the Funds in order to try and accomplish such a feat.''

This had been Fanny's precise intention. She went quite white. ''You are very acute, sir,'' she gasped.

''You overwhelm me, child.'' As ever, sarcasm coloured the Duke's voice, but watching him Ellen detected a frisson of pleasure flit over his cold reserved face. Aye, he enjoyed his wicked reputation, if she was any judge!

Ellen barely managed to restrain a sniff of disdain. His precious grace was as big a poseur as that poet fellow Byron, him as had all the swells dancing to his tune until only last week. Not all his fancy connections had saved Byron from disgrace, though she didn't believe all the nasty rumours she'd heard—as if any gentleman would behave in such a dreadful way! But he'd liked to shock people had Lord B. Just like the Duke, Ellen thought shrewdly. The pity of it was that his children were fooled along with the rest and there was no one to try and penetrate the shell a lonely and embittered old man had built around himself.

When he had gone, Fanny sank trembling into a chair. Taking one look at her white face, Ellen bustled to mix her a glass of hartshorn and water and, placing the restorative in Fanny's hand, said firmly, ''Come along, Lady Fanny, you drink this.''

Fanny smiled at this reversion to her old nursery manner, but shook her head. ''Ugh, pray take this vile stuff away, do, Ellen.'' She thrust the glass at Miss Clay. ''You may give me another glass of Madeira instead.''

''Indeed I won't!'' exclaimed Ellen, scandalised.

Fanny sighed at this tyranny. ''Oh, very well, but I need it. I can quite see why an interview with my father drives Marc to the bottle!''

Relenting, Ellen poured a little wine and handed it to her in a disapproving silence. Fanny sipped it and stared unseeingly at the Meissen figurine of a street musician which decorated her mantel.

What had really inspired her father to visit this morning? Why had he been so interested in Corisande? She did not like it!

THE MARQUIS OF DENE, who had passed a sleepless night, rose at an unprecedented hour, which almost caused Peabody, his faithful valet, to have a heart attack, as he later confided to his cronies over a glass of daffy in the tavern he favoured with his custom. Peabody was of the opinion that the Marquis had not been himself since the recent visit to Lavenham Place.

"Gorn all quiet-like. Not so much as thrown a boot at me head," lamented the valet whenever he could find anyone to listen. "No drinking sprees, no high-flying Cyprians, no crazy wagers. Turning monk he is, sickening for something like as not."

This morning it was his lordship's Tiger who was the recipient of his dark prophecy. Dickon had other ideas on what was ailing the guv'nor, but preferred to keep his own counsel.

"You ought to stow your gab, you old fidget," he retorted disrespectfully, scorning the middle-aged valet's loquaciousness. "You know he don't like to have his affairs talked about." A jerk of Dickon's head towards the parlour, where the Marquis was partaking of his breakfast, indicated his meaning.

Peabody sniffed and removed himself in a dignified silence, leaving Dickon to finish brushing his livery jacket in anticipation of a summons to duty. Whistling as he worked, Dickon recalled a certain young genty-mort, now living with the guv'nor's sister, and his gamin face split into a grin.

Gloomily contemplating a plate of cold beef, his master evinced no such signs of cheerfulness. The Devil take it if he knew what Corisande was about! He could have sworn her ardent response to his kisses was genuine and yet not five minutes later she had been flirting shamelessly with Harry Vernon.

There had been no chance to talk to her during supper, but she had avoided him afterwards. Her dance-card was filled to overflowing and without her co-operation it was impossible to snatch a moment alone. His patience worn to the bone, he had quit the ball seething with temper. Now he wondered if he would have done better to have stayed and somehow insisted on an explanation.

The arrival of the post brought an end to these dismal reflections. His glance quickly scanned the single sheet of one letter and then the Marquis was up out of his chair and calling for his curricle to be brought round.

Within a very short space of time he was driving towards the City where his man of business was soon startled to learn from his senior clerk that Lord Dene was in the outer office, and desirous of an immediate interview if it were convenient.

Suppressing a gasp of surprise, Mr. Dibden hurried out to greet his noble client and beg him to step into his private office. "Please be seated, my lord." Mr. Dibden indicated a chair and proceeded to assure his visitor that he would have been very happy to have waited upon his lordship at his lodgings, if he had known his lordship had wanted to see him.

"Dibden, it is excessively civil of you to see me at such short notice. There was not the least need to drag you out." Marc had a fondness for the elderly man who had looked after his affairs since his majority and set himself to soothing his solicitor's ruffled feathers. "As a matter of fact, I've been meaning to come and see you for the past couple of days. The thing is, I want to set my affairs in order. Settle my debts and so forth."

"I see." Mr. Dibden regarded the tips of his fingers.

He was a spare little man with a thatch of grey hair tied back in an old-fashioned queue. His features were sharp and combined with his sober raiment and scratchy precise voice to give the impression he was a very dry old stick indeed. However, when he lifted his eyes it could be seen that they were a bright cornflower blue and held a merry twinkle, quite at odds with the rest of his appearance.

"In short, my lord, you wish to be beforehand with the world?"

"Exactly so."

Mr. Dibden permitted himself a small smile. "May I make so bold as to enquire the lady's name?"

"What! How did you guess?"

"It is the obvious conclusion, my lord," Mr. Dibden replied. "Still, as I can see that you do not care to discuss the matter, I must apologise for my impertinence."

"No need. I am thinking of marriage," admitted the Marquis. "But I rely on your discretion to keep the information to yourself," he added, recovering from his surprise.

The solicitor nodded. "Of course. Now, may I ask the nature of your present obligations?"

Marc, who had spent several hours in rescuing what bills had escaped consignment to the fire from their oblivion in various drawers, pockets and other sundry resting-places, handed them over, together with a piece of paper on which he had written a rough estimate of the total, so far as he knew it.

"I know I'm badly dipped, but surely there's no need for such a long face, man," he exclaimed impatiently after a pause of several minutes. "My holdings in the Funds will cover it, won't they?"

Mr. Dibden was unable to share this sanguine belief. "If you remember, my lord, I did warn you a few months ago that this might happen if you continued at your current rate of expenditure."

"And if I sell my yacht, the racing-string and my hunters?" The Marquis enumerated his most valuable disposable assets in a perfectly level voice.

Mr. Dibden inclined his head and contemplated the list once more for a few moments of busy calculation. A dry cough was the result. "I'm sorry, but even then I think you must disabuse yourself of the hope of meeting your creditors in full."

"So, if I am to come about, I shall have to sell some of my lands."

Mr. Dibden glanced at him sharply. The Marquis was rather white about the mouth, but was otherwise calm and composed.

"I would not advise that course," he replied with a deceptive meekness. "You are scorched this year, but with gradual retrenchment I think you can pull clear. Another mortgage, perhaps, would serve?"

His lordship shook his head. "That would not answer my purpose." He coloured slightly. "I will be frank with you. Everyone will know soon enough, in any event, if my father decides to go ahead ... the thing is, Dibden, his grace is likely to leave his fortune elsewhere."

The solicitor's mouth fell open. Horrified, he could only gasp, "My lord, surely you are mistaken?"

"No. Wish I were, but I'm not," Marc declared frankly. "Told me so himself. Unless I marry Miss Marlow he'll disinherit me, but I'll not do it and that's flat."

"Amberfield," murmured his solicitor in a strangled whisper.

"Not for Amberfield or any other reason." A flash of amusement lit the dark eyes. "Do you keep any brandy, sir? You look as if you could do with it."

Too shocked to quibble over the proprieties, Mr. Dibden allowed his client to pour him a glass of sherry, which was all the Marquis could find by way of a restorative.

"I can't believe his grace would be so vindictive, so foolish!" A little colour had returned to the solicitor's cheeks. "The injustice of it, the scandal such an improper action would cause!"

"Much that would worry my father," shrugged his lordship. "Devil take it, you know what he is like when he has made his mind up! But I refuse to be a puppet to dangle on his strings."

Something in the younger man's tone warned the solicitor that further discussion would be useless so he returned to their original topic. "I think it might be possible to raise the sum required by a less drastic method," he ventured. "Perhaps your lordship might consider disposing of your hunting-box in Leicestershire. It is not a family property, but it is a good little house in an excellent situation. It should fetch a tidy sum, which added to the money raised by the sale of your other assets should cover your difficulties."

This suggestion gave Marc something of a pang, since he was a bruising rider to the hounds, but having already accepted the necessity of selling his hunters he saw the sense in Dibden's plan. It

would be a wrench, but not so shocking as to be selling his lands.
He had inherited Denehurst, his Yorkshire estate, with the title and
since it was free of any entail it was his to dispose of as he saw fit,
but he had been very conscious that no Richmond had ever sold a
foot of land for the last hundred years and more, and God knew
some of his ancestors had been regular loose-screws!

"That is a capital notion, Dibden," he exclaimed. "I am very
glad I laid the matter before you. I wish I had done so earlier, it's
been giving me uneasy nights, I can tell you."

Relief sent Marc's spirits soaring. He hadn't realised he had been
sailing so close to the wind. Anxiety over debt had never been a
characteristic of his, but a man had to think of the future when he
was contemplating marriage!

"Thank you. It is something to know that I shall be able to
support my wife in comfort, if not the first stare of luxury," remarked his lordship when all the arrangements had been concluded.

"Shall your lordship require me to draw up a notice of your engagement to be inserted in the *Gazette?*" asked Mr. Dibden craft-
ily.

The Marquis met his eye and then grinned. "No, I can see to it
myself, thank you." Regarding the solicitor's disappointed look,
he relented. "To be honest, I haven't asked the lady yet, but you
shall be one of the first to know if she says yes."

Mr. Dibden beamed and thanked him. Turning to the other
matter which had brought him hot-foot into the City, the Marquis
drew out the letter which had arrived for him that morning.

"You may have heard that my sister has a young friend staying
with her?"

The solicitor nodded; very little escaped his notice.

"She is an orphan and her uncle, Sir Robert Clifford, will neither provide a home for her nor make any push to help her. Here,
read this letter for yourself." He handed it across the desk. "I sent
word to him in the belief that he would consent to act as her
guardian."

"A very sorry business, my lord." Mr. Dibden handed back the
missive with a disgusted shake of his head.

"A regular miser, ain't he?" remarked the Marquis. "He refuses to acknowledge any responsibility for her welfare. Probably
worried she might take the shine out of the daughters he men-
tions." The Marquis's tone was jocular but his mouth was grim.
"I've half a mind to post up there and tell him what I think of his
paltry behaviour to his face."

Alarmed, his solicitor bent all his energy into dissuading the Marquis from this course of action. He was very fond of his hot-headed young client and inclined to hope that Lord Dene would not go ahead with what sounded suspiciously like a misalliance which would infuriate the Duke of Weston. Too astute to venture this opinion, he confined his attention and advice to the matter of Miss Clifford.

"So there is no way I can force the fellow to act as he ought?" asked the Marquis with a curl to his lips.

"I'm sorry, my lord."

The Marquis got to his feet. "I dare say she would not be happy living there in any case," he said abruptly. He picked up his hat and gloves. "Thank you for your time and your help. Please let me know how the other business we spoke of goes on," and with a brief goodbye he strode out of the dusty office which seemed very quiet after he had gone.

Mr. Dibden straightened a pile of tidy papers with an automatic gesture, his gaze anxious.

Why was his young client taking such an interest in a penniless orphan? It was possible, of course, that Lady Linton had asked for his help, but that did not explain the expression which had soft-ened the Marquis's dark features whenever he mentioned the girl's name.

Could it be, could it possibly be that the Marquis's mysterious bride was this penniless Miss Clifford? The solicitor sighed. "Dear me, I hope the boy doesn't do anything rash!" he murmured to himself.

"OH, THERE YOU ARE, my love, where in the world have you been? I declare I am quite distracted," Fanny greeted Corisande, as she walked into the morning-room shortly after the Duke's departure.

"I was taking the air in the Green Park." Corisande was sur-prised to see Fanny so agitated. "I'm sorry if my absence incon-venienced you, but I stayed to drink chocolate with Augusta Marlow."

Fanny emitted a loud groan. "That wretched girl! I wish you had not become acquainted with her!" She sank on to the sofa.

Corisande gazed at her in astonishment. "What is wrong? Do you dislike Gussy? She is most respectable, you know."

"I am aware of that!" said Fanny tragically. "She is so entirely respectable in every way that Papa has determined that she must be Marc's bride."

"Oh!" Corisande's hand flew to her mouth. "I did not realise he was to be married."

Fanny tried to pull her scattered wits together. In a calmer tone she bade Corisande sit down. "While you were out I sustained a visit from his grace. He is set on the marriage."

"Does Marc know his father wishes him to marry Gussy?"

Fanny nodded. The look of bleak misery on Corisande's face made her want to burst into tears. "My dear, I did try to warn you it would not do to fall in love with my wretched brother. Even if Marc returns your regard it would be impossible for him to marry you."

"Pray do not distress yourself. My feelings are not deeply engaged," Corisande lied. "Moreover, I do not think his lordship has any serious intentions towards me."

"I can assure you that Marc would not dream of offering you a *carte blanche*," Fanny said, alarmed by Corisande's bitter tone.

"And I would not accept if he did," snapped Miss Clifford, sitting up very straight, red flags of temper flying in her cheeks.

Attempting to redeem her mistake, Fanny explained the Duke's edict and Marc's reaction.

"How perfectly Gothic of your papa to behave so! No man of spirit would agree to such monstrous terms," Corisande declared roundly.

Fanny blinked at her vehemence. "Yes, but it would be an exceptional match in many ways, you know. Miss Marlow would make an excellent duchess, such elegance and poise!"

Corisande raised her eyebrows. That didn't sound much like the Gussy she knew! And yet now she came to think on it, they had spent most of their time together in private. Perhaps Gussy's company manners were more formal.

At any other time this hint of mystery would have been enough to whet Corisande's abundant curiosity, but she had no wish to dwell upon it now. With a sudden chilling certainty she realised she could never accept any offer, of whatever kind, from the Marquis of Dene.

Tempted though she was to abandon her principles for the pleasure of lying in his arms, Corisande knew she couldn't do it. She was too honest to pretend it was virtue that prevented her. She wanted all of Marc's love! It would be torture of the most hellish kind to share him with anyone else, which as his mistress she would be forced to do!

"Will you excuse me please, Fanny?" she begged, and fled to the sanctuary of her room where she could think in peace.

Quelling her inner turmoil as best she could, Corisande forced herself to consider the situation with all the practicality she could muster. The Marquis had not made any improper suggestions to her yet, but she was convinced it was only a matter of time. What was less certain was her power to deny him! She loved Marc with all her heart and soul but, putting her romantic notions aside, there was a high price to pay for abandoning respectability.

A mistress had to live in the shadows, her life made insecure by the knowledge that she could be cast off at any time, with no provision made for her future except by the charity of her former lover. Corisande did not think Marc would ever treat her unfairly if he tired of her, but there was one further problem that could not be resolved.

She must face the fact that he would marry one day. His position demanded an heir, a legitimate heir. She could never dare give him children. They would be bastards!

The thought sent icy shivers down her spine. She might be besotted, willing to count the world well lost for love, but how could she brand her children with that hateful name? She wanted a real home, babies and most of all the right to belong to him without shame or deceit. She wanted to be his wife!

So, she could not become his mistress, but the thought of becoming his Marchioness was absurd. He must marry a girl of his own degree, a well-bred, well-connected young lady who could bring him a proper dowry and who would make him a suitable duchess one day.

Grandmama was right when she always used to say that the aristocracy and the gentry did not mix together well, Corisande thought to herself sadly. There was still that vast gulf of class dividing them. On the surface she appeared to have fitted in, but what did she really know of Marc's world?

If he asked her to marry him, she would be expected to play the part of a great lady, to run his homes and act as his hostess to the leading members of society. Failure to do so would reflect badly upon her husband. Corisande did not lack courage, but she was not a fool; she knew she hadn't the training for such a daunting role. Her success would have to depend on hard work and luck, particularly as she could not look for support from the Marquis's relatives, since such a misalliance would hardly meet with their approval.

The peer and the pauper—Corisande could not help remembering that she had once described their relationship to herself in this light-hearted way, but it was no longer a comparison which made her smile. The gulf between them was too great for laughter to ease the pain.

Could love bridge that gap? A tempting little voice inside her head whispered that it could, but Corisande forced herself to ignore it.

Love? If she truly loved him how could she let him ruin himself for her sake?

CHAPTER TEN

CORISANDE WAS JUST emerging from Hookham's Library when a voice hailed her. She looked up to discern the Marquis of Dene's curricle bowling along Bond Street towards her. He pulled up and she walked across the flagway to meet him.

"Will you give me the pleasure of seeing you home?"

The formal words were infused with a warmth that made Corisande's heart begin to race. "Thank you, but it is only a step," she faltered, longing to accept and knowing it was foolish.

"Please." He stretched down a hand. "Send your maid home and come with me."

Corisande could not resist his smile. "His lordship will see me home, Alice," she said, climbing into the carriage.

Alice, who was carrying the two novels, in the marbled covers of the Minerva Press, which were Corisande's choice from the Library, looked a little doubtful, but she nodded obediently and stepped back.

Seated next to him in the close confines of the curricle, Corisande found she was having trouble with her breathing. This was the first time they had been alone since the Rutledges' ball, if the silent unobtrusive presence of Dickon could be discounted, and she found it easy to forget the little groom. It was too easy to forget everything save the man by her side, but she knew she had to try!

If only her pulse would stop hammering! She could not think sensibly. The memory of their passionate embrace burned in her mind and she wondered if he thought of it, too.

"Corisande, there is something I want to say to you," the Marquis began as they drove through the crowded streets. He knew he must tell her of the reply he had received from Sir Robert, but he did not know how to break the news of her uncle's perfidy to her.

Dreading he might say something else entirely, Corisande rushed to fill his hesitant pause, "Shall you attend Lady Norbury's Venetian Breakfast the day after tomorrow? I understand it is being given to celebrate Princess Charlotte's marriage. Fanny tells me that Lord Thorne has arranged for us to watch the actual wedding procession itself. It sounds most exciting, I am quite longing to see it.''

The Marquis was alarmed. Corisande's cheeks were unusually flushed and her nervous chatter was a far remove from her normal easy friendliness. Suddenly hope flared in his breast. Did she regret her teasing behaviour the other night, but find it hard to say so?

"Is there anything you want to tell me, about Harry Vernon, I mean?'' Marc's manner lacked its usual confidence and Corisande sensed the longing behind his simple question.

Her heart ached with pain as she shook her head and answered brightly, "Why, no, my lord.'' She had given Harry her word, but she wished she could break it when she saw the confusion in Marc's dark eyes. She wanted to fling her arms around his neck and beg him to forgive her for hurting him.

Instead she began to chatter about the forthcoming festivities, which would mark the wedding of the Prince Regent's only child to Prince Leopold of Saxe-Coburg, as if her life depended upon it.

The Marquis's brows met in a black frown. So, his provoking little love did not wish to discuss Harry! He took his attention from his horses long enough to glance at her cameo profile and involuntarily his anger softened as his gaze absorbed her delicate beauty. If only they were not in such a public place! Alone, he was certain that he could persuade her to tell him the truth.

The memory of the last time they had been private could no longer be buried in the recesses of his mind, try as he might to contain it there. She had felt so warm and soft in his arms, but there had been nothing fragile about her answering passion! Marc wanted to get to the bottom of this infuriating mystery, but even more strongly he burned to take Corisande in his arms and kiss her again.

"Fanny said she met Prince Leopold two years ago when he came to England in the suite of Tsar Alexander. She thinks him quite handsome, although his manner is rather solemn.''

The Marquis dragged his thoughts to the present.

"What a pity his attributes do not include wealth. I dare say Prinny wishes his daughter had followed his suggestion and accepted William of Orange.''

His ironic tone brought Corisande's frantic prattle to an abrupt halt. "Do you despise the Prince for his poverty?'' she asked in a strangled whisper.

The Marquis shrugged. "They say Charlotte is sincere in her attachment to the fellow, but such an unequal match does not bode well. She is the Heiress of England! For once I think Prinny had right on his side to try and persuade her to a husband more suited to her station."

Depression swept over Corisande. He could not know it, but Marc had just confirmed her worst suspicions. His haughty attitude to the Princess's marriage unconsciously echoed all she had feared. He could not shake off the effects of his upbringing any more than she could and, even worse, he did not appear to believe that love could overcome the difficulties of a mixed marriage!

Determined not to let Marc see her heartache, Corisande kept up a flow of innocuous conversation that lasted until their arrival in Hill Street. Fanny was at home and her presence encouraged Marc to broach the delicate subject of Sir Robert's letter, though he did his best to wrap the refusal in clean linen.

A gurgle of her silvery laughter reassured him that Corisande was not likely to need Fanny's comforting ministrations. Indeed, it was his sister who displayed the most outrage.

"Of all the shabby behaviour! I know he is a relative of yours, my dear, but I think him a miser!"

Corisande shook her head in genuine amusement. "Fanny, pray do not come to blows on my behalf, I beg you! The poor man has seven children and four of them daughters to be provided with dowries, it seems. No wonder he does not wish to add me to his household!"

She turned to the Marquis, the smile still on her face. "There is no need to apologise, sir. I never expected my uncle to solve my difficulties for me."

"So you told me, but I was too pig-headed to believe that you could know best."

"Oh, no, do not blame yourself for trying to help. It was well meant."

He made her a small bow of thanks. "I am relieved his refusal causes you no grief. However, there is one more thing. He sent you this. To sweeten the bitter pill, no doubt."

The Marquis handed over a fifty-pound banknote. It was his own idea, and he would have made it more but for the thought that it might make her suspicious.

"How very generous of him! I must write and thank him," Corisande exclaimed in delight. "If I do it now could you frank it for me, sir?"

"Of course." Privately Marc resolved to destroy the letter. Otherwise, the baronet might let the cat out of the bag and, in any event, after the way he had behaved Clifford didn't deserve any communication from his niece.

While Corisande was composing this ill-fated epistle in the privacy of her bedchamber Lady Linton acquainted her brother with the details of the Duke's visit.

"Cold-hearted swine," commented his undutiful son.

"Marc!" Fanny made the protest automatically, but without conviction.

"I'll not allow myself to be a sacrifice to suit his whims. One of us was enough."

Fanny gazed at him blankly. "But Marc, I wanted to marry Jack!" she exclaimed when she realised his meaning. "Indeed, Papa was against it!"

Marc's expression betrayed his bewilderment. He had only been fourteen at the time of Fanny's betrothal and furious at the thought of his beloved sister being manipulated into marrying a man he had disliked on sight.

He ran a hand impatiently through his unruly locks as he strove to adjust to this new information. "Then, in God's name, why did he let you go ahead?" he asked slowly. "Jack Linton was a loose-screw, if ever there was one."

Fanny winced. Any mention of her late husband made her feel almost ill with unhappiness. It brought back all the black despair, the anguish of a love gone sour, a love she had once believed would last a lifetime. But she owed Marc an answer and it was not fair to her father to let Marc go on thinking that she had been pushed into a marriage of convenience when nothing was further from the truth!

"In those days Jack had only recently inherited the title, he had not had time to make more than a slight dent in his fortune. He came of a good family, of course, and he swore to mend his reputation if only Papa would give his consent to the match." She sighed. "At first Papa refused, but I threw fits of hysteria. I wept for days! In the end Papa washed his hands of me. I dare say he found my tears inconvenient."

"Did I not say he was a cold-blooded monster? Why could he have not tried harder to make you see reason!"

Fanny laid her hand on his arm, distressed to have aroused such passion. "My dear, do not get so heated. It all happened so long ago. I do not blame Papa. I was a silly young girl in the throes of first love, I would not have listened to him if he'd been ten times as patient. He did his duty by me."

"Duty?" The Marquis snorted. "Duty be damned! You are his daughter, he owed you more than that."

Fanny smiled at him wryly. "Papa holds women in low esteem. The subsequent events of my marriage showed he was right to doubt my good sense. I didn't deserve sympathy from him when I behaved in such a ridiculous way."

"Perhaps, but then our dear Papa is not noted for his loving consideration. Frankly, he doesn't give a rap for either of us."

His sister paled. "That is a dreadful accusation, Marc. You judge him too harshly. He never displays affection, I agree, but he is not devoid of family feeling. He would not permit harm to befall us if he could prevent it. Without his insistence on the lawyers tying up the settlements so tightly I would most likely have lost my jointure along with everything else Jack gambled away."

"Why have you never spoken of this before? I had always assumed you were tolerably happy with Linton," Marc asked after a moment.

"I tried to put a brave face on it, my pride would not permit me to do otherwise, but the memories are painful." Fanny shuddered. "Please, let us not continue this discussion. It does no good to rake over old coals."

Her brother nodded in silent understanding, but Fanny found she could not dismiss her demons so easily now that they had been raised.

She had been so happy on her wedding-day, but within three months Jack had resumed his former rackety ways. She might have forgiven him the gaming, but he took mistresses by the score and her love for him had withered away under the onslaught of endless quarrels and recriminations. The marriage had disintegrated, until in the end they had become hostile strangers, polite to one another only in company.

Then an unexpected inflammation of the lungs had carried Jack off with shocking suddenness, ending her ceaseless daily torment of living a lie. The pain had taken far longer to heal. In its place it had left behind a depressing sense of having failed and the resolve never again to expose herself to the harm love could do.

"I suppose this is the wrong time to ask, but have you given any further consideration to Papa's demand?" Fanny said after a short tense silence. "Would it really be so bad, when even a love-match like mine could not be guaranteed?"

"And you think I should do no better?" Her pointed remark caught Marc on the raw. "That is in the lap of the gods, dear sister, but, as I told you before, I'll never marry Augusta Marlow. I'd as lief enlist."

"Oh, pray, do not speak of that crazy notion!" Fanny had heard of this possibility from Tom. "You are a clothhead, Marc, if you think you should like to serve in peacetime. You would be bored out of your mind within a month."

He grinned at her. "So I would! Anyhow, don't fret, I've got different plans now for my future." But he wouldn't tell her what they were.

"Don't rush into any cork-brained schemes, I beg of you, Marc. There are still some weeks until the end of the Season, when Papa's ultimatum runs out. Give yourself until then, at least, before you make any decisions. Don't do something you may regret in the future," Fanny implored, catching hold of his sleeve in her agitation.

"I won't," he promised, patting her hand reassuringly, but something in his smile made Fanny's heart plummet to her dainty satin slippers.

THAT EVENING, Fanny and Corisande were engaged to visit the Drury Lane Theatre. Absorbed by the exciting melodrama, the first she had ever seen, Corisande sat forward in her seat, her eyes drinking in every detail of what was going on behind the footlights.

During the interval, there came a tap at the door of their box and Sir Lucius Orsett entered. He bowed low over Corisande's hand with exaggerated gallantry and engaged her in conversation until the curtain was about to rise. Before he took his leave he succeeded in obtaining a promise from Corisande that she would attend the pic-nic he was giving for a party of several young people, including his niece.

Fanny's face set into a frown and, seeing that their escort was Tom Lavenham, she did not scruple to say, "I wish you would not associate with that old roué! Orsett is one of the Regent's profligate set; his reputation is a disgrace!"

"Shouldn't acknowledge the fellow if I were you, Corisande," chimed in Tom. "He's a bad man."

"He is Augusta's uncle and she is my friend," said Miss Clifford simply. "He has always been extremely civil to me and I should not like to hurt his feelings."

Fanny groaned and exchanged a wry look with her cousin. And during supper at the Piazza, after the play had ended, she managed to whisper a request to him that he visit her the next morning.

Mr. Lavenham was very nattily attired when he arrived to pay this call, but Fanny scarcely noticed this elegance in her honour. Turning to her butler she said peremptorily, "Deny me to any other callers, Turnbull. I do not wish to be disturbed."

"Very good, milady," replied Turnbull at his most wooden.

Miss Clifford, pretty little thing that she was, had already been despatched to the Soho Bazaar under the auspices of Ellen Clay to match a difficult shade of ribbon, so it was obvious that her ladyship intended to have a cosy chat with her cousin and no interruptions permitted.

Fanny handed Tom a glass of sherry and urged him to try one of her cook's home-made macaroons.

"Trying to turn me up sweet, Fanny?" Tom joked.

A guilty look appeared on Fanny's face.

"Thought as much! Let's have the worst! What do you want me to do this time, Fanny?" said Tom with placid resignation.

"Oh, Tom, you are an angel!" Fanny beamed at him. "Do you think you could bear to attend the Norburys' breakfast? Marc is to escort us, but I want someone to keep an eye on Sir Lucius Orsett. Corisande will not pay any heed to what I say and I don't want him following her around."

Tom frowned. "I wonder why that old court-cad is paying her such marked attentions. It's well known that his pockets are pretty much to let."

Fanny shrugged irritably. "I don't know. He is received everywhere so Corisande thinks I'm exaggerating about his shady reputation. She is still very innocent and so kind-hearted she is inclined to see good in every one."

Mr. Lavenham agreed with enthusiasm.

"Tom, never say you have developed a *tendre* for the girl?"

"Lord, no!" Mr. Lavenham was aghast. "She is a dear little soul, but no! Dash it, Fanny, take care you don't go saying such things around Letty. I'd never hear the last of it." Tom wiped his brow uneasily.

Fanny hid a smile and solemnly assured him of her discretion. "Your mother is planning to stay in town, then, before going on to Worthing?"

Tom nodded. "Aye, she's going to stay for at least a week. Letty will want to prolong it, I've no doubt." He cleared his throat. "Er—do you think Marc is *épris* in Corisande's direction? I'm devilishly fond of him, you know, my cousin and all that, and it seems to me that the gossips will have a field-day if he carries on the way he had been doing. Dash it, he ain't her guardian! Very delicate situation! I'll lay you a monkey that the tabbies will be saying next that he is honour bound to marry her, especially if it ever gets out how she went gallivanting all over Somerset with him!"

Fanny shuddered. "Don't!"

"Lord, Fanny, it has to be said! You'd think the silly nodcock would see it for himself, but he nearly bit my head off for asking if she was going to go and live with that uncle of hers. No one is going to believe his motives are disinterested at this rate. She's too beautiful by half, and he will look at her like a hungry dog after a bone!"

Fanny couldn't help laughing. "Oh, Tom, you have him off exactly!" Sobering, she continued, "I am dreadfully afraid he intends to ask her to marry him."

"What?" Tom's mouth fell open. "He's dicked in the nob, that's what he is."

Fanny puzzled over this for a moment. "If you mean that he is mad, I'm half-persuaded you are right. Corisande is of gentle birth, but she has no fortune and Marc could look a lot higher."

"As if Marc cares a straw for that!" Tom retorted scornfully.

A nod of assent answered him. "True, but the real problem is my father's ridiculous blackmail scheme."

"Perhaps Miss Marlow will refuse him."

"And give up the chance to become a duchess?" Fanny shook her head. "No, I think my little brother is in love for the first time in his life. I'll wager he barely remembers his grace's order, and ignores it when he does."

Tom concurred sadly, "Heaven help us all when Uncle Montague finds out!"

This melancholy reflection prompted Fanny to refill their glasses. Taking a strengthening sip of sherry, she said, "Is Marc's interest in Corisande common knowledge, do you think?"

"There are a lot of rumours flying about," Tom admitted reluctantly.

"I suppose the next thing is that they will start laying bets on his pursuit of her in your horrid clubs!"

Her anger startled Tom. "Ain't bad as all that, but I wouldn't put it past one of m'uncle's cronies to write to him and tip him the wink." A worried frown creased Mr. Lavenham's brow. "You don't think Marc has actually proposed to her yet, do you?"

"No, but I am certain he will do so now this wretched uncle of hers has disowned her." Fanny sighed and proceeded to tell him about Sir Robert's letter.

"What curst shabby behaviour!" exclaimed Tom.

"I know and what an irresistible combination! Marc feels a protective responsibility for Corisande in addition to everything else."

"A damsel in distress, yes, I see." Tom stroked his chin thoughtfully. "Do you think Corisande will accept him?"

Fanny shrugged. "I'm not sure." Her fingers played nervously with the velvet streamers adorning her morning-gown. "I believe she cares something for him, but he is not the only gentleman who has been paying her marked attentions."

Her stifled tone reminded Tom that Sir Harry Vernon was one of the leading members of Miss Clifford's court of admirers. He decided to tactfully change the subject. "Well, I'm your man if you can think of any way to help Marc, but, if you'll take my advice, you'll leave things alone. Marc's old enough to take care of himself and I fancy he won't welcome any interference in this issue even from you."

"Perhaps he would heed you if you talked to him—"

"Good God, Fanny, you cannot be serious!" Tom was roused from his usual calm. "Marc would want to blow a hole in me if I dared interfere. Even if he restrained that impulse he'd likely tear me limb from limb. Very handy with his fives, my cousin, you know!"

"So we are to watch Marc whistle his inheritance down the wind for the sake of a girl who may only be flirting with him!" Suppressed passion made Fanny's voice shake.

Oh, she had tried so hard to curb her wicked suspicions, but it was hard to swallow her resentment, for all that she had grown very fond of Corisande. A dozen times a day she had to tell herself that she was just jealous and there were no grounds for believing ill of Miss Clifford's character, but the thought that her adored brother, as well as Harry Vernon, had fallen victim to those celestial blue eyes made her burst into noisy tears.

Utterly confounded by this unexpected development, Tom awkwardly patted Fanny's shoulder, but his clumsy wordless sympathy was not enough to dry the flow of her tears.

The door opened. "Tom, how nice to... oh, my dear ma'am!" Abandoning her greeting, Corisande flew across the room to Fanny's side. In a trice she had her hostess feeling more comfortable before turning a reproachful gaze on Mr. Lavenham.

Tom's courage failed him. "I dare say I am only in the way," he mumbled, edging towards the door. "I will call to see how you do later, Fanny, and I shall be happy to do as you asked in that other matter we spoke of."

"Thank you," Fanny sniffed tearfully and Tom made his escape.

Inclined to be indignant, Corisande stared after him and said roundly, "I would not have believed Tom had so little consideration!"

"Do not blame the poor fellow, my vapours are not Tom's fault." Fanny pressed her hands to her hot cheeks, trying to calm herself. "Tears invariably embarrass gentlemen. Jack always used to fling out of the house at the least hint that I might cry."

"You rarely speak of the Viscount," Corisande observed curiously.

She regretted her remark the instant it was made, for Fanny's expression hardened and her hands clenched angrily into her lap.

"I'm sorry, I should not have pried," Corisande was contrite.

"It does not matter," Fanny replied stiffly. Then she sighed, unbending a little. "Perhaps it is I who am at fault. I should have told you that I do not like to speak of the Viscount because we were not happy together."

She gave a small bitter laugh. "It seems that one cannot ever completely escape the past. Only yesterday I broke my own rule of silence! Very well, let me put an end to your speculations and then perhaps we can be done with the subject for once and all.

"I married Jack Linton thinking he loved me as much as I loved him, but it was only infatuation on his part. Perhaps my own feelings did not run deep enough. In any event, they did not withstand the pressure his return to his rakehell pursuits put on them. The match went sour. You cannot imagine how painful was my situation until his unexpected death released me. Now do you understand my reluctance?"

Corisande felt she suddenly understood far more. A mystery had been explained, but when she exclaimed, "Is that why you have fought shy of marrying again?"

Fanny's reaction startled her. "Pray do not presume to read such a meaning into my words or I'll regret having taken you into my confidence," Fanny snapped.

"I beg your pardon. It is just that it seems so unfair to Harry if you won't tell him why—"

"If you are speaking of Sir Harry Vernon, I wish you would not!"

Fanny's eyes flashed with a fire that suddenly reminded Corisande of the Marquis. It seemed that Lady Linton possessed a little of the Richmond temper after all, though she did not allow it to gain the better of her.

"I do not wish to quarrel, Corisande," she continued in a calmer voice. "You mean well, no doubt, but you are meddling in something that does not concern you. I will not have my affairs discussed!"

"But Harry loves you—" Again she was interrupted.

"This is intolerable! Have I not made my meaning clear?"

Corisande blinked. This was a side to her benefactress's character she had never seen before. It was easy to forget Fanny was the daughter of a duke, but not in this mood; she had suddenly become a haughty stranger!

She nodded silently, shocked by the change her unthinking words had wrought.

"Good. I am glad to hear it." Fanny was very much on her dignity as she rose to her feet. "Please understand that I will not brook interference in my private life, Corisande. If you wish us to continue as friends, then you must permit me to know what is best in such matters."

She swept to the door but halted abruptly at Corisande's next words.

"Would you prefer me to leave your house, Fanny? I swear I had no intention of offending you, but since I seem to have done so I shall quite understand if you wish me to make those arrangements I mentioned for my return to Oxfordshire." Corisande's back was very straight and she held her head high as she made this offer.

"Now I have upset you! Of course I do not mean you to leave, you absurd girl!" Fanny sighed and passed a weary hand over her brow.

Corisande claimed Harry loved her, but what of Corisande's own friendship with him? Could it really be so innocent or was the girl playing the hypocrite for some devious reason? Fanny's feelings were in such confusion she hardly knew what to think any more. Yet in spite of everything she still liked Corisande. It seemed unfair to send her away when she had nothing to support these vague suspicions, though perhaps it would be safer for her own hopes and her brother's future if she could bring herself to do so?

She stared at the slight proud figure standing silently before her and hesitated. If only the girl were not so lovely! Even if she broke her promise to help Corisande, what was there to prevent Marc, or Harry, from leaving London to follow her? She might achieve nothing but an uneasy conscience.

"We have both said a little too much, I think," Fanny murmured. "It would be best if we could both forget it and try to go on as before."

When Corisande had consented with eager relief Fanny was anxious to get away for a space to think and pray she had made the right decision. "Now I must go and change my gown if we are to view the paintings at Somerset House."

Left behind Corisande found her nails had bitten into the soft flesh of her palms. Fanny's cold haughtiness had upset her more than she had realised. It was all the more puzzling for being so unexpected.

She looked at me with such dislike, Corisande thought in bewilderment. Surely my curiosity could not have offended her so deeply?

"Oh, no, it cannot be that! She cannot think Harry is serious about me!" The exclamation was torn from Corisande as this idea forced itself into her mind.

When the Marquis had accused her of trying to steal Harry from Fanny at the Rutledges' ball Corisande had been so angry with him for thinking her mercenary that it had blotted out all other considerations. He must have seen her as a rival to his sister, but Corisande still could not believe anyone could take such an idea seriously. Fanny was so much more sophisticated and elegant!

"But it was only a game of make-believe," Corisande murmured in consternation.

Unfortunately, it seemed that the game had gone awry!

CHAPTER ELEVEN

WHEN CORISANDE, dressed for the Norburys' Venetian Breakfast in a very pretty gown of eau-de-Nil jaconet, emerged from the morning-room, it was just in time to see the Marquis handing his glossy beaver hat and York tan gloves to Turnbull.

"You are in good time, sir," she greeted him with a sunny smile, which revealed nothing of her inner turmoil as her heart leapt at the sight of him. There had been no opportunity for them to be private since he had driven her home from Hookham's Library, but the heightened awareness that existed between them had not abated.

Marc raised her hand to his lips. "You look as fresh and lovely as a spring morning," he murmured softly.

Corisande shivered deliciously. When he smiled at her with such intimacy it turned her blood to fire. She wanted to draw his head down to hers and kiss him until they were both as breathless with passion as they had been on the night of the Rutledges' ball. From the look in his dark eyes she knew he felt the same.

How am I going to resist him, she thought helplessly, unable to tear her gaze from his. Desire, sharp as a knife, quickened her pulse as he turned her hand gently over and with a slow seductive deliberation pressed a kiss against the soft skin of her inner wrist.

Oh, God, he knows how I feel! Panic fluttered along Corisande's nerves and her knees began to tremble. Now he would think her shameless!

To her intense relief the Marquis did not look in the least shocked. Instead an expression of delight spread slowly across his handsome features.

"Dearest girl, I can hardly believe in my good fortune," he breathed.

He was still holding her hand and Corisande made no attempt to withdraw it. She knew she was behaving recklessly, but she didn't care, she was too happy.

The very air seemed to shimmer with a special magic as they stared at one another in an enchanted silence.

"Ah, Marc, you have arrived on time."

Fanny, resplendent in rose-coloured silk, swept towards them, breaking the spell which held them in thrall.

Corisande could have wept with vexation. In another moment he would have kissed her and she had so wanted him too! But perhaps it was as well. Loving him could only result in heartache. She must try harder to steel herself against his charm.

In the carriage, Fanny's mood was as sparkling as the sunshine and Corisande was glad that yesterday's quarrel had blown over. Seeing her hostess so lively, she longed to put an end to the scheme which now threatened Fanny's peace of mind. Without breaking the confidence she had promised to keep, she must find a way to let Harry know that their plan had succeeded.

For both of them, it would be a relief to finish with the pretence, but Corisande could not regret suggesting it. Whether or not Fanny was prepared to reconsider her decision to marry him, at least it had made her see Harry was not a lap-dog she could neglect at whim!

It was a hot day and Corisande was glad of her parasol. "I freckle so easily," she lamented.

"You must try Denmark Lotion to remove them if you are unlucky today, or perhaps crushed strawberries. Emily Cowper swears by them, I believe, and they will be in season any day," Fanny advised. "By the by, Marc, Emily asked me yesterday why she had not had the pleasure of seeing you at Almack's lately."

The Marquis, who was busy thinking that Corisande's creamy complexion looked good enough to eat, said vaguely, "I will take you there next Wednesday if you wish."

"Shall I be so cruel, I wonder, as to hold you to that rash promise?" Fanny teased. "What do you say, Corisande?"

"For my part I must admit to finding Almack's something of a disappointment." Corisande had paid two visits to King Street and had been unimpressed. The stiff formality was not to her taste and she said so. "I thought the masquerade we attended at the Argyle Rooms much more entertaining," she added.

Marc laughed, but Fanny was aghast. "Never say so in company, I beg of you, my love," she warned.

Corisande grinned. "Lady Cowper was kind to me," she continued blithely. "She presented Sir Harry to me as a partner for the waltz."

Corisande, who had been taught the steps by her dancing-master, had been longing to test her skill and her gratitude to Harry for engineering the necessary approval had shown itself in her most dazzling smile as he had led her on to the floor.

Fanny restrained a wince at the memory Corisande's unthinking comment evoked. To see Corisande's slender form held in such proximity to Harry's broad chest had done strange things to her own diaphragm, leaving her oddly breathless. Only the strictest self-discipline had enabled her to conceal her feelings on that occasion.

A tiny sigh escaped her, but she stifled it quickly. After yesterday's quarrel with Corisande she had felt wretchedly guilty. It would do no good dwelling on her unworthy suspicions again today and spoiling what promised to be one of the best parties of the season.

On arrival at the Norburys', Fanny was immediately claimed by Mr. Devlin who bore her off to meet their hostess, his aunt. Corisande followed on Marc's arm and by silent agreement they slowed their steps, savouring their brief moment alone, knowing it could not last long.

"What a charming house!" Corisande was enchanted by the white villa, which was built in the Italian style and surrounded by flower gardens and green lawns running down to the River Thames.

"Norbury brought some of the statuary back with him from Italy when he made the Grand Tour, I believe," said the Marquis when Corisande expressed admiration for the white marble figures which elegantly decorated the terraced steps. He was watching her animated little face rather than these objects, but nodded when she said they were very fine.

"I like them better than those of Lord Elgin. I dare say I did not understand them properly, but they seemed sadly damaged to me," Corisande dimpled.

The Marquis chuckled at this cavalier dismissal of the artistic worth of these antiquities. "You are very honest. Lots of people admire them dutifully because fashion dictates it."

"You are teasing me again," she laughed. "Harry told me I must not say such things. He was quite shocked."

"Was Vernon your escort on that occasion also?" There was a slight edge to his voice.

Corisande deliberately ignored it. "Why yes, I had expressed a desire to see them and he was so obliging as to take me."

"Did my sister accompany you?"

Corisande's eyes dropped to the carved handle of her parasol. "No, she had the headache and did not join the party, though she was engaged to do so." Only her conviction that her actions would ultimately serve Fanny's best interests gave her the courage to meet his stormy gaze with a look of limpid innocence.

Marc was confused, but he was given no time to pursue his enquiries as Fanny came to sweep them into the house. In the press
of the four hundred guests who had been invited Corisande was
soon borne from his side on a tide of polite conversation.

An enormous silken tent had been erected on one of the lawns
and here refreshments were being served. Marc came across his
cousin Tom, keeping Sir Lucius Orsett under discreet observation
while trying to balance a plate of lobster patties and other delica-
cies in one hand and a glass of iced champagne punch in the other.

"Of all the infernally stupid affairs!" he hailed Marc with relief. Tom thought he had found a kindred spirit, judging by the
Marquis's well-known thunderous aspect and the way in which he
took the glass of champagne from a waiter and downed it in one
gulp.

Recognising these signs, Tom decided to steer the conversation
to a safe topic. Unfortunately, he chose to describe a cock-fight he
had attended the previous evening where one of Sir Harry Vernon's birds had won its bout.

"Very handsome winnings I collected on it, too."

"Damn the man, must I hear his name everywhere!" The Marquis ground his teeth.

"I say, steady on, Harry's not such a bad fellow, Marc, Marc..."
Tom's protests fell on empty air.

He began to follow his cousin, shouldering his way through the
throng only to fall alive into the clutches of Mrs. Overton, a lo-
quacious crony of his mother's, who demanded all the latest news
of Lavenham Place.

The Marquis went striding back towards the house, but his hasty
footsteps were arrested by the sight that greeted him on the lawn
before the balustraded terrace. A maypole had been erected and
several people were engaged in trying to dance around it, holding
on to long silken streamers. A crowd of spectators watched,
amused by the difficulties encountered by some of the perform-
ers.

"Set of sapskulls!" The Marquis curled his lip at this rustic
posturing. One of the men who had been tangling himself up
stopped just then and urged a slim figure clad in pale green to accept his ribbon. Marc stood entranced as the girl joined in the
dance with a light gracefulness all her own.

Corisande's red-gold hair gleamed in the sunshine as she danced
and Marc could hear her delicious laughter floating towards him
on the breeze. His anger softened. He did not always understand
her, but it made no difference. He loved her and before this day was
through he was resolved to put his fate to the touch.

THE ROSE GARDEN was deserted. Lady Norbury had rounded up her guests to hear the famous Italian soprano she had hired at great expense and a few hardy souls who had escaped her clutches were congratulating themselves over the card-tables set out in the Yellow Salon, a piece of forethought engineered by Lord Norbury, who joined them there after giving his wife the slip.

"Do you think we should turn back? Lady Norbury will be offended if she notices our absence."

"Among so many we won't be missed," replied the Marquis, his tone brooking no argument.

Corisande's fingers trembled on his arm, but she allowed him to lead her towards the pretty little mock Grecian temple at the end of the garden. The interior of this round marble structure was unfurnished, but it was refreshingly cool and the dimness was soothing to the eyes after the sunshine outside.

"What was it that you wanted to say to me, that you did not desire an audience?"

Corisande had tried to inject a note of teasing gaiety into the silence, but Marc ignored it and stepping closer said abruptly, "Will you do me the honour of becoming my wife?"

Unaccustomed nervousness made his voice gruff and he mentally cursed his inept manner as Corisande's eyes widened in stunned surprise.

Corisande swallowed hard. She had been expecting a different kind of proposal!

It made her feel quite giddy with happiness to know that he cared enough to offer marriage. She hadn't dared let herself believe that he would, and her heart ached at the thought of what she must do now.

"Your wife?" Her voice shook and she strove valiantly to steady it. "I think you must be bamming me, sir."

"You know I'm not!" Marc gripped her by the shoulders. "Sweetheart, I was never more serious in my life."

When he bent and would have kissed her Corisande quickly averted her head so his lips merely grazed her cheek. No matter how she had longed for his embrace earlier she could not allow herself that luxury now, for if she did her resolve might weaken.

Marc stared at her. "Corisande, I don't understand. Has something happened to upset you? We were in such harmony it seemed a good time to ask you to marry me, but this new mood of yours . . ." His voice faded to nothing.

His look of hurt puzzlement almost stopped her in her tracks, but Corisande screwed up her courage and forced herself to simper. "La, sir, what a mournful face! Where is the need for this seriousness? You cannot have thought our flirtation meant anything! Heavens, why should you want me as a wife or I you as my husband?''

Her arch tone made her cringe inwardly but she pressed on with the vulgar charade regardless. ''To be sure, a Marquis would be a wondrous catch for a poor girl like me, but you'd make a devil of a husband.''

''Explain yourself, if you please.'' Anger stirred now in his taut reply and Corisande suppressed a shiver of apprehension.

''When I wed I want a complaisant husband. One willing and able to indulge me in every luxury. I have had enough of doing other people's bidding and would call the tune myself for a change.''

''You desire an older indulgent man you could rule to your own satisfaction. Is that what you are saying?'' Marc's tone was rough with disbelief.

''How very quick you are!'' Corisande tittered, despising herself. Oh, God, if only he would believe her and she could crawl away and hide the pain that threatened to consume her!

''Someone like Harry Vernon perhaps?'' the Marquis went on relentlessly, his tone fringed with menace.

She nodded swiftly before she lost the courage. His grip on her shoulders was now so hard it almost made her wince and it was the bravest thing she had ever done in her life to continue to smile up into the dark eyes that were blazing into her own.

''Come now, admit we should not suit. You ought to marry someone of your own milieu, a meek and biddable girl who will not argue with you,'' Corisande continued, masking her desperation with an airy unconcern. ''We would be forever at odds.''

''Corisande, all that you say is true, but it doesn't matter to me.'' He shook her slightly. ''I love you and, God damn it, I thought you loved me!''

Corisande closed her eyes for an instant. Fierce joy swept through her, but she dared not let him see how his declaration had affected her. Instead, she took a deep breath; this was the critical moment and she must not bungle it! ''I am fond of you, I'll admit, but love?'' She laughed lightly and shook her head. ''I do not think I could love a man with your reputation, my lord. You are too wild for me.''

For an instant murder flickered in his eyes and then without warning his mouth descended on hers so swiftly she could not muster her defences. This time there was no gentle sweetness in his passion, only a demanding urgency that made her head swim. To her horror, Corisande felt something within herself respond to this savage handling. Her blood ran thick with desire she could not control and she clung to him blindly, all her good intentions thrown to the winds.

Suddenly he let her go, almost flinging her from him.

"Too wild for you, my girl? What a rich jest!" His laughter had an ugly, jarring ring which made Corisande long to clap her hands over her ears. She resisted this impulse, but she began to tremble in every limb from sheer reaction. "What a fool you must think me if you imagined I'd swallow such feeble lies!"

Crimson stained Corisande's cheeks. She wished the ground would open up and hide her rather than have to meet his scornful gaze. "I'm afraid I do not understand you," she said in a voice which came out as a whisper.

A thin smile touched his mouth. "Don't you? Well, you led me on finely, my dear, but I'll be your gull no longer, so there's no need for those maidenly blushes." The grim humour faded from his tone. "I wonder just how much of your original tale is true."

When she would have interrupted he flung out a warning hand. "Spare me your protests. I dare say there's enough truth in your claim to be a respectable orphan to allow for a little, shall we say, judicious embroidery? What's more, I don't deny you the right to fend for yourself as best you may. I told you once before that's what I believe most women do when it comes to marriage, but I dislike anyone trying to dupe me, my dear Miss Clifford."

Corisande had recovered a little of her composure. "You are talking in riddles," she answered coldly. He quirked one eyebrow at her and his scorn made her angry. Forgetting her role, she glared at him. "I haven't the faintest idea why you should think I have tried to deceive you."

"Oh, come, why so missish, Corisande? Surely, my plain speaking cannot offend a bold piece like yourself?" His tone dripped mockery and Corisande flushed. Her shameless response to his brutal kiss had robbed her of the right to object to this disdainful remark.

"Was it Fanny who told you my pockets were to let?"

The sudden question made her jump and her eyes flew to his in dismay.

"I suppose my protection offered the best prospect at the time, but now you aim to find another fool who can offer more."

"There is no need to insult me because I have refused to marry you." Bitterness filled Corisande. She had wanted him to think she was fickle, a silly flirt who did not know her own mind, but he'd decided she was coldly calculating.

"Then tell me I'm wrong." Marc swiftly enfolded her hands within his own and held them tightly. "Tell me this is all some vile mistake and that you have never heard of my father's scheme to disinherit me if I marry outside his wishes." A barely repressed eagerness filled his voice but his hopeful expression died as Corisande shook her head.

"I cannot!" she cried wildly. She pulled her hands out of his, wanting to run and hide rather than disappoint him. She had never dreamt he would link her refusal with his father's threats. It was supposed to be a secret, yet he had guessed Fanny had let the truth slip. Oh, God, after all she had said just now about wanting a rich husband it would look as if she wanted to throw him over merely because he would be cut out of the Duke's fortune!

"Answer me! Did you know?"

"Yes, Fanny told me of it. Now are you satisfied?"

He stepped back. "Yes, I'm satisfied," he said dully.

"Marc, please, it was not how it sounds." Corisande was distraught. "Let me explain."

"No! I'll not listen to any more of your lies. I should have trusted my judgement on the night of the Rutledges' ball instead of letting myself be blinded." His voice cracked as the sweet memory caught him, but he crushed it. He had thought he had frightened her with his passion, but all the time she had been pretending. Pretending and scheming to discover where lay the richest prize.

"You told me that you wouldn't marry for money, but you were lying even then. Now that you have given it due consideration you've concluded Harry's wealth outweighs my title."

"You, you coxcomb!" Rage flared in Corisande, giving her new strength. "Because I dare refuse you there must be some terrible reason behind it. You have the manners of an ox!"

His jaw tightened. "Don't push me too far, I'll not take insults from a two-faced little jade like you. Your conscience might not stop at betraying the woman who has befriended you, but I'll see you have no chance to do my sister any harm. Out of sight is out of mind, so they say, and Harry's passing fancy for your desirable little person will fade quickly enough if you are not around to remind him of it."

Corisande went pale. In spite of her rioting emotions she perceived the pit opening up beneath her feet. The Marquis was quite capable of carrying out such a threat. It might not affect the fruition of her scheme to help Harry, but it would prevent her from carrying out a new plan. Only an hour ago she had thought of a way of saving Marc from the Duke's wrath and nothing since had altered her wish to do all in her power to secure his happiness. Though he might hate her now, she still loved him with all her heart.

"Just so, my dear," Marc said in a silky drawl as he watched the dismay spread over her expressive features. "I don't intend to take risks with Fanny's future."

"Are you so sure she wants Harry?"

"I know my sister," he nodded, confirming her own beliefs.

"Very well, I'll swear to you on a stack of bibles or by any other sign you want that I will never accept any proposal of whatever kind from Harry Vernon." Corisande gave a careless shrug. "There are plenty of other gentlemen around who would suit me as well."

Marc's lips compressed to a thin line, but he said nothing.

"Well, do you still intend to drag me screaming from Hill Street or am I reprieved?" she demanded. It didn't matter if he thought her hard so long as he agreed and she had time to work against the Duke's edict.

"Jupiter, but I have to hand it to you!" He swept her a mocking bow. "Your act as an innocent maiden was faultless, my dear; you had me properly fooled. You should consider a career on the stage; you would be a great success, I'll wager."

Corisande bit back a sharp retort. "I prefer something more respectable, thank you. Not that I'll find the husband I want in the wilds of Oxfordshire," she continued with perfect truth. "But I'll retire there to my old home at the end of the season if I don't manage to find myself a better alternative, I swear it."

She clasped her hands tightly to hide their trembling from his gaze. "Fanny has told me that she intends to remove to Brighton at the end of June. Will you give me until then?" Desperate to convince him, she hurried on. "What harm can it do when I have promised to leave Harry alone? Please, it is not much to ask, and you did give me your word once that you would help me."

"Your audacity compels me to accept," the Marquis said on a slow intake of breath, staring at her as if he had never seen her before. "It is a bargain, on condition that this entire conversation remains a secret between us. I've no mind to become the subject of gossip or have people know I was ever such a fool as to offer marriage to one such as you! Is that agreed?"

She nodded quickly. It would be too painful to speak of this to anyone, even a good friend like Gussy!

Marc locked away his despair and assumed a nonchalance he was far from feeling. "I have always admired spirit in a woman, and it was clever of you to remind me that I had given my word to see you settled." A thin self-mocking smile appeared on his handsome face.

"How very foolish of me to make such open-handed promises to a stranger, even one with a face like an angel," he said softly.

Before she knew what he was about he stepped close again and took her throat in one of his shapely hands. There was an iron strength in the long fingers and he let her feel it for an instant.

"But you are no angel, are you, my sweet?" he murmured.

The blood drummed unpleasantly in Corisande's ears but she forced herself to stand still and not struggle. Suddenly she could believe in all the wild tales told about him!

"Don't try to be too clever, will you, my dear? Consider this a little warning of what will happen if I discover you have crossed me, for now that you have opened my eyes to your true character you'll not fool me again."

He let her go and Corisande's hand moved involuntarily to massage her sore throat.

"It would be a pity to break that pretty little neck, so don't force me to it." The mocking voice drawled on relentlessly. "My friends tell me I've a shocking temper. Do you understand me?"

Tears sprang to Corisande's eyes and only pride prevented them from falling. She had let loose the devil in him and must pay the consequences of her folly.

Oh, why had she not listened to her heart and confessed her fears instead of thinking she could handle him? In this mood he would never believe her if she tried to explain that she had never cared a curse for Harry, or anyone but him. It tore her to shreds to know that she had made him despise her, even though her motives had been pure.

She had hurt him and he would not forgive her lightly. The fierce glow in his dark eyes, so much at odds with his icy disdainful voice, warned her of it, but Corisande could think of no immediate way of mending her error. The only thing she could do for now was continue with the charade.

"I understand you, sir," she replied with all the lightness she could muster. "Now, may we rejoin the party?"

CHAPTER TWELVE

IN THE HAPPY position of a young lady who finds herself with no less than five engagements for the evening, Corisande was kept too busy to reflect over much upon the events of the afternoon. Strolling on the arm of Mr. Bentley through the foyer during the interval at the Opera she encountered Miss Marlow, and it was the work of a moment to dispatch that amiable young gentleman to fetch her a glass of lemonade.

Augusta's icy company manners dissolved at his departure, much to Corisande's relief. She found it uncanny how her friend could assume her iceberg pose so easily and now understood why Fanny had thought Augusta a suitable candidate to be the next Duchess of Weston.

She readily agreed to meet Corisande in the Green park. "But I thought Lady Fanny did not like you meeting me there. Cannot you tell me what it is now?"

"There isn't time, look, here comes your uncle already. I'll try to meet you as soon as I can manage it." Corisande schooled her expression into civility as the baronet approached.

Sir Lucius was accompanied by a young man dressed in the first stare of fashion and Corisande gave a start of recognition. "Why, it is Mr. Swindon, is it not? Do you recall we met at Lady Linton's, sir?"

Mr. Swindon stammered an assent, his blushes revealing his delight at her acknowledgement.

"Well, well, you young dog, and you never told me you were already acquainted with the prettiest lady in town! 'Pon my word, you have stolen my thunder, sir!" A jovial nudge and wink accompanied this remark from Sir Lucius, who hid his irritation under a cloak of cordiality. He had hoped to increase his hold over this plump pigeon by the introduction and it annoyed him to find the ploy useless.

"Sir Lucius has been kind enough to show me all the sights," Mr. Swindon confided to Corisande in a low voice as the baronet was addressing his niece. "I only met him by chance at the Vauxhall Gardens, but he's been devilish good to me. Taken me everywhere.''

Corisande was a little surprised. She would not have imagined Sir Lucius to be interested in the company of such a callow youth, but this information caused her to smile warmly upon the baronet. Letty's friend was a pleasant if green boy and she thought better of Sir Lucius than ever for being kind to him.

On her return to her box she happened to mention the meeting to Fanny and was startled to see Fanny frown. ''What is wrong?''

As luck would have it, their escort that evening was Sir Harry Vernon and it was he who answered this question.

''Lady Linton is right to be concerned,'' he said in a serious tone, at odds with his usual cheerful good-humour. ''Orsett is no fit companion for young people.''

''Well he has always been kind to me at least. I think he is rather a dear,'' replied Corisande with a stubborn tilt to her chin.

Fanny exchanged a rueful look with Harry, their awkwardness with one another forgotten in the face of this problem. Fanny had been reluctant to accept his escort, but now she found herself grateful for his presence. There was something comfortably solid and dependable about Harry, a quality she had been inclined to scorn in the past, but one she now recognised as desirable. All of a sudden it occurred to her that Harry would make an excellent father, and then she blushed furiously at the direction of her thoughts.

Harry was trying to make Corisande see reason, but not wishing to distress her he let the subject of Sir Lucius drop when she showed signs of becoming angry and upset. Privately, he resolved to have a word with Tom Lavenham. Perhaps together they could drop a warning hint to young Swindon. The discreet little establishments in Pall Mall favoured by Orsett played for devilish high stakes, and if that damned sharp had got his hooks into the fledgling it might be urgent to persuade Swindon to give up such a dangerous excitement. The Marquis of Dene was well acquainted with the excitements of faro. Experienced enough to avoid the sort of places frequented by flats like Peter Swindon, where a successful first night's play was the lure to swift ruin, the Marquis preferred to confine his considerable skill to his various clubs, which included Watier's and Boodle's.

About the time Corisande was disputing the merits of Sir Lucius Orsett's character with Lady Linton, the Marquis was sitting sprawled in a chair at one end of the fifty-guinea faro-table at the Nonpareil, his latest haunt, where the night-long gambling was deep enough to satisfy even the most hardened gamester, providing he could meet the exclusive requirements to gain entry.

His lordship's cravat was loosened and this, combined with the dead men at his elbow, warned Mr. Lavenham that his cousin was in the grip of one of his black moods. His devil appeared to be finding expression in the cards, for the play was wild enough tonight to suit even his temper. In the blaze of candlelight, his tanned face looked unusually pale and his dark eyes held a curious glitter as he looked up to see Tom walk over.

The long fingers were curled about the stem of his wine glass. He raised it in salute. "Hallo, Tom, are you going to join us?" Half drunk the Marquis might be, but neither his speech nor his intellect were impaired. Knowing that wine had little effect on his cousin's hard head until the third bottle had been broached, Tom guessed he must have been drinking steadily, an assumption which was correct. No sooner had his lordship returned from the Norburys' than he had dined at the Great-Go, from whence he had repaired to the Nonpareil and he had not risen from his place at the faro-table since.

Tom shook his head. "Not tonight," he answered Marc's question, but he took up a position behind his lordship's chair, joining the crowd of spectators who obligingly made room for him. One of them whispered quietly, "Dene is plunging deep, but he's had the Devil's own luck so far."

The bank at the Nonpareil was normally run by a syndicate, but tonight the rules had been relaxed and it was held by the Earl of Cranbourne, a friend of Brummell's. It was strongly rumoured that the Beau was on the verge of bankruptcy, but no such ignominious fate threatened the Earl, who was reputed to be one of the richest men in England.

"Waiter, a fresh pack if you please!" The Earl had just completed a deal as Tom entered and had thrown the pack on the floor. "Your stakes, gentlemen."

The Marquis had a large pile of rouleaus in front of him, each worth fifty guineas, and with one languid movement he pushed the entire heap towards his chosen card, the queen in the livrat.

A gasp went up when the Earl turned up the Queen of Hearts. "Devil a bit!" he exclaimed, but cheerfully picked up the rake beside him and thrust his winnings towards the Marquis.

Several of the men at the table were punting on tick and the Earl had a heap of scrawled vowels in front of him. "Scorched again!" groaned Mr. Devlin who was sitting on Marc's right.

"Never mind, Dev, you know what they say. Perhaps you'll have better luck with the ladies." The Marquis stretched out his long legs and smiled lazily at his cousin. Tom gritted his teeth. That mocking smile told him all he needed to know! The crazy madman had quarrelled with Corisande and was seeking solace in his favourite game.

Bending forward he said softly, "Marc, you lunatic, will you quit now while you are ahead?"

His lordship raised his brows, pained. "My dear coz," he drawled, "The night is yet young."

Contrary to Tom's conviction that this course must inevitably lead to disaster, the luck ran decidedly in Marc's favour for the next hour. The Marquis continued to drink steadily, his expression growing bored. "God rot you, Cranbourne, this is poor sport! What say you to raising the stakes to a hundred?"

The Earl nodded blandly, though someone at the other end of the table complained that this was too deep.

"Stand out if it don't please you," said the Marquis, and tossed off what remained in his glass. To Tom he seemed to have put all thought of the possible consequences of his actions out of his mind and his sheer lack of nerves enhanced his skill. The former ill-luck which had dogged him for months seemed to have turned at last.

Rouleaus passed backwards and forwards and at the end of another couple of hours' play Lord Dene's winnings had increased in a breathtaking fashion.

Mr. Devlin pushed back his chair. "I'm out."

"So soon? Sit it out, Dev, your bad luck can't last forever. Lady Fortune will smile on you soon if you continue to chase her," drawled his lordship in a faintly mocking tone.

"It's nearly four!" protested Mr. Devlin.

"Tell you what, I'll wager you my Samson against that pretty little bay mare of yours that I break Cranbourne's bank within the next hour."

Mr. Devlin laughed. "Done!" he cried. "Waiter, bring up the betting-book."

Tom groaned. The horse was one bred from his stables. "Good God, you'll never risk losing Samson to a roadster like Dev!"

Mr. Devlin took exception to this and while they exchanged insults in a spirited fashion the wager was duly entered.

"Hush, Tom, hush!" reproved his cousin gently. "You disturb the game." He shot a mocking look at the Earl. "Can I tempt you to two hundred, my lord?"

The Earl bit his lip. He was a very rich man, but only a fool pursued his ill-luck and the cards had been against him all evening. However, the odds favoured him in the long run since he held the bank. "You cannot win forever, Dene," he declared. "Playing two hundred!"

A wild laugh escaped the Marquis. "Play or pay," he agreed and thrust forward his money.

At first it seemed fortune had decided to favour the Earl. The bank won several times in succession and gradually the remaining players dropped out of the game.

"Too deep for me," said General Ravenscar, who was the last of them as he signed his final vowel and pushed it over before sitting back in his chair.

Ignoring Tom's frantic advice, the Marquis played on. "I'll stay the course. Not shy of a bit of bad luck, are you, coz?"

The luck veered. It irked the Earl considerably and a desire to get the better of his opponent overmastered his good judgement. The fumes of the brandy he was consuming at a rate to match the Marquis's own mounted to his brain, clouding his senses, but increasing the reckless excitement which had him in its grip.

In contrast Lord Dene remained cool, almost, Tom could have sworn, a little indifferent.

"Good God, man, you've done it!" Mr. Devlin exclaimed in awe. He looked at his watch. It wanted ten minutes to the hour. "And you've gained yourself my mare!"

Wild excitement rippled through the dense throng of spectators who had come crowding into the room, those at the back standing on chairs to see the play. Mr. Lavenham mopped his brow in relief, feeling almost light-headed as he clapped his cousin on the back, murmuring words of congratulation.

With a faint edge to his voice the Earl said, "I'll send you a draft on my bank, my lord." He rose to his feet and shouldered his way out of the room. The Marquis remained lounging in his chair, a faint smile on his lips.

"What's the tally?" demanded an excited voice from the back of the crowd.

"Fifteen thousand," someone else replied in a hushed tone.

A stunned silence fell to be broken an instant later by the sound of laughter. "I told you, Dev," choked the Marquis. "Fortune's a fickle jade, like all women."

THE STORY OF THE Marquis of Dene's amazing luck was round the town like wildfire. Corisande heard it the next day when she accompanied Fanny, as the guests of Lord Thorne, to watch the procession in honour of Princess Charlotte's wedding.

The diplomat had arranged an advantageous position for them to view the Guard of Honour of the Grenadier Guards go marching past. There was music by the band of the Coldstream Guards, in full dress uniform, but Corisande liked the Lifeguards troop best of all, with their splendid uniforms and great crested helmets.

The Princess rode to Carlton House with her grandmother, the Queen, and her aunts Augusta and Elizabeth, in an open coach so that the crowd had a good view of the Princess's gown, which was of white silk net over a white and silver slip glittering with silver lamé embroidery. Diamonds flashed in her blonde hair, around her neck and arms and on the clips fastening her white and silver manteau.

"She looks very happy. Don't you wish you were at Carlton House, Aubrey?" teased Lady Linton.

"Spare me, my dear. Prinny's parties are vulgar at the best of times. Heaven knows what he will make of this opportunity," replied his lordship. Rather bored by the proceedings, he was glad when it was time to usher his charges back to his house in Berkeley Square where he was giving a supper party, a form of entertainment he found much more amusing.

During the drive, he noticed that Corisande was unusually quiet and looking at her distinctly pale face wondered if the warmth of the day had been too much for her. When they had been shown up to a guest-chamber to rest and refresh themselves before the party began Fanny remarked upon it.

"Did you hear what Miss Wynford was saying?" Corisande demanded in agitated reply.

"Why no?" Fanny turned from the mirror in surprise.

"She was telling Lady Mary that Marc . . . the Marquis, I mean, broke the faro-bank at the Nonpareil last night. He won fifteen thousand pounds."

Fanny sat down abruptly. "Dear Heaven! How could he have been so reckless?" she gasped. Then joy lit up her thin features. "But he won, Corisande, he won!" She jumped up and with a beaming smile clasped the younger girl's hands. "I believe this means he will be free from pressure to obey Papa! Perhaps we shall find a way to persuade his grace to consider another bride if we can bargain for more time."

"Wait, Fanny." Corisande gripped her friend's hands tightly. "You haven't heard it all yet. It was too noisy to catch everything that was said but I got the distinct impression that he had wagered his entire winnings backing himself to beat Sir Harry in some sort of race!"

"What? He's mad!" wailed Fanny. "And Harry too . . . oh I'll never forgive him! How could he!"

It was a question Corisande was determined to put to the baronet. He had been invited to the supper party by the wily Lord Thorne, who was hoping to encourage him in his pursuit of Miss Clifford. Several other admirers of Miss Clifford's had also been bidden to attend, but Corisande had profited from her experiences as an accredited beauty well enough to detach herself from a mild flirtation with one of these gentlemen the moment Sir Harry walked in, summoning him to her side with one swift movement of her fan.

Fanny's ivory brisé fan had been poised to execute the same signal, but Lord Thorne was too old a hand to be sent to the right-about so easily and so Fanny had to swallow her chagrin and hope that Corisande succeeded in persuading him to abandon the race. She watched Harry lead Corisande over to a small table in a secluded spot by one of the long windows and tried to tell herself she was not jealous.

Corisande was glad that Lord Thorne's sister, who was acting as his hostess, had decided to serve the meal in the Russian style, with separate small tables, rather than seat all her guests at one board. She stared with a frosty hauteur copied from Mrs. Lavenham at the two eager young gentlemen who would have joined their table. Abashed, they retreated in disorder, leaving the field clear for her to pose her question to Harry.

Harry, who had just taken a mouthful of the succulent oyster pie, almost choked. "Damn . . . I mean dash it, Corisande, how the devil did you come to hear that?" he spluttered.

"Never mind, it doesn't signify," she replied impatiently. "Is it true?"

"Aye, it's true, unfortunately."

She stared at him, her brow creasing. It was well known that Harry Vernon was an excellent sportsman, but his tone did not indicate enthusiasm. "But I thought you issued the challenge?" she exclaimed.

"It was the other way round," Harry grimaced ruefully. "Does Fanny think so ill of me that she suspects I would egg Marc on to ruin? I had just walked into White's intending to eat there and everyone was talking of Marc's feat."

Harry paused and took a fortifying sip of champagne. "I didn't realise he had come into the dining-room until I heard him answer my comment to General Ravenscar that cards were not my game. As soon as I looked round I could see he was in one of his wild humours so I tried to turn it off, but he was determined to pick a quarrel with me."

He gave Corisande a level look. "Am I a fool for wondering if that young man has offered for you?" he asked shrewdly.

A blush mantled Corisande's cheeks. "Pray do not speak of it, sir!"

Her suffocated voice and agitated manner checked him.

"Very well, I'll not tease you for an answer, but it's my belief Dene was mad with jealousy when he forced the challenge on me." A slight grin lit his homely countenance. "I dare say he would have preferred it to be with pistols, but he made do with a race. That looby, Devlin, gave him the opening by asking me if my Firebird was for sale and saying that she was the only horse he knew which could beat his Molly, which he had just lost to Dene. He then announced he would even back Firebird against Dene's Samson and before I knew where I was everyone was calling for a race with Marc, declaring he'd stake his winnings from the Nonpareil on the outcome."

A grimace of frustration tugged Harry's eyebrows together. "I tried to laugh it off, but then he said he would engage to race his grey against any horse I chose over any distance and on any day I cared to set! What's more he offered the odds of two to one. Impossible to go on refusing!"

"That's thirty thousand pounds!" Corisande squealed, almost oversetting her glass of orgeat. "He's mad!"

"So I mentioned, my dear." The baronet's tone was dry. "It will go very hard with me to find that kind of money if I lose, but none so desperately as Dene. He will have to sell virtually everything he owns."

Corisande swallowed hard. Her feeling of guilt intensified.

"It's all my fault! If only he had not thought I was going to marry you, he would never have provoked you into this race."

Somewhat startled, Harry demanded an explanation. Considering that the possible sacrifice of thirty thousand pounds entitled him to it, Corisande gave him a scathingly honest version of what had transpired at the Norburys' breakfast.

"The young fool! How can the silly gudgeon think you could be so vulgar and mercenary!" expostulated Harry.

"Well, I did behave like a . . . a grasping harpy," murmured Corisande hanging her head in shame. "He was so furious, I dare say he never stopped to think, but I knew he wouldn't believe me if I tried to tell him I was merely indifferent to him. It was the only way I could think of to throw dust in his eyes. In view of my circumstances I knew it would sound reasonable to pretend I was on the catch for a rich husband and had only used him to serve that end."

She lifted stricken eyes to meet Harry's gaze. "It was all lies of course. I love him, you see," she said with a simple dignity that touched the baronet's heart. "Too much to entangle him in a misalliance which would end in his disinheritance. But look what has been the result of my meddling stupidity!" She bit her lip to still its trembling. "Could . . . could you cry off?" she whispered pleadingly.

"I'm sorry, but it's gone too far. I didn't want to accept, but I cannot withdraw now without staining my honour," Harry said gruffly. He gripped her hand across the table. "Don't blame yourself, my dear. I asked you to pretend an interest in me, so I can hardly cavil at the results."

"But that was my idea, too!" A tiny groan forced its way past her compressed lips. "I suggested you try and make Fanny jealous." Tears shone in her eyes. "I wish I'd never come to London! I've done nothing but cause trouble."

The baronet gave her hand a comforting little squeeze. "I do not agree with you there, but if it helps I know someone who would be glad to give you refuge in the country. My god-daughter, who lives in Cornwall, wrote to me only the other day and mentioned that she was seeking a governess for her son. If you wish, I could recommend you. Think about it, my dear. It might prove a solution and I know you would find them agreeable."

"Thank you," Corisande whispered. "I shall consider your kind suggestion, sir."

Perhaps it would suit her better to look after a lively little boy than mope in her old home, but Cornwall was so far away! Not that it mattered now, she supposed bleakly.

Harry made another effort to cheer her. "It was very good advice you gave me. I adore the woman, but I was doing myself no service acting like a blasted lap-dog, no, nor Fanny either!" he said firmly.

A faint smile touched Corisande's mouth. "I thought so too."

"Well then, my dear, let's pluck up our courage and hope for the best," he continued in bracing tone. "It isn't like you to refuse to jump your fences."

"But I don't want either of you to lose," she exclaimed, marvelling at his calm acceptance.

"I can afford it," Harry shrugged. "And to tell you the truth, I shall enjoy racing against Dene. He is a superb horseman, you know."

"Then you think he'll win?"

He hid a wry smile at her sudden eagerness. "I'd say there was a good chance of it, though, at the risk of sounding like a coxcomb, I'm no slow-top in the saddle myself. I won't hold back, but I doubt if I can beat him."

Corisande's smile broke out like dazzling sunshine. She felt as if a great weight had suddenly been lifted from her shoulders. "Thank you for being so honest with me," she said. "Do you know, I think I could eat supper after all!" And Harry joined in her sudden laughter.

CHAPTER THIRTEEN

AUGUSTA HAD AGREED to meet Corisande by the Ranger's Lodge in the Green Park, but she was some twenty minutes late and Corisande was wondering what could have gone wrong when she came hurrying into sight.

"I do beg your pardon," she gasped over Snowy's enthusiastic greetings. "Papa wished to speak to me just as I was leaving. He was determined to impart some news and I thought I should never get away."

"Heavens, Gussy, whatever did he say to you? You look quite worn to the bone." Corisande's irritation vanished. "Shall we find somewhere to sit and talk?"

The two maids who had accompanied them were ordered to take a stroll, but Snowy refused to leave. He did not approve of such a tame activity as sitting still, but was pacified when Corisande hunted out a stick to throw for him. Since he thought himself a famous retriever it was safe to release him from his leash as he would return the stick again and again for as long as anyone had the patience to keep up the game.

Recovering her breath, Gussy asked curiously, "What was that you wished to ask me? You said that you hoped I could help you and I shall be glad to do so if I can." The twinkle which appeared in her pale eyes would have astonished the *ton*. "I do not make friends easily, but when I do I stand true!"

Corisande considered her thoughtfully. "Why do you try to fool everyone you are such a cold fish, Gussy? In company you are a different person."

"I know. An iceberg!" A peal of laughter greeted Corisande's candid remark. "I know I can trust you not to repeat this, so I shall tell you the reason. My cold behaviour is to discourage any possible suitor."

"Don't you wish to get married?" Corisande was delighted by this unexpected news. It would make her awkward task much easier!

"Not to any gentleman in England," Gussy affirmed with an odd smile.

Consumed with curiosity Corisande waited for her to continue, but Gussy hesitated. "I have never spoken of this to anyone outside my family," she murmured indecisively.

Corisande threw the stick again for Snowy, letting her friend take her time. Until recently she would have pressed Gussy to confide in her, but she had learnt to be more patient thanks to the confusion she had created in trying to help Sir Harry. It did not always pay to jump in with both feet, even if the intention was excellent, she realised. She had paid dearly for the lesson, but perhaps she was growing up at last, she thought to herself with a bitter amusement.

Gussy bounced her blonde head as if she had come to a decision. "You see, when I was seventeen I fell in love with someone my parents considered ineligible," she began. "Hector had been sent to serve as our vicar's temporary curate. He is the son of a gentleman, but there are three elder brothers and two sisters, so his father could do nothing for him. It was decided that Hector should go into the Church, but without a patron he found it difficult to obtain a living and his career did not advance."

Gussy sighed. "It was dreadful when my parents discovered our secret. Papa made a fuss to the Bishop, which placed Hector in a very awkward position and I was packed off to London to be presented. Naturally I protested, but I was told to forget such nonsense."

Never having dreamt of such an answer, Corisande took a moment to recover from her stupefaction. "But you have not forgotten him, is that it?"

"One of the things I like about you, Corisande, is that I do not have to explain every little detail for you to understand me." Gussy smiled at her gratefully. "I simply could not give Hector up. He is seven years older than I am and quite impoverished so he was worried he might be taking advantage of me, but I told him I should never marry anyone else, which helped him overcome his scruples. We wrote to one another using my old nurse as a go-between. Hector thought it wrong in view of my parents' objections, but we could not stop loving each other and there was no other way we could keep in touch."

A grim frown descended on her brow. "Those first few weeks of separation were a nightmare. I was in such a daze I hardly spoke a word to anyone in spite of Papa's threats. Then, before I knew it, I discovered I had gained a reputation for haughtiness."

"So you decided to turn it to your advantage?"

Gussy nodded. "I dare say it was wrong of me, but I soon realised it was the best way to put suitors off." She chuckled. "Mama was angry with me for a time, but she is not a person who cares to exert herself so eventually she ceased to scold, particularly as she knew I did not care a button if I was sent home in disgrace."

Snowy came bounding up to have the stick thrown for him again and Gussy obliged.

"To make matters more awkward for my parents, my godmother, Lady Bartlett, died and left me her fortune when I was nineteen. It is all tied up in a trust, but I receive a handsome allowance, which I might add has kept the bailiffs from the door on more than one occasion these last four years! The capital I cannot touch until I reach twenty-five, unless I marry first, but there was nothing in the will to prevent me from marrying wherever I please."

A triumphant smile lit Gussy's face. "It is my intention to marry Hector Drummond. He is abroad at present, but he is to return soon and nothing my parents can say will alter my decision. I am of age now and with my godmother's money I shall be completely independent."

Relief washed over Corisande. "Oh, I'm delighted to hear of your secret attachment!" she exclaimed.

"It is very kind of you but I'm afraid I don't see why you should be so deeply concerned?" Gussy was a little puzzled.

"If you are going to marry the Reverend Mr. Drummond then you cannot accept an offer from the Marquis of Dene," Corisande pointed out.

"How on earth did you know of the Duke of Weston's proposition? Papa only received the letter from him this morning. That is why I was late. Papa was trying to persuade me to agree."

"The Marquis told his sister and Lady Fanny confided it to me, under terms of strictest secrecy, of course."

Gussy nibbled her thumbnail reflectively. "I see, but I still don't understand why my choice of husband should interest you so greatly."

"Well, it does, because Marc doesn't want to marry you," Corisande stated baldly and then gasped, her hand flying to her mouth in dismay. "Forgive me, I put that very badly. I am sure the Marquis esteems you but . . ."

"Nonsense," Gussy laughed. "Lord Dene dislikes me and I'm not surprised at it, since I have taken the greatest pleasure that he should." Gussy's expression clouded and a little shiver ran through her buxom frame. "I detested his brother. I know it is not good manners to speak ill of the dead, but he was the most abominable man. I hated him paying court to me and did all I could to discourage him, but Papa prevented me from saying anything outright. I believe he wanted to marry me, but I would have refused him if he'd asked, no matter what Papa threatened." She sighed. "He gave me a dislike of his entire family. It was irrational, I know, but I could not help it."

"And your feelings have not altered since Lord Edward's death?" Corisande probed.

"A little, but it is hard to shake off my prejudices. That is why I have not accepted your invitations to visit you in Hill Street, though of them all I like Lady Linton the best."

"Do you still dislike Marc, the present Marquis, I mean?" Corisande corrected herself hastily. "Don't you think him handsome?"

"I do not admire his style of looks," Gussy stated calmly. "Nor do I approve of his reputation, though I must admit he has a certain rakish charm." She smiled. "I can see you do not share my opinion, Corisande, but then you have not met my Hector."

"You mentioned he was living abroad?"

Gussy nodded. "He had relatives living in the Cape so he decided to go out there soon after we parted in the hope of improving his fortunes. Thanks to Papa's monstrous interference he could not obtain a decent living here in England. Africa seemed to offer more opportunity."

She smoothed her skirts and then looked up with a proud little smile. "He has done very well for himself and recently wrote to me that he had obtained the promise of a respectable parish in Norfolk, so that he could now support me as his wife. If my parents still refuse to countenance the match when he returns to England I shall marry him without their blessing."

The slight edge in her tone told Corisande a great deal about her friend's strained relations with Lord and Lady Marlow. Corisande had guessed before this that Gussy was not happy, but now she understood how difficult it had been for the older girl.

"Papa will bellow and rage, but he cannot force me to marry to suit his purse. He would like to see me a Marchioness, of course, my brothers are very expensive and he is none too plump in the pocket, which is why I shall keep my intention secret until all my arrangements are made."

Corisande had rarely heard such determination in anyone's voice before and she hid her amusement by patting Snowy and giving him a scratch in his favourite spot. It struck her as most odd that Gussy should not wish to marry the Marquis, but it was very welcome news.

"Thank you for taking me into your confidence, Gussy. I shall keep your secret about the Reverend Mr. Drummond, of course, but there is someone else I should like to tell about your decision to refuse the Marquis, if he should offer for you. If you will grant me permission?"

Gussy looked at her with doubt in her eyes and Corisande came to the conclusion it was not fair to expect her friend to agree unless she explained everything.

"Oh, how infamous of the Duke to threaten his son in that way!" Gussy exclaimed. "It isn't very flattering, but I can quite see Lord Dene's aversion to me, though I would have refused his brother. I do not like to boast of my conquests, but in fact I have refused several gentlemen. If his lordship feels forced to ask for my hand I will certainly reject his suit, and you may tell him so with my blessing!"

"I thought perhaps to mention it to Fanny and let her deal with her brother, if you don't object?" Corisande asked, adding that she hoped Gussy wasn't too offended.

"No, I'm not offended with you, you goose," Gussy shook her head. "I'm just angry at being used as a pawn in the Duke's game. What a very unpleasant man he is, to be sure."

"I have never met him. He is in Belgium now, I believe, but from all I've heard about his character I'm sure you are correct."

"When Hector returns I shall point out to my Papa that we do not want a penny from him, whereas he would have been burdened with finding an expensive dowry if I had agreed to marry the Marquis. Furthermore, I doubt Weston would have allowed Papa to bamboozle any handsome settlements out of the contract anyway, which is what Papa is hoping for, of course."

She shrugged her shapely shoulders. "No doubt I sound an undutiful daughter, but the truth of the matter is that Papa and I have never got on. He refuses to listen to me when I tell him I shall marry Hector and Mama is too indolent to care. In fact, of all my relatives, only my Uncle Lucius has ever shown me any sympathy or consideration."

"Indeed, he seems a most kind gentleman," Corisande agreed.

THIS FAVOURABLE description would have surprised Sir Lucius, had he been privileged to hear it. His behaviour towards his niece was not entirely altruistic. In so far as his selfish nature allowed, he was fond of Gussy, but he was more devoted to the portion of her allowance which found its way to him through the doting fingers of his sister, Lady Marlow.

Without Gussy's money, Lucinda was far too improvident to continue making him loans, which he rarely repaid. Lucinda had only her meagre pin-money, which wasn't enough to cover her own needs, let alone his! Gussy's generous help was necessary to them both.

It was all very disagreeable, but Sir Lucius's affairs were in very bad order. His shady dealings with certain discreet gaming-halls had not been very profitable of late and for some inexplicable reason the most promising young greenhead he had lured to his hand had taken sudden fright. His hopes of fleecing Peter Swindon dashed, Sir Lucius was in no good frame of mind as he took himself off to pay yet another morning call upon his only sister.

"Lucius! Just the man I wanted to see!"

This greeting from his brother-in-law, who was not apt to be so effusive, brought the baronet to a wary halt in the middle of the marble hallway of the Marlows' town house.

"Come in here a moment. I want a word," ordered Lord Marlow firmly and, refusing to listen to any protests, he ushered the visitor into his bookroom.

"Yes, yes, you can go up and see Lucinda directly if you wish," he said impatiently. "Not that she got a feather to fly with at the moment, I warn you."

Sir Lucius's plump face fell dramatically.

"And before you ask, my pockets are in no better state," his brother-in-law added hastily.

The baronet's smile dimmed, but revived a trifle as Lord Marlow continued, "However, I do have hopes of raising the wind, and if you'll help me I'll cut you in for a share."

Sir Lucius accepted a glass of wine and sat down. "What do you want me to do?"

This simple question appeared to afford Lord Marlow great satisfaction. "I knew I could count on you. It's a bit of a dirty business, but you'll not mind that," he went on, and ignoring his brother-in-law's pained expression proceeded to outline his plan in detail.

"Well, it's no secret I find the little Clifford a tasty morsel, but are you sure she's no innocent? I ain't keen on virgins. They tend to make such a fuss. Quite puts a man off!"

"Of course she ain't a virgin! She's Dene's fancy piece, I tell you, no matter what Fanny Linton might pretend. Damn it, you only have to look at the way he pants after her!" retorted Lord Marlow testily.

"All right, I believe you, but what's in it for me?"

"Oh, don't worry, you'll get your fair share. Weston is bound to cut up warm. There'll be plenty to go round if we can bring this wedding off," Lord Marlow announced with an expansive wave of one hand.

"Well, I can easily see to it that the lovely Clifford is got out of the way," Sir Lucius consented. "But I hope you're right in thinking that will induce Dene to look with favour on Gussy."

"It will if his father has anything to do with it, and when have you ever known Weston fail to gain his objectives?"

"True, but what about Gussy? Will she accept him?"

"She'll do as she is told for once, by God!" Lord Marlow's expression was grim. His daughter's obstinacy frequently infuriated him, but this time he would brook no disobedience. If something wasn't done soon it would be the River Tick for him, the way his affairs were going!

"If you ask me, she's still hankering for that young parson," remarked Sir Lucius thoughtfully as he heaved his bulk out of the chair ready to take his leave.

"Gammon!" retorted his brother-in-law.

LADY LINTON'S PLANS to curb Miss Clifford's unsuitable association with the Marlow family were thwarted by the onset of a summer chill which developed into one of her feverish colds. Ellen ordered her to bed with saline draughts and water-gruel, refusing any other member of the household admission to the sufferer's bedchamber.

Left to her own devices, Corisande found herself spending a great deal of her time in Arlington Street. She brushed aside her faint guilt with the sophism that her hostess had not actually forbidden her to visit there. Fanny was clearly prejudiced, but she did not know the real Gussy. Corisande preferred her to anyone else she'd met in London and she was not willing to give up the friendship just on Fanny's say-so.

With regard to Sir Lucius, Corisande could not understand why the Richmond circle disliked him. He was always extremely charming and she admired his support for Gussy. Opposition had set Corisande's back up and she did not stop to examine why she defended Sir Lucius. Impulsively, she had decided he was the victim of spiteful rumour. This aroused her ready sympathy and did away with any need to probe the battlefield of her own emotions. She did not wish to admit, even to herself, that the main reason she thought well of the baronet was a perverse desire to go against Lord Dene's advice!

For his part, Sir Lucius was glad he had always behaved to Corisande as if he were an indulgent uncle. When he had grudgingly handed over a roll of the soft, Marlow had warned him not to frighten the wench off, an aspersion on his skills Sir Lucius resented. He could behave with perfect propriety when he wished and he was not such a sapskull. The little Clifford needed handling with kid gloves and he flattered himself he had gained her confidence.

He was teaching her to drive his phaeton. This clever move had not only gained him Corisande's delighted gratitude, for she had long wanted to learn to handle the reins of such a vehicle, but it also gave him the perfect excuse to frequent her company. His visits to Hill Street continued throughout Fanny's brief illness and, when she at last left her bedchamber and learnt of the situation, it was too late to put a stop to such an established custom without causing a great deal of difficulty and offence.

"I have no real grounds to prevent him calling," she complained bitterly to Mr. Lavenham one evening. They were at Lady Byrant's soirée—Fanny's first outing since her recovery—and Corisande was dancing.

"Perhaps Harry might drop a word in Corisande's ear," Tom suggested. "He handled Peter Swindon beautifully and got him to see sense in no time. Why don't you ask him?"

Fanny's lips thinned. "I think he would heed such a request better if you made it of him, Tom." She laughed artificially. "Still, Harry does seem to have influence with her, she might listen to him."

"Fanny, have you and Harry quarrelled because of Corisande?" Tom blurted. "She's devilish pretty, but if Harry's head has been turned I'll swear it's only a temporary infatuation."

"Harry Vernon is entitled to pay court to Corisande or any one else he pleases." Fanny's fan fluttered in agitation. "It's of no consequence to me."

Recognising defeat, Tom abandoned his efforts. He could only hope Harry had more success with Corisande than he'd had lately trying to persuade sense into Marc's head.

His lordship had plunged into every kind of excess. He was drinking too much, spending a great deal of money, flaunting a different dazzling lightskirt on his arm every evening, and indulging in every form of high play. However, as fortune continued to favour him, no serious ill had come of his reckless behaviour. On the contrary, he had won several hundred pounds backing a goose against a turkey in a hundred-yard race in Hyde Park and a runner he had backed at Epsom, against all odds, came romping home, an unexpected winner.

The minute Tom saw his cousin cross the Byrants' elegant salon, he perceived that the Marquis was still in the same wild mood. Sally Byrant's parties were usually lively affairs with vast quantities of excellent champagne flowing freely. Judging by the glitter in his dark eyes as he strolled up to them, Lord Dene appeared to have been imbibing deeply of this beverage.

"Servant, Fanny." He bowed over his sister's hand and saluted Tom before turning to greet Corisande, who had just rejoined them. It was the first time they had met since the Venetian Breakfast at the Norburys' and Corisande's knees were knocking together beneath her rather décolleté evening dress of burnt orange Indian mull over a gold satin slip. She had spent hours altering this gown of Fanny's with Ellen's help and had been feeling pleased with her new sophistication, until she met the derision in the Marquis's eyes.

"Admirable!" He put up his quizzing-glass and surveyed her through it. "Our little snowdrop has put off her virginal muslins and blossomed forth as a lily, gilded of course!" he said outrageously in his most mocking tone.

Corisande would have liked to have slapped his dark face, but she gritted her teeth instead. Before she could protest he seized her hand, clad in one of a pair of yellow kid gloves which had depleted her purse by a whole five guineas. "Come and dance with me, my sweet," he said and whisked her away into the next room before any of the horde of her eager admirers could descend to claim her.

Her dance-card had been filled the instant she arrived and Corisande glared at him indignantly. "You must be foxed!" she accused as he swept her out on to the floor. The fiddles had struck up for a waltz and his arm encircled her waist, holding her close. She was so much shorter than he that her head barely reached his shoulder, but all of a sudden Corisande's gaze dropped. Her heart began to pound and she felt strangely shaken. He was holding her far too tightly for convention, but she had no desire to draw away, only a longing to confess her love.

The delicate perfume of her hair reached him and Marc's arm tightened involuntarily. She had looked so lovely this evening, he had been unable to resist the impulse of waltzing with her. In his arms she felt so fragile, so deliciously feminine.

When Corisande looked up there was a shy appealing look in her beautiful eyes. For a moment he was aware of a tug at his heart, but he had no intention of letting himself be fooled again.

"I am drunk," he conceded. "But do not let it worry you. I won't tread on your toes, it don't affect my co-ordination." He grinned. "It might even be better."

"Then I hope you may be foxed when you race Harry Vernon," was her tart retort as she regained her composure.

"So you've heard about our little contest." His mocking expression was pronounced. "The tattlemongers have been busy."

"Marc, don't do it, it is too risky," Corisande implored, forgetting her vow to remain aloof.

"Do you fear for Harry's neck, or mine, I wonder?" The dark eyes glittered. "You needn't waste your breath, my sweet. Nothing shall prevent me from the pleasure of beating him."

"You are quite detestable!" Corisande swallowed hard on the tears rising to choke her. "No wonder Gussy Marlow doesn't want to marry you."

The instant the words had left her mouth Corisande wished them unsaid. She felt him stiffen and prayed the floor would open up beneath her feet. Why did she have to blurt it out like a fool, when she hadn't even found the right occasion to tell Fanny yet!

"Why do you say that? Have you been discussing my affairs?" he demanded roughly, coming to an abrupt halt.

"Why should I discuss you?" Corisande attempted careless indifference, but she was shaking.

The Marquis was frowning blackly, regardless of the stir they were creating. Corisande was equally oblivious to the fact that their spectacular quarrel was providing unexpected entertainment for Lady Byrant's guests. She did not want to answer his fierce questions in case she betrayed her own emotions to that searching intelligence.

"Gussy is a friend of mine," was all she would admit to in the end. "I happen to know that she hopes to marry another gentleman."

Marc felt a surge of tremendous relief. If this were true . . .

"How can I believe you? Are you spinning me another tale to satisfy some obscure ambition? If you've changed your mind and think to accept my offer, let me inform you that it is no longer open."

Corisande went white. "How dare you?" she raged.

"Try for a little more originality, my sweet, you sound as if you still had straw in your hair. You'll never catch a husband if you don't learn a modicum of wit," he mocked.

Wrenching herself from his hold, Corisande grated, "I would sooner die an old maid than marry you! I haven't changed my mind and I wouldn't if you begged on your bended knees!" and with this declaration she marched off the floor leaving him standing alone and furious in the midst of the other dancers.

CHAPTER FOURTEEN

THE QUARREL between Miss Clifford and the Marquis of Dene, which had entertained the polite world at the Byrants' soirée, flourished when Corisande refused to receive his lordship when he called to see her the next day. She remained in her bedchamber and would not descend to the drawing-room in spite of Fanny's urging. Such unreasonable behaviour naturally put all thoughts of apologising for his uncivil remarks out of Lord Dene's head and he went away incensed.

His place was taken soon afterwards by Sir Lucius Orsett who had called to see if Miss Clifford cared to come driving with him. Determined to be contrary, Corisande agreed with a charming smile.

Corisande was about to depart for another of these lessons the next afternoon when Sir Harry Vernon called. Fanny was out, so Corisande received him alone, much to Turnbull's disapproval.

"Fanny has gone to the Botanical Gardens with Mr. Devlin," Corisande explained. Harry's expression became grim. "I should have called this morning," he muttered, and then apologised for the unusual hour of his visit. "I am not detaining you, am I?" he added, eyeing her carriage-dress adorned with braid and epaulettes in the military fashion.

"I expect Sir Lucius any minute," she admitted.

"I wish you would not go driving with that fellow," Harry expostulated.

"I cannot see why you are all so against him," replied Corisande with a stubborn look. "His manners are beautiful."

Harry clenched his fists and gazed heavenwards. "You are mistaken in trusting that court-card, but I haven't the time to argue the case with you. I called merely to tell you that the date and time for my race with Dene has finally been fixed. We are to race across the Heath from Highgate to Hampstead Village at three o'clock the day after tomorrow."

He shrugged. "I'd hoped to settle it sooner and take advantage of this fine weather. Firebird ain't keen on heavy going, but from the look of that sky I'm afraid we might be in for a storm."

Certainly the clouds had been building up all day and Corisande half-expected Sir Lucius to cry off, but no sooner had Harry departed than the baronet arrived.

"Do you think you might like to try fresh pastures, Miss Clifford?" asked Sir Lucius after they had taken a turn about the Park.

Corisande, who had just caught sight of the Marquis of Dene's curricle pulling up beside the gig of Mrs. Tavistock, a very pretty, but very fast young matron, was only too pleased to agree. "I have been longing to try my skill elsewhere," she affirmed. "This is very tame work."

The baronet nodded and patted her hand. He congratulated himself on the trusting way she followed his directions through the London streets and gradually the cobbles were left far behind.

"As a matter of fact, Miss Clifford, I have a small matter of business to deal with at my house near Chelsea Village. It is quite urgent. I have some medicine to deliver for my housekeeper's sick child. Some pills." He patted one of his coat pockets. "Do you have any objection to us calling there?"

Corisande hesitated. The clouds were now distinctly black and the hour already past four, but she did not wish to be uncharitable.

"The visit would only take a few moments. My house isn't very far and we shall be back in good time for dinner," he reassured her persuasively. "Or do you think Lady Linton would object?"

Fanny would, of course, and this decided Corisande in his favour, as the baronet had suspected it might. "Of course I shall be happy to accompany you, sir. There cannot be anything improper in such a brief visit, particularly as it is in a good cause."

"Excellent, my child." He beamed at her. "I warned my housekeeper to have refreshments ready today and, of course, I shall drive us home if you are tired."

Corisande was grateful for this prospect by the time they reached their journey's end. Their route had taken them deeper into the countryside than she had anticipated, although she failed to appreciate just how far they had come, being taken up with controlling her pair. He arms were aching with the strain, and to make matters worse, it had started to rain.

They turned into a pair of open gates and rattled up an uneven drive and she wondered if the downpour was the reason why everything seemed so bleak and desolate as they stepped down. Dripping lilac bushes formed part of a shrubbery screening an overgrown lawn and the house was smaller and less handsome than she had expected, knowing the baronet's love of finery and ostentation.

The front door was opened to them by a large individual with a bent nose and a cauliflower ear, who wore his ill-fitting livery with an awkward air that Corisande scarcely noticed as they hurried in from the rain. Inside, the house was even more shabby and Corisande decided that Sir Lucius's fortunes must be at a low ebb indeed. Instead of having her ushered upstairs by a housemaid to remove her wet pelisse and bonnet, the baronet directed her into a sparsely furnished parlour.

Thankful to at least see a fire burning in the grate, Corisande hurried towards it. However, the flames were fitful and she soon realised why, as a gush of smoke came rushing back down the chimney. "Heavens, sir, I think you need this chimney sweeping," she exclaimed, coughing and turning surprised eyes upon her host.

"I dare say," Sir Lucius answered without interest. His glance brightened as he spotted a decanter residing upon the sideboard and he crossed to pour himself a glass from it. "Can I give you some of this claret, my dear?"

"I should prefer some tea," Corisande replied, trying to repress a feeling of uneasiness. "If it is not too much trouble."

"I'll see what I can do." Sir Lucius waved a casual hand. "Take off your bonnet and get warm. It's turned damned chilly with that rain."

He went out of the room on this offhand speech, leaving Corisande prey to the most unsettling doubts. Was it her imagination, or had the baronet's manner altered towards her in the last few minutes? His respectful courtesy seemed to have vanished, to be replaced by a familiar, appraising look in his pale eyes that she could not like.

The house was very quiet and she jumped when at last the door reopened. "Oh, it is you, sir," she exclaimed, whirling round from her bored contemplation of a dreary oil painting. To her surprise the baronet himself was carrying a tray on which reposed a teapot and assorted crockery of the rough earthenware sort. A slab of cake with a knife sticking out of it accompanied the tea. Her doubts crystallising in the most horrid fashion, Corisande said, "Where is your housekeeper, sir?"

Sir Lucius ignored this question and set down his burden on a badly scratched Pembroke table. "Help yourself," he ordered and moved towards a sofa near to the fire. Corisande stared at him indignantly as he sat down and made himself comfortable, putting his feet up to the warmth. She was not one to stand on ceremony, but his behaviour was frankly impolite!

"I should like to return to London, Sir Lucius," she announced in a tight voice, drawing on her gloves. "At once!"

"Now don't fly into a pelter. Be a good girl and drink your tea."

Corisande gulped in dismay. There was no mistaking his familiar tone this time. "I'll have you know, sir, that your behaviour is not at all that of a gentleman!"

"Hoity-toity little madam, ain't you," laughed the baronet. "Now stop ripping up at me and sit down while I explain."

Corisande hesitated, but something in his tone warned her that nothing would be gained by disobeying. When she had done as he had ordered he smiled at her, cordial once more.

"That's the ticket, m'dear. Just do as you are told and we'll get along famously. Now, as you must have guessed, I didn't bring you here on a social visit. This house ain't mine, it's hired for the purpose, and there ain't a housekeeper. The only servants are the one you've seen and a slattern in the kitchen."

He smiled at her. "It's up to you how long we bide here. If you are the sensible wench I take you for, you'll accept me without fuss and we can make ourselves cosy in a comfortable little inn I know of. I don't mind sporting Marlow's blunt while he fixes up the marriage settlements." A fat chuckle accompanied this remark.

Corisande stared at him in disbelief. "Let me understand this clearly," she choked, wondering if he'd run mad. "Are you saying that Lord Marlow has arranged for you to kidnap me and keep me out of the way while he forces Gussy to become engaged to the Marquis of Dene?"

"Clever little puss," admired Sir Lucius. "Or has Gussy been tattling to you? Not that it matters. Yes, that's about the size of it. Marlow's paying but I would have been happy to take on a luscious little peach like you, m'dear, without his bribe, and that's a fact." He leered at her and Corisande realised he intended it as a compliment.

"Now what do you say? Will you take me in Dene's stead or do I have to tie you up to keep you here? I'd rather not be obliged to do so but, make no mistake, I will if you force me to it, m'dear."

Fighting down her nausea, Corisande willed her brain to function. She was no longer the little country miss who had been terrified into flight by Horace Hepburn. She had grown up a lot since then and she wasn't going to allow herself to be frightened now. But she must think quickly!

"Come, let's have your answer, Corisande."

The hint of impatience in the baronet's tone spurred her to a decision. It was obvious he would not believe her protests. He was convinced she was Marc's mistress and it might be wiser to let him go on thinking so rather than risk increasing his lust with the knowledge of her virginity.

Corisande tried to repress a shiver. If she kicked and screamed he would only summon assistance to subdue her and once she was tied up her chances of resistance and eventual escape would be lessened. Her best hope was to convince him his revolting proposal was agreeable to her.

She forced a sweet smile to her lips. "There is no need for threats, sir. I accept my situation."

Sir Lucius was relieved. He'd been vaguely worried she might kick up a dust, hence this lonely house where no one would interfere. Of course there was no avenging family to concern him, and not much likelihood that the Marquis would want her back once he learnt she'd taken a new lover.

Dene was well known for his fastidiousness in such matters. It was one of the factors Lord Marlow was counting on. Marlow insisted that Dene wouldn't chase after another man's leavings. Sir Lucius decided Corisande might not like this brutal truth mentioned, but he did essay another comment.

"You realize, don't you, puss, that Dene will be kept too busy to miss you? Wouldn't be good form, in any event, to be dangling after you while he was getting hitched to Gussy. A man should keep that sort of thing for after the wedding."

A flash of wry amusement made Corisande's eyes sparkle. What an elastic notion of morality the baronet had!

"Does your brother-in-law rate my chances of snaring the Marquis in wedlock so highly?" Corisande asked, moving gracefully towards the table. "All this seems a little excessive," she added with an airy wave of one hand before she poured out some tea for herself.

"Let's say Marlow likes to hedge his bets."

Corisande was wondering if she could extract the knife and hide it for later use, but when she tested it on the cake the blade was almost too blunt to cut off a slice. The baronet's casual manner was not as careless as first seemed!

"You are a very pretty wench, you see," Sir Lucius was continuing. "Thanks to Fanny Linton you've been accepted by the *ton*. A very shrewd move on your part, m'dear. You might even have brought the marriage off given time, except for one thing."

"Indeed?" Corisande sat down in the chair opposite, as far away as she could get without seeming too obvious.

"Weston," said the baronet succinctly. "He's got his heart set on Gussy for a daughter-in-law and he's a man of iron determination."

"And Gussy, will she obey her father's wishes?"

"She ain't keen," he admitted, rubbing the side of his nose thoughtfully. "But in the end Marlow will make her. He needs the money even more than I do."

Corisande reflected that Gussy's family did not know her as well as they imagined, but she had no time to dwell upon the fate planned for her friend. Her own future was in the balance and she must try and discover what the baronet's immediate plans were.

She fluttered her eyelashes at him in the most roguish manner she could assume. "Do you intend to abandon me here once Lord Marlow's aims are achieved, sir?"

"Nay, I could stand your protector longer than that, I reckon." Surprised pleasure broadened his smile.

"Thank you. I had not dared set my sights so high," Corisande continued to ladle on the flattery. "You know, of course, that I have no fortune, but the plain fact is that I am dependent on Lady Linton's charity. I had hoped to find myself a rich husband, but none of the gentlemen I have met so far in London has offered marriage."

"Too scared of Dene, I'll warrant. Anyone can see his interest in you, even if they don't all guess how far things have gone between you."

"It is true I've never been acknowledged as his mistress, but I don't suppose you would believe me if I told you we weren't lovers?"

The baronet laughed. "I'm not such a greenhead, m'dear. Sensibly, you've kept it very quiet to protect your reputation and I'm not the man to blame you. It is only fools who openly flout the rules of society."

Corisande covered her frustration with an admiring smile. It had been worth a try, but Sir Lucius was even more cynical than she had supposed. He was determined to think her an adventuress!

"Why should a girl as pretty as you have to waste her youth just because she's poor, eh?" said the baronet.

"I did not enjoy being a paid companion," Corisande admitted, playing idly with a curl of bright hair.

"Wouldn't expect you to, m'dear," he chuckled.

Sir Lucius had been pleasantly surprised by the little Clifford. He'd been half afraid she would weep over some romantic attachment to the Marquis, but it appeared she was as coolly calculating as himself when it came to putting her own interest first.

"'Course, once word of our little adventure gets out your reputation will suffer and your sojourn at Fanny Linton's will have to come to an end," he said, stating the obvious, without the least sign of remorse that Corisande could see. "It's unfortunate, but you won't regret exchanging her protection for mine," he promised. "I can be generous, and something tells me we shall get along like a pair of turtle doves."

Corisande turned a squeak of disgust into a cough. It seemed that she had succeeded in reassuring him. He was so mercenary himself, he had fallen into the trap of judging her by his own immoral standards!

Knowing she must take a swift advantage of his error, she coughed again, more loudly this time. "Lord, this house is very damp!" she complained. "And that fire is smoking so much it is making me cough. Are you not uncomfortable, sir?"

"It is a plaguey nuisance." The baronet bent forward to kick at the logs in the grate, but the sulky blaze did not respond. "Pah, the whole house is fit for naught!"

"Since it is so horrid, why don't we repair immediately to that inn you spoke of?" Corisande asked with a limpid smile, taking a casual bite of her cake. It tasted like sawdust in her mouth, but she continued to meet his suddenly suspicious look with an air of unconcern.

"Not so fast, puss." Sir Lucius's eyes narrowed. "Marlow wants his money's worth. Dene must learn you have spent several days alone with me lest he continue to hanker after you."

Corisande controlled her despair with great effort. She winked at him saucily and wagged a reproving finger. "Let us leave his lordship in the past where he belongs. I was only thinking of our future comfort."

"Aye, well, you've a point." The baronet visibly relaxed. "But, all the same, we'll stay here a while." His expression grew lustful. "I dare say we won't take much heed of the surroundings, eh?"

Corisande swallowed the bile that rose in her throat. Oh, God, she mustn't be sick!

"But are you sure we shall obtain a tolerable dinner, sir?" she asked with her warmest smile, knowing he was a noted trencherman and might think more of his stomach than the lack of other comforts.

This appeal brought a thoughtful frown to his plump face. "I trust it will not be too inedible." He sighed regretfully. "Perhaps we shall move tomorrow, if that woman can't cook, but I'm damned if I'm going to stir again tonight. Listen to that rain!"

Seeing he would not be persuaded, Corisande abandoned the attempt. She could not afford to make him suspicious. Beneath his amiable manner and self-indulgent laziness there was a hard ruthlessness. He would not be moved by any appeal for mercy, even if he thought her as innocent as a newborn babe and clearly he believed nothing of the sort.

Oh, why did I not listen to Fanny? Corisande began to shiver with apprehension. What should she do now?

"Why don't you come and sit nearer to the fire. You look frozen." The baronet smiled broadly. "Or shall I come and warm you up myself, eh?"

He began to lumber to his feet and sheer panic gave Corisande a new idea.

She held out a hand to ward him off. "Actually, I am feeling queasy, sir," she gasped.

The baronet halted in his tracks, his expression of playful amorousness changing to one of indignation.

"Queasy!"

He sounded so insulted Corisande made haste to elaborate. "It was that rich cake on top of our long drive. I am not a good traveller," she lied. "I shall feel as right as a trivet if only I could rest for an hour or two. Please, sir. I shall make it up to you."

Sir Lucius surveyed her carefully. He noted how pale she was and how her lovely skin was bedewed with a faint sheen of perspiration, although the room was decidedly chilly.

"All right, you can rest for an hour," he said in a begrudging tone. "Not a minute longer, mind. I'm in no mood to kick my heels in solitary silence all night."

Corisande thanked him effusively and he rang for the slovenly maid to show her up to a bedchamber.

Almost fainting with relief, Corisande followed the woman who opened a door for her and stood aside, her expression bored.

The room was damp and cold, but after the servant had gone Corisande noticed that the wide bed had been made up with good quality furnishings. There was a fire ready to be lit in the hearth too, and Corisande gulped at the ominous implications of such preparations for the night ahead.

"I must escape. It is the only answer," she muttered to herself through gritted teeth.

She moved to the window. The bedroom was on the back of the house, overlooking a large garden, rank with weeds and tall grass. The rain made it seem very gloomy, but she was glad to see that the downpour was easing.

Lord Marlow's infamous plan would come to nothing because Gussy would never agree to marry the Marquis, but it would be too late to save her reputation! The thought of Sir Lucius's podgy white hands touching her made her feel truly sick and yet she doubted her ability to flatter him out of his intentions. She had to get away from here!

Corisande tried to open the sash window. It was stiff. Worse, it was a long way down to the ground, although there was a vine to aid her descent. Perhaps she should risk the stairs after all. Sir Lucius had seemed settled with his decanter when she had left him.

Unfortunately, when she tried the door she found it had been locked and she released the handle with an unladylike exclamation. Sir Lucius might appear to trust her, but it seemed he was prepared to take no chances.

A fresh wave of anger swept over Corisande. How dared he have her locked in? Detestable man, she would not sit here like some sacrificial lamb to be taken at his pleasure!

She returned briskly to the window and attacked it once more. This time it yielded to her efforts and she eased it up as quietly as she could. Next she removed her half-boots of orange jean and kilted up her skirts with a cord she purloined from the curtains to make the descent easier.

Her boots went out first and, praying that the overgrown vine which rioted in thick profusion all over the brickwork would take her slight weight, Corisande swung her legs over the sill.

THE MARQUIS OF DENE watched Miss Clifford turn Sir Lucius Orsett's phaeton with neat precision and drive off. Abruptly curtailing his flirtation with the vivacious Mrs. Tavistock, he set his chestnuts in motion. Without knowing quite why it should be so, it disturbed him that they had stayed so short a time in the Park, and some instinct made him follow them at a discreet distance.

The press of traffic in the streets made his task a difficult one, but his lordship's eyebrows met in an even more fierce frown when it became clear that the baronet intended to travel into the countryside.

"Damn the stupid girl!" he muttered furiously.

Dickon regarded his master with deep suspicion. "Where we going, guv'nor?" he demanded.

"I don't know."

"Dang me and I never suspicioned you was boozy! You carries it very well, guv'nor!"

"Blast you, I'm not drunk," retorted the Marquis. "But I'm going to follow that phaeton if it takes all night!"

Dickon pondered this in silence for a moment. "Be that tallow-faced old cull a-running off with Miss Clifford?" he asked cautiously.

The Marquis's eyes began to kindle. "If he is, I'll break every bone in his fat body," he vowed, forgetting he had intended never to so much as speak to Miss Clifford again.

Once they turned off the main pike road, the Marquis was forced to hang back for fear that they should be spotted, but the phaeton continued to bowl along at a brisk pace without stopping. When it began to rain his worry that any pursuit might be noticed lessened, but his necessary caution landed him in a quandary when they reached a country crossroads. There was no way of knowing which direction the other carriage had taken, the rain having obliterated the tracks in the dusty surface.

"We'll try the left-hand fork first," his lordship announced, but was soon obliged to slacken the fast pace since the chosen lane dwindled into little better than a cart track. Lord Dene became convinced the baronet could not have come this way, and when they rounded another bend to behold a farmhouse he was sure of it.

A man with a piece of sacking thrown over his head and shoulders was just closing the big yard-gate and in reply to the Marquis's shouted question answered that no other vehicle had passed this way this afternoon and, no, the lane didn't go no further unless you was wanting Widow Mamble's cottage.

The Marquis thanked him, and without wasting any more time turned his curricle around with a speed and skill that left the farmer gasping in admiration and drove off. Reaching the crossroads once more, he took the other lane and was soon rewarded by the sight of a pair of rickety gables hanging open and a weed-infested gravel drive.

"Wait here for me," he ordered Dickon, convinced now that Orsett was planning mischief.

"Be careful, guv'nor," admonished Dickon with a worried frown.

The Marquis nodded. Orsett was the type to turn vicious if cornered, and there was Corisande's safety to think of.

The heavy rain was easing as he trod cautiously up the drive, but it was still enough to render it unlikely anyone would be abroad. It didn't seem that Orsett had set guards, but then he would not be expecting visitors! Cutting through the overgrown garden, he made his way stealthily round to the back of the house to be met by the astonishing sight of Miss Clifford descending the last few feet of the creeper on the wall like an agile cat.

He blinked at the exquisite pair of legs thus revealed and then as she reached the ground hissed softly, "Corisande!"

She whirled round with a gasp of alarm, but then her expression relaxed into thankfulness.

"Marc!" She cast herself into his arms with a sob of fright. "Sir Lucius locked me in. He means to make me his . . . his . . ."

His arms tightened protectively. "Hush now, sweetheart. You are safe."

Corisande felt his lips brush gently across her hair and rest in a tender kiss on her forehead for an instant. The convulsive shudders which racked her slim frame stopped, but she could not control her voice as she blurted, "He . . . he thinks we are lovers."

The Marquis's eyebrows rose, but he said firmly, "This is no time to talk. Has he set guards?"

His question recalled their danger and Corisande shook her head. "I'm sorry," she gulped. "I don't think so, but do let us get away from this horrid place."

The Marquis gave her an arm to lean on while she swiftly pulled on her boots and then he led her quickly back the way he had come. To Corisande's relief they encountered only weeds and soon reached the carriage.

Dickon greeted them joyfully, though Corisande's kilted skirts made him blink. He discreetly averted his interested gaze while she restored her dress to rights before allowing the Marquis to hand her up to her seat.

"Marc? Where are you going?"

"To throttle Orsett, of course. Dickon will look after you. Drive away at the first sign of trouble," he added to Dickon in the same calm tone.

"No! Wait! You mustn't go back there, he has got this big ugly brute with him," Corisande shrieked.

When she had described Sir Lucius's peculiar-looking footman the Marquis shrugged. "One of the prize-fighting fraternity, I imagine," he concluded. "Not that it signifies in the least."

"If you move one inch from here, Marc, I shall scream that house down and so I warn you!" Corisande pushed a wet ringlet out of her eyes. "I'm soaking wet and chilled to the bone, to say nothing of having been scared half out of my wits. I will not have your death on my conscience on top of everything else!"

The Marquis began to chuckle. "Very well, infant, I'll deal with Orsett later." He stared at her. "You're shivering. Here, take my driving-coat."

"But then you'll catch cold," Corisande protested.

"Nonsense." He stripped off his coat and then sprang up into the curricle to arrange it around her.

Corisande thanked him shyly. There was the faintest hint of the lemon cologne he sometimes used in the thick folds and she huddled into it with a voluptuous sigh.

"Lord, you look the most complete romp!" the Marquis exclaimed, giving his horses the office to start. "Where's your bonnet?"

"I left it behind. Well, I could hardly climb down that vine with it on. It has three curled plumes," she pointed out reasonably.

"Yes but what the devil shall we do when we get back to London?" he frowned. "I'll lay you a monkey we drive slap bang into a parcel of tabbies. One look at you and your reputation will be in shreds!"

Dickon who had been following the conversation with interest, interposed his opinion that nothing could be more prejudicial to their chances of keeping this adventure secret. "She didn't ought to be sitting up there beside you for any chub to see, guv'nor, and that's a fact."

"Shall I hide? I could sit on the floorboards," Corisande offered.

"There's no need for such drastic measures yet, but it might serve when we get closer home," agreed the Marquis.

They regained the main road and the conversation lapsed as his lordship appeared to give his attention to driving.

The immediate danger averted, Corisande was suddenly conscious of a ridiculous impulse to cry. It was impossible to forget how she had last parted from him in anger and yet he had rushed to save her.

It was becoming an absurd habit, she thought miserably, and I don't deserve it.

"Are you comfortable?"

This polite enquiry made Corisande gulp back her tears even as she hastily murmured assent.

The Marquis touched her hand in a brief gesture of reassurance. "Don't refine too much upon Orsett," he advised in his kindest voice. "You cannot help your looks."

"My looks?" Corisande was puzzled for a second before she understood his meaning. "Sir Lucius was not taken with my beauty. He kidnapped me for money."

"Money?" The Marquis glanced at her sharply.

Corisande blushed. "He and Lord Marlow seemed to think you would look more kindly upon Gussy if I were out of the way," she said in a low voice.

The Marquis looked thunderstruck for a moment. "So Marlow was paying him! Was that what you meant when you spoke of Orsett's thinking we were lovers?"

Corisande nodded, her colour deepening.

There was a silence and Corisande could hear her heart beating like a wild thing against her breastbone. The feel of his strong arms around her only minutes ago—no matter if he had only been offering her comfort—the warmth of his body next to hers now! Her pulse quickened, as longing for his love surged in her stronger than ever. Lovers! If only they were!

One swift glance at his profile told her that his thoughts were travelling the same path as her own.

"Corisande, could you consider, would you...oh, damn it!" The Marquis's deep voice was almost hoarse but she knew the question only Dickon's restraining presence prevented him from asking. He wanted her too!

Like a field of gorse after a dry summer, desire crackled between them, needing only a single spark to set it ablaze and consume them both in a rage of passion.

Oh, God, what am I going to do? Desperately, Corisande strove to master her emotions. Nothing had changed! She could not allow herself to be swayed by her senses. Becoming his wife would have led to his ruin, becoming his mistress would lead ultimately to hers!

"Do you know, sir," she said shakily, "I have been offered the position of governess to a little boy in Cornwall and I am thinking of taking it."

A muscle quivered beside his well-cut mouth. "Indeed. Then I must congratulate you."

Marc's calm tone cost him a great deal. His unthinking response to Corisande's danger had been to fly to her rescue. His jealous fury had not stopped him and now he realised that nothing ever would. It didn't seem to matter that she was an unprincipled little baggage, who didn't care a rap for him in any real sense. She would not have him, she had just told him so, but still he loved her and would do so until his dying day.

The Marquis was just wondering if there was any insanity in his family, when Dickon piped up, "Here, guv'nor, there's a cove a-waving at you."

Corisande had also noticed this unusual sight and she tried to pull herself together as the young man came hurrying towards them.

It had stopped raining and there was still light enough to see that he was respectably dressed in sober garments of an old-fashioned cut and that his decidedly weather-bronzed face wore a worried look. Beyond him, a short distance ahead, a chaise could be seen with one wheel off.

"Careful now, infant." The Marquis muttered the warning as he reluctantly drew rein.

Corisande did not waste time replying. She was too busy trying to straighten her hair and tidy her wretched appearance. Fortunately, the benighted traveller did not seem to notice that anything was amiss and after one brief nod in her direction confined all his attention to the Marquis.

"Thank you for stopping, sir. I had begun to despair that any other traffic would pass this spot tonight," he said. "I wonder if I could make so bold as to ask you to convey my companion to the nearest inn? Our postillions have gone for assistance, but it may be some time before they return and my friend is unused to this evening chill and only recently recovered from a bout of seasickness."

The traveller's frank countenance grew even more grave.

"Indeed, I am anxious that he may become ill, for he is not a young man and his recent mode of life was filled with privations which have affected his health."

"Where are you headed for?"

"London, sir. We landed yesterday at Portsmouth and we have pressing reasons for making haste to the capital. However, any inn along this road where my friend could rest would suffice until I can set about hiring another carriage if this one cannot be mended."

His determination met with Corisande's approval. "Can't we help them?" she whispered to his lordship.

Marc nodded and said to the man, "I hope your friend is not fat. There's little room for three." This was a complication they could have done without, but he urged the chestnuts forward at a walking-pace and pulled them up close to the post-chaise.

The young man hurried to open the door and let down the steps while the Marquis descended from his own vehicle.

"I want to get down," Corisande said pointedly.

"You'd be better off staying where you are."

She shook her head. "Our new companion is too busy with his own concerns to take any notice of me and I dare say his friend will be the same."

The Marquis sighed, but extended his hand to help her. "He don't seem tonnish, but be careful what you say. We don't want them learning your name or mine, for that matter, if it can be avoided."

Corisande ignored this admonition.

A middle-aged gentleman was alighting awkwardly from the chaise and she stared at him with a peculiar fixed rigidity. His grey head was bowed to watch where he stepped, but when he lifted it she gave a choked cry of recognition and to the Marquis's astonishment ran forward to fling her arms about the frail traveller's neck.

CHAPTER FIFTEEN

"YOUR *Papa?*" Lady Linton gazed in astonishment at the trio of weary travellers who had just been shown into her drawing-room.

Fanny had been waiting for her protégée's return in a fever of alarm. No one seemed to know where Corisande had got to, but now her worry and annoyance vanished in an instant, banished by this totally unexpected but wonderful news.

When all the introductions were over and refreshments had been brought Fanny said, "I hope you will stay the night with us, Mr. Clifford. And you too, Mr. Drummond."

"Thank you, ma'am. It is kind of you to offer, but I wouldn't dream of imposing upon you. You have been too kind already." Mr. Clifford patted his daughter's hand.

Corisande was sitting next to him on the sofa. It had been a very long and eventful day, but she was too keyed up to feel any fatigue. The fact that her father was alive was something she still had difficulty in comprehending.

They had dined at an inn in Chelsea while the wheelwright had very obligingly mended her papa's chaise. A handsome *douceur* from Mr. Clifford had assured speedy attention and it was another source of wonder to Corisande that he seemed to have acquired wealth during his lost years.

It had been a strange meal. Mr. Clifford was too worn out to eat and Corisande far too excited, while the other two men were much preoccupied with their own private thoughts. Corisande's bedraggled appearance had necessitated a sketchy explanation of what had occurred and, though the Reverend Mr. Drummond had raised his sandy eyebrows, her father had been too exhausted to ask any questions.

When the chaise was repaired, the Marquis suggested that Corisande travel with her father. Since this plan would eliminate the difficulties she might encounter if she continued the journey with him, Corisande agreed.

"I will not call on my sister tonight," Marc added, to her disappointment.

She guessed that he was trying to be tactful, so did not press him, but bade him farewell. It was impossible to say the things she wanted to say to him, but from the way he kissed her hand, with far more warmth than convention decreed, she knew that their quarrel was over and he had forgiven her for spurning his offer of marriage in so brutal a fashion.

Corisande did not realise how her expressive little face betrayed her feelings. Her glowing smile as she stared after the Marquis's retreating figure made her father frown and turn a puzzled look of enquiry upon Hector. Hector Drummond shrugged eloquently, shaking his sandy head.

In the carriage, Mr. Clifford confided a little of his story, but part way through a sentence he fell asleep.

"Pray do not be offended, Miss Clifford." Hector Drummond spoke up swiftly. "I know for a fact, since he has often told me of it, how your father esteems you. He was so looking forward to meeting you again, but we did not expect it to be until he had recovered from the rigours of our journey."

"I am not in the least offended, sir. Papa was never a good traveller and from what little has been said it is plain that he has had a hard time of it lately. I am only sorry that I spoilt his plan to surprise me, though I cannot regret that fate brought us together so much the sooner."

Her curiosity was like a raging torrent, but Corisande had tried to keep it in check. Her father was much thinner than she remembered and looked older than his years. It was obvious he was not in good health and a wave of protective tenderness swept over Corisande once again as she saw how he was struggling to mask his fatigue in order to respond politely to Fanny's remarks.

"If you are determined to put up at Grillon's hotel, Papa, perhaps we could continue this conversation tomorrow," she suggested.

He gave her a grateful smile, as Hector Drummond seized the opportunity to get to his feet and begin thanking Fanny for her hospitality. "Forgive me, my dear," he whispered. "I shall try to make it up to you in the morning."

Corisande smiled and shook her head. "There is nothing to forgive, Papa. I am just so happy to have you back! My only regret is that Grandmama never knew the reports of your death were mistaken, though I think she never entirely gave up hope."

"She was a marvellous woman. I shall miss her greatly. My poor dear, what you must have gone through during her illness and afterwards, and I not there to help you!"

Corisande gave his hand a little loving squeeze. "It is all behind me now, Papa. You are home and that is all that matters."

Corisande scarcely slept a wink and was up betimes, restless for the hour when she might reasonably visit her father. She dressed in her prettiest morning-gown of almond-green cambric muslin lavishly trimmed with blond lace and went down to breakfast.

For once Fanny joined her. "I could not sleep, for all that it was so late when we retired last night," she said, taking her place at the table.

Corisande poured a cup of coffee for her. "Thank you for not scolding me, Fanny. I know I richly deserved it after ignoring all your warnings. It was sheer perversity that made me go off with Sir Lucius, but I have learnt my lesson now." She shivered a little at the memory of the baronet's leering smile.

After her father had departed they had sat up talking half the night and Corisande had told Fanny all that had occurred. The only thing she had held back was the way Marc had kissed her and almost asked her to become his mistress.

"Are you sure it wasn't a fit of pique against my brother?" Fanny asked shrewdly.

Corisande coloured. "Marc and I have made up our estrangement," she murmured.

Fanny sighed. "I hope so, my love. There are too many people with vulgar minds and, though they might not jump to quite the same conclusion as Lord Marlow, disastrous scenes like that at Sally Byrant's can only give rise to unwelcome gossip. It looked so plainly a lover's quarrel! Thank God, my father is in Belgium!"

This reminder of the Duke made Corisande exclaim, "His grace cannot quibble if Marc fails to meet his demands! Not in the circumstances."

Fanny laughed. "I suppose not. Having met Mr. Drummond, he strikes me as a man of determination, and from what you have told me Augusta Marlow seems equally set on having him." She took a sip of her coffee. "Not that he is my idea of a hero of romance," she added with a chuckle.

Corisande grinned. She couldn't understand why Gussy thought Hector more handsome than the Marquis, though she was glad of it. "I must admit he is not as I imagined."

"I was thinking that perhaps we could hold a simple supper party for your father tonight," Fanny announced, spreading a little conserve upon a slice of bread and butter. "Nothing elaborate of course. It would not do to tire him, but I thought it might make a nice gesture of welcome?"

"How kind of you, Fanny! I'm sure he would like to come and perhaps we could ask Gussy too, if you intend to invite Mr. Drummond along, that is?"

Fanny blinked. "Why yes, of course, if you wish it, my love. Shall I write her a note or perhaps it would come better from you?"

"I'll go and do it now." Corisande pushed back her chair, leaving her breakfast half-eaten. "Though something tells me that Hector will have contrived to have sent her a message already!"

THIS SUSPICION was confirmed when Corisande was shown up to her father's private parlour at Grillon's, to find him alone.

"Corisande, my dear." Mr. Clifford came hurrying across the room to greet her. "You have just missed Hector. He has gone to meet his Miss Marlow and I declare I never saw him so agitated before!"

"You are looking much better this morning, Papa," Corisande said thankfully as she removed her bonnet and gloves.

"I'm quite restored after the best night's rest I've had in months, my love," he affirmed. "Come, sit down here near me and we can talk in comfort."

Corisande noticed that his limp, which had troubled him last night, seemed much improved as he moved to a side-table and poured a glass of wine, which he handed to her.

"Your health, my dear." He raised his own glass. "And to our new future."

He sat down and smiled at her. "Well, where shall I begin my story? It seems a lifetime since I left England. You were only a little girl. I never dreamt you would grow up into such a beauty, 'pon my soul!"

Corisande laughed. "Africa has turned you into a courtier, Papa."

"Never that, my dear, but it has made me a rich man. I don't know if you realise it, but you are quite an heiress now."

"An heiress? Are you bamming me, Papa?" Corisande stared at him. "I guessed last night that your fortunes had improved, but surely plants, no matter how rare, cannot have brought about such a change?"

"Not plants, my dear, but diamonds."

"Diamonds!" Corisande squeaked, almost oversetting her wine. "Papa, I am afraid I don't understand."

"It is quite simple." His smile broadened. "Ah, I must not tease you. It all began, you see, on the day that I foolishly ignored good advice and decided to make the trek to cross the Orange River alone..."

Wide-eyed with wonder, Corisande listened to his strange tale unfold and when it was done she gasped, "Oh, Papa! And Hector was the one to rescue you from your captivity!"

"Aye, I owe the lad a great deal. If it were not for his help I should still be a prisoner of the Baralongs. It is my intention to give him a share of the money that the diamonds fetch. He has told me he will not accept, but it shall be my wedding-gift to him, so he'll not be able to refuse."

"Gussy will be delighted." Corisande's smile held the faintest tinge of sadness.

"And you, my daughter, won't you enjoy your new status, or does it come too late to be of any help to you, eh?" Mr. Clifford asked shrewdly. "If I'm not mistaken, I fancy that young man you were with last night may hold the key to this mystery."

He put down his wine glass. "Just what were you doing out so late with the Marquis, Corisande? Why did you have no chaperon other than his groom?"

She flushed. "It is not how you think, Papa."

"No? Then you are not in love with him?"

"My feelings have nothing to do with why we were on the road at that hour," Corisande replied quickly.

Her father frowned. "Come, my dear, don't treat me like a fool. I may have forfeited my rights over you, thanks to my own carelessness, but I am still your father. In the past I have been guilty of neglect, but during my captivity I had time enough in plenty to regret my selfish behaviour towards my family and vow I should do better if I ever won my freedom."

Corisande's hands twisted in her lap. "It is a long story, Papa, and I am not proud of myself. My behaviour has been foolish on several occasions."

"My dear, I don't seek to condemn you! Through no fault of your own you were cast adrift upon the world with no one to guide you. If you have formed an unwise attachment perhaps I can help."

Tears stung Corisande's eyes. She had forgotten how wonderful it was to be wrapped in the warmth of family affection. Haltingly she told him all that occurred since she had met the Marquis of Dene on the Bath road.

"My poor girl." Mr. Clifford patted her hand. "But now that your friend is to marry Hector perhaps this Duke of Weston will relent. After all, my dear, why should you not make a suitable duchess? We do not possess noble blood, but you come of a genteel family. You have shown that you are intelligent enough to learn how to conduct yourself in Society. Surely you could also learn how to act the part of a great lady? Not least of all, you shall have a considerable dowry. That much, at least, I can contrive for you."

"Perhaps I could." Corisande tried to smile, grateful for his support. Strangely, it ran counter to the views her grandmama had held, which had influenced her own thinking so heavily. Now it occurred to her for the first time that maybe Mrs. Dalton had been mistaken to think moving out of one's own class was automatically wrong. "But I do not think the Duke would welcome me as a daughter-in-law. The size of my fortune would not impress him; he is too proud. His son's wishes do not seem to count with him and there is no other reason why he should agree to the match."

"You suspect he will order the Marquis to marry another well-connected young woman like Gussy?"

Corisande nodded sadly and, anxious to change the subject, asked him if he would like to dine in Hill Street, explaining Fanny's notion to him. He was in the middle of accepting the invitation when there was a knock at the door and in walked Hector with Gussy on his arm.

"Corisande! Oh, isn't it wonderful?"

Corisande had never seen her friend look so radiant.

Gussy embraced her and then was introduced to Mr. Clifford and they all sat down again to drink more wine and talk. After a while Corisande mentioned the proposed supper party.

"Can you forget your prejudices and accept, Gussy? I think Fanny believes it is time peace broke out and I feel sure she is right."

"I should be happy to accept if Hector wishes to go," Gussy said, giving her beloved a warm smile. "I feel too content with the world to go on disliking anyone. For the first time in years I can be myself. It is time to bury my iceberg image and all the pain it masked. Soon we intend to tell my family that we are to be wed, but I want today to be unmarred by recriminations and arguments. It is a little time of perfect happiness we have decided to steal for ourselves."

"Amen to that!" Hector raised her hand to his lips.

Watching them, Corisande felt a pang of envy, which she tried hard to suppress. Gussy deserved all the happiness she could get, but oh, how she wished she could sit here with Marc and have his arm around her shoulders too!

AT THAT PRECISE MOMENT the Marquis of Dene was engaged in a search for Sir Lucius that was proving as fruitless as it was frustrating. He had returned to the house near Chelsea, but the bird had flown and, on returning to London, there was no scent of the baronet in any of his usual haunts. His enquiries were hampered by the need for discretion, but his determination to extract vengeance only grew as the day wore on.

He contemplated paying a call in Arlington Street, preferably with a horse-whip, but Fanny pleaded with him not to risk causing a scandal that might rebound upon Corisande's innocent head.

He had been disappointed to find Corisande out when he had arrived in Hill Street, but he took the opportunity to pick Fanny's brains to see if she could think where Orsett might be hiding, consoling himself with the thought that he would see Corisande at supper.

With Fanny's help he concocted a curt note informing Lord Marlow that they knew of his part in the plot to ruin Miss Clifford and warning him of what the unpleasant consequences would be if they heard the slightest whisper of gossip concerning that lady's name in the future.

"Thank you for your help, Fanny. I shall see you tonight, then," he said as he bade her farewell.

"Don't forget to ask Tom to come. I only wish Letty could be here to make the party of Corisande's friends complete. We had another letter from her two days ago, you know. They shall be in London very soon now and I know Corisande is looking forward to seeing her again."

"You ain't asked Harry Vernon, though," Marc pointed out.

Fanny coloured slightly. "It would be most improper. Or have you forgotten you are racing against him tomorrow?"

"With thirty thousand pounds at stake I am hardly likely to let it slip my mind," the Marquis retorted drily.

Fanny shuddered. "Pray do not speak of it! One of the reasons for this party is to take my mind off your folly, little brother."

"Then I shall contrive to be on my best behaviour." He bowed over her hand.

"Good. And don't you dare tease Mr. Drummond about wishing to marry Augusta Marlow. Corisande told me how you laughed when the poor fellow mentioned it last night." Fanny tried to look stern.

Marc grinned. "I shall do my humble best, though you must admit it is a startling notion that any man should wish to shackle himself voluntarily to the Iceberg!"

"Oh, go away, do!" Fanny began to laugh. "And remember your promise tonight."

LATER THAT EVENING, Lady Linton gazed with great satisfaction at the small informal group assembled in her drawing-room. Corisande was looking her best in a simple gown of cream silk and she could quite understand the look of glowing pride upon Mr. Clifford's face whenever his eyes lit upon his beautiful daughter.

"I beg you will allow me to reimburse you for any charges you have incurred on my girl's behalf." He turned and said quietly to her, "Corisande may have mentioned that I have amassed considerable wealth during my exile and I do not wish to seem niggardly in paying our debts.''

Fanny smiled and managed to refuse this offer in a charming manner which did not offend his pride.

"I count Corisande as one of my dearest friends,'' she concluded simply.

Corisande who caught the tail end of this conversation experienced a *frisson* of guilt that she had ever hurt Fanny's feelings, even in a good cause. She wished Fanny's scruples had permitted her to invite Harry tonight. Looking at Gussy and Hector laughing together over some remark Tom Lavenham had made, she couldn't help wishing the same happiness for Fanny that she had earlier wished for herself.

As if her thoughts had conjured him up, Turnbull announced the Marquis, who walked into the room looking very handsome and self-assured in his dark evening-clothes.

"How are you, sir? I trust they are making you comfortable at Grillon's?'' He shook hands with Mr. Clifford.

Mr. Clifford replied politely to this enquiry but he was shocked by the stab of jealous resentment he experienced when the Marquis turned to greet Corisande and his daughter bestowed one of her lovely smiles upon the young man. Firmly, he curbed the unwelcome emotion. He had no wish to try and tie Corisande to him. It was too late, in any case. From the way in which she suddenly sparkled as if the Marquis's presence had brought her truly alive he knew his daughter was no longer a child, but a woman in love.

Discreetly he edged away, leaving them momentarily alone.

"Thank you for your note. It was kind of you to call and enquire how I did. I'm only sorry I was not here to receive you,'' Corisande murmured, feeling suddenly shy as she remembered how he had helped rescue her from Sir Lucius.

"Then you are feeling quite recovered after your ordeal?'' Marc sounded relieved. "Do you know, when I left you last night it occurred to me that our journey yesterday was rather like the very first one we undertook together.''

Corisande chuckled. "My appearance left a lot to be desired then, too!''

He smiled. "I wasn't thinking of that, but of the sense of comradeship we shared. No matter what else has happened we are still friends, are we not, infant?''

Corisande nodded quickly, not trusting her voice.

At that moment Turnbull announced supper and Corisande didn't know whether to be glad or sorry when they were parted in the general move towards the dining-room. She loved him so dearly that she didn't know if she could stand the strain of being nothing more than his friend, but it was the most she could hope for, so she would have to steel herself to bear it.

Fanny was delighted by the way her impromptu party was turning out. Everyone appeared to be enjoying themselves and the mood around the table was relaxed, with the conversation flowing as easily as her choice of fine wines.

The Marquis exchanged an amused glance with his cousin when Miss Marlow launched into an animated story that set everyone laughing. Tom's face mirrored his own disbelief. It was still hard for him to credit Augusta with a secret passion, but at least he could now begin to understand why Drummond wanted to marry her. The transformation of the Iceberg was miraculous!

"Do not linger too long or we shall not forgive you, gentlemen," Fanny announced with a smile as she gave the signal for the ladies to withdraw when the meal was over.

Once the port was circulating, Mr. Clifford said, "I must thank you, my lord, for your care of my daughter. I shudder to think what might have befallen her if she had met up with a rogue like Orsett on leaving Lady Maltby's employ."

The Marquis accepted this gratitude with some embarrassment, which he turned off by saying quickly, "If you should not mind relating it, sir, I should like to hear about your adventure. You said something last night about a trek into the interior, I believe?"

Mr. Clifford nodded. "I was in search of rare plants, as you know," he began, not realising that the very same subject was being discussed at that moment in the drawing-room.

"Look," said Corisande. "These are some of the diamonds King Moroka gave Papa as a reward for saving the life of his favourite son." She had just removed a worn leather pouch from her reticule and now she shook out the contents on to the surface of one of Fanny's small card-tables.

Gussy picked up the largest of the stones. "It feels rather soapy and it is so dull."

Corisande smiled and, picking up another one, held it up to the light. There was a sudden flash of fire, a promise hidden in the heart of the diamond that correct cutting would eventually release.

"How odd to think that these may one day form a sparkling necklace," Fanny remarked, running her fingers lightly over the several stones that remained on the table.

"I know, they look so uninteresting at the moment," Corisande agreed. "Papa said that King Moroka didn't seem to realise that they were valuable and only bothered to collect because they made handy counters for his gambling games." She grinned. "Some of his wives used the shiniest stones as decoration. They stuck them into the fat they used to smear on their bodies. Only fancy!"

"And it was Hector who advised your Papa that they might be real diamonds, I understand," Gussy contributed proudly.

"Yes, the King had clay pots full of them and he let Papa take his pick."

Fanny was still examining the other stones with fascinated interest. "Mr. Clifford told me that he has taken the biggest ones to Storr and Mortimer in Regent Street. These are to go to Rundell and Bridge, and then he will consider offers from both jewellers."

"Papa says that the opinion is that they may be worth as much as forty thousand pounds!" Corisande shook her bright head. "I have scarcely taken it all in yet."

"No wonder, my dear." Fanny put an arm around her shoulders. "It has been a shock."

"But a pleasant one." Corisande's smile was sunny as she began to gather up the diamonds. "It is very comforting to know one is not an orphan after all!"

"I declare I could almost wish myself one." Gussy's fair skin flooded with embarrassed colour. She had dragged the story of her father's perfidy out of Corisande after Fanny had unthinkingly made a tart remark about Sir Lucius when they had returned to the drawing-room.

Corisande had tried to conceal the worst, but Gussy had been very shocked and angry. Producing the diamonds had been an attempt to distract her, but it was obvious she was still feeling the humiliation very deeply. "I don't think I ever wish to speak to either of them again. If Papa dares say a word about *my* questionable behaviour—"

"Hush, my dear, you must not upset yourself so," Fanny said soothingly, inwardly boggling at this change in a girl who had always seemed devoid of any real feelings.

"I beg pardon." Gussy shook her head. "I'm behaving like some tragedy queen, when it was Corisande who suffered such distressing hardship."

"Well, I shall not pretend it was in the least pleasant, but maybe it will teach me not to be so foolhardy in the future." Corisande smiled, dispelling the tension. "But to speak of genuine suffering, I must ask you not to mention my papa's imprisonment by the Baralongs to anyone. He has a horror of becoming the subject of cheap gossip."

"But I thought he stayed with the tribe because of his injured leg," Fanny said with a slight air of puzzlement. "Was that not the case?"

"At first, yes, but when the broken bone finally mended King Moroka would not let him leave. Papa offered him half his oxen in exchange for his freedom, but he refused. He is quite capricious, Papa says, and considered that Papa belonged to him because the tribe had found him lying delirious amid the wreckage of his waggon and saved his life. One of the old women nursed him back to health and though he swears he was lucky, because his leg did not become infected, I'm sure such primitive treatments must have been agony."

Fanny shivered. "I have noticed he has a slight limp. I suppose it did not heal quite straight."

"Will your Papa give up his travels now, do you think, Corisande?" asked Augusta.

"He has said he intends to settle in Portugal, Gussy. Our climate is too cold for him after so long in Africa and he has several friends there." Her fingers played nervously with the fringe of her silk shawl. "Papa is an excellent linguist, of course, and used to living in foreign places, but I am not sure if I shall be happy in Portugal. It is probably very selfish of me, but I do not think I want to accompany him there."

"You may make your home with me for as long as you like," Fanny cried, catching hold of her hand and giving it a little comforting squeeze.

"Thank you, but Papa has already told me that if I wish to remain in London he will find a suitable house and chaperon for me so that I may continue to enjoy a fashionable life. Certainly there is no need now for me to look for employment!"

Corisande's voice faltered as she remembered how she had told the Marquis that she meant to be a governess in Cornwall. It had been her only defence! She knew how much he wanted her and in that moment she had realised he must love her a little, too, or he would not have humbled his pride. But she had rejected him once more, though it had almost broken her heart to do so.

The possibility of anything other than friendship is all over for us, she thought sadly. Marc was telling me tonight that he understood that I will not accept any offer of his. He will not ask me to love him ever again. Despair swept over her at the realisation. Perhaps Portugal would not be so terrible after all, if the alternative was to breathe the same air as Marc, knowing that this pain would never end.

IN THE DINING-ROOM Mr. Clifford was concluding his tale. "I doubt if I would have had the nerve to save that child from drowning if I hadn't been out of my head again with fever, for though I was a good swimmer in my youth there were crocodiles in that river." He chuckled. "That's why the King let me have the pick of his possessions. His own people were too afraid to attempt it, even though the boy was Moroka's favourite son."

He gave a self-deprecatory shrug. "My bravery was nothing of the sort, but it impressed the King and made him willing to give me my freedom when Hector turned up at the kraal."

"How did you know Mr. Clifford was there?" asked Tom, who was fascinated.

"We heard rumours of a white man living with the Baralongs," Hector replied. "However, it was impossible to send anyone to see if the story was true until my relief came up from the Cape. Ours was only a small Mission Station, you understand."

"You spent all your time in Africa as a missionary?" questioned the Marquis.

"Most of it. My uncle found me the position soon after I landed in Cape Town, but, to be honest, the life did not really suit me. Once I heard that I had a promise of a living here in England I asked to be replaced. However, it seemed worthwhile investigating such an extraordinary rumour before I left."

"I was lucky you did. I should never have managed the trip to the Cape on my own," Mr. Clifford stated. "Without your help I would have died before I got there."

A fierce blush rose to the roots of Hector's sandy hairline as he disclaimed this praise.

At first glance he was not a very prepossessing figure and his manner was rather awkward and lacking in social polish but, watching how those bright hazel eyes gleamed with intelligence and determination, the Marquis decided that there was a lot more to Hector Drummond than appearances indicated. His slight frame was deceptively wiry and there was an energy about him that was compelling. Marc could quite see what had attracted Augusta Marlow to so unlikely a suitor.

When the gentlemen returned to the drawing-room Fanny asked if anyone would like to play cards, but this suggestion was rejected in favour of some music. Fanny began with a sonata on the pianoforte, followed by a duet with Tom. Hector then took his turn, singing a rousing sea-shanty in a surprisingly tuneful voice before Gussy was persuaded to play a short piece, which she did with considerable skill.

Fanny turned to Corisande to ask her to sing for them.

"You have such a beautiful voice, my dear, but you are too shy normally to show off your talents. But here you are among true friends, so won't you oblige us?" she coaxed.

Corisande smiled. "My voice is nothing compared to the way Grandmama could sing, is it, Papa?"

"She sang like a golden nightingale," Mr. Clifford agreed with a reminiscent smile.

Seeing Fanny would not be put off, Corisande laughingly admitted, "Well, my singing is better than my playing. That is on a par with Letty's—or has your sister improved lately, Tom?"

Tom shook his head. "No such luck," he grinned.

"It is a very long time since I have had the pleasure of hearing you sing, my dear," said Mr. Clifford and this appeal won the day.

A hush fell upon the company as Corisande's pure voice poured out into the room and the Marquis listened in astonishment. He had never suspected his little love had such a marvellous talent and it suddenly occurred to him that his father, who was a great connoisseur of music, would have appreciated this treat.

A storm of applause greeted the end of her song and the clamour for another brought a blush to Corisande's cheeks.

"Very well, just one more," she agreed shyly.

"Drink to me only with thine eyes,
And I will pledge with mine;
Or leave a kiss but in the cup,
And I'll not look for wine..."

The haunting words of Ben Jonson's "To Celia" filled the silence with the pleasure and pain of love. This old favourite was an unconscious choice, but no one in the room doubted that she sang from the heart.

Marc could not take his eyes off her and as their gazes met it was as though they kissed.

Wishing she had never suggested that Corisande should sing, Fanny happened to catch the glance of Mr. Clifford. He raised his eyebrows at her, but there was a sympathetic understanding in his expression and her discomfort fled. No one could blame her beloved brother for this impossible situation. He had not asked to fall in love with Corisande. In affairs of the heart one did not always have the luxury of choice.

LATER THAT EVENING, strolling home with his cousin, the Marquis discussed the amazing reappearance of Mr. Clifford.

Tom was elated. "Uncle Montague will have to cry off," he remarked.

"I'll lay you anything you like he will simply switch his demand to another bride of his choosing," Marc retorted.

It was a wager Tom was not prepared to take. "I suppose so," he answered gloomily, but cheered up when his cousin invited him in for a nightcap of hot rum punch.

The Marquis was preparing to boil the kettle, but he turned to look sharply at his cousin when Tom said, "At least Clifford's return solves the problem of Corisande's future. I heard him telling Fanny that they were going to live in Portugal."

"Did he say when?" Marc asked a shade too casually, as he busied himself getting out the sugar and lemons he needed.

"No, but I got the impression he meant as soon as he had settled his affairs and sold those diamonds to the highest bidder. Jupiter, did you ever see their like?"

The Marquis nodded absently as he sliced a lemon in half and measured out the rum. Why had Corisande not told him? Did he mean so little to her after all, in spite of the way she had sung that song?

Tom was chattering on in his usual cheerful fashion about Mrs. Lavenham's plans to pay him a brief visit before she and Letty went on to spend the summer at Worthing.

"Letty would prefer Brighton, of course, but Mama won't budge. Says Brighton is too raffish. Lord, but she will be put out to learn that every word of Corisande's story was true, when she kept insisting it was all a hum!" Tom laughed heartily.

Marc winced. Mrs. Lavenham was not the only one who had behaved like a fool. "Tom . . . do you think that Corisande might have been deliberately flirting with Harry Vernon to open Fanny's eyes to the truth of her own feelings?" he demanded abruptly, giving voice to the suspicion which had been haunting him for days.

Tom stared at him thoughtfully and took a moment to consider his answer. "It's possible," he said slowly. "Aye, I think you are right." Tom nodded emphatically. "Fanny is wary of marriage, not that you can blame her after Jack Linton, but I think she's finally begun to realise that Harry is the right man for her."

"You don't think Corisande is attracted to him, in earnest, then? I wondered if she might be," said Marc, squeezing lemons into the silver punchbowl as if his life depended on it.

"What poppycock!" Tom eyed his cousin with a bland innocence. "Took a notion tonight that she was in love with you, coz," he murmured, and had to hide his satisfied grin at his cousin's eager response.

A fragrant aroma arose from the bowl as the Marquis stirred his mixture with a long-handled spoon and pronounced it ready. He ladled it into two glasses and handed one to Tom before taking his own and sitting in his favourite chair with a dreamy smile on his lips and a far away look in his eyes.

"What time do you intend to set out for your race tomorrow?" Tom said bringing Marc back down to earth with a bump. "They are laying heavy bets on it in the clubs."

"I wish I had never challenged Harry," burst out his lordship. "It was a damned fool thing to do, when I was clear of debt for the first time this year."

"The 'green-ey'd monster', eh, coz?" remarked Tom, displaying an unexpected scholarship.

"Shakespeare, Tom? I am speechless with admiration."

"Gammon!" Tom retorted. "Learned it at Harrow," he added with a deprecating cough to explain this piece of erudition. "Never thought I would remember any of it, but it just goes to show!"

He hesitated and then decided to pursue the point. "You were jealous, of Harry, I mean, weren't you?"

Marc nodded. "I could have killed him," he said simply.

Tom shuddered. "Thank God you didn't! What a dust-up that would have caused, Fanny wouldn't have spoken to you!"

The Marquis roared with laughter and Tom joined in when he realised what he'd said. When they had recovered they needed another glass of punch and Marc got up to ladle it out.

"Still, the harm's been done, I can't back out now." Marc's gaze brightened. "Harry's Firebird is a lovely creature, but not up to Samson's weight, I fancy!"

A vigorous nod greeted this pronouncement. "It should be a devil of a race," Tom declared enthusiastically, almost wishing he stood in his cousin's shoes. "Harry is a bruising rider and too game to cry off, although I'm pretty sure he knows why you challenged him."

"Good God, so he must!" said the Marquis faintly. "I shall have to hope he will forgive me, since there is no way we can mend matters at this late hour."

The thought of defaulting on a wager made Tom blanch. "No, by Jove, there isn't!"

CHAPTER SIXTEEN

UNFORTUNATELY for Sir Harry Vernon's hopes, the following day was also showery. Corisande viewed the rain through the breakfast-parlour window with a sigh. It was impossible to summon up any appetite and she took her place at the table to nibble at a piece of bread and butter, which she left unfinished, before drifting into the morning-room.

Fanny's copy of *Glenarvon,* Lady Caroline Lamb's recent novel, lay on the rosewood tripod table. Corisande picked it up. It had caused quite a scandal, since it made fun of certain prominent members of society, but Corisande thought it rather silly and melodramatic. She put it down with a sigh, doubting anything could hold her interest for long this morning.

Fanny did not appear and Corisande suspected she was putting off the moment when, racked by worry, she would have to face the world and pretend nothing was wrong.

When I see Harry, Corisande thought, I shall tell him that I think this is the moment to try his luck. It is quite obvious Fanny is at last ready to acknowledge that she is in love with him.

Corisande would be very glad to end the deception and confess her part in it. The colour stole into her face as she wondered how the Marquis would receive the news. She had longed to tell him the truth, but she could not break Harry's confidence.

Somehow the morning was passed. Fanny finally emerged looking pale, but composed. She asked if Mr. Clifford was to visit, but Corisande told her he was busy, conferring with Mr. Thruxton, who had come up post-haste from Oxford, but Hector came to call on them and Gussy was another visitor. Hector's principles were too nice to permit him to entertain Gussy in private and Fanny had kindly agreed to let them meet at her house.

Fanny invited them to stay and eat luncheon, but Hector informed her that he had hired a tilbury to drive Augusta out to Highgate to watch the start of the Marquis's race. He asked if she and Corisande would like to accompany them and Fanny blanched.

"No, oh, no, I couldn't bear to watch it," she gasped and then recovering her composure turned to Corisande and told her that she must go if she wished.

Corisande longed to go, but it seemed unkind to leave her hostess. Noticing her hesitation, Fanny insisted and ordered the meal to be served early so that they could get off in good time.

Corisande went upstairs afterwards to put on the silk spencer which matched her pale blue tricot de Berlin gown and a most becoming bonnet with a high-poke lined in gathered silk of the same celestial blue as her eyes. When she was ready they bade Fanny goodbye and set off.

When they arrived at the Spaniards inn at the top of Highgate Hill, Corisande was surprised to see what a large crowd had gathered. They were lucky enough to manoeuvre into an excellent position and sat waiting for the contestants to arrive. Sir Harry was the first, on his glossily beautiful mare, and Corisande admired Firebird's glorious, rippling ebony flanks. However, she quickly decided that the mare, who was prancing nervously, her great eyes rolling, might be too highly strung for such a venture.

Of the Marquis there was no sign, but it still lacked some ten minutes to the appointed hour.

"I think I'll just go and see if I can catch a glimpse of Lord Dene. I'll be back in a moment," Corisande announced impatiently.

She felt as if she would scream if she sat still for a moment longer. Hector was too busy conversing with a man on their right to notice, but Gussy emitted a squeak of protest. "Wait, Corisande. Please, you must not..."

Corisande ignored this plea. The impulse to snatch a moment alone with Marc if she could was too strong to resist. She desperately wanted to wish him luck, knowing how much the race meant to him and aware he would never have suggested the wager if not for her.

After some active elbow-work she managed to win through the throng and stood surveying the road. Her vigilance had just been rewarded by the sight of the Marquis astride a big raking grey and accompanied by Mr. Lavenham when a voice spoke respectfully in her ear.

"Miss Corisande Clifford?"

She turned to see a tall man clad in sober riding-dress. "Yes, I am Miss Clifford," she assented rather impatiently.

"I have a message for you. It concerns Lady Linton."

There was nothing to alarm Corisande in the man's appearance. His air was entirely respectable, his bow deferential and his manner refined. He glanced disdainfully at the nearest spectators within easy earshot and moved away slightly. "A private message, miss."

"What is it? Is Lady Linton feeling ill?" demanded Corisande jumping to conclusions in her impulsive way.

The man nodded. He moved away from the crowd; again Corisande followed him automatically. "Do please tell me!" she exclaimed.

He bowed again and then, as he straightened, exclaimed, "Oh, miss, a bee on your collar!" And before she knew it he had closed with her and his strong fingers were grasping the velvet collar of her spencer. At the same time she felt something sharp pressing against her ribs and heard his voice whisper, "Stay silent, miss. If you scream I'll be forced to use this knife. Now nod if you understand me."

She nodded, her mouth dry with sudden terror.

"Take my arm and we will walk towards that carriage over there. Just act natural, miss, and there'll be nothing to worry either of us."

Corisande obeyed him and moved at his side on legs that trembled. "That's it, miss," the man said, still employing the same oddly respectful tone.

"Are you in Lord Marlow's employ?" Corisande forced the words through her stiff lips.

"I'm not at liberty to say, miss," was the unhelpful response.

It did not reassure Corisande, who could not think of anyone else who might wish her harm. They reached the plain closed carriage and the knife at her side was removed.

Sheer terror gave her the sudden strength to wrench away from the grip on her arm, preparatory to making a dash for freedom, but the man was too alert.

Before she could scream or take another step he had clamped one large hand over her mouth and almost in the same movement swung her up off her feet. The next instant Corisande was thrust into the dark interior of the waiting chaise.

IT WAS WELL KNOWN that the Marquis of Dene had an eye for a pretty woman. The slender female form clad in blue on the outskirts of the crowd which had gathered to watch his race caught his attention as he rode towards the inn and he interrupted his discourse with Tom Lavenham to remark upon the excellence of her figure.

They rode a little closer and the Marquis exclaimed with a chuckle, "Good God, it's Corisande! Isn't it, Tom?"

"I think so, yes. Fanny must have nerved herself to watch you after all."

"I don't see her." A note of concern entered Marc's voice. "Tom, do you know that fellow Corisande is talking to? The Devil take it, I hope she hasn't come here without an escort!"

These words had scarcely left his mouth when they saw Corisande take the stranger's arm and begin to walk off with him in the opposite direction. Loud cheering arose at this moment as they were spotted and several people began to run towards them.

"I can't see...Tom, can you make out...why is Corisande getting into that chaise?" The Marquis shouted above the din, ignoring the acclamation to turn a baffled look upon his cousin.

"I can't see anything for this press," muttered Tom, his attention on controlling his mount. "Stand away there, my good fellow," he exclaimed as someone came too close, making his young horse, one of Solomon's offspring, rear nervously.

The Marquis returned the greetings of his friends, but his attention was taken up in trying to keep the carriage in view. When the man jumped in and it drove off at high speed his eyebrows met in a black-barred frown.

"Damn it, Tom, I don't like this!" His instinct was to go chasing after the carriage, but it was impossible to resist the dense tide of humanity bearing them towards the starting point where Harry was waiting.

The noise was tremendous. People had poured in by the hundred to see who would win. Lord Dene was the favourite, but many had backed Sir Harry. A breeze had got up, fluttering the skirts of the ladies and vendors wandered about selling hot pies, sweetmeats and ale. A carnival atmosphere prevailed in spite of the grey skies. Modish costumes, rough homespun and farmers' smocks all mingled, while children and dogs ran round everywhere in mad noisy circles.

Marc saluted Harry and the baronet raised a hand in acknowledgement. "A tidy crowd, my lord," he called, a wide grin splitting his homely face as his strong hands held in Firebird's tapering.

"Have you seen Fanny?" Marc shouted back but Harry shook his head.

The Marquis's frown deepened. Tom, who had fallen behind came up. "I've just spoken to Augusta Marlow. Corisande gave her and Drummond the slip and he is out looking for her now."

Marc's dark eyes flashed. At that moment the starter raised his flag and a hush fell over the crowd. Excited faces turned to fix their gaze upon the white handkerchief snapping in the breeze.

In that breathless moment his lordship swore loudly. "Orsett! By God, he's had her abducted!"

Tom's startled face turned to him. "Marc, you don't know...you can't! The race...Marc, you madman!"

The flag fluttered to the ground. Firebird leapt forward galloping down the hill but, to everyone's utter astonishment, the Marquis of Dene hauled the big grey's head round and Samson went plunging through the crowd in the opposite direction.

ALL THAT WAS IMPORTANT was the surge of powerful muscles beneath him, the thunder of hoofs and the thought of the carriage ahead. There was a toll at Highgate Archway and a gig pulling up before it, the fresh-faced young groom blowing his yard of tin with great enthusiasm for the pikeman to come and open the gates.

The owner of the gig fumbled for his purse and painstakingly found the correct fee. Fuming with impatience, the Marquis decided he could brook the delay no longer. He shot between the narrow gap twixt the vehicle and the gatekeeper, flinging a guinea at the man with a shouted warning. Murmuring encouragement to Samson, he tightened his knees and leant forward and man and beast went soaring over the gate as if they were flying in one beautiful co-ordinated movement.

Indignant gobbling from the elderly gig-driver, admiring laughter from the groom, and cries of, "Sir, your change!" followed him, but Marc paid no heed and galloped on. The road was thick with mud, but crouching low in the saddle Marc urged Samson to a greater speed and felt the horse gallantly respond. He patted the grey neck, his spirits rising. The coach could not be far in front of him, he must come up with it soon.

A large herd of cattle suddenly filling the road ahead was a setback to this optimism. The drover who was herding them down to Smithfield shrugged phlegmatically at Marc's frantic curses. He was forced to pick his way through the confusion, swearing furiously at this loss of precious time. At last he was free and picking up speed as he reached Finchley Common, too angry to give any thought to its possible lurking dangers as Samson sped on in hot pursuit.

"Damnation, where is the curst thing!" Marc strained his eyes, but could see nothing that resembled the vehicle he wanted. With grim determination he carried on, but he could feel Samson beginning to tire. His hat had gone, whipped away by the wind, a wind which was blowing drops of rain into his face with increasing ferocity. Rain, which would only add to the sticky mud clinging like glue to Samson's burnished hoofs and plastering Marc's boots and breeches.

Barnet was the first main stage from London and as he cantered into the town Marc was already debating where the chaise would have halted. The Green Man and the Red Lion were the most noted houses, catering exclusively for the gentry, where best change of horses could be hired. Knowing that the driver of the chaise must have sprung 'em to stay ahead of him, Marc was sure that the weary beasts must be spent and changed here rather than anywhere further along the road.

He drew a blank at the Red Lion and rode out of its yard cursing at the wasted minutes he'd spent in trying to get some sense out of the various servitors he'd interviewed, but in the end none of them remembered seeing the chaise he wanted. The Green Man was further up the street and his shouted question to an ostler produced the welcome response that, yes, a private chaise drawn by four handsome bays had pulled in about ten minutes ago.

The Marquis sprang down from the saddle and thrust the reins into the ostler's hand. "Take good care of him," he ordered tersely and strode into the inn.

"Landlord...landlord! Damn it...ah, there you are. The chaise which arrived just now, where is the owner? Quick now, man!"

The landlord bowed obsequiously. Lord Dene might be hat-less and plastered in mud, but the innkeeper knew an aristocrat when he saw one. "The gentleman is upstairs. He hired a chamber and my best private parlour, sir."

"Take me to him," Marc ordered. "Hurry, fellow, I have business with him and I haven't got all day to waste."

"Yes, sir, immediately, sir. Jem, show this gentleman up to number twelve."

Jem, a middle-aged dreamer in a waiter's apron, cherished his own ideas as to the suitable pace to maintain up the leg-wearying stairs and it was all the Marquis could do not to thrust a booted foot up Jem's plump backside to hasten it. Instead, he pushed a coin into the man's hand as they reached the room and said curtly, "Thank you. My business is private, you need not wait."

Jem nodded and, sniffing catarrhally, padded off back down the stairs, leaving Marc to knock sharply upon the door. No one answered and he hammered it again relentlessly.

"Coming! I'm coming!" a testy voice called.

Even as the door opened the Marquis was shouldering his way into the room. It was empty save for a corpulent young man clad in a dazzling silk dressing-gown and smelling strongly of attar of roses and scented hair pomade.

"Sir, what is the meaning of this outrage?"

Marc, blind to everything except that Corisande might be in danger, swung round, his expression ferocious. "Where is she?" He grasped the man's arm in one lightning swift movement, forcing it up behind the silk-clad back. "Answer me, damn you, or I'll break it," he growled savagely.

The protuberant gooseberry-coloured eyes popped. "Sir, are you mad? I demand to know...oh my arm! You are hurting me, damn your soul!"

The Marquis vouchsafed no answer to this petulant cry, but his eyes began to glitter dangerously. "You have a girl here. Are you going to talk or am I going to have the pleasure of breaking every bone in your body, you fat flawn?"

Gobbling and spluttering with indignation, the portly exquisite pointed to the closed door of the adjoining bedroom. "She's in there. But if I'd known there was going to be all this pother I'd have never taken up with the wench! No, no matter what she promised!"

Scarcely hearing a word of this, the Marquis ignored him and strode single-mindedly across the room to fling open the door. A feminine squeal greeted this action and he gazed in total stupefaction at the half-undressed young woman thus revealed. Impossibly brassy blonde curls rioted in profusion about the pretty painted face and a vulgarly bright striped gown lay in folds about her feet. A string of very ungenteel curses smote the air as the beauty snatched up her discarded petticoat to veil her opulent charms from his bewildered gaze.

"Good God!" said the Marquis faintly.

CORISANDE CAME to herself slowly. Nausea threatened to overwhelm her and for a few moments she lay with closed eyes. By degrees she shook off the effects of the drug and struggled to sit up, her hand going to her head, which was aching. She looked about her and discovered that she was alone, lying on a bed in a dimly lit room. Someone had removed her bonnet and spencer and taken off her shoes, but otherwise she was fully dressed and uninjured.

There was a jug of water and a glass on a small table next to the bed and she reached for it eagerly. Remembering caution, she sniffed it suspiciously, but it seemed untainted and she drank a little, for her mouth tasted vile and she was desperately thirsty.

Bit by bit her memory returned.

After pushing her into the coach that dreadful man had climbed in beside her and before she knew what he was about had thrust a flask to her lips. She had struggled, aided by the rocking of the chaise as it rumbled into swift motion, but he had pinched her nose tightly and in opening her mouth she had involuntarily swallowed.

"And slept, I suppose, since I can't remember anything more!" Corisande exclaimed aloud. "Whatever it was, it must have been strong, I think." She got up and found that her legs worked, although they felt a little shaky and she moved to the window, which was draped in heavy velvet curtains. Drawing them aside, Corisande experienced shock. "Heavens, it must be tomorrow!"

Glancing round wildly, she saw an ormolu clock upon the mantelpiece, showing the hour of eight. This evidence confirmed the position of the sun in the morning sky.

Corisande's bewildered gaze travelled around the room. She willed her brain to function and gradually she took in the rich furnishings and the air of elegant luxury.

"No inn, but the home of a wealthy man, I think." She chewed thoughtfully at her lower lip. Lord Marlow must have persuaded someone, perhaps Sir Lucius, to make another, more successful attempt to remove her from the scene. He would soon discover it had been a waste of time. Gussy had intended to tell her family of Hector's return after the race.

"But I shall have to make shift for myself in the meantime." She turned back to the window. She was on an upper storey and there was no hope this time of climbing down, that stone was too smooth.

Corisande's mouth set in a grim line and resolutely she moved towards the door, but before she reached it she heard footsteps outside and sped back to fling herself upon the bed and feign sleep. Someone entered quietly and through virtually closed eyelids Corisande saw that it was a neatly garbed maidservant.

She tip-toed closer and then began to back silently away so Corisande sat up abruptly. "Don't go yet!"

"Oh, miss, what a fright you gave me. I thought you was asleep." A country burr thickened the girl's voice but her pleasant face was wreathed in a smile of welcome.

Corisande was puzzled, but demanded, "Who are you and where is Sir Lucius?"

"I'm Kate, miss, but I don't know of any Sir Lucius. Oh but you was poorly when you arrived last night, miss. You had to be carried in from the coach and Mrs. Merivale, that's the housekeeper, said as how you might not be feeling quite yourself this morning. We had orders to keep a watch on you and to send for the doctor if you took worse."

Corisande's bewilderment increased. The girl looked honest enough, but none of this made sense. Marlow couldn't care less about her well-being. Why should he have given such orders?

"If Sir Lucius isn't here, then I want to speak to Lord Marlow or his representative," she said, trying to sound confident.

"Begging your pardon, miss, I've never heard of such a gentleman." Kate's expression was apologetic.

"Then, for God's sake, what am I doing here!" Corisande burst out. She raised her hand to her aching head. "I'm sorry, I should not have shouted, but I don't understand. I don't even know where I am."

"I suspicioned you was feeling mazed! Why don't you lie back and have a nice rest," Kate suggested in a soothing tone.

If her head hadn't felt as if it were splitting Corisande would have screamed in frustration. Instead she sank back against the lace-trimmed pillows and sighed. Either the girl knew nothing or she was a better liar than she looked, but there was no point in continuing to argue.

"Would you like some tea, miss?" Kate made the offer hesitantly. "Or mebbe some hot chocolate?"

"Thank you, tea would be very welcome." If she had somehow strayed into a lunatic asylum, at least she was to be treated kindly! "Do you think I could have some hot water for washing as well?"

"Of course, miss. I'll fetch it up directly." Kate looked pleased at the way events were settling to a normal routine. "And mebbe you'd like me to press your gown for you while you drink your tea?"

Corisande accepted. It was all she could do except be ready to escape when the chance arose.

EMERGING FROM the Green Man, the Marquis of Dene was hailed by his cousin and Sir Harry Vernon, who came cantering into the innyard at a breakneck pace.

"Tom . . . and Harry! What are you doing here? I had expected you to be in Hampstead by now."

"What and leave you to stand buff without my helping hand? Shame on you, man, you want to keep all the adventure to yourself!" Harry's tone was deliberately light, but the Marquis was touched by his show of comradeship.

"But the race," he murmured. "I forfeited—"

"Damn the race! Corisande's safety is worth a hundred such wagers," Harry interrupted. "As for forfeits, I had barely gone a quarter of a mile before I realised that there was no sign of you and knew something must have gone wrong. So I turned back and Tom told me what had happened."

He grinned. "We managed to square it with the judges and came after you as soon as we could. So neither of us completed the course, my lord."

The twinkle in his eyes brightened. "We can run it again, man, on another day if you've still got a mind to test that mangy brute against my Firebird. But for different stakes, eh? Agreed?"

"Agreed!" The Marquis held out his hand. "Forgive my curst temper, Harry. I had no business forcing you to accept such a wager."

Harry thought that he'd done equally stupid things himself in the name of jealousy, but decided it was more prudent not to say so as he accepted the apology and they shook hands.

"Did you come up with that chaise, Marc?" Tom's question brought them swiftly back to the matter in hand.

When the Marquis had finished his explanation his dark complexion was tinged with unaccustomed colour and his two friends were helpless with laughter.

"Jupiter, I'd give a hundred pounds to have seen your face!" Tom choked.

A crooked grin answered him. "It was devilish awkward, I can tell you. What with trying to apologise to that coxcomb and the doxy screeching fit to bring the rafters down!" A shudder ran through his tall frame. "I don't think I ever want to set foot in Barnet again."

They soon sobered as they began to discuss where the chaise could have vanished to.

"Unless they switched carriages they must have turned off here. They cannot have gone any further without fresh horses," Tom said.

"Unless I missed them earlier on the road somewhere, but damn it, I'm sure I didn't," Marc frowned.

"It might be worth a try checking all the other inns," Harry suggested.

"Aye, but quicker if we all split up and rendezvous later," nodded Marc.

When they met up at the agreed point they discovered that the time had not been wasted. Tom had picked up a clue. Sir Lucius Orsett had passed through the town a short while ago and was thought to be heading north.

"I'm going follow Orsett," the Marquis said grimly.

"Then I shall come with you," Tom declared, with Harry swiftly seconding him.

"Harry, Fanny will be frantic for news. Perhaps it would be better if you returned to town," the Marquis suggested. A smile touched his worried face for an instant. "If I were you, I'd take the opportunity to settle my differences with the silly baggage. It's high time the pair of you had the banns announced!"

"Thank you, the same thought had occurred to me," Harry grinned. "Good luck and Godspeed your safe return with Corisande."

He did not delay them further. They did not need his help, but Marc was right. Corisande's friends would be frantic with worry and he had best get back to London as fast as he could.

He reached Hill Street just in time to see Hector and Gussy descending the steps of Fanny's house.

"Sir Harry, have you any news?" Gussy flew to meet him.

"Not a great deal, I'm afraid," he replied and told them all that had occurred. "Do you think we should try and conceal the matter from Mr. Clifford?" he added anxiously. "You know more about him than any of us, Drummond. Will his health stand the shock?"

Hector frowned. "I do not think we have the right to hide the truth from him, but you are right, sir, in supposing that it will strain his resources. Perhaps it would be better if I broke the news to him?"

Harry had no objections to this plan and Gussy went on to say she had every faith in the Marquis before she and Hector made their farewells, leaving him to enter the house they had just left.

Lady Linton did not appear to share this confidence. Her face was drawn and her eyes were shadowed, but to Harry she had never looked lovelier as her frown changed to a smile of welcome when he walked into the room.

"Harry! Oh, thank God you have come!" She cast herself into his arms and burst into tears.

By degrees he was able to calm her and restore her to a more cheerful frame of mind once her worst fears were allayed. He dried her face with his handkerchief and led her to sit down with him upon a sofa. "You mustn't agitate yourself, it will be all right," he soothed.

"Thank you." Fanny was suddenly shy. "You will think me bird-witted!"

"Never," he promised.

"I pray Marc will be able to bring her off safely. I am very fond of her, you know."

"She's a sweet girl, full of pluck to the backbone."

Fanny swallowed hard, her expression clouding with dismay. Any moment now he was going to tell her he loved Corisande and she could not bear it!

Harry decided it was now or never. "I'm very fond of Corisande too," he began.

"Oh, don't!" Fanny stared at him, unable to continue for the lump in her throat.

"But I don't love her," Harry ignored the interruption. "You are the only woman I have ever loved, Fanny."

"But I thought you wanted Corisande!" Fanny gasped, releasing the breath she didn't even know she had been holding.

"I've a confession to make. I wanted you to believe I was in love with Corisande." Harry gave her a faintly rueful smile. "You had fallen into the habit of taking me for granted and so when Corisande suggested the ruse I leapt at the chance to prove I wasn't some lap-dog to be petted or kicked aside at whim.''

Fanny coloured painfully. ''I treated you abominably,'' she admitted. ''But I didn't realise at first that I had come to care for you. When Jack died I swore I would never love again. I was scared of being hurt, but then while I was in Italy I discovered that I missed you. It frightened me to think how much I enjoyed your company, how much I depended upon you.''

She raised her eyes to his. ''I didn't want to admit I was in love with you.''

A radiant smile lit up Harry's homely face. He had waited a long time to hear her say she cared, but it was worth it!

''But once Corisande came to be my guest my coolness did not seem to matter to you.'' An indignant sparkle brightened Fanny's eyes. ''Do you mean to tell me that I need not have worried myself half to death, that your flirtation with her was all a trick—''

Sir Harry, who intended to tell her nothing of the sort, thinking the least said, the soonest mended, interrupted this promising tirade by taking his indignant love into his arms with a masterfulness she found as surprising as it was agreeable.

''All I mean to tell you, my dearest goose, is that I love you and must marry you as soon as it can be arranged or lose what little sanity I have retained!''

Whereupon he began to kiss her and Fanny forgot her aggravation in the pleasurable task of convincing him that his obliging sentiments were wholly reciprocated.

CHAPTER SEVENTEEN

"ONE MOMENT, dear creature," said a soft voice. "You require the key."

Corisande whirled to face the man entering the conservatory at a leisurely pace.

"I always keep the outer doors locked. So many undesirables roaming the countryside and my plants are my passion. Do you admire exotic specimens, Miss Clifford?"

"No, I do not." Corisande moved away from the glass door and the tantalising glimpse of freedom it had seemed to promise.

"A pity," mused the gentleman, who was dressed plainly, but in well-cut clothes. His hair was silver-grey and his figure thin, with nothing to distinguish his appearance but a pair of keenly intelligent blue eyes.

In one hand he carried a cane and as he came towards her Corisande saw that he leant upon it slightly. The sunlight streaming in through the enormous panes of glass which illuminated this magnificent conservatory also showed up the lines on his face and Corisande realised that he was older than she had first supposed.

"As you do not care for plants, shall we return to the salon?" He spoke with an air of calm authority which Corisande found difficult to dispute. She curtsied in dignified acquiescence and marched back into the nearby salon, which she had quit only moments before.

It was a beautiful room, tastefully decorated in gold and ivory, but Corisande was in no mood to appreciate its elegance. After she had dressed, breakfast had been brought to her in her room and then a footman had arrived to escort her here, through what had seemed miles of corridors and dozens of splendid staircases. She had waited for a moment or two in a bewildered and resentful silence before deciding to see if she had any avenue of escape, but her attempt had proved fruitless.

"Pray, do be seated. I find it fatiguing to stand, you see." The old gentleman offered this information with a mocking smile she found oddly familiar.

Feeling she could not very well refuse to obey, since he had put it in such a way, Corisande took her place upon a gold brocade sofa. He waited until she was seated and then lowered himself rather stiffly into a chair arranged directly opposite.

Corisande felt at a loss. Her anger was deep, but it had become overlaid with a nervous agitation in the last few minutes. His impassive face told her nothing and it seemed absurd to accuse such a dignified old man of having had her abducted. Yet it must be so! In spite of his unobtrusive dress there was no mistaking him for a mere underling, though she could no more fathom his reasons than she could fly.

"Sir, I must ask why I have been brought here," she began in a rapid voice.

She fell silent as he raised one white hand. "I cannot deny that you have the right to demand whatever answers you wish, Miss Clifford, but first I must beg your indulgence in allowing me to question you."

Corisande eyed him uneasily.

"I mean you no harm, child. If any of my servants caused you distress, I apologise. My orders were that you should be treated as gently as circumstances permitted."

Corisande sniffed indignantly, remembering the knife held to her ribs and the vile-tasting drink.

A faint smile touched his thin lips. "Ah, I see you remember everything. I must present William's fervent apologies and assure you that he would never have used that knife, no matter how it must have seemed at the time. A good man, but inclined to be a little over-zealous, I fear. He mentioned that your struggles were most spirited."

"I bit him hard," Corisande recalled with satisfaction. However, she was mollified by the apology and, losing some of her nervousness, she stared at her unknown host with her customary candid gaze. "Very well, sir, I'll answer your questions providing you promise in return to tell me the reason behind my abduction."

He nodded. "I shall do more, my dear. You have my word of honour that you may leave this house whenever you wish once this interview is over."

Her eyes flew to his in a startled look of interrogation. "I . . . I don't understand," she faltered.

"To begin, may I ask how you came to be under the protection of the Marquis of Dene?" said the gentleman, suavely ignoring her confusion.

Corisande jumped and then, realising her face must betray her, knew it was too late for any denial. "How did you learn of that? It is generally supposed I am Lady Linton's protégée."

"I have my methods and certain rumours reached me . . . but we have agreed, have we not, that I shall ask the questions?" was the smooth reply.

Corisande apologised meekly. She folded her hands in the lap of her blue gown and waited.

"Thank you. Perhaps you will tell the story from the beginning?"

"It is rather a strange one, sir. I should not like you to think I am lying," she warned.

"I fancy you are too honest to make a convincing liar, Miss Clifford, and so I believe your word may be trusted. Pray do not omit any details. I am not easily shocked."

With this encouragement Corisande launched into the morass of flight, deception, counter-deception and rescue which had attended her dealings with Lord Dene.

"Dear me," remarked the elderly gentleman mildly when her rapid account ended. "I had no idea such romance existed in the souls of the modern youth!" He felt for his quizzing-glass and raised it to survey her. "You have achieved what few persons manage these days. You have surprised me, Miss Clifford. I apprehend you are a female of great resource."

Corisande's dimples flashed. "Thank you, sir," she laughed. "Truly, it wasn't very romantic to be the butt of Mrs. Lavenham's condescension or to be obliged to climb down that vine when I had been locked in by Sir Lucius!"

"Ah, do not disappoint me." A slight smile warmed his cold gaze. "I have ever admired a woman of spirit."

His remark touched another elusive chord of memory. Corisande wished he would tell her his name, but she did not dare ask, realising he would raise his brows haughtily at such impertinence. She had the oddest feeling she had met him before, but she knew she could not have done so for he was not a man one would forget.

He opened his snuff-box and took out a pinch with delicate precision. "I deplore Orsett's lack of finesse, but do pray continue, my dear. What happened after the Marquis rescued you?"

"Oh, the oddest thing of all, sir." Corisande gave a little chuckle. "We met my Papa on the road to London returning home with a fortune in diamonds."

The hand closing the snuff-box checked. "I do not think my understanding is poor," the gentleman said pensively. "But surely you said your papa was dead?"

Corisande acknowledged it, but proceeded to explain how the reports had been inaccurate.

"I congratulate you, my dear. No doubt you shall find it entertaining to be an heiress and set the Polite World by the ears."

"I don't think I shall," Corisande replied quietly. "Papa wishes us to live in Portugal."

"And you, do you wish to live there, Miss Clifford?" A shake of her downcast head answered him. "Then shall you accept his lordship's offer of marriage?"

The red-gold head came up instantly. "You are very astute, sir!" she gasped. "I did not tell you that he had proposed to me..." Her voice faltered to a halt.

"Forgive me. I was not kind to trick you into confirming my suspicion was correct, but I needed to know the truth."

Corisande bit her lower lip. "I declined Lord Dene's offer. If he marries me he will be ruined!"

"But you are an heiress."

"You may mock, sir, but it is not an amusing situation for me," Corisande said hotly.

He inclined his silver head. "I beg your pardon. The role of a confidant is new to me." A satirical smile curved his thin lips, but Corisande received the impression it was directed at himself, not her.

"You have no family then, sir?"

He raised his quizzing-glass haughtily at this impulsive question, but then his expression softened and the glass was lowered as he regarded her blushing embarrassment.

"Shall we just say that my relationship with the members of my family has never been particularly intimate."

Corisande managed not to gape at him, but her expressive little face left no doubt that she considered this a very strange statement.

"Pray proceed. You were about to tell me why you will not marry the Marquis."

"Was I, sir?" Corisande gave him a very direct look but then she shrugged. "I suppose it does not matter now. I will not marry Marc because his father will disinherit him if he does not obey a command to wed another lady." A faint gleam of amusement lit Corisande's blue gaze. "Not that Marc could marry her even if he wished to do so! She has become engaged to the parson who accompanied my papa home. Indeed, you may well look surprised, sir, but it is an attachment of long-standing and there is no doubt that the marriage will go ahead."

The elderly gentleman appeared to recover from his astonishment. "You think this may throw a spoke in his grace's wheel?" he inquired.

"I hope it may," Corisande answered with a candid smile. "I am not acquainted with the Duke, but he seems monstrous unkind!"

"Really? You interest me, child. How did you form this unfavourable impression? Was it from something said by his grace's children, perhaps?"

"Oh, no! I think at heart both Marc and Fanny would welcome closer relations with their father. But he holds them off and treats them as mere chattels, to be directed at his will. My opinion rests on common gossip only, sir, but I suspect that the Duke is a very lonely and unhappy man, for all that he is so powerful. Respect and fear are no substitutes for love."

"You draw a convincing conclusion, Miss Clifford. I will not contradict you for I too am—er—acquainted with the Duke of Weston."

Corisande blanched. "I did not mean to criticise . . . that is . . . I—"

"Pray do not feel discomposed, my dear." He smiled at her with what appeared to be genuine amusement. "I can assure you that his grace would not take your remarks amiss. However, I must correct you on one point. No matter what he may have said to his son, when it came to it he would never disinherit him."

"No? Are you quite sure of that, sir?"

"Positive, Miss Clifford. It would be a very crude solution, and his grace deplores vulgarity."

"I see. Still, there can be little doubt he will soon seek another bride for the Marquis." A sigh escaped Corisande at the thought and, conscious of the sharp gaze scrutinising her, she averted her face to hide her heartbreak. "I should prefer not to discuss the Marquis any more, sir," she said in a small voice. "It is rather painful for me, you see."

He had been regarding her with a thoughtful frown, but Corisande did not see the satisfied smile which flickered over his narrow face at this request. "Very well, we shall leave the Marquis and his unknown bride, though undoubtedly she must be an heiress, and turn to the other matter which prompted me to have you brought here in, unfortunately, so rough and ready a fashion."

Corisande lifted her head. She had almost forgotten how she came to be here in this lovely sunlit room. "You need not dwell upon your guilt, sir. I don't bear you any resentment," she said honestly. "If it were not for the anxiety my absence must be causing I should be happy to stay longer. This is a beautiful house and I have enjoyed talking to you."

"Thank you. Had I known you would be so reasonable, my dear, I should never have resorted to such drastic methods." His thin shoulders were shaking slightly, but his countenance remained grave.

Corisande regarded him in puzzlement. Was he laughing at her? She could not think why he was amused.

There was not the least doubt in her mind now that he intended her no harm. His bark was far worse than his bite, but she sensed he liked her and she waited with interest to hear what he would say next.

Slowly he got to his feet and moved to a bureau of gleaming walnut. He opened one of the drawers and drew out a miniature portrait set in a gold frame. Returning, he handed it to her in silence.

Corisande let out a gasp of surprise. Allowing for the differences in the old-fashioned hairstyle and glimpse of gown, it could have been a head and shoulders painting of herself! The same red-gold hair, the same blue eyes, feature for feature it was a remarkable likeness.

She turned a bewildered gaze upon her host. "Who is this lady?"

"Another Corisande." He smiled faintly as her look of puzzlement increased. "It is your grandmother, child. Painted when, like you, she was eighteen."

"How...how on earth does such a thing come to be in your possession?" Corisande stared at the portrait once more. In her memory Mrs. Dalton had always been grey-haired, her face lined and rather care-worn towards the end. It gave Corisande the weirdest feeling to look at this image from the past and know it was the twin of the face she beheld in her mirror each morning.

"She gave it to me. It was a token of her regard. Ah, now I have surprised you! Did you think I'd stolen it somehow or picked it up at auction?" He shook his head. "I wanted to meet you because I suspected you might be her grandchild, although my enquiries were not entirely conclusive. Yes, my dear, I did have men searching out your background. How do you think I knew where to find you so easily if I had not been having you watched?"

"I do not care for the notion of being spied upon, sir," Corisande said with dignity.

"Regrettable, I agree, but necessary. I did not want to lose you. Then last night, as soon as I set eyes on your face I knew you must be Corisande Wade's kin."

"My grandmother's name was Dalton, sir."

"I speak of her maiden name." Impatience shaded his tone. "She was not married when I first knew her."

"Did...did you love her, sir?" asked Corisande incredulously.

He laughed rather wildly. "How perceptive you are, child. Yes, I loved her. In fact, I wanted to marry her from the moment I first laid eyes on her." His expression became reminiscent. "I was staying with some friends in the country and accompanied them to church. She was in the choir and sang in the most beautiful voice I'd ever heard. I fell in love with her on the spot."

Corisande suddenly realised her mouth was open like a fish and shut it promptly, but the sense of amazement remained. "But she married someone else," she murmured.

"I did not say that she loved me." His reply came softly like a sigh. "In spite of all my attempts to woo her, she remained faithful to the man picked out for her by her parents, a man I could have bought and sold a hundred times over without feeling the pinch!" Old anger stirred in him and he finished curtly, "However, they were already betrothed and my suit was rejected."

"Do you now seek some sort of revenge for that rejection, sir?" Corisande asked in a carefully controlled voice. His unexpected vehemence was alarming. "I think it very shabby of you if you do!"

"What? No, you foolish child, that is the last thing on my mind." He laid a hand on her shoulder in swift reassurance. "Your grandmother would not have me, but I never stopped loving her."

Carefully he eased himself back into his chair and took up the story once more.

"I dislike to admit it even now, but she loved her fiancé. Sometimes I wonder if things might have been different if she had met me first, for she did have a certain regard for me, but perhaps that is mere wishful thinking. I loved her too much to care that she was not my equal in birth, but the disparity in our backgrounds troubled her. We came from different social worlds, as she was fond of reminding me, and our paths would not have crossed except by accident."

A shiver ran through Corisande. Only too well did she remember her grandmother's insistence that people should stick to their own class. It was a view she had allowed to colour her own ideas until her father's remarks had opened her eyes to the fact that it was an old-fashioned opinion.

"On her wedding-day I wanted to kill myself, but I had too much pride. I attempted to go on seeing her afterwards, but fearing a scandal she made me promise to let her go." He smiled faintly. "That's when she gave me the portrait. I swore an oath never to seek her out again and they went to live in another part of the country. She would not tell me where."

A sigh escaped him. "I could not forget her, but eventually, for the sake of an heir, I gave way to my mother's urging and married a creature of her choosing. To be honest with you, my dear, it didn't much matter to me; all women seemed inferior after your grandmother."

"Then your marriage could not have been very happy, sir," Corisande remarked recklessly.

His eyebrows rose, but to her surprise he answered her. "It was the usual arrangement, I believe. We went our separate ways and did not trouble each other."

"How very sad, sir!"

He shrugged as if the conversation suddenly bored him and Corisande sensed that he was a man normally impatient of sentiment.

"So now you know why I was desirous of making your acquaintance, Miss Clifford."

"Forgive me, but I still don't understand."

"It grieved me to think of anyone of her blood in want. For her sake I had intended to provide for you, to make you an allowance and furnish you with a dowry, but events have overtaken me. Your father's return has robbed me of that satisfaction." He paused. "However, perhaps I can give you your heart's desire instead."

This enigmatic remark made Corisande hesitate. She swallowed hard, grateful for his kindness, but wondering how to answer him.

He did not let her silence deter him.

"My reputation is damaged, child. I bear a noble name, but my actions have never brought it honour. To no woman have I been faithful, to few men a friend. I do not ask pardon for these faults, I am as I am, but I did love your grandmother. I loved her as I have never loved before or since. You are her image. It would give me a great deal of pleasure to be your friend and to help you if you will let me."

Corisande hurried from her seat and, sinking to her knees by his chair, took his thin cold hand in her own.

"I should be happy to have you as my friend, sir. Indeed I should." Her smile trembled on her lips. "But you cannot give me what I want most in the world; no one can!"

"Can I not, my dear?" said the old gentleman softly and with a smile told her his name at last.

THE MARQUIS OF DENE, Mr. Lavenham and Sir Harry Vernon were sitting together at a table in the back parlour of the King's Arms. This tavern was owned by Thomas Cribb, the ex-champion of the Ring, but not everyone was admitted to this inner sanctum where young bloods of the Fancy, scarred veterans and promising novices gathered to blow a cloud and drink daffy.

It was nearly midnight and they had retired here to Cribb's Parlour to cudgel their brains after a wearisome and fraught day, rather than to discuss the merits of any rival pugilist.

"So Orsett had nothing to do with Corisande's disappearance? Damnation, I was sure he must be at the back of it!" Sir Harry took an angry pull at his glass of gin.

"I thought so, too," said the Marquis. He was white about the mouth and looked as if he was keeping his emotions in check only by exercising stringent self-control. "When we finally caught up with him he was halfway to Grantham and had nothing more on his mind than a good dinner at the Angel." He made an exclamation of disgust and lit another of his thin cigars with a hand that shook.

"He swore he hadn't seen Corisande since she left him in Chelsea," Tom took up the tale. "Claimed that was all a mistake too. Had the effrontery to pretend that the bedroom door must have stuck! Said it must have been damp, since he never locked her in and was intending to bring her straight back to Fanny's as soon as she was rested. Swore she must have misunderstood him."

"Damned villain!" Harry commented.

"He was lying through his teeth," agreed the Marquis with a savage frown. "I wanted to drag him out of his coach and teach him a lesson, but he's too old and fat."

"Issuing a formal challenge would have done no good either," Tom sympathised. "He took every insult you threw at him and still kept that sickly smile of his in place. There was nothing more you could do but let him go." Tom wiped his brow, reliving the uncomfortable memory.

"I should have known better than to waste time on that fat flawn," Marc said bitterly, not cheered by these words of comfort.

Sir Lucius, having formed the opinion that he would be safer rusticating on his mouldering estate in Scotland, had been on his way north when they had stopped him. It had been a distinctly unpleasant shock and the terrified baronet had been convinced that if Mr. Lavenham had not intervened to save him the furious Lord Dene might well have ignored the code of honour and beaten him to a pulp!

This disconcerting belief had encouraged him to talk. He had revealed all the knowledge he possessed, taking care to place the blame on his brother-in-law's shoulders. Sir Lucius rather thought it would serve Marlow right if the Marquis came thundering on his door demanding retribution. He'd had the devil's own job persuading the old crab-squeeze to fork out the readies for this journey to Scotland and the delay had enabled Nemesis, in the form of the Marquis, to catch up with him.

Sir Lucius's very real astonishment at being accused of engineering further harm to Miss Clifford had told its own story. He so patently believed he was being pursued for past crimes, that he was outraged to discover they held him responsible for this new kidnap. His vehement denials had had a rare ring of truth and they were forced to conclude both he and his brother-in-law were innocent.

"We wasted the whole afternoon and most of the night on a damned wild goose chase!" The Marquis's fingers gripped the table as if he would have liked to throttle it. "And we are no nearer a solution. Who could have taken her and, in God's name, why?"

Tom called for another round and they sat drinking in depressed silence.

"It'll have to be the Runners, then, I suppose?" Harry said at last. "Will you send round to Bow Street, Marc?"

The Marquis winced. The scandal that would result was the last thing he wanted but, as he was about to agree, a commotion on the outer fringes of the room attracted his attention.

"It's Dickon!" Tom exclaimed as the slight figure came dashing towards them.

"What the deuce can he want?" demanded his lordship.

The Tiger pushed and shoved, scattering patrons in all directions as he fought his way through the crowd to their table.

"There you be, guv'nor," Dickon was breathless. "I've bin everywhere looking for you."

"He's lushy!" declared Harry.

"No, I ain't." Dickon glared at the baronet in affront. "I never touched a drop tonight." He turned back to the Marquis and there was an expression of genuine concern on his sharp gamin face. "It's the Dook," he blurted.

"What do you mean? My father's in Belgium."

"He ain't, guv'nor. He's at Amberfield and he's sent for you. This fat chub comes a-banging on our door and I heard him telling Peabody as how you is wanted there immediate."

"Well, I won't go," declared his master with a stubborn frown. "I've more important matters to attend to."

"Might be as well not to set Uncle Montague's back up," Tom murmured placatingly.

"We can deal with the Runners, Marc. You can leave it to us."

"Thank you, Harry, but I do not mean to desert Corisande now."

"But that's just it, guv'nor." Dickon committed the solecism of seizing his master's coat-sleeve and, having gained his attention, continued hastily. "This here cull says as how Peabody is to tell you that the Dook knows the whereabouts of Miss Clifford and if you want the information you must come to Amberfield for it."

"What?" The Marquis felt as if the floor was heaving beneath his feet.

"Sounds like a hum to me. How should his grace know?" Tom demanded.

"I can guess!" The Marquis had the sensation of viewing the world through a red mist. His chair crashed backwards as he leapt to his feet.

"Good God, you don't think the Duke is responsible?" Harry said, appalled.

"It fits," replied Lord Dene tersely. "Dickon, I want my curricle at the door as quickly as you can."

The Tiger nodded and ran out.

"Marc, what are you proposing to do?" Tom was uneasy. "If you are going to Amberfield I think I'd better come with you."

"And so will I," added Harry. "Can't have my future brother-in-law murdering my future father-in-law!"

This forced an unwilling laugh from Marc and he was smiling as he said, "Thank you, gentlemen, but I don't require your assistance." He waved aside their protests. "Aunt Lavenham is expected tomorrow and you must be here to greet her, Tom, or she'll never forgive you. As for you, Harry, my sister would never forgive *me* if I dragged you away from town just now."

His flash of good humour faded. "Never fear. I shall strive to remember he is my father, though I would prefer to choke the life out of him!" He laughed harshly. "If the old fox thinks he has found another way to coerce me, he is in for a surprise when I inform him Augusta Marlow is to marry elsewhere."

"But you'll pay the price he wants for Corisande's freedom?" Harry asked softly.

His jaw tightening, the Marquis nodded abruptly and without another word strode out of the room.

CHAPTER EIGHTEEN

THE BLUE DRAWING-ROOM at Amberfield overlooked a lake, created by Capability Brown some forty years ago to celebrate the accession of the present Duke to the title. The lake was part of a plan to turn the grounds into a new fashionable landscape, which succeeded even the famous gardener's expectations. In the noon-day sunshine the placid waters sparkled peacefully and a dozen swans glided along in a dream-like silence broken only by bird-song. But the tall young man viewing this charming scene had no eye for its pastoral beauty and turned from the window with an impatient exclamation.

The Marquis had driven halfway through the night, racking up for just a few hours' sleep at a wayside inn. A final change of horses at Warwick had brought him home to his ancestral acres, deep in the heart of the leafy countryside, but Amberfield's impressive classical splendours interested him not at all this afternoon. Once more he pulled out his gold watch and consulted it. An hour, he had been kept waiting for a full hour!

"Ah, Dene. I trust you have not been discommoded. An unavoidable delay."

The Marquis whipped round at the sound of this soft cool voice. "Sir." He bowed with stiff formality.

A gleam of amusement shone in the Duke of Weston's pale blue eyes. "Do be seated," he invited sweetly. "May I offer you some of this claret? A tolerable vintage, I fancy."

"All you can offer me is the information I have come for," retorted his son with a grim-faced bluntness.

His grace raised pained brows at this lack of finesse. "Such heat, my boy. Bad temper can unbalance the blood; take care you do not do yourself a mischief."

"I should like to do you a mischief," ground out his lordship between clenched teeth. "However, your age and our relationship forbids it, as you very well know!"

"You think me unsporting to take advantage of the fact?" His father gave him a faintly mocking glance. "Well, you are right. I have not dealt fairly with you in the business of your marriage, aye, and other matters too, and I regret it.''

The Marquis just managed to smother an exclamation.

"I can see you are astonished and, egad, I cannot blame you!" The Duke toyed with the head of his cane. "I have not been a good father to you. My only excuse is that I have never understood you.''

Rocked off balance, the Marquis exclaimed bitterly, "Did you ever try?" His memory filled with the many occasions when a small boy's love had been rejected with indifference. "I doubt it.''

"No, I must admit, I did not." The answer was given quietly and with an absence of his father's habitual mockery. "I did not much care for children. What interest I had I reserved for your brother, who was my heir. Moreover, in appearance, at least, you are entirely your mother's son. I could never see any trace of myself in you, which did not encourage my affection, of course.''

"You always looked at me as if you measured me and somehow found me wanting." The Marquis shrugged. "There was never any way I could win your approval.''

"I do not deny it." The Duke sighed faintly. "When Edward was killed in that stupid accident I was furiously angry with all the world. My grief made me behave like a fool. I should not have insisted you leave the army, but persuaded you into seeing the sense of doing so. It was illogical of me to expect you to offer your services freely, but your reluctance to obey annoyed me intensely.''

The Duke stared at the wall behind his son's head, keeping his gaze firmly upon the pattern of the silk wallpaper as he continued this confession.

"We quarrelled and the chance to get to know one another was lost. Thereafter you seemed bent on committing all the follies I had performed in my own youth. Having travelled that road, I knew the dangers and did not desire you to repeat them. Liberal experience, at least, gives one the capacity to judge! Unfortunately, I could not find the way to warn you of the unhappiness you were storing up for yourself.''

"I did not realise you cared. You masked your concern very well, Father,'' said the Marquis, much shaken by these revelations.

"Many years ago, after a disappointment in love, I decided it was simpler to live without close ties. I did not want to risk intimacy and considered myself incapable of offering my affection to anyone. Now it is difficult to change, to accept that one has a need of other people. Since I was your age I have lived only for myself.''

The Duke paused, seeking for the right words to explain. "I will not apologise for my past selfishness. What is done is done, and my words will not alter it, but I would like us to start afresh. Perhaps we can salvage something if we try."

His son stared at him in troubled silence and the Duke guessed correctly that cynical disillusionment warred with Marc's desire to welcome this offer. A faint sigh escaped him and swallowing his pride he continued quietly, "I want grandchildren, Marc. I want to see our name carried on. It seemed to me that marriage might settle you. Oh, I know now that I went about it the wrong way, but my reasons were sound! It was foolish of me to try and force you into Edward's shoes, but Augusta Marlow did appear to be an excellent choice."

"She is to marry someone else." Marc produced this information with none of the pleasure he had anticipated. It grieved him in some strange way to see his cold, haughty father so humble. It seemed almost against nature, as if one of his horses had begun to spout poetry!

"Sir," he began impetuously. "We have both been at fault. We have both misjudged each other. You were right to take me to task for my recent behaviour. It was naught but folly for the most part."

"I had begun to be afraid you might gamble away everything you owned or, worse, kill yourself in some crazy escapade!" the Duke revealed. "You were so wild, Marc, I did not feel I could hand over any of my responsibilities."

"I believe I have learnt my lesson," Marc answered, thinking of his insane challenge to Harry and how fortunate he had been it had not turned into a financial disaster. "Thanks to a stroke of good luck I'm clear of debt now, and I aim to stay that way."

"I'm glad to hear it. Temptation can be hard to avoid sometimes in town but, of course, when you are married I hope you will spend more time in the country. It is time you took an active part in running the estates."

The Marquis stiffened. The initial purpose of his visit had been deflected by his father's totally unexpected disclosures, but this mention of marriage brought it swiftly back to him. "You sent for me to tell me your information concerning Miss Clifford. Where is she, father? I assume you did have her kidnapped?"

"You are right, of course, but not for any reason you might suppose," the Duke spoke quickly, hoping to avert the anger gathering on his son's handsome face, but it was too late.

"Don't play at words with me, for God's sake!" Marc exploded. "If you want me to believe you are sincere in the overtures you have just made then tell me the truth. Is she safe?"

"Of course she is safe! I may lack morals, Dene, but I draw the line at murdering innocent young girls—or did you think I'd had her abducted for the pleasure of seducing her?"

The Marquis begged pardon. "I thought nothing of the sort, but I presumed you meant to use her to force me into marrying Augusta Marlow," he said stiffly. "Now you know that is impossible, will you release her?"

Slowly the Duke shook his head.

"I see. So you have decided I must marry another of your choices, is that it, Father?" Marc's voice shook in spite of his efforts to control his rage. He took a deep breath. "If that is your price for Corisande's freedom then I am willing to pay it."

"Even though you love Miss Clifford?"

A muscle twitched beside the well-cut mouth. "Because I love her."

The Duke's blue eyes filled with satisfaction. "Very well, I'll strike a bargain with you," he said with a briskness that grated on his son's taut nerves. "Wed the lady I choose for you and Miss Clifford shall be restored to her friends with all honour and comfort."

The Marquis nodded bleakly, hope fading. He might have known the old fox had not really changed. He had been willing to give up his inheritance for Corisande's sake, but it seemed a greater sacrifice was required.

"You have an odd way of showing your affection, sir, forcing me into a marriage you know I will find distasteful," he murmured bitterly.

"Believe me, I have your interests at heart. Trust me to know what is best for you. You will thank me for it one day, and sooner than you think," replied the Duke with a jaunty good humour his son found as inexplicable as it was offensive. "Go now. You will find the lady in question walking in the Chinese garden," the Duke continued. "Pray be so good as to speak to her without delay."

"Here? Now?" The Marquis blanched.

"She is expecting you." His father pointed inexorably to the door.

Manfully the Marquis squared his shoulders. He walked to the door and then he paused. "I hope you enjoy your victory, Father. It may amuse you to order me around like a puppet, but I'll have you know I'm not doing this out of fear of losing my inheritance, but for the sake of a girl who deserves far better than the love I would willingly give her if I had the right to choose."

He bowed with exquisite grace and walked out of the room with a dignity that made his father want to applaud.

"Oh, I'm sure I shall enjoy my victory, my dear boy!"

A chuckle of pure amusement accompanied this remark, but the Marquis was already too far away to hear it.

THE CHINESE GARDEN, with its exotic trees and colourful shrubs, its winding walks and charming grottos, was a contrived contrast to the rest of the smooth serenity of the landscaped grounds of Amberfield. Corisande thought it enchanting.

She had enjoyed her walk, but it was time to return to the house and her nerves were fluttering with excitement as she abandoned her inspection of the tall brightly painted pagoda which dominated the heart of the garden. The pagoda stood on a small island in the middle of a miniature lake and she was just crossing the rustic bridge back to the main path when she saw the tall figure striding towards her. Her hand went to her throat in a quick nervous gesture as she came to an abrupt halt. He was frowning savagely!

The Marquis spotted the girl standing on the bridge and his rapid advance checked. Her figure clad in a blue gown was alluringly slender and her uncovered hair blazed a rosy gold in the sunlight. He continued to stare at her for one disbelieving moment and then started forward saying in a thickened voice, "Corisande! Oh, my dear love, you really are safe!"

Corisande melted into the arms that seized her feeling as if she were coming home. Tenderly she smoothed back a lock of dark hair which had fallen over his brow.

"My love, my darling girl! I did not know you were here at Amberfield. I was so worried!" Marc gave a wild laugh that was almost a groan and began kissing her with a passion that left Corisande breathless. Her lips parted eagerly beneath the urgent pressure of his and she hungered for him with a desire that made her tremble in his crushing embrace. She loved him so much, he was all she had ever wanted, all she would ever want!

Marc's hold slackened as he finally recollected himself, but he did not let Corisande go. Instead he stared down silently into her small delicate face for a moment, imprinting it upon his memory for ever. "Forgive me," he said shakily. "I should not...must not kiss you!" The glow in his eyes betrayed his reluctance, but he released her.

Corisande curbed the impulse to put her arms around him. She wanted to wipe the worried frown from his face, but did not know how. What had gone wrong? Why was he looking at her as if she was forbidden fruit? It was as if she was only a dear memory already out of reach.

"Corisande, where is the other lady who was walking in this garden?" Marc strove for a correct formality, but could not keep the strain from his voice. "Did you see which way she went? My father told me she was here, but I have not found her."

Corisande's puzzlement vanished. "Why did you want to find her?" she asked with a limpidly innocent expression.

His jaw clenched so hard that a muscle flickered at the corner of his mouth. "My father wishes me to propose marriage to her."

"And, you? What are your feelings?" Corisande breathed, apparently unperturbed by his blunt revelation.

"Damn you, Corisande, you know the answer!" he exploded, unable to maintain his pose of calm an instant longer. "You provoking little witch, you are the only woman I want to marry!" He pulled her back into his arms. "Oh, God, don't you know by now how much I adore you!"

Corisande slid her arms up around his neck. "Even though I am a vulgar scheming trollop?" she enquired, glancing up at him provocatively through half-closed eyes.

His arms tightened. "Minx!" he replied appreciatively. "Not that you can cozen me any longer. Harry has confessed all! Fanny has accepted him, you see."

"Oh, Marc!" Corisande beamed at him in delight.

Her radiant smile was too much for the Marquis's self-control. His lips found hers in a kiss so sweetly tender that Corisande's heart filled with joy, but it was a brief embrace and over too soon for her.

Marc let her go. "Corisande, I have made a bargain with my father," he said in a constricted voice. "I cannot tell you why, but we must not . . . Where did this other lady go?" His gaze caressed her longingly. "Please, I gave him my word. If I don't go now I fear I never shall . . . but I must leave you!"

"Oh, Marc, I am a horrid wretch to tease you!" Corisande exclaimed with swift repentance. She had wanted to make sure of his feelings, but she could not bear to see him tortured like this. "Don't you realise, my love, that there is no other girl?"

"But there must be! My father told me she was in the Chinese garden . . . My God, did he mean *you?*" He seized her by the shoulders. "Did he?"

She nodded, impish mischief dancing in her eyes.

The Marquis was looking understandably bewildered. "But he wants me to marry someone like Augusta, surely?"

"Ah, but I am an heiress!" Corisande broke into a peal of laughter at his thunderstruck expression. "Truly, I have it upon your papa's authority." She smiled lovingly at him. "Come, let's walk back to the house and I'll try and explain it to you as we go." She tucked her arm into his and they began to stroll along the winding path. "Perhaps I had better start from the moment I woke up here at Amberfield. Not that I knew where I was at the time."

When she reached the point where the Duke had revealed his identity she began to laugh. "Can you imagine my feelings? I vow I did not know where to look. I think my face must have turned white with shock and then scarlet with embarrassment, but your father merely smiled. He even apologised for his deception."

"He is very fond of his little jokes," Marc said with feeling.

"I agree he has behaved badly, but he is so lonely, Marc. When he explained that he had ordered my abduction because he feared I would refuse to see him if I knew his identity I couldn't help feeling sorry for him."

"Sorry for him!"

They were now in sight of the house, but the Marquis halted their slow progress across the greensward. "Does that mean you have forgiven him, infant, in spite of the way he has treated you like one of the pieces on his chessboard?" There was a hint of wry humour in his lordship's tone.

Corisande nodded. "I think his autocracy is a shield to ward people off," she said thoughtfully. "It is an ingrained habit, a means of proving his importance to himself as much as to the outside world. To persuade him out of such high-handed behaviour will take a lot of time and effort, but perhaps if we can help him to trust us he will have no need of it."

A sudden grin appeared on her face. "Perhaps his grandchildren will soften him."

Marc ruffled her hair. "Saucy brat."

Corisande laughed. "You must forgive my presumption, sir. I thought you might want children with me?"

"Dozens," he replied promptly and the glint in his eye told her that he was thinking with relish of the prospect of begetting them.

A faint blush coloured Corisande's cheeks. "His grace has already sent a message to my father. I think they will get on famously," she murmured in a rather distracted voice, trying hard to control her wayward longings, but finding it impossible when he was standing so close. "Did you know your father was extremely interested to hear about Papa's travels to collect exotic specimens? He asked me all about them and then gave me a tour of his conservatory to show me his favourite plants."

"A rare privilege." Marc's arm slipped around her waist.

Corisande swallowed hard, wishing that her pulse would not race so fiercely when there were still things they needed to discuss. "He . . . he wants to hold the wedding very soon, Marc. The invitations are already awaiting dispatch."

The gentle exploration of his hand along the fascinating curve of her hip halted. "The old fox, all the time we thought he was in Belgium he was engineering events like a puppet-master!" Marc exclaimed. "But this hurried ceremony, is it what you wish, Corisande? Knowing my father, it will not lack for splendour no matter how quickly it is arranged, but I shall tell him to cancel his plans if you have other ideas in mind."

"I don't give a fig where or how, so long as it can be soon," Corisande declared with an honesty that made the Marquis long to shout for joy. "A quiet wedding would be less of a strain on my papa, but there is nothing to prevent us from asking all our friends. The chapel here at Amberfield is big enough to hold everyone we might like to invite. Your father showed it to me this morning." She smiled. "I shall ask Letty to be my bridesmaid, and Gussy, too, if she is not on her honeymoon."

"Letty would like that."

Corisande's smile deepened. "But none of it really matters, Marc. For a long time I never thought it would be possible for us to be together. You would have been ruined if you had disobeyed your father's edict and I could not face the prospect of becoming your mistress, because it would never have been enough for me. I think you must know by now that is why I refused you, but I have loved you all along. Let your father arrange the ceremony as he will. All I need is you."

He raised her hand to his lips. "I don't deserve you, my darling," he said softly. "But may I roast in hell if I fail to make you happy!"

For a long moment they stared into one another's eyes in a rapt silence that had no need of words. Then Corisande let out a naughty chuckle. "I don't know about that, sir, but I cannot promise not to hit you over the head with the nearest vase if I discover you had been reverting to to your disgraceful old habits!"

"Minx!" laughed his lordship. "Come here and I'll teach you how a good wife behaves."

Oblivious of the fact that they were standing in the middle of the great lawn in full view of the house, he caught her to his broad chest and kissed her with a long slow expertise until they were both breathless.

"There, Miss Clifford, let that be a lesson to you," said the Marquis unsteadily when he at last raised his dark head.

Flushed with rosy colour and eyes sparkling with pleasure, Corisande traced the line of his jaw with one small loving finger. "I shall promise you to be a very good wife," she said solemnly, but her dimples danced irrepressibly. "But only if you swear to repeat the lesson most regularly every single day."

"Every hour," he vowed, smiling down into her bewitching little face.

Then, taking her hand in his, the Marquis of Dene led his bride towards the great house that was her destiny as his future, most suitable duchess.

AT HIS BEDROOM WINDOW, overlooking the great lawn, the Duke of Weston gave a sigh of satisfaction and, with one swift smiling glance at the little portrait now restored to its place of honour by his bed, hurried down to meet them.

PENNY JORDAN

Sins and infidelities...
Dreams and obsessions...
Shattering secrets
unfold in...

THE HIDDEN YEARS

SAGE — stunning, sensual and vibrant, she spent a lifetime distancing herself from a past too painful to confront... the mother who seemed to hold her at bay, the father who resented her and the heartache of unfulfilled love. To the world, Sage was independent and invulnerable— but it was a mask she cultivated to hide a desperation she herself couldn't quite understand... until an unforeseen turn of events drew her into the discovery of the hidden years, finally allowing Sage to open her heart to a passion denied for so long.

The Hidden Years—a compelling novel of truth and passion that will unlock the heart and soul of every woman.

AVAILABLE IN OCTOBER!
Watch for your opportunity to complete your Penny Jordan set. POWER PLAY and SILVER will also be available in October.

HARLEQUIN
Romance

A Christmas tradition...

Imagine spending Christmas in New
Orleans with a blind stranger and his aged
guide dog—when you're supposed to be
there on your honeymoon!
#3163 Every Kind of Heaven
by Bethany Campbell

Imagine spending Christmas with a man
you once "married"—in a mock ceremony
at the age of eight!
#3166 The Forgetful Bride
by Debbie Macomber

*Available in December 1991, wherever
Harlequin books are sold.*

HARLEQUIN HISTORICAL

CHRISTMAS

STORIES·1991

Bring back heartwarming memories of Christmas past
with HISTORICAL CHRISTMAS STORIES 1991,
a collection of romantic stories
by three popular authors.
The perfect Christmas gift!

Don't miss these heartwarming stories,
available in November
wherever Harlequin books are sold:

CHRISTMAS YET TO COME
by Lynda Trent
A SEASON OF JOY
by Caryn Cameron
FORTUNE'S GIFT
by DeLoras Scott

**Best Wishes and Season's Greetings
from Harlequin!**